"For my family in the UK and Ethiopia"

Semira, Ben, Matt, Emily, Pete, Alice, Rose

ቤተሰብ

ዘላለም ሀይዛ አቢኒዘር ልእልት ልዮወርቅ አብራሃም ኑፉሁሴን.

"Occasionally life provides us with unexplained abilities allowing us to see into the darkest of corners."

Mike Hardy.

PROLOGUE

S ome say there are places in the world where true evil thrives, festering like a cancerous tumour too deep to remove. I used to think they were talking about specific spots on the map—those cursed, broken places you can point to and say, 'there it is'. And sure, I've seen enough of the world's dark corners to know evil can take root in a place like weeds in the cracks of a wall. But here's the thing. What I didn't see, what I wasn't ready to see, is that evil doesn't just sit in dark, forsaken places, waiting for us to stumble in. No, it breathes in all things, walks in the sunlight, mingles with crowds on bright streets, hides in plain sight. It's the spark behind a quick, simmering rage, the twist in a smile that fades too quickly. It's always there, patient, waiting for an opportunity.

The truth clawed its way into me, and I realise now it doesn't matter where you are, how safe you feel. Evil doesn't need an abandoned house or a dark alley to thrive. It only needs us—open, unaware, ripe for the taking... And once you see it, really see it... well, there's no unseeing it. I know now It takes many forms. Twisted predators lurking in the shadows, feeding on the weak and vulnerable. Sometimes, it's a group of men grooming girls barely old enough to understand, shaping them into victims before they even know what innocence is. Other times, it's the figure who operates in the dead of night, bound to a twisted ritual, perhaps a serial killer whose violence rises and falls with the cycle of the moon. But in this truth—in this dark and bitter story—it's innocent women and children caught in the crosshairs of monsters, their lives taken by unimaginable acts of cruelty. The world is a hard and brutal place. Some of us grow up believing in the safety of daylight, the idea that there will always be someone to protect us. But the reality... It's colder. Much harsher. It's important to remember—for every kind soul, there's a shadow that hovers, slipping between thoughts, hiding in the places we pretend don't exist. That's where the real horrors live—the kind that don't need blood to terrify. You see, it's not just the darkness outside you have to fear; it's the darkness that waits within—behind friendly faces, whether it's the unassuming neighbour next door, the seemingly charitable friend, or as close as a stranger's gaze lingering too long in a crowded bar. I have seen its true capabilities. I have seen the power it holds. The full extent of its abilities is terrifying. What frightens me the

The Story Behind The Story...

Originally from Scotland, Hardy now calls Cardiff home, where he lives with his wife, Semira. Their story began in Ethiopia, a country that remains profoundly significant for both of them. They married in Addis Ababa in 2014, and Ethiopia continues to be a place they return to, reconnecting with family and lifelong friends. Hardy is the proud father of three adult children—Ben, Matt, and Emily—from a previous marriage.

Hardy's professional background is diverse, rooted in his service as a Royal Marine Commando, which evolved into a 30-year career dedicated to safety and security. Today, he brings the same dedication to his writing, drawing from the discipline of his military background and the rich tapestry of experiences that have shaped his life. As someone who has personally battled PTSD and received treatment at Cardiff University, Hardy understands firsthand the therapeutic power of storytelling.

Writing initially acted as a means of processing his traumas and gradually became a creative outlet for Hardy. This path led him to fiction, where real-life events and nightmares often inspire his characters. Hardy's debut novel, Blood, Dust, Hyenas, is a work of fiction, yet through its protagonist, Tommy, it echoes aspects of his own life.

In addition to writing, Hardy is an avid reader of horror, with a particular affinity for Stephen King's work, holding a prominent place on his bookshelf. Storytelling, in its many forms, remains a constant source of solace and inspiration. Alongside his writing, Hardy continues to work full-time as a safety consultant in the quarries and mines of Wales and England, applying his knowledge to an industry where safety is paramount.

BLOOD-DUST-HYENAS

most is evil isn't something that prowls only in "others." It's within us all. You are probably thinking this is just another horror story. And yes, in part, you'd be right. But what I want you to understand is that terror doesn't care about borders or boundaries—it doesn't check passports. It slips through the cracks of the everyday, settles into forgotten spaces, and waits. Even now, as you read these words, something dark and relentless is watching from a shadowed corner, waiting for its moment to breathe. The memories come in fragments, blurred at the edges like a filmstrip left too long in the sun. Yet, even through the fog, they strike with the sharpness of a blade, cutting past bone and marrow, straight to the heart. I'm there, lost somewhere in that mist—a younger version of myself, just another man who thought he understood what life could throw at him. But the story I found myself in… well, some might call it love. Others might call it insanity. And both would be right. If love can be tangled up in shadows and sharp edges, if it can thrive in places where no light dares to go, then maybe that's what it was. Or maybe it was something darker altogether. Either way, I've lived it, felt it sinking its claws deeper than I thought possible. Now, when I close my eyes, I feel the weight of it all, the raw, blood-stained memories that refuse to fade.

It is about how far one soul will go when he's lost it all, only to reach for it again. It's stitched with loss and loyalty, where family bonds are unbreakable, and yet, depravity lurks close enough to touch. Together we will walk through the villages where laughter is just a memory, see children with eyes aged by horrors they should never know, and watch a mother clutch her child like it's the last thread holding her to this life. I witnessed firsthand real evil—not the kind from children's tales, but relentless hatred that destroys people, corrodes communities. Like a rot spreading through the veins of a family. Sometimes, it's a look, a word, a silent betrayal. No, true evil isn't always obvious. Sometimes, it's a quiet presence, disguised as kindness or camaraderie, biding its time. By the time you do notice, it's too late. The pieces of you that mattered are already gone, chipped away bit by bit, and you're left staring into an empty reflection. You'd fight back if there were enough left to care. But now, that part of you is just… gone.

Looking back, I can't say for sure if I lost my mind or just reached a breaking point. All I know is once you've been through a storm like this and manage to come out the other side —well, if you're lucky enough to come out—you're never the same. This is my truth. I have to tell it, not for sympathy or redemption, but because if anyone's going to understand, they need to see what I saw, feel what I felt. They need to understand how easily it can happen— how one small shift in your world can tear you apart. I tried to resist the pull of those memories, like a soldier straining against the fog of some long-forgotten combat zone. In the Ethiopian Highlands, wars aren't fought only with blades and bullets; they're waged with the very spirit, with raw, primal forces that seem to rise up from the land itself. Out there, in the thin air of those sacred mountains, a man can find himself crossing into realms he never knew existed, places where reality blurs and myth breathes. Sometimes, a wounded warrior is just a vessel, a bridge between the tangible world and something far older, far stranger. The horrors I encountered… no training could have prepared me for them. No matter how many times I close my eyes, those images linger. The things I saw—the things I did—still haunt the edges of my mind, shadows that refuse to fade. Even now, I struggle to put them into words, like they're secrets too heavy, too dark for language to bear.

The woman who had once saved me was the one I had to save. The irony of it hit me like a fist to the gut—almost poetic, if it hadn't been so terrifying. The thought crept in, unbidden but fierce—maybe I was her only hope. Maybe I always had been, even before either of us realised it. Destiny? Fate? I couldn't care less about those things back then. All I knew was that whatever bond had drawn us together, whatever love or duty I felt toward her, it drove me, sharpened me. The air was thick, weighted, as if the world itself held its breath, waiting to see if I would falter.

CHAPTER 1

"Throughout history, it has been the inaction of those who could have acted; the indifference of those who should have known better; the silence of the voice of justice when it mattered most; that has made it possible for evil to triumph."

— *Haile Selassie*

"Tommy." The voice cuts through the darkness. "Tommy." It's closer now, insistent, pulling me from the void. My eyelids feel like lead, and panic grips me as I strain to open them. Who's calling me? What do they want? My mind claws for answers, but all I find is fear. I want to scream, shout that I'm here, alive, but nothing escapes my lips. Silence. Am I dead? Is this what death feels like? I can't move. The murmurs swell around me, growing sharper, like a storm gathering strength. Feet shuffle closer, the heat of bodies pressing in, trapping me. Their voices buzz like angry bees, a low hum that makes my skin crawl. I feel their breath, hot and stifling, on the back of my neck, and for the first time, I know real terror. Objects swim before my eyes, blurred and indistinct, like they're dissolving into the pale backdrop around me. Everything else is a dull haze of grey, with flickers of light and shadow playing tricks on my mind, but nothing sharp enough to grab onto. There are no faces, no clear shapes—just a foggy mess. I blink hard, trying to force my vision into focus, squinting at the harsh, flickering light above me. The rush of relief that I'm still alive hits, but it's quickly swallowed by a cold wave of fear. What the hell happened? My limbs feel like they're pinned under something heavy, refusing to respond. My chest tightens, each breath coming faster, more frantic, like I'm running out of air. Panic grips me as the walls seem to close in, the room shrinking until the air itself feels heavy and suffocating. I fight to steady my breathing, but the harder I try, the more it spirals out of control. I force myself to focus, turning inward. There's a faint tingling in my fingers, like they're waking up after being numb for too long. I try to flex them—slowly, stiffly—they respond, but it feels unnatural, like I'm moving through water. I try to sit up, but something holds me down—restraints. Shapes move in the blur beyond me, figures in white, drifting like ghosts. A voice calls my name, soft and distant, but I can't make out the words. Machines hum and beep around me, their mechanical sounds filling the room, blending into the fog of confusion. A figure leans in close, speaking, but it's like their voice is underwater, lost to me. I don't know how I got here, or where here even is. Am I in a hospital? An institution? A cold dread seeps in. None of this is familiar. None of it makes sense. A woman's voice, no wait, a man's voice. Not sure, the words are muffled and disconnected, like they are coming through a thick fog. "Fuck," What are they saying? I need to regain consciousness. Where the hell am I? I need to figure this out. Remember what I see. I can't focus; too much noise; The sound of screaming fills the room, echoing off the walls and piercing through my ears. But as I look around, I realise that the screams are coming from me. My body feels numb, as if I have no emotions left. Could this really be me? Am I still alive? Nerves are starting to fire up, subdued, but they are there. Wait, oh no. Pain is creeping in. Stronger now. I remember...pain. I fucking remember pain. Struggling to catch my breath, a heavyweight crush down on my chest. My head throbs and throat burns. Even my fucking feet hurt. Finally, my vision is clearing, I see a large face materialising over me, foul breath assaulting my nose. I desperately wish they would take a step back. Fuck! Suddenly, it all comes rushing back. I know this man's face - it's the same ugly bastard who keeps me here. *Sinclair*.

I try to speak, but my mouth feels heavy, my body sluggish as the drugs wear off, leaving me trapped in slow motion. Tubes run through my throat and nose, making it hard to breathe, every inhale laboured and unnatural. They keep pressing me with questions, digging into a past that feels distant and foreign. Each time I wake, it's the same—this confusion, this dull ache of not knowing where I am or why I'm here. The pain is dulling now, fading into the background, and as soon as they remove the thing jammed down my throat, I'll tell them everything I've been holding back. But my mind is still foggy, tangled in questions I don't have answers to

A voice cuts through the fog—Doctor Sinclair. His words yank me back to reality. I force my eyes open, squinting as he leans in close, his dark eyes sharp, too focused, like he's expecting a revelation any second. His pen hovers over his notepad, ready to trap every word that slips from my mouth. The fluorescent lights above are searing, making me wince, and I turn my head to escape the harsh glare. The room feels overwhelming, like everything's turned up too high—too bright, too loud, too real.

"Tommy, are you with me?" His voice is tight with concern, maybe frustration. He's always pushing, always digging for answers I can't give him. I try to nod, but my neck won't cooperate, stiff and weighted like it's forgotten how to move. Fantastic. My heart pounds against my ribs, each beat louder than the last, and my palms are slick with sweat. Then it hits me—fragments coming together, cold and sharp. I remember where I am. Or at least, I think I do.

"You were panicking while you were under," Sinclair says, his voice softer now, almost like he's trying not to spook me. "Your breathing was shallow, erratic. We had to intubate you to help you breathe." His words trigger flashes—disjointed fragments of a nightmare I can't fully shake. My fists clench on their own, and my heart pounds as I try to bury the memories Sinclair keeps dragging to the surface. But he never stops. Never lets up. I shift in the bed, uncomfortable, trying to escape his relentless gaze. It's too intense, like he's peeling back layers I'm not ready to expose. He sighs, reaching out to place a hand on my arm, like that's supposed to comfort me. "Talk to me, Tommy," he urges, his tone gentle but insistent. "We want to help you remember."

Remember. The word sinks like a stone in my gut. I can't meet his eyes, my stomach twisting with shame, anger bubbling up inside me. How the hell can I talk about something when I don't even know what it is? Guilt gnaws at me, but I don't know why. It's just... there. A heavy weight I can't shake. But Sinclair doesn't stop. He never stops.

"Talking is a powerful tool in your recovery," he repeats for what feels like the hundredth time, and all I can think is—what if I don't want to recover? He glanced down at his clipboard, flipping through the scribbled notes before locking eyes with me again. "We're making progress, Tommy," he said, leaning in a little closer. "Each session is taking us deeper into your subconscious, and we're uncovering more about your past trauma."

As he spoke, images I didn't want to remember started creeping into my mind—sharp, vivid, and impossible to ignore. I clenched my fists, squeezing my eyes shut in a desperate attempt to push them back down, to block them out. But his voice kept going, a steady drone that never gave me a moment to breathe. I let out a long, frustrated sigh. The way he talked to me—like I was a puzzle he was so close to solving—made my skin crawl. It always did. The condescending tone grated on my nerves, as if he thought he had me all figured out. And yet, as much as I hated to admit it, there was a sliver of truth in what he said. As irritating as CBT *(Cognitive-Behavioural Therapy)* is, I couldn't deny it had worked before, at least in small ways. The nightmares weren't as constant. But knowing that didn't make his voice any less irritating, or the flood of memories any less overwhelming. Now, it felt like trying to coax life from dying embers, barely flickering in the dark. Therapy had taught me how our past shapes everything—how memories twist and distort, how trauma lingers in the shadows of our minds, waiting to surface. Sinclair paced in front of me, his white coat swishing with every step, and my muscles tightened as he kept probing. My mind screamed for him to stop, to pull back before he dragged up something I wasn't ready to face. But he never stopped. They never do. He's just one of the many white coats that haunt these sterile hallways, their voices echoing off the walls of this place they claim is for my own good. But

I don't feel safe here. I feel like a specimen under a microscope, and Sinclair is determined to dig deeper, to drag out the memories I've locked away, convinced they hold the key to something—something I'm not sure I even want to understand. I stare hard at a crack in the wall, silently willing it to open up and swallow me, to pull me out of this moment, to save me from the memories clawing their way back to the surface. Suppressing them has become second nature, a survival instinct in this place. But Sinclair keeps pushing, telling me it's for my recovery, for my own good. I wish I could believe that.

The truth is, they want something from me. Something buried deep in my subconscious. Maybe it's something important, something crucial they think can help. Or maybe it's too terrible for me to confront, too dark to acknowledge, let alone share. Either way, I know this much: whatever it is, it's locked away for a reason. I know something's wrong here. I can feel it—a creeping sense of danger, like I'm being watched, studied. This place, whatever it was meant to be, feels more like a detention centre than anything designed to heal. I'm sure it was once a hospital or a clinic, but now it's cold, sterile, with the unsettling quiet of an empty building. And somehow, I seem to be the only one left. No other patients. Just me. I spend every day fighting to keep the past locked inside, avoiding the pain I know it holds. But it's like those memories have a mind of their own, clawing their way to the surface when I least expect it, demanding to be felt, to be remembered. The people here— the doctors, nurses, whoever they are—are relentless, their insistence bordering on desperation. They prod and push, practically begging me to give them something, to crack open the memories I've buried. The constant pressure is suffocating, closing in on me with no escape. I tried to resist, especially in the beginning. I fought them with everything I had. But the harder I pushed back, the tighter their grip became, like they could squeeze the truth out of me if they just held on long enough. Still, one memory breaks through the fog, clear and horrifying. It's seared into my mind, too vivid to ignore. It's the one thing I know is real, but it terrifies me. I need to figure out what's real and what's just a nightmare—a twisted creation of my mind. Because if I don't, I'll never get out of this place. Physically, I might be trapped here, but this emotional prison is worse. To escape, I have to confront the past, no matter how much it hurts.

My name is Tommy Thompson—at least, that's what they keep telling me. But the name feels like it belongs to someone else now, a stranger I barely recognise. They said I woke up in this very room after a year-long coma. A coma I don't even remember. That was eight years ago, but it feels like a lifetime has passed, with each day bleeding into the next. I've seen doctors come and go, their faces all blending into a blur of white coats and tired eyes, asking the same questions, offering the same hollow reassurances. False hope dressed up as a medical concern. But lately, something's shifted. They've started treating me a little differently, like they've decided I'm more than just a puzzle they can't solve. There's an edge of compassion now, or at least they pretend there is. Sometimes, if I look hard enough, I think I catch a flicker of humanity in their eyes. Or maybe that's just wishful thinking. Either way, it's the smallest gesture, but it's something. And in this place, something is all I have to hold on to. Every now and then, I ask if I can go outside—feel the sun on my face, the wind on my skin. But I already know their answer before I even ask. *'Not today, Tommy. Maybe soon. It's too risky right now.'* Always the same refrain. Some of them won't even meet my eyes, as if my request is too much to bear. Others just give me that blank look, like they've stopped seeing me as a person altogether.

This isn't like the mental hospitals you see in movies—there's no Nurse Ratched, no rebellion brewing under the surface. At least in *'One Flew Over the Cuckoo's Nest,'* there was some spark of life, some sense of control, even in the madness. But here? Here, there's no comfort, no comedy. Just endless waiting, endless questions, and the feeling that I'll never really be free of this place—or of the past they keep trying to drag out of me.

CHAPTER 2

I wake up screaming again, drenched in sweat, my heart pounding in my chest. None of this makes sense—none of it. Are the nightmares real? Did those things really happen? The images cling to me, refusing to fade: a dark room, the sharp tang of metal in the air, flashes of searing pain. And always, the crushing weight of loss, like a heavy blanket suffocating me as soon as I open my eyes. The dreams are getting stronger, more vivid, like they're clawing their way out of my mind, no longer content to stay hidden in sleep. I fight to push them back, but it's getting harder. Even in daylight, they linger, creeping into the corners of my thoughts. I'm scared—scared that soon, I won't be able to push them away at all. That the horrors in my head will become my reality. It has to be the treatments, the drugs they pump into me, numbing me, dulling everything around me. Every session feels like slipping into a coma, a deep, dreamless sleep where they have complete control. The whitecoats say it's necessary, that it's part of the healing process. But I can't shake the feeling that they're stealing pieces of me, sifting through my subconscious for answers I don't even know I have. I glance around the room—small, colourless, lifeless. The walls close in on me, just as they have for years. No windows, no clocks, no way to mark time except for the guards who drift in and out. They're the only sign of day or night, but even they feel detached, like they're moving through the motions without really seeing me. Vacant eyes. Blank faces. But that doesn't stop me from trying. I've made a game of it, in my own small way—trying to make them smile. Just a flicker of something human. It's pathetic, I know, but it's the only way I've found to keep my mind occupied. Anything to keep the nightmares from creeping in during the hours when I'm supposed to be awake, supposed to be safe. But I'm starting to wonder if I'll ever feel safe again. I cling to whatever scraps of sanity I can find. Sometimes, when the walls feel like they're closing in, I close my eyes and take myself somewhere else—anywhere but here. I picture a winding path, one that cuts through a quiet forest, where the sounds of birds and rustling leaves fill the air. I can almost feel the cool breeze on my skin, the scent of pine. And then, in the distance, I see her. She's walking toward me—a woman with long, flowing hair and a smile that feels like home.

As she gets closer, a strange warmth spreads through me, something familiar, something safe. When she takes my hand, it feels like we've known each other forever. She leads me to a clearing, a peaceful spot where the grass is soft beneath us. We sit there, and her presence helps me remember pieces of my past—fragments of joy, moments buried under layers of doubt and pain. I don't know if she's real or just some figment of my imagination, but I want to believe in her. In the happiness, she stirs within me. In the possibility that I was once whole, once content, once someone with a life that made sense. Maybe this woman holds the answers to the questions I can't even form—about who I am, about who I was. Every night, she comes to me, her dark hair falling in waves down her back, her brown eyes locking onto mine with a silent promise. She beckons me from a place that feels just beyond reach, and I follow her. I have to. She's the only dream I don't want to wake from. The only vision that doesn't dissolve into something darker. I tell myself she must be out there somewhere, that she's real, and that somehow, I need to find her. I can feel it deep inside, as if her name is carved into my very soul.

Zahra.

I'm confined to a small, sterile room with walls so white they almost hurt to look at. There's not much here—just a metal-framed bed with a thin mattress that barely offers any comfort, covered by a scratchy wool blanket that's more irritating than warm. It keeps the chill off on cold nights, but just barely. In the corner by the bed, there's a tiny sink with a cracked basin, the tap constantly dripping onto the chipped porcelain. Next to it, a child-sized toilet, like a cruel joke, making even basic needs feel like an afterthought. This bare-bones setup offers little solace during the long hours of isolation. Across the room, there's a chair—sturdy, with a worn wooden frame that shows its age and the signs of too many bodies slumping into it. Beside it sits a small, round table, scratched and stained from who knows how many years of neglect. That's it. That's my entire world, unless they're moving me somewhere. The only break in this monotony is when they drag me out for meals or meetings with the doctors. The orderlies—or guards, depending on how they feel that day— lead me down a soulless hallway, long and bare, with the smell of bleach hanging in the air and the hollow echo of footsteps on linoleum flooring filling the silence. I'm stuck in these damn grey overalls—one of only two pairs they've given me. No pockets, buttons up the front, heavy and too big, but they do their job, especially at night when the room gets cold. My feet are stuffed into plastic shower slip-ons, the kind you'd expect in a prison. No socks. My feet are always cold, pressed against the unforgiving ground. As for underwear? They gave me a few pairs of ill-fitting men's briefs, stiff and awkward. That's all I have. Just enough to cover my body, but never enough to feel like a person.

When I step into the dining hall, the assault on my senses is immediate. The rancid odour of spoiled vegetables hits first, sharp and sour, followed by the greasy, sickly-sweet stench of old oil that clings to the air like a film. There's a metallic tang too, like rusting steel, mixing with the damp, musty smell that seems to seep from the very walls. It's like the room itself is rotting from the inside out. Once, the smell alone would've turned my stomach, maybe even made my eyes water. Now, it's just part of the background, something I've learned to ignore, like so much else in this place. I scan the room, my eyes drawn to the heavy wooden tables and chairs, each one bolted down, a permanent reminder that there's no escaping. No change. Maybe this is it—this bland, grey existence. Maybe this is my life now. I glance up at the small window near the ceiling, barely big enough to let in a sliver of sunlight. It's not enough to warm the room or me. The fluorescent lights overhead buzz faintly, casting an artificial, clinical glow that makes everything look even more lifeless. I pick at the food on my tray—if you can call it food. It's a colourless, tasteless lump, something they probably scrape together without much thought. I try not to make eye contact with the guards, but I can feel their eyes on me, watching. They're always watching. I finish as much as I can stomach, then push the tray away, the uneaten food barely distinguishable from what I started with.

A guard comes over and escorts me out, down the hall to Sinclair's office. The moment I step inside, my eyes go to the round cameras on the walls, their lenses tracking me like predators. There's a two-way mirror too, like in a police interrogation room. I catch my reflection—sweat on my forehead, hands trembling slightly, a nervous smile that doesn't belong on my face. My feet shift on the cold tile, and I can't stop glancing at the mirror, wondering who's watching from the other side. I feel exposed, like a specimen under glass. Sometimes, in a desperate attempt to escape the reality of it, I imagine myself on a talk show. I'd be the guest of honour, telling my story—about how I survived, how I overcame. Or maybe, in this case, how I failed. But then there's another part of me, the part that secretly hopes this is all just some elaborate joke, that any moment someone—maybe my family, maybe even an old friend—will burst into the room laughing, yelling, "Gotcha!"

But I know better. No one's coming. And the joke, if there ever was one, is long over.

Sinclair gestured toward the plush recliner with a smooth, practised hand. "Sit, Tommy," he said, flicking his wrist as if the chair itself were some kind of solution. The cushions looked soft, almost too inviting, like they belonged in a different place entirely. A new tactic, maybe. I'd never been offered anything like this before—comfort. I hesitated, my eyes glued to the floor, avoiding Sinclair's sharp, expectant gaze. Eventually, I sat down, sinking into the unfamiliar luxury, my body tense, unsure what this new approach was meant to accomplish. A cough broke the silence, low and throaty, muffled by the walls. Probably behind the one-way mirror. There's always someone else watching, listening. They've asked me a thousand times to dig into my past, but today it felt different. More staged. Cameras already littered the room, but Sinclair still reached for his own device—a small, outdated recorder, like something from a different era, complete with cassette tapes. He placed it on the table between us with a deliberate thud, like he wanted me to know it was there, capturing everything. Every word. Every slip. I want to talk. I want to spill everything, to unravel the mess in my head and finally get it out. But I'm terrified. What happens if I let it all out? What if those memories break free and can't be contained again? I'm stuck between the need to rebuild whatever's left of me and the instinct to protect myself, to stay hidden. I don't know how much I can safely share—how much I even 'can' remember.

This isn't about changing anyone's opinion or proving anything. This is supposed to be for me. That's what they tell me, at least. An attempt to piece together a man who's been broken for longer than I can remember. And as I sit here, in a room that smells faintly of antiseptic and desperation, I realise something: my voice is my only weapon. It's all I have to fight the nightmares that claw at me, the beasts from my past that still circle, waiting for the right moment to pounce. Here, in these walls that seem to close in every time I try to breathe, I'm forced to be a participant in my own story, no matter how badly I want to walk away from it. I'm being pushed, again and again, to confront the hyenas of my past who cackle in the face of my recovery, as if it's a joke to them. I never wanted this fight. But here I am, facing it head-on in hopes of finding peace within myself. A chance to be whole again.

Doctor Sinclair—if that's even his real title—looks more like an old-fashioned professor than a therapist. He's a short, slender man, the kind you'd expect to see lecturing in a dusty classroom, not poking around inside someone's mind. He sits behind his oversized mahogany desk, a small round table between us, scribbling on a yellow legal pad. His glasses sit low on his nose, and his white coat is pristine, almost too pristine, every button fastened neatly. When he crosses his legs, it's with this deliberate, almost pretentious flair, like he's performing for an audience only he can see. And here I am, the captive in this little routine, sitting across from him, once again submitting to his well-rehearsed act of attentive listening. He nods at all the right moments, makes a show of scribbling down my words, and then repeats them back to me, like a parrot with a diploma. He says stories can help 'reorganise a disturbed mind.' Maybe he's right. Or maybe it's just some line from 'Therapy for Dummies' that he memorised. Either way, I brace myself. I know what's coming—digging up the painful pieces of my past, prying open old wounds, all for the hope of finding some peace. Or at least a shred of it. I sink deeper into the plush leather chair, letting my head rest against the soft cushion as it reclines. I'm about to close my eyes, ready to go through the motions, when something catches my attention—his shoes. Immaculately polished, brown lace-ups that seem absurdly out of place in this sterile, fluorescent-lit office. A slight grin pulls at the corner of my mouth. If those shoes don't belong here, maybe I don't either. Maybe this whole place, this whole process, is just as out of place as I feel.

CHAPTER 3

"Start from the beginning," Sinclair says, like it's that simple. Like there's some neat, clear point where my broken past begins, something easy to unravel. He sits across from me, pen hovering over his notepad, eyes fixed on me, waiting for the story to spill out. But the memories I need—the ones he wants—don't come easily. They're distant, blurry, always slipping just out of reach. So, I do what I always do: focus on the present, on the relentless pressure of this place and the weight of the emotions that threaten to crush me every time I try to remember. The nightmare. That's what I know best. It's been with me for nearly a decade, as familiar to me as my own skin, though I wish it wasn't. These aren't just dreams—they stick to you, cling to your bones. Even now, I can still feel it, like it happened just yesterday, like it's waiting to happen again. They tell me it's 2024, but the passage of time makes no sense to me anymore. The years blur together, just like the faces, the doctors, the endless white walls of this place. Sinclair's been at this for a while, pushing me to speak, to record everything, no matter how fragmented. He says it'll help unlock more memories, help me piece together what I can't seem to remember. His face is blank, unreadable, as he moves a little closer, pressing the record button on his device.

"OK, Tommy," he says, his voice soft but relentless. "Ready when you are."

I take a breath and start with the clearest piece, the one that won't let me go. I know he's waiting for more, for the flood to come once I open that first door. But the truth is, I don't know if I'm ready for what's behind it. I take a sip of water, letting the cool liquid soothe my throat. For a moment, I focus on that small comfort, something real, something solid. When I'm ready, I set the glass down gently, careful, like it might shatter if I move too quickly. I take a deep breath, and then I start to speak—telling them my truth. Or at least, what I think is my truth. The things I see in my sleep… they aren't just dreams. They're more like fragments of something real—tragedy, love, horror—stories so intense, it's hard to believe they aren't pieces of my past. I'd like to think they're just nightmares, that my mind is playing tricks on me. But I know better. They're too vivid, too detailed. They feel like memories, even though I wish they weren't. And lately, I can't seem to tell what's real and what isn't anymore. The lines are blurring, and the more I try to separate fact from fiction, the harder it gets. These images—they're not new. I've had them for as long as I can remember, but now they're relentless, always there, waiting for me. And the feeling they bring with them is like something out of a horror novel—dark, unnatural, something that doesn't belong in this world. I don't know exactly when it started. Sometime around 2015, maybe 2016. The dates are fuzzy, but that doesn't really matter. What matters is that this one is different. It's persistent, always lurking in the back of my mind, a shadow I can't escape. It's not the kind of story you'd expect. I didn't grow up in chaos. I wasn't some troubled kid from a broken family. I had a good life—a loving home, parents who cared about me, who did their best to protect me from the ugliness of the world. I had everything I needed. And yet, these memories—these visions—won't leave me alone. It's like something beyond this world is playing with me, pulling at the edges of my sanity. Sometimes, I wonder if it's just my own guilt and fears, twisting themselves into something monstrous. But deep down, I can't shake the feeling that it's all connected—that these images, these moments, are real, and that they're hiding something I haven't figured out yet. Something I'm scared to confront.

I'm being forced to relive nightmares that blur the line between what's real and what's not. Every time I wake, I cling to the hope that it was just a dream. But deep down, I know better. The dread hits me before I can even open my eyes, a wave of anxiety that crushes me. This isn't just some bad dream—it's something far worse, something I can't shake, something threatening that I don't understand. The scariest part? Knowing I'm under the influence of God-knows-what. I'm not in control. It's like I'm watching everything from a distance, trapped behind glass while my body moves, speaks, reacts—only it's not really me. It's a twisted, distorted version of me. The sound of my own voice, warped and foreign, sends a chill through me.

Then the memories hit, flashing like a broken reel. The bed. Empty. Alone. Trembling. Fear grips me, and I see those old family photos—smiles frozen in time, offering a momentary comfort. But the images twist, distort, and shift into something more sinister. Flashbacks flood my mind. A life that feels like it belongs to someone else. And then, as quickly as I blink my eyes, another memory pulls me in, dragging me somewhere I don't want to go. Suddenly, I'm back in our home. The smell hits me first—familiar, comforting. This was our place. Zahra. My wife. Her face, her presence, it's all coming back to me. This is real. She is real. Her perfume lingers in the air, wrapping around me like a lifeline. I'm in bed, our bed. The sheets are cool against my skin, grounding me for just a second. Without thinking, I reach for her, expecting to feel her warmth. But she's not there. Panic shoots through me, sharp and immediate. I call out for her, my voice too loud in the empty room.

'Zahra!" I yell again, but the silence presses down on me. My heart hammers in my chest, frantic. Where is she? I call her name again, my voice desperate, but the room swallows my words. Then, a souna. A cry. It's faint, distant, but it's hers. She's calling for me.

'I can hear you!" I shout into the darkness. 'Where are you? Please, come to me!" But all I see are shadows, shifting in the blackness. My heart races, pounding so hard it hurts. I need her. I need to find her. Instinctively, my hand fumbles for the medication on my nightstand. The cool plastic of the pill bottle meets my fingertips, and I snatch it up, relief flooding me for a brief second. But then, as I shake it, the bottle rattles. Empty. Mocking.

'Shit." The word tears from my throat, filled with frustration and fear. I'm spiralling, out of control, and the darkness is closing in. I scream into the empty room, but nothing answers me back. Nothing.

"Fuck!" The word tears out of me, sharp and loud, as I jerk awake again. I open my eyes, and there's Sinclair, staring down at me like I'm a monster that just crawled out of a nightmare. His face is pale, eyes wide, lips quivering. He looks like he's seen a ghost. Hell, maybe he has. I try to sit up, but my body feels leaden, weighed down by exhaustion and whatever they've been pumping into me. How long was I out? Minutes? Hours? Days? I can't tell, but the look on his face tells me it was longer than I think.

I try to ground myself, reminding myself of who I am. "I'm Tommy fucking Thompson," I mutter, the words harsh and bitter on my tongue. That name used to mean something, used to carry weight. It wasn't just a name—it was a symbol of everything I'd been through. Brutal battles fought, hard-won victories. I was strong. Disciplined. A soldier. A brother. A father. A husband. The name isn't just letters strung together—it's my history, my identity, a lifeline to a life I'm struggling to remember. But it's there, somewhere inside me, and as long as I hold onto it, I can keep clawing my way back. I'm starting to remember now. Little pieces. Who I am. What I was. And what happened. I know what I have to do.

But then Sinclair's voice cuts through the fog, pulling me back. "Tommy, you're not just recounting events. You're weaving a narrative, trying to piece together the meaning behind it all." His words hang in the air as he fidgets with his device, eyes darting around the room like he's searching for something—or someone. I nod, not because I agree, but because I don't want to argue. He doesn't get it. My goal isn't just to tell a story. It's to find the truth. The truth that's been buried, the one that's going to tear me apart if I don't confront it. That's the thing about fear—it only grows when you run from it. The only way to break free is to face it head-on, even if it destroys you in the process.

For my own sanity, and for those who can no longer speak for themselves, I have to keep going. The memory that haunts me the most is the smell—the thick, choking stench of blood and dust, mixing together in the air. I can still hear the hyenas, their laughter echoing as they circled the mangled bodies scattered across the ground. It's everywhere I look. I try to push it away, but the scene follows me, a shadow that never leaves. After years of struggling to piece it all together, I'm finally starting to confront the details, bit by bit. I'm forcing myself to face the fear, the horror, and the grief of everything I've lost. It's agonising, but I have no choice. I have to drag the truth out into the light, even if it's been buried so deep for so long that it feels like it's become a part of me. I'll make sure the truth bleeds through these walls, exposing the darkness I've carried, showing them what really happened.

The doctors here—these pitiless people who keep poking and prodding at my mind, searching for answers—have no idea what it's like. They treat my pain like it's a riddle to solve, something clinical and detached. But maybe, just maybe, when I finally tell them about the blood-soaked soil of Ethiopia, where the lives of so many were crushed into the dirt, they'll start to understand. Maybe they'll realise that the nightmares they poke at are more real than they could ever imagine. Every day, that place—the horrors of it—plagues the darkest corners of my mind, and I carry it with me like a weight I'll never shake. One day, they'll know the burden I live with. And when they do, maybe they will finally have a taste of the horrors that invade my dreams, stop seeing me as just a broken man in a bed and just maybe, they will begin to understand the truth.

Chapter 4

"Coffee and love taste best when hot."

Ethiopian Proverb

Another day, another bowl of tasteless, lumpy porridge. I force it down like I do every morning, choking it back because I know I need the energy, even if the thought of eating it makes my stomach turn. Sometimes they'll toss me a piece of fruit—something small and bruised, like it's been salvaged from someone else's plate. The bare minimum. But I take it, because I don't have a choice. The doctors are relentless, always pushing pills on me, saying they'll help me remember. Help me find the missing pieces of my life. But I don't want their pills. I want to remember on my own terms, without the fog they keep trying to shove down my throat. It's like they don't understand that some things aren't meant to be forced. I'm alone most of the time—at least, I think I am. But on quiet nights, when everything is still, I hear things. Faint, muffled cries, like they're coming from somewhere deep in the building. Maybe there are others here, but I've never seen them. The isolation is wearing me down. The absence of any real human contact gnaws at me, making me feel like I'm unravelling. The sterile white walls, the constant hum of the fluorescent lights overhead, it all grates on my nerves. It's too much and not enough all at once. My mind's turning on me. Without anything to hold onto, without any kind of stimulation, it's conjuring things—visions, hallucinations that feel too real. The line between reality and fantasy is starting to blur, and I can't always tell which side I'm on. Each day the walls feel closer, like they're slowly closing in. The silence here is deafening, amplifying every little sound, every creak and whisper until it's all I can hear. Paranoia's wrapping around me, making me question everything. I don't even know if I'm still me. Is this place real? Am I real? Or am I just another ghost trapped in a nightmare I can't wake up from?

A bulky figure strode toward me, his pace steady, his eyes locked on mine. Every instinct screamed for me to brace myself for a fight. Adrenaline surged, my muscles coiling tight, ready to spring. As he got closer, I saw the bottle in his hand—white pills rattling inside. You've got to be kidding me. No way was I swallowing any more of that crap. He was massive, a hulking presence that made me feel small, insignificant. His shadow seemed to stretch in every direction, and his face—cold, expressionless—looked like something straight out of a bad movie villain line-up. I tried to tell him to back off, to piss off, but my voice caught in my throat. Still, he kept coming, silent, unflinching. I could hear the sound of his boots on the floor, each step louder than the last. Then I noticed them—two more men creeping in from behind, boxing me in. My heart raced. There was no way I could take all three, but hell, I wasn't going down without a fight. If I was going to bleed, so would they. These clean white tiles beneath our feet would be slick with blood before it was over. I squared up, took a fighting stance, every nerve alive, ready. They had no idea what they were about to face. Ripping off my shirt, I grabbed what was left of the butter from the breakfast tray and smeared it messily over my skin. It wasn't much, but it'd buy me a minute, maybe. That's all I needed—to turn this into hell for them. The first guy closed the distance—10 feet, 8 feet, 6. And then, suddenly, he stopped dead in his tracks.

A voice rang out from the doorway. Familiar. Controlled. "Leave us!"

Sinclair. I exhaled hard, my eyes darting to him. He stood there, his presence freezing the room. Without a second thought, the three men—like soldiers given a command—turned and marched out, leaving just as quickly as they'd come. As their footsteps faded, I couldn't resist.

"Guess today's not the day," I muttered under my breath, feeling the adrenaline drain from my body. I'd just narrowly avoided the kind of beating that would've left me on the floor. "Yeah, fuck off. Lucky for you the doc showed up," my voice loud and clear.

I turned toward the doctor, squinting as the harsh fluorescent light stabbed at my eyes. He was almost in front of me now, the same white coat, the same smug expression, like he knew everything, and I knew nothing. Today, though, he was wearing a tie under his coat, dark blue with some writing on it, but I couldn't make out the words. His presence filled the room, but not in a comforting way. He stopped, and just as he did, two nurses walked in. I stumbled back onto the steel chair, the freezing metal biting into my bare skin. My head swam, and the room blurred at the edges as a wave of dizziness hit me.

"Stay there, relax," he said, his voice dripping with condescension. "Tommy, we're going back to my office, and we'll start today's session." It wasn't a request. It never was.

I tried to respond, but the words felt heavy, stuck in my throat. "What...what did you say?" The world spun, and I could barely string my thoughts together.

"Tommy, you might feel a little lightheaded," he said, not even bothering to hide the arrogance in his voice. "We've given you something to calm your nerves today."

His words hit me like a punch in the gut. "What?!" The anger surged up, quick and hot, like a fire roaring out of control. My voice echoed off the cold, sterile walls, bouncing back at me in a mocking chorus.

I leaned back, recoiling from the bowl of half-eaten porridge on the tray beside me, my stomach twisting with disgust. They drugged me. Without a word, without a warning—drugs in my breakfast, like it was nothing. Betrayal clawed at me, sharp and unforgiving, and my head swirled with the realisation. It wasn't just the drugs—it was the lie, the deceit woven into every interaction here. I felt my world closing in, darkening, like a trap tightening around me. I looked up at Sinclair, his cold, detached stare boring into me through those damn glasses. He didn't care. None of them did. To him, I wasn't a person—I was just another problem to fix, another case to check off. The betrayal stung deep, deeper than I could even process in that moment, and all I could do was sit there, feeling my grip on reality slip further away.

I struggled to find the words, my throat tight with frustration. "You... you bastard," I finally spat out, but the rest of my sentence crumbled before it could form. It was like my brain was working against me, refusing to give me anything but rage and confusion. Recovery had been a nightmare since I woke up in this hellhole. Every interaction with the people here felt like a battle, their probing questions and clinical detachment pushing me further into a corner. I'd reached the point where life felt pointless, but I wasn't ready to give up. Not yet. I fought my demons daily, hoping for something—anything—to change. As the years dragged on, the lack of sunlight had turned my skin ghostly pale, and the strength I once had in my muscles faded, leaving me weak and brittle. Each day I spent locked in this sterile box, I could feel myself slipping, both body and mind deteriorating bit by bit. My spirit was wearing down, eroding like stone under constant rain. I'd tried so many times to prove I was still in control of my thoughts, that I wasn't some broken thing they could fix with needles and pills. But it was getting harder. Every conversation was a struggle, my emotions like a dam about to burst. There were some questions I couldn't answer, not because I didn't want to, but because I honestly didn't know. My focus was simple—survive and get the hell out of here.

He stood there, speaking in that calm, measured tone of his, talking about trust like he didn't see the fire burning behind my eyes. I wanted to scream, to tell him he was full of it, but all I could do was stare, seething. Then I felt the nurse's hand tighten around my arm, and the sharp sting of the needle hit me. Something cold coursed through my veins, and my body betrayed me, pulling me down into the dark. I fought to keep my eyes open, but the medication worked fast. My limbs felt heavy, my words slurred, drool pooling at the corner of my mouth as I tried to form any coherent thought. I could hear his voice, Sinclair's voice, still droning on about controlling my mind, but it was fading, slipping into the background. I knew it didn't matter anymore. I was at their mercy—completely. Then, just as I started to sink deeper into that drugged fog, something unexpected happened. Amidst the chaos of Sinclair's voice, the flickering lights, and my sluggish thoughts, an image broke through—the vivid, intoxicating image of Zahra. Her face appeared so clearly, cutting through the confusion, and with it came a flood of emotions I wasn't ready for. I could feel her presence, the pull of her, a rush of memories and longing. The room around me blurred as her image flickered in and out, like a light trying to fight the darkness. Voices whispered, calm and soft, telling me to let go, to relax, to stop resisting. But, how could I?

Zahra moved closer, her hand brushing mine, a soft touch that brought a flicker of comfort. We stood in a place that felt almost unreal, a hazy dreamscape with no clear landmarks or sense of direction. But her smile—it was radiant, filled with the warmth of a past I could still remember. In that moment, with her beside me, nothing else seemed to matter. My mind let go of the endless battle I had been waging with myself, with them. I was tired of trying to make sense of it all. With Zahra by my side, I didn t have to. We walked together along the water s edge, a gentle breeze off the ocean carrying the salty air with it. It felt cool against my skin, grounding me in the present, in this perfect moment. I stared out over the bay—Cardiff Bay, shimmering under the sunlight. The water sparkled like it was alive, reflecting the bright sky and the green hills in the distance. It looked like something out of a painting, too beautiful to be real. For a brief, stolen second, it was just us—Zahra and me, no past, no pain.

Then it all came rushing back. The stark white rooms. The doctors. The endless pills. The blank faces. The needles. And the pain. Always the pain. I couldn't stop it—the memories, the flashes of fear, the choking isolation. *Help me. Please. Stop. Stop it.* My mind spiralled. *Screaming. Questions. More questions.* I was confused, terrified, lost. There was no escape. No way out. I could feel the tears, the sobbing, the breaking.

But then... Zahra. Zahra was here. We were back at our home, where we belonged. And suddenly, the chains that had bound me fell away. The weight, the fear, the past—it all evaporated. I was free. Empty. A blank page, ready for something new. No more nightmares, no more prison. Just me. And Zahra. Here. Now. But even as I held on to that thought, the feeling started to slip, unravelling as fast as it had come.

Because maybe... I wasn't free. Maybe I wasn't even here. Maybe I was nothing more than a memory, drifting in and out, just like her.

Chapter 5

The sunbathed everything in a soft, golden light, casting a warm glow across the still waters of Cardiff Bay. In the distance, sailboats swayed gently in the breeze, their masts cutting against the clear sky, while smaller motorboats skimmed along leaving trails of white foam in their wake. The air was filled with the sounds of life—dogs barking as their owners strolled along the promenade, the happy chatter of children begging for ice cream, their voices carrying on the wind. Days like this were rare in Cardiff, especially this late in September. The sun usually kept its distance, but today it lingered, an unexpected gift of warmth in the midst of an Indian summer. These kinds of days felt like they stretched longer as if time itself slowed down to soak up the sun. It made everything seem brighter, and more alive. And in a city where grey skies were the norm, this stolen bit of summer felt even more precious.

We sat on an old wooden bench by the water, the warmth of the sun gently touching our skin. The air was alive with the sound of seagulls screeching, diving for scraps of food, while swallows cut through the sky above in perfect formation. The hum of cars in the distance mixed with the birdsong, an odd but perfect blend of nature and city life. Around us, the aroma of freshly brewed coffee and sizzling steak drifted from the upscale restaurants lining The Bay. It was busy, noisy, chaotic even, but sitting next to her, I felt nothing but peace. She was beautiful—God, she was beautiful. Her floral sundress moved with the soft breeze, and her smile... it was like the sun itself, lighting up everything around us. When she looked at me, her eyes sparkling, my heart skipped more than a few beats. I found myself staring longer than I should have, completely caught up in her. I loved her completely, stupidly in love and anyone watching could probably see it plain as day. But for once, I didn't care what anyone else thought. This moment was ours, and we'd earned it. After everything we'd been through, all the hurdles we'd faced, this was our time to just be—to live, to love, to enjoy the now. In this minute. And every minute that followed.

She caught me staring and raised an eyebrow, playful. "What?" she asked, knowing exactly what she was doing to me.

"Nothing. Just admiring the view," I said, trying and failing to hide the ridiculous grin spreading across my face.

She laughed softly and teased, "Don't just sit there gawking. Come kiss me," and with that, she pulled me closer, our lips meeting in a kiss that felt like it could last forever. Her fingers traced the back of my neck, sending shivers down my spine, and in that moment, nothing else mattered. It was just us, the way it was always supposed to be. As our lips parted, I leaned back, trying to catch my breath.

My heart pounded, a mix of dizziness and exhilaration coursing through me. I couldn't help but mutter, "Wow, that was... amazing," feeling my face stretch into a goofy grin. My mind raced with anticipation, already imagining getting her alone, picking up right where we'd left off.

We kept walking, the air between us charged, and soon I spotted the Pierhead Building, its iconic red brick standing tall against the skyline. It had this almost castle-like presence, something solid and proud, a constant reminder of Cardiff's maritime past. But beyond it, sleek modern skyscrapers rose into the sky, markers of how much the city had changed. Progress, I thought. The perfect blend of history and what's to come, all right there in one breath-taking view. We found a quiet spot by the water, a place where we could watch people pass by. We'd always loved making up stories about strangers—where they were headed, what they might be talking about. It was one of those silly things that made us laugh, and as the sun dipped toward the horizon, its golden light stretched across the bay, casting everything in a warm, peaceful glow. It felt like time had slowed down like this moment was meant to last.

My first visit here had been like that too unforgettable. The blend of old and new, the streets filled with history, yet alive with something fresh. The grand theatre with its dome, and the Millennium Centre's copper façade catch the light just right. And then there was that pub, one of my favourites, squeezed between an Indian restaurant and a Chinese takeaway. Its red lanterns swayed gently in the breeze, a little slice of character that felt like home during all that change. It was one of those evenings that would stay with me forever— where the city itself felt alive, and the moments shared seemed to stretch on, suspended in time. Today, the market stalls are empty, though I'm pretty sure they'll be open tomorrow. It's always worth a visit—there's something satisfying about finding little treasures and supporting the local traders. As I stand here, taking in the view of our corner of the world, I can't help but smile at the patchwork of homes that surround us. Each one is different, a reflection of the people who live inside. I often catch myself wondering about the stories behind these walls, the lives being lived just beyond my view. As I watch the flow of people moving through the streets, it's clear everyone has their own path, and their own battles. A homeless man huddles in a doorway, his coat pulled tight against the wind. A mother pushes a stroller, lost in thought. A group of friends laughs together outside a café, the sound of their joy cutting through the noise of the city. We're all part of this bigger thing, this chaotic adventure called life, even if our roads rarely cross in any meaningful way. Cardiff wasn't part of our original plan. We didn't expect to stay, much less fall in love with the place. But somehow, despite the challenges, it's become home. Funny how life works out like that. The rain we'd been expecting finally starts to fall, and we head back to our apartment, weaving through the damp streets with the rest of the city's late afternoon crowd.

As soon as I step through the door, I'm hit with the familiar, comforting scent of our little sanctuary. The air is thick with the earthy aroma of spices—berbere, Zahra's favourite, lingers strongest. Its mix of chilli and garlic fills every room, a reminder of her homeland. Beneath it all is the rich smell of freshly ground coffee beans, a staple in our daily routine. It's a blend of scents that's come to define our home, a place we've affectionately started calling "Little Ethiopia." Pictures cover our walls, each one a snapshot of our lives, moments we couldn't bear to forget. Some we carefully framed, placing them just right, while others we hung in a rush, not caring about perfection because they all meant something. Each photograph brings back a memory—stories we've told a hundred times, yet somehow, they always make us smile when we pass by. We may not have expensive artwork, but these photos are our own gallery, far more meaningful than any painting could ever be. They tell the story of us; of the life we've built together. Our living room is like a canvas of memories, every picture frame is another brushstroke in the mural of our family. Walking down the hallway, I feel a swell of love as I pass each image. In one, my daughter's eyes are lit up with laughter, her face caught in the middle of a joke that still makes me chuckle. In another, my son's brow is furrowed with concentration as he tackles a puzzle, the kind of determination only a child can have. Each frame pulls me back to those moments, and for a second, it's like I can feel them here with me, their energy filling the room. Above the bed hangs a beautiful canvas, Zahra's home village of Hayak brought to life with every stroke. It's a bustling marketplace at the centre, surrounded by fields of colour, the distant mountains rising tall and proud. I glance at it again, noticing how it's slightly crooked, making a mental note to straighten it later. Across from the bed, another favourite hangs—a photo of a dusty field, framed by towering mountains. In the foreground, barefoot children run, laughing and carefree. It's simple, but there's so much joy in that moment, a reminder that the best things in life aren't complicated. This apartment isn't just a place to live—it's home. The walls may be ordinary, but inside, it's filled with memories love, and safety. Every photo, every memento, tells a story, and together, they make this place feel like more than just bricks and mortar. It's the heart of who we are. As I glance at the photo, memories flood back—Hayak's winding streets, the rich smells of street food, the warmth of Zahra's family as we shared stories and laughter. I remember my first Christmas in Ethiopia as if it happened yesterday. It was so different from the familiar, monotonous routine I was used to back home—pubs, overeating, TV, and then more of the same the next day. In Ethiopia, Christmas wasn't about excess. It was called *Gena* or *Lidet*, meaning Christ's birthday, and it was unlike anything I'd ever experienced. What struck me most was the deep spirituality woven into everything—church services that seemed to go on forever, fasting (which, to be honest, I didn't exactly excel at), and a sense of community that permeated the entire celebration. Unlike the frenzied December rush, I knew, their Christmas came in January, a peaceful observance guided by the Julian calendar and the Ethiopian Orthodox faith. It wasn't about gifts or shopping. It was about something purer, something I'd almost forgotten back home. The festivities kicked off with a special church service the night before, stretching well into the early hours of January 7th. We dressed in traditional Ethiopian attire, and Zahra's family gifted me a *Kuta*—a simple, white garment worn by most Ethiopian men. It was the only gift I received, but it felt more meaningful than any of the piles of presents back home. Zahra, her sister, and her aunt fussed over me, adjusting the Kuta, adding little touches until I looked the part. I couldn't keep up with their rapid-fire Amharic, but their laughter and care made me feel like I belonged. After the long service, we returned home for the real highlight—the family feast. As we approached the house, a goat bleated from the yard, happily chewing on grass, oblivious to its fate. Zahra's brother, Abraham, and I had woken at dawn the day before to visit the local market, carefully selecting the best goat we could find. Arriving early meant we could pick a strong, healthy animal for the occasion. It wasn't just food; it was tradition, and being part of it, even in such a small way, filled me with a sense of pride and connection I hadn't expected.

That Christmas was a world away from the chaotic, commercialised holiday I had known all my life. There was no stress, no pressure—just family, faith, and a simple joy in being together. I could feel the weight of the men's disapproving stares as I offered to help the women with the meal. In this family, it was tradition—unspoken, but firm—that the women ran the kitchen, especially for these special feasts. They were the heart of the home, the ones who kept everything together. As the newest addition to this family, I wanted to fit in, to contribute wherever I could. So, when it came time to slaughter the goat for the meal, I didn't hesitate. I'd killed animals before during my time as a Marine, but this… this was different. The whole family gathered in a clearing behind the house, a small space surrounded by trees, the sounds of the forest blending with the murmurs of those around me. Abraham, the family elder, stepped forward with a sharp blade in his hand. He recited a blessing, and we all bowed our heads, thanking the goat for what it was about to give us. There was a reverence in the air that I wasn't used to. Abraham approached the goat, whispering words of gratitude, laying it on its side as gently as one might cradle a child. He tied its legs with care, and in one smooth motion, he drew the blade across its throat. The blood flowed into a hole dug in the ground, a perfect channel for what felt like a sacred act. The goat's eyes met mine as its life slipped away, and for a moment, I was struck by how raw and honest it all was. There was no cruelty, no haste—just respect for the life we were taking. I stood there, watching as the light faded from the goat's eyes, feeling a sense of awe at the whole process. I'd seen death before, plenty of it, but this… this was something else. Once it was over, I stepped back, leaving the women to their work. They'd handle the rest—skinning, cleaning, cutting the meat into the pieces that would feed us for the day and the days ahead. I joined the men inside, but my mind was still outside, lingering in that clearing, feeling the quiet power of what I'd just witnessed. This wasn't just about food. It was about family, tradition, and life itself.

Chapter 6

I was married once, long before I met Zahra. It was the early nineties when it started, and almost twelve years later, it ended in a painful, drawn-out divorce. But despite the heartache, it wasn't wasted time. It gave me the three greatest gifts of my life—my children. My youngest daughter, who must be 22 now, is the epitome of unconditional love, and I am grateful for her, and her two older brothers every single second of each day. We were just two young teenagers when we married, filled with hormones and curiosity, and we couldn't resist the pull towards each other. Before we even knew what was happening, we were parents, trying to navigate a life we weren't quite ready for. We stood in front of our families and friends, promising forever. And in the beginning, we believed it. We were inseparable, spending every waking moment together, holding hands like we were afraid to let go. But over the years, things changed. I noticed it slowly at first—her smile wasn't as bright; her laugh didn't come as easily. She stopped reaching for my hand when we walked down the street, and I didn't know why. The spark between us, once so vibrant, began to flicker and fade until it was just embers. She grew colder, more distant. I could feel her slipping away, and there was nothing I could do to stop it. Then there was him. The way her eyes lit up when she talked about him—it was a look I hadn't seen from her in years. That's when I knew. He had taken my place, and no matter how hard I tried, there was no getting it back. The day she left, taking the kids with her, I felt something inside me shatter. Our connection, our history, everything we'd built—it all fell apart in an instant. I was left standing in the ruins of a life that had once been full of love, wondering how it all slipped through my fingers. The agony that followed was unbearable—a storm of self-loathing and a burning rage that I directed at everyone, especially at her. Each day was swallowed by misery, a cycle I couldn't break, no matter how hard I tried. I pushed away anyone who tried to help, convinced I didn't deserve it, and in the end, I found myself utterly alone, trapped in the torment I had built. Looking back now, the weight of guilt and regret is almost too much to bear. The damage I inflicted on the people I cared about was deep and permanent. I carry that with me every day, knowing I caused so much pain and suffering. It took years for me to even begin accepting the consequences of my actions, and in that time, I was consumed by sorrow, by this gnawing hatred for myself. But somehow, through all of that, there was a spark of hope. My children—despite everything they had witnessed, despite seeing the worst parts of me—grew into strong, kind, resilient people. They were my saving grace, a reminder that even in the darkest moments, something good could still exist. And for them, I will always be grateful.

After what felt like a lifetime of rejection letters and dead-end applications, an email with the subject line "Job Offer" appeared in my inbox. I stared at it in disbelief, and as I read through the details, the salary, the possibilities, tears welled up in my eyes. Finally, a chance. A job that would allow me to afford a tiny one-bedroom apartment—a fresh start. When I stepped inside that place for the first time, the wooden floors creaked beneath my feet, and the smell of fresh paint hung in the air. But it didn't matter. This was mine. My space. A new beginning. I couldn't stop smiling as I imagined the possibilities. But the real change came when I met Zahra. God, she was everything I could've ever wanted—smart, kind, empathetic, and always seeing the best in everything. She was a light in a world that, for a long time, had felt so dark. We never really talked about starting a family, but I knew, deep down, she would've been an incredible mother if we'd gone down that path. I loved her more than I knew was possible. I think back to those rainy evenings, the two of us curled up on the couch, wrapped in a thick fleece blanket. The rain tapping on the balcony door, the rich smell of Ethiopian coffee in the air. We'd binge-watch sitcoms, tangled in each other's arms, laughing at the dumbest jokes. Zahra's eyes sparkled with mischief as she sipped her coffee, infecting me with her playful energy. We had been in this new city for a year, and it already felt like home. We were content, happy even, in this quiet, ordinary life we'd built together. And for the first time in a long time, I believed that maybe I deserved that happiness.

CHAPTER 7

As the sun set behind the storm clouds, and the city lights reflected off the wet streets, Zahra's voice broke through the sound of rain tapping against the windows. "Tommy!" she yelled; her energy contagious as always.

I turned to face her and raised an eyebrow at her mischievous smile. "What's up?" I asked, trying not to let my own excitement show.

She leaned in closer, her eyes sparkling with mischief. "Do you trust me?" she asked, a playful glint in her eye.

I chuckled and gave her a confident nod. "Of course."

Her grin grew wider as she whispered, "Good, because I have an idea."

My curiosity was piqued. "What is it?"

"It's just a quick walk," she said teasingly.

A burst of laughter escaped my lips at her spontaneous suggestion. "In this downpour? Are you serious?" I asked incredulously, already imagining our drenched clothes. She waved off my concerns with a flick of her hand, sending her bangles jangling on her wrist.

"Don't worry, we've got everything we need," she said, pulling out a bright yellow umbrella from her bag. Her eyes sparkled with excitement as she beamed at me "Let's go dance in the rain!" Her energetic demeanour never failed to lift my spirits, and I found myself nodding along. She bundled up in multiple layers and joked about being an Arctic explorer, while I opted for practicality with my old military boots and windbreaker. As we emerged from our apartment, the bright neon lights of the Bay enveloped us in a warm glow. The rain pelted down around us, but she held her umbrella high above our heads as we made our way towards the waterfront. We stumbled over uneven pavement and dodged streams of water flowing down the gutters. For a second, we paused, huddled under her bright umbrella, and laughed at ourselves. Then, with a mischievous glint in her eye, she twirled the umbrella like a circus performer's baton. I pushed it aside and pulled her in for a passionate kiss. Our clothes were drenched, and our shoes squelched loudly as we ran hand-in-hand through the empty streets, feeling like two kids who had just jumped into the ocean fully clothed. Although we were both completely dripping wet, it did not matter; I was having the time of my life. But as the night wore on, the chill in the air crept into our bones, and we sought shelter at a nearby café. With steaming cups of hot chocolate in hand, we snuggled into a corner booth and shared sweet kisses. It felt like we were transported back to our first date, every moment full of magic and nostalgia.

As the morning light filtered in through the curtains, I stretched out my limbs and took a deep breath. For once, there were no haunting images or disturbing thoughts plaguing my mind. Instead, I was greeted with the comforting sight of Zahra lying beside me, her dark skin glowing in the soft light. Her peaceful expression and the warmth of her body next to mine brought a sense of calm over me that I hadn't felt in a long time. I closed my eyes and let out a content sigh, grateful for this moment of peace and love with the person who meant everything to me. She stirred next to me, her almond-shaped eyes blinking slowly as she woke up. I reached out to caress her cheek and she leaned into my touch with a soft smile. In that instance, all my worries and unsettling nightmares seemed to fade away, replaced by the love and inner peace I felt with Zahra by my side. I closed my eyes and savoured every second we had together before starting another day.

I stretched my arms above my head and let out a content sigh. "Last night was amazing," I said, unable to contain my glowing smile.

Zahra's face lit up in response, her eyes sparkling with joy. "I've never felt so alive before," she exclaimed, her happiness filling the room and making it impossible not to smile back at her.

I reached for the coffee mugs, and Zahra gracefully glided past me to grab the milk from the fridge. I couldn't help but admire the way her dark hair caught the morning light and seemed to shimmer. She poured us each a cup and handed me one with a warm smile. We moved around the kitchen in perfect harmony like a well-rehearsed dance routine, our years of living together evident in every fluid motion. I marvelled at how effortlessly she made even the most mundane tasks seem elegant. Together, we worked like a seasoned team, me handing her utensils with practised precision while she flipped eggs on the stove like a pro. In between sips of coffee, I paused to take in the picture-perfect view of a waterfall hanging on our living room wall, its cascading streams seeming to release a peaceful aura into our home. I couldn't wait to experience it in person one day with Zahra by my side, exploring new places and making more memories together. Zahra's hand brushed against mine, bringing my attention back to our dance in the kitchen.

"More sugar?" I asked, holding the sugar bowl out to her, already knowing she would want more in her coffee. She smiled gratefully, and I couldn't help but feel a sense of peace as I watched her stir it in with a small silver spoon. A grateful smile stretched across her lips, revealing the dimples I loved so much. I reached out and smoothed down the collar of her blouse, feeling the soft fabric beneath my fingers. It was a small gesture, but it spoke volumes about our unspoken promises and deep understanding of each other. Her warm eyes met mine, and I saw everything she wanted to say without a single word. The jasmine-scented fragrance that lingered on her skin stirred up a rush of emotions within me. Zahra had always been able to evoke such intense feelings with just a simple glance or touch, and I couldn't help but be swept away by her once again. We finally settled onto the creaky wooden chairs at the scratched, oak table, our plates were piled high with steaming fluffy eggs mixed with diced tomatoes and spinach. The smell of freshly toasted bread wafted through the air as we eagerly dug in, savouring every warm, buttery bite. The worn table may have seen better days, but nothing could dampen the joy of this simple breakfast together. Zahra's bright smile and infectious laughter eased my worries about her upcoming trip. After breakfast, she perched on the kitchen counter, swinging her legs as she excitedly planned our day. The sunlight danced through her curly hair, catching every glimmer, and making it seem like she had a halo around her head. At that moment, it was just the two of us and all the endless possibilities ahead. We were fearless, ready to explore the vibrant market and leisurely stroll through the lush park nearby.

Chapter 8

As we strolled through the bustling market, vibrant laughter echoed around us. The sun caught in her eyes, making them sparkle like jewels, and I couldn't help but smile. She turned to me, her voice soft and sweet as she asked about my expression. "Just happy," I replied, pulling her close for a hug. "Just happy," I said again.

With a sense of nostalgia, Zahra led me through the bustling market, her vibrant eyes shining with memories of her childhood. She expertly weaved through the crowd, stopping at various stalls to carefully inspect each vegetable before choosing the freshest ones for her basket. We made our way to her favourite section, where she conversed effortlessly with the vendors in her native Amharic. And I couldn't help but feel a strong connection to her and the culture that surrounded us. The spicy scents and vivid colours filled my senses, transporting me to a world that was both foreign and familiar at the same time.

At the market, my senses were inundated with the sights, sounds, and smells of vendors selling handmade crafts and delicious food. Zahra's face lit up as she caught a whiff of freshly ground coffee beans, and I knew how much she cherished her authentic Ethiopian coffee at home. With a smile on my face, I suggested we grab some beans to make her day. Zahra eagerly agreed and practically skipped over to the coffee stand, expertly selecting the perfect bag of beans. Her eyes sparkled with joy as she proudly held up her selection and we continued browsing stalls with our arms now loaded with bags from different vendors. We decided to forgo our plans for the park as we headed home, both content with our successful shopping trip. As someone who typically dislikes shopping, even I had to admit that it had been a wonderful day well spent with my wife.

Back in our kitchen, I couldn't help but smile as she carefully laid out bags of pungent Ethiopian spices and exotic ingredients. "Can you teach me how to make your famous Doro Wat?" I eagerly asked. Her face lit up with pride, and she replied, "I promise, you'll love it," she said with a satisfied smile.

We sat on the sofa, sipping coffee and catching up on our day. The sun beamed through the window, highlighting the network of scars on my scalp. She reached out and gently traced her fingers along them, a silent acknowledgement of our shared struggles. In her embrace, I felt safe and loved no matter how far apart we may be. Excitement filled her voice as she spoke about her upcoming trip to visit family back home. My mind couldn't help but drift to images of violence and political unrest that I had seen on the news. My apprehension grew stronger with each passing minute, and I struggled to push away the thoughts that threatened to ruin our day. My mind screamed for me to stop her—to say no. But how could I refuse her? She hadn't been back since the conflict began. Now they say it's safe. But is it? Doubt creeps in like a toxic gas. I'm lost, helpless, my mind racing. How can I stop her from leaving? Fake an illness? Hide her passport? Did she miss the flight? No, none of that feels right. Reality hits me hard - it's time to do the right thing for once.

"Just make sure to stay safe," I urged, my voice strained trying to hide my unease. I was about to say something but thought better.

Anyone in my shoes would be feeling the same. My wife's going to war-torn country. What can I possibly do? Can I even do anything? My throat tightens with anxiety. I place my steaming cup of coffee down on the table and turn towards her, extending my hand in a gesture of invitation. She smiled playfully before making her way over to me, sliding perfectly into the nook of my arm. The heat radiating from her body instantly calmed my nerves, and for a moment, everything else faded away. We were close, our bodies touching and moving to the soft music. I had to have her, so I pulled her in for a deep kiss that stole my breath. Our lips met in a fervent kiss, and a tingle of electricity shot through my body. She tasted like mint and faintly of coffee, her soft moans filling the space between us. I could feel the heat radiating from her body. Her eyes were bright with passion and her hands roamed eagerly over my skin. I traced circles on her cheek, feeling the smoothness beneath my fingertips. The sun peeked through the curtains, casting a warm golden glow on our tangled limbs as we moved in sync, lost in the intensity of our desire for each other.

As Zahra's lips parted, she whispered the three words that made my heart skip a beat and tears well up in my eyes. "I love you," she said, her voice trembling with emotion. I pulled her closer, feeling the warmth of her body against mine and hearing the sweet sound of our synchronised breaths. Lost in the beauty of our connection, we continued on our way to the bedroom, still intertwined as one.

Our clothes were soon scattered around the room, discarded like fragments of our past lives. All that mattered now was our skin against skin, as we lay intertwined on the luxurious silk sheets. The room filled with the intoxicating scents of sweat, passion, and love as we explored each other's bodies. My fingers traced every curve and crevice, committing them to memory. She arched towards me when my lips found her neck, her breath catching and moans escaping as she uttered my name. Her hands roamed over my body, mapping out every inch until there was nothing left between us but raw desire. My tongue continued its exploration of her body, savouring the taste of her salty skin and causing her to shudder and cry out in blissful release. Our physical union was more than just a pleasurable act; it was an intimate unveiling of our deepest selves. When we finally reached satisfaction, our bodies remained connected, basking in the euphoria of the moment. Zahra rested against my chest, tracing patterns on my skin with her fingertips. I leaned down and pressed a gentle kiss to her forehead, inhaling her intoxicating scent. She looked up at me with a soft smile, propping herself up on one elbow to meet my gaze.

My eyes are drawn to her intense gaze, which seems to hold a million unspoken thoughts. "What's on your mind?" I ask, intrigued by her captivating presence.

Her smile widens, causing her eyes to crinkle at the corners. "Just how happy I am," she replies softly.

As we lie there, savouring the moment, she lets out a satisfied sigh. "That was incredible," she breathes out, her voice brimming with pleasure. Her warmth spreads to my own cheeks and I can't help but agree, finding myself grinning uncontrollably.

"Definitely one for the books," I say, my smile mirroring hers as we revel in the afterglow together.

CHAPTER 9

I watched as Zahra reorganised the spice rack; I couldn't help but study her delicate fingers carefully arranging each jar with precision. A glimmer of admiration filled me as I realised how much love she poured into every aspect of her life. Zahra moved around the kitchen, her hair twisted into a messy bun, I couldn't help but watch in awe. She reached for the jar of berbere spice, delicately measured out a perfect amount, and expertly tossed it into the pot on the stove. The spices sizzled and filled the room with a tantalising aroma. I wanted to help, but I felt like I was just getting in the way. As I watched, I couldn't help but admire her effortless movements around the kitchen. "You make it look so easy," I said with a smile. She turned to me, her eyes sparkling mischievously. "Well, you know what they say... I only let you help because you're cute." she teased, nudging my arm playfully.

I impishly nudged her back. "Hey, I have skills too." I countered.

Standing alongside her in the kitchen, dicing onions for our second attempt at making Doro Wat, memories flooded back of our first disastrous try. Onion tears streamed down my face as we both laughed uncontrollably, covered in flour and spices. Zahra playfully nudged me with her elbow. "Do you remember how many tears you shed?" she teased, taking over my one and only task.

I playfully feigned offence. "Hey, my tears added extra flavour," I joked, adding a sprinkle of salt to the pot. Our bond had grown even stronger through that hilarious and messy cooking experience.

We shared a moment, no words needed, then got back to work in the kitchen. The clatter of pots and pans joined the steaming water and sizzling meat. As we chopped and stirred, our eyes locked in silent understanding. Strangers turned lovers, appreciating the path that brought us here. I took a break, and let the pro handle it. I pulled out my phone and scrolled through Zahra's photos. There she was, in that damn red apron. The stains from our cooking experiments couldn't hide her smile. "BOSS LADY" embroidered in bold letters, a perfect fit for my wife.

"Admit it, you're just jealous because I'm the queen of spice and you're just Tommy the taste tester." She teased; her eyes filled with mischief.

"Quit playing, you know I'm the true king of flavour." I retorted, a smirk playing on my lips. She met my challenge with a mischievous glint in her eyes.

"Ha! You couldn't handle the heat if it slapped you in the face."

The scent of spices filled the air as we playfully bantered back and forth. "Oh please," I scoffed, "I could spice up anything better than you." We both burst into laughter at our silly competition, enjoying the familiar banter between us.

She leaned into my arms, her body fitting perfectly against mine. Her hot breath grazed my skin as she spoke in a hushed tone. "Promise me."

"Anything," I replied without hesitation.

"Promise that we'll always find our way back to each other, no matter what," her eyes held a fierce determination.

"Always," I promised, sealing it with a passionate kiss that left us both breathless. We exchanged grins, but suddenly her face changed. Something was bothering her.

"Ethiopia," she said, as she set down her mug on the countertop. "I've been thinking about the trip.

The thought of her returning to her family home made me sick. "Let's go together," I offered, trying to stay composed.

Her eyes searched mine, reading me like an open book. "I have to see my family. It's been too long."

I couldn't argue with her unbreakable bond with her family. Through gritted teeth, I asked the one question burning in my mind, "Is it safe?"

She squeezed my arm reassuringly. "I won't be anywhere near trouble." I wanted to protest, but when I looked into her eyes, my words died in my throat.

All that came out was a weak "okay." I forced a smile that felt more like a grimace. I agreed to something I knew deep down was a mistake. The tension between us was suffocating. I couldn't bring myself to say the words. My mind was a jumbled mess of worries and doubts.

"What if something goes wrong? What if—" I bit my lip, trying to push away the doubts.

"It won't; trust me," she said, her thumb lightly tracing circles on the back of my hand—a small gesture that held a flicker of hope.

I couldn't let her leave. I wanted to keep talking. But all I could manage was a weak "Wait." My eyes followed her figure, graceful and strong, as she walked away. Zahra, with her dark hair flowing and summery clothes, looked like a dream. "Not Zahra," I murmured as I watched her, this small, fragile, yet confident woman. A small sigh escaped my lips as I tried to calm down.

A voice, cold as death, shattered the silence, and my heart leapt into my throat. *'Hello, Tommy.'* It resonated with an icy detachment that sent my heart racing. I longed for it to be Zahra's voice, but deep down I knew it couldn't be her. It was distant yet menacing, like a ghostly whisper from beyond.

'Are you ready for the next chapter?' The words slithered out. I stopped dead, unable to move or even breathe. The voice felt hauntingly real. Trembling, I called out to her, hoping against hope for a different response.

"Zahra," I shouted, my voice trembling with anxiety.

"Almost done," she responded, her footsteps reverberating down the hallway as she approached.

Standing before me, she gave me a questioning look, offering to assist. "Did you call for me?" I asked nervously, still startled by the shadowy voice.

"No," she replied, just as confused. "I thought you called for me?"

My senses prickle with unease as I try to pinpoint the source knowing that whatever or whoever it is, it is not welcome here.

Confusion swirled in my mind, and before I could voice my thoughts. Zahra's phone blared to life.

"Three Little Birds" by Bob Marley, one of our many favourite songs, filled the room. She answered quickly, listening intently to whoever was on the other line. After a brief pause, her face twisted with concern. Sweat blooms across my body. I knew this was serious

I impatiently demanded; my voice laced with fear. "What's wrong?" she stuttered, her voice quivering.

"Tommy," she choked out, "we have to go. Your dad..." Her words trailed off as tears welled in her eyes and fear set in. "He's in the hospital. Heart attack."

My body turned to lead, my heartbeat quickened, and I struggled to catch my breath. Each word was a sucker punch, knocking the air out of me. We weaved through traffic, every red light a cruel obstacle as we raced to my dad's hospital room.

CHAPTER 10

"Regret, like a tail, comes at the end."

Ethiopian Proverb

The lack of funding is painfully evident in the crowded hallways of an NHS hospital. Patients on gurneys line the walls, some tended by weary relatives and some unaccompanied. Each person lies facing the flickering fluorescent lights as if pleading for forgiveness. Among these patients who are not able to pay the excessive private charges, there are occasional gaps, revealing the pale blue walls bear deep scratches from metal-framed trolleys, revealing the drywall beneath like white scars. The generic prints on the walls are so dull and lifeless that they seem bleached by the non-existent sunlight in this windowless corridor. The confined space amplifies the cries and whimpers, but the nurses have become numb to it all, desensitised after being constantly exposed to such suffering and overworked as a result. Doctors and nurses hustled with purpose. Zahra squeezed my hand tightly as we moved through the chaos. Every door we pass has a hand sanitiser dispenser on the wall and large plastic signs over the door; they are dark with white writing—no fancy fonts, just bold and in caps. We leave behind the maternity ward, paediatrics, oncology, geriatrics, and the acute care unit. We bypass them all heading for the ICU, as that's where dad is. With each step, my heart raced faster and faster. We had to get to him before it was too late. We dodged trollies and nurses like they were landmines, our footsteps heavy with dread. But we didn't stop until we reached his room, praying it wasn't too late.

"Nearly there," I grunted between breaths, more to convince myself than anyone else.

We reached a set of double doors in front of us. We paused, tilting our heads up to take in one more sign similar to the ones we had passed earlier. This reads 'Intensive Care.' I nudge the door open, and it swings smoothly and soundlessly on its hinges. A gust of air greets my face, its warmth mingled with a hint of bleach. Old photos of hospital staff adorn the creamy white walls before me. Most likely those who have either passed away or retired to nursing homes by now. The width of the hallway is narrow; if I stretch my arms out, I can almost touch both sides.

I hurried into the room, my heart racing. My eyes immediately found my dad lying in the bed, his skin pale and almost translucent against the stark white sheets. Each breath sounded like a struggle, and I saw the faint sheen of sweat on his forehead.

"Dad," I said, trying to keep my voice calm as I approached him. I gently placed my hand on his forehead and felt the heat radiating from his feverish body. "I'm here," I reassured him, willing him to get better.

My mom sat in the stiff hospital chair; her fingers intertwined with my dad's. Her knuckles were white from grasping his hand so tightly. Her eyes were red and puffy, and tears streamed down her face as she whispered words of love and support to him. I tried to hold back tears as I watched her suffering. Zahra stood behind me, her hand a warm weight on my shoulder. She had become a part of our family, supporting us through this difficult time without needing to say anything. Just having her close brought me comfort. I sank into the only other chair next to my dad's bed.

My eyelids were heavy, and my back ached from sitting in the rigid hospital chair for hours. Zahra's fingers dug into my hand; her nails left crescent-shaped imprints on my skin. The heart monitor beeped in a steady rhythm; it seemed to mock us. Each beat felt like a countdown, stealing precious minutes with our dad. Sitting there helpless, memories swirled in my mind: childhood holidays, family celebrations, and special moments together; those memories felt like a lifetime ago. Mom remained as when we arrived, her shoulders slumping and her eyes much darker than before. Her fingers trembled as she clutched my dad's hand, his once strong grip now weak. I could see the weight of forty years of marriage etched on her face, the lines deepening with each passing moment. He lay motionless on the bed, machines beeping and whirring around him. I knew he was fading away, and I felt a heavy weight settle on my chest. This was the moment I had been dreading—when I would have to step up and become the man my parents had always wanted me to be. But as I looked at my dad, his face colourless and frail, I couldn't help but feel a rush of emotions—love, fear, and sadness—all mixed together. I squeezed his hand, silently praying for more time with him.

The steady beep of the monitor began to slow, and my heart sped in response. A nurse appeared at my father's bedside, her movements precise and efficient. She checked his vitals with a detached professionalism, her expression betraying no emotion. I longed to beg her to do something, anything, but my words caught in my throat. I felt as though I were suffocating on my own breath as I stood up to give the nurse space. As the beeps slowed, I stood frozen, completely lost, unable to move. Two more faint beeps sounded before the monitor fell silent. My world stopped with it.

My legs trembled, then buckled beneath me, and I crumpled to my knees on the cold linoleum floor. Hot tears streamed down my face as I finally released all hope with a whisper, "It's over."

Zahra rushed to support me, her arms wrapping tightly around my shaking body. But even her strong grip couldn't bear the weight of my grief. Dad was my pillar of strength.

"Was!" With venom dripping from each syllable, I spat out the word.

Suddenly, a blur of white shapes burst into the room, their urgent voices creating a cacophony of chaos.

"We need the crash cart, stat!" one nurse shouted above the din.

Another nurse turned to us, gesturing for us to move away from the hospital bed.

"Please, sir, give us some space to work," she commanded firmly, her eyes filled with purpose and compassion.

My heart thudded against my chest, and I stumbled backwards in shock. It couldn't be real. I reached out, grasping for something solid to hold onto. Zahra's grip on my hand was the only thing keeping me grounded.

"Tommy," she whispered, barely audible over the flurry of medical activity and frantic attempts to save our dad.

It was all too much to process. My dad, my rock, was slipping away right before my eyes. And I was completely helpless. Despite the overwhelming urge to lash out and scream, I remained frozen in place, unable to tear my gaze away from the doctors' desperate efforts.

"Please," I shout out, my voice hoarse with desperation. "Not yet."

And then it happens—the flatline tone that always signals death in movies. But this is real life, and it's so much worse.

"Nooooo…!" I screamed, not even recognising my own voice. At that moment, my world crumbled as waves of anguish and regret washed over me.

The incessant noise from the machine shows no signs of stopping, and each passing moment only makes it more aggravating. The nurse glides in her movement's fluidity and confidence as her experienced hands quickly silence the obnoxious tone with a single button press. I could tell she had performed this task countless times before. My mom was now standing by my dad's side, grasping his hand. She was talking nonstop, but I couldn't make out her words through the anguish in her voice. When she finally called my name, I looked up to see the same emptiness reflected in her eyes that I felt in my own. It was like we were both just shells of our former selves. Mum stood in front of me, her shoulders trembling with sobs. Tears streamed down her face, carving glistening paths over the years of worry etched into her skin. "Tommy," she choked out, her voice barely recognisable. Zahra and I stood by her, helpless and speechless, unsure of how to comfort her. Even as I tried to offer words of comfort, they wouldn't come. Trying to be the rock for my family, I uttered words that felt hollow even as they left my lips. "We'll figure this out," I said, trying to sound sure of myself. But inside, I was crumbling under the weight of our new reality.

"I'm scared," she whispered, tears streaming down her face.

"I know, Mom. Me too," I replied honestly.

Her sobs shook her body as she clung to me, tears staining my shirt. I wrapped my arms around her, and we stood there in the hospital hallway, both of us trembling with grief. But even in this moment of vulnerability, she held on to me tightly, seeking comfort and strength.

"I can't do this without him," she whispered.

"Yes, you can," I replied firmly, wiping away her tears. "And so, can I. We'll get through this together."

My thoughts were pulling me down, but I had to stay strong for her so instead of wallowing in my sorrow, I chose to persevere.

"He's gone, Zahra," I said quietly, my voice heavy with sorrow. "He's really gone."

The words hung in the air, carrying a sense of finality that none of us were ready to accept. Our dad was dead, and nothing could change that. Her hold on me strengthens, and I surrender, my face wet with tears. These are not tears of sorrow for a dad who won't see another sunrise; they are silent sobs for all the moments that will never be relived, every story that remains unspoken, and every 'I love you' left unsaid.

"Let's go," I said softly, urging her towards the exit.

Together, we guided our mom out into the cool night air, leaving behind the harsh brightness of the hospital. The outside world greeted us with a dampness that matched our emotions. Climbing into our car, the familiar scent of aged leather and musty air greeted us, reminding us of simpler times.

"Are you tired?" I gently asked my mom as she closed her eyes, leaning against the window for support. She nodded weakly in response. "We'll be home soon," I reassured her.

The car engine hummed as we drove down the road home; our only company was the fleeting shadows from passing headlights. With the back of my hand, I wiped away tears, tasting salt on my lips.

When we arrived, I helped mom out of the car, her fragile figure leaning heavily on me as we made our way to the front door. As soon as we stepped into our home, the familiar scent offered some comfort. Zahra immediately took charge as she led us into the kitchen, her activities were a much-needed distraction. With practised ease, she prepared the tea; the familiar ritual offered a sense of normalcy to our disordered world. We gathered around the table. Silence took hold, as words at this moment were insufficient. As we sipped our tea, a point of calm settled around us, if only for a minute. I shifted in my seat and cleared my throat, feeling awkward.

"How are you doing?" I asked tentatively, immediately regretting my words. Her eyes were red and puffy, and her hand felt cold and lifeless in mine as I gave it a gentle squeeze. She gave me a weary smile, her eyes reflecting the weight of her struggles.

"I'll manage," she sighed, her voice barely above a whisper. "One day at a time."

"Yes, one day at a time," I repeated, trying to convey a sense of conviction in my tone.

Chapter 11

*"When one is in love, a cliff becomes a
meadow."*

Ethiopian Proverb

Zahra and I sat side by side at the kitchen table, surrounded by stacks of papers and pamphlets with sombre images of angels and crosses. Sunlight streamed through the window, casting a bittersweet glow on our faces as we worked together to plan the final farewell for our dad. Now and then, one of us would pause and wipe away a tear, but we stayed focused on the arrangements. My brother and my children came by to assist. We gathered around the table, sharing stories and laughter amidst the tears. Together, we chose a simple, yet elegant wooden casket adorned with sunflowers and daisies, his favourite flowers. We carefully selected songs and readings that reflected his life and values, making sure to include all of his favourite hymns. And then, we drove to the cemetery to choose the perfect spot for him to rest peacefully. It was a difficult and emotional journey, but we faced each hurdle together as a strong and united family.

As the sun dipped below the horizon, shadows crept in and draped over us like a heavy blanket. Zahra and I huddled close on the sofa, surrounded by old photo albums with faded covers. She lightly flipped through the pages, pointing out photos of dad with his infectious smile and legendary storytelling skills. I joined in, reminiscing about fishing trips and the exhilaration of reeling in a big catch, or enjoying the stillness of being out on the water, just dad and me. We laughed as we remembered the sporting events we attended; our voices raised as one. We clung to each other, tears mixing with smiles, finding comfort in memories and our shared love for him. Zahra has always been my support, then and now. Her touch is a lifeline in this storm of pain. But even she can't shield me from the relentless demons that haunt me. My past is a black cloud hanging over everything. Zahra's hand squeezes mine, a small gesture of support amidst the unquenchable shadows. But even her touch can't shield me from the approaching darkness.

I never told anyone about my dark side. Not even Zahra. Too difficult. Too much pain. Like many men, I buried my emotions, afraid of the stigma surrounding it. I wanted to tell her, let her in on the shit that's been eating away at me. But it's fucking hard, too much pain. I stuffed everything down and pretended it didn't exist. But when I finally opened up to Zahra, it was like a weight had been lifted off my back. The battle with demons still raged within, but at least now I had someone by my side. I finally mustered up the courage to confess everything to Zahra while we were living together in Ethiopia. It was around 2015, just over a year ago. It was difficult at first, the words hesitant as they left my lips, but then they came pouring out like a flood. Tears streamed down my face as I relived the pain and fear that had haunted me for so long. And yet, as I spoke, Zahra listened without judgement, offering only support, and understanding. Confessing my struggles was terrifying, but also liberating. And I knew that no matter how challenging my journey towards healing may be, Zahra would be there every step of the way, my unwavering ally and supporter.

Chapter 12

Finally, the day of the funeral arrived. Dad had always remarked he wanted it to be simple—just a celebration of his life rather than a sad ceremony. And so, with heavy hearts but also gratitude for having such an incredible father, we said farewell. The funeral home was quiet, except for the hum of hushed whispers and the faint sound of shuffling feet. Each person was moving like a lone figure in a sombre procession.

My eyes scanned the crowd, searching for her among the sea of mourners. Then, I saw her- Zahra- with her dark hair cascading down her back. Our gaze locked and a subtle nod conveyed our unspoken understanding. She has always had a profound impact on my life, and even now, in this moment of loss, she somehow manages to make me feel better. During the service, she squeezed my hand tightly as we listened to people drone on about my father. The atmosphere was heavy and oppressive, mirroring the weight of my own helplessness. The air was heavy with the scent of flowers, adding to my already overwhelming feelings of grief. The Sun was bright and had started its descent. When the ceremony ended and we said our final farewells, they lowered his casket into the ground, I couldn't hold back my tears any longer. I didn't look down into the earth. Looking down would be to see him cold in a box without any hugging or goodnight kiss. My mother's tears were more than just tears; they were an outpouring of deep grief. That instant the awareness that life would go on without him, and time only stopped for her, shattered her completely. Her sorrow seemed to seep out of every pore of her body, and her anguished cries echoed through the cemetery. A cry so raw that even the eyes of the strangers around us were suddenly wet with tears. In her black dress and dirt on her pale hands, she knelt at the edge of the freshly dug grave as if trying to be closer to the husband she had just lost. There was the chill of autumn that hung in the air, making her anguish even more intense. My brother came to her aid, nodding at me before leading her away, still weeping, to the waiting black limousine that had brought them here.

"Tommy." Zahra's voice cut through the silence. Her hand found mine, and she whispered in my ear, "I'll be careful. I promise."

I squeezed her hand tightly, knowing that she was talking about her upcoming trip to Ethiopia. I implored softly, "Please, just take care of yourself."

She took my hand in hers, her grip firm and unwavering. As she met my gaze, I saw the same intense connection we've always had. "I promise," she said, her words filled with determination and trust.

Her voice softening, she added, "And please watch over our mom while I'm gone." The weight of responsibility settled on my shoulders as I nodded in understanding.

Our footsteps echoed on the gravel path, each crunching louder than the last. Zahra's eyes met mine, and a silent understanding passed between us—she knew the weight of grief I was carrying. Her hand found mine, and I squeezed it gratefully. We stopped and gazed into each other's eyes, our unspoken love and emotion speaking volumes that words could never capture.

"You are my rock, my everything," I told her with all my heart.

Tears welled up in her eyes, and she spoke with a quiet but steady tone. "Tommy, you're never alone. No matter how far we may be, I will always be by your side." We held each other tightly, surrounded by the silent gravestones, as the sun set, casting a warm golden light over everything. Zahra pulled away slightly to look up at the sky, a small smile playing on her lips.

She gripped my hand tightly and pointed towards the sky. I followed her gaze and saw a flock of birds soaring gracefully above us.

Her eyes lit up with wonder as she said, "Those are our loved ones, finally finding their freedom." I watched the birds glide gracefully through the air. At that moment, I realised just how much hope she carried within her, even in the darkest times. I let out a shaky breath and swiped at the tear that rolled down Zahra's cheek.

"Thank you," I whispered. She gave me a small smile before leaning in for a tender kiss. Our foreheads pressed together as we both struggled with our emotions.

"He was my father too," she whispered, her voice barely above a sigh. We stood there in silence for a few moments before Zahra pulled away and took my hand. "Let's go home," she said softly, leading me towards the car.

The sky appears to be on fire. I've not noticed a thing comparable to this before. The sun, so blinding just a few minutes ago, is now this glowing ball of molten orange, sinking gracefully behind the trees. It's like it's being drawn downward by a hidden force, taking the day with it. The clouds: are they usually this colour? They're streaked with pink, like someone smeared a paintbrush across the sky, leaving trails of light and shadow. I can actually see the colours change. The orange melts into red, then softens into purple, and the blue of the sky becomes deeper. Everything looks... different. Even the air feels different—cooler, quieter. The birds have stopped singing. It's as if the whole world is holding its breath, waiting for whatever comes after the sun. I can't stop staring. It's almost like watching magic—something that doesn't feel real but is right in front of me. Zara gave me a tug, keeping me moving to the car. The cemetery gates closed behind us, leaving behind a faint echo of prayers and hushed farewells for the loved one we laid to rest. The drive home was familiar, but a heaviness hung in the air. The streetlights cast long shadows that seemed to stretch out endlessly before us. The routine sequence of lights reminded me of the instructions my mom gave to both my brother and me. At the time, I would have been about eleven or twelve years old; this was a time and place before everyone became obsessed with their mobile devices. Our mom's voice echoed throughout the neighbourhood, a familiar sound whenever we left for somewhere. As she spoke our names, her call was urgent and necessary. When she used that tone, we knew not to ignore her.

'*Make sure you're home before the streetlights come on!" she would shout. 'Do you hear me?! If not, you'll get a good hiding.*"

Chapter 13

"Confiding a secret to an unworthy person is like carrying a grain in a bag with a hole in it."

Ethiopian Proverb

When I reflect on my time in Addis Ababa, my mind drifts to the first day I met Zahra. You see, at the time, I was working as a close protection specialist—a fancy term for bodyguard—for some pretty important people. Let me tell you, it was no easy job. I was constantly on edge, always on high alert for potential threats. But hey, I've got eyes like a hawk and can blend into any urban setting like a chameleon, thanks to my military training. Sometimes I would just use everyday objects as cover while keeping a watchful eye on my client. It was all part of the role. Trust me, blending in without detection is not as straightforward as it sounds. I had escape routes memorised. I kept safe houses and hospitals on my speed dial. Always a plan for any situation. Money was decent, but not as glamorous as the movies make it seem. I never had to use my weapon in three years. But I still clean that damn thing every night, as if my life depends on it. I couldn't afford to let my guard down.

I remember one morning; the air was buzzing with enthusiasm. Outside my hotel, the air hums with the sound of honking horns and people's constant babble. Minibuses, which they called "blue donkeys," swerve in and out of traffic, with their drivers shouting out their windows to commuters hurrying by. The roads are bursting with taxis, motorcycles, and pedestrians, everyone in a rush to start their week. The smell of roasting coffee wafts through the air from small street-side stands, where vendors brew Ethiopia's famous buna in clay pots over open flames. The scent of fried dough from sambusa stalls, their crispy, golden triangles piled high, prepares for the usual morning rush. Everybody is moving quickly. Businessmen and women stride with a purpose, donning modern outfits, their polished shoes clicking on the pavement. Some gathered immediately outside the hotel to have their shoes polished by the show-shine guy. Others wear colourful traditional dresses—white cotton *shemmas* with intricate, sharp patterns along the edges. Students in uniform carry frayed backpacks, and women balance baskets of goods on their heads with proficient grace. With all this going on, I couldn't shake off the feeling that something significant was going to happen. It wasn't even a special day or anything I could think of—just a regular Monday. Yet, I still couldn't help feeling this electric energy coursing through me as I headed to work. I sat at my usual spot at the 'Buna Roastery,' my favourite coffee place, and I eagerly told my friend about my feelings, but he just chuckled and said something about caffeine-induced optimism. Still, I knew deep down that today was going to be different, a turning point for me, in a positive way. My mind was clear, and for once, the usual images didn't bother me. The silence from all the noise allowed me to concentrate on the present moment. And boy, am I glad I did, because something incredible happened that day. I set out to watch over the ambassador in lively Addis; everything seemed routine.

I had checked all the equipment and was feeling pretty good about things. But there was this nagging feeling that had been with me since dawn. Still, I pushed it aside as I approached the ambassador's hotel, feeling light and ready for whatever the day might bring. While conducting my routine perimeter inspection, I observed the vendors lining the pavements, actively searching for anything unusual. Their stalls overflowed with everything from fresh fruits—bananas, oranges, and mangos—to small electronics, cigarettes, and phone chargers. A woman sitting on a low stool calls out in Amharic, waving bundles of green eucalyptus leaves. Then I saw her—a woman—a lady. Wow. Just wow. She glowed. She exuded an air of elegance as she engaged in negotiations with a vendor, her hair flowing down her back. In these bustling city streets, she was a striking contrast. Her beautiful white *habesha*, enhanced with colourful patterns around all the borders, swayed in the wind like a rare gem, while her dark hair cascaded down her back. I noticed that she was wearing a wooden cross over her dress. Her beauty was blinding. I desperately blinked away the swirling dust of passing cars. The world around me blurred into nothingness; all that mattered was her. This woman before me. Who was she? I couldn't take my eyes off her. Although cliché, it was love at first sight for me, and I knew it then. While I watched her, I felt an exhilarating rush flow through me, and without even realising it, my feet started moving towards her. My mind was solely focused on getting closer to this captivating woman. I pushed all my other responsibilities to the back of my mind. I just had to talk to her. Know her. With an anxious opportunity, I crossed the street. As if under a spell, I walked, drowning out all other noises with the pounding of my heart. But just as quickly as she appeared, she disappeared behind a passing bus. I couldn't believe my luck—finally meeting someone—well, nearly meeting someone. Their beauty immediately brought me to life, only for them to disappear before my eyes.

As the sun beat down on me, I followed the ambassador's entourage through a maze of ornate buildings and manicured gardens. She smiled and exchanged pleasantries with important officials, but I couldn't focus on anything else except for the brief encounter I just had. My job felt meaningless compared to the fiery spark this stranger had ignited in me. Exhausted and lost in my thoughts, I trudged back to my hotel. The doubts that had been nagging at me all day surfaced once again. Was this all there was to my life? Did my life consist solely of endless disappointments and fleeting moments of happiness? Or was there something more meaningful waiting for me out there?

The streets outside my hotel were alive with activity, like a beehive humming with energy, buzzing with the pulse of a city that never seemed to slow down. It's a symphony of urban energy, pulsing with life and vibrancy; there's a shared sense of purpose—everyone has their own destination to reach, their own task to accomplish. I stepped into the bustling hotel lobby; my mind was in a daze. In a trance-like state, lost in reflection, I spotted her. The woman who had captured my interest earlier stood in my hotel lobby. Her radiant presence caught my eye. She stood out among the crowd, still wearing her beautiful white habesha. I stopped dead. I felt rooted to the spot. My fingers twitched at my sides as I tried to find something to do with them, but I couldn't take my eyes off her. Admiring her. She seemed to glow under the warm lights of the lobby; every curve and angle of her face left me spellbound.

My feet shuffled forward on autopilot, and I coughed awkwardly before nervously clearing my throat. "Uh... hi," I stuttered, my heart pounding in my chest despite my attempts to act cool.

She met my gaze with a warm smile. "How was your day?"

"Good, thanks," I replied, my voice betraying my nerves. "How about yours?"

"I'm Zahra," she introduced herself, extending her hand. Her touch was gentle yet strong, instantly connecting us.

"Tommy," I said, attempting to exude confidence. My own name felt foreign on my tongue like it belonged to someone better suited to her attention.

Her smile widened when she heard my name. "Tommy," she repeated, relishing it. "You seem preoccupied."

I let out a nervous chuckle. "Just tired, a long day of security-type stuff." I added quickly, "But it's pretty boring."

But instead of breaking eye contact or passing judgement, she only smiled and remarked, "It must be quite a responsibility."

Her words caught me off guard, but in the best possible way. Finally, someone who saw past my walls and scars. Perhaps she even saw me as someone of value. "Yeah, it can be," I admitted. My interest was piqued; I couldn't resist asking about her.

"And what about you?" I finally asked.

Her lips curled into a playful smirk as she spoke. "I usually work the morning shift at the front desk here, but you probably already knew that," she said, her eyes sparkling with warmth and mischief.

"I'm sorry, I'm not very observant in the morning," I admitted with a sheepish smile.

I decided not to mention the time I saw her on the street, just in case she didn't remember me.

She let out a bubbly laugh. "I've always been a bit of an adventurer," she confessed dreamily. "Working at the front desk pays the bills, but my heart always yearns for the mountains and lakes." Her English was perfect—better than a few of my friends back home.

Intrigued by her sense of adventure, I couldn't help but ask. "I would love for you to show me your favourite spot some time," I said boldly, hoping I wasn't being too forward. After all, my divorce had robbed me of most of my self-respect, and I had nothing to lose.

Her eyes lit up with excitement. She eagerly described a place where the sky met the earth in perfect harmony and tranquillity reigned.

"That sounds incredible," I replied, trying to contain my eagerness at the thought of potentially going on a date with her.

We stood in the crowded lobby, surrounded by people rushing about. She shifted her weight from foot to foot, avoiding my gaze. I should get back to work," she said, glancing at her watch.

As she turned to leave, I noticed the faint scent of her perfume lingering in the air. Something inside me began to shift, feeling a surge of hope and possibility. I couldn't help but stare after her, admiring her confident stride and the way she effortlessly commanded attention. A sense of hope and possibility filled me as I made my way towards the elevators.

Just as I reached out to press the button, I caught a glimpse of her reflection in the shiny metal doors. She was standing behind me, a small smile playing on her lips.

"Hey," she said confidently, tucking a stray strand of hair behind her ear. "Want to grab a drink later?"

My stomach did a somersault as I turned to face her fully. This beautiful girl was asking me out. Me?

I couldn't contain my excitement as I replied with a grin, "Yes, definitely!" I replied eagerly. "Eight o'clock in the bar?"

She nodded, her own smile widening. "Perfect."

As we parted ways, I couldn't stop grinning from ear to ear. Who knew that this chance encounter could lead to such an exciting opportunity? I couldn't wait for eight o'clock to come around.

<h1 style="text-align:center">CHAPTER 14</h1>

I spent the next few frantic hours trying on my limited clothes, having no idea what I was doing—a task foreign to me. I hated it. The clock crawled towards eight, and my palms were already sweating. The elevator bell rang, and my heart started racing. I took a quick glance at myself in the reflective doors, trying to calm my nerves before stepping out. "She's way out of my league," I thought to myself. As the seconds ticked away, I stepped out into the lobby. Excitement and anxiety mixed in my stomach. My nerves were on edge as I made my way to the bar, constantly second-guessing what I was wearing and if I should have asked for her number.

Then her voice shattered my reverie: "Tommy?"

Her white dress, with its flowing fabric and intricate lace details, hugged her curves in all the right places, making her look like a vision of beauty. She took my hand and led me through the crowded room to the bar. We settled onto our stools at the end of the bar. Rihanna's 'We Found Love' blasted through the speakers, adding to the already buzzing atmosphere. I couldn't help but feel nervous as I thought about where this night might lead. But as we chatted and laughed over our drinks, her genuine interest in getting to know me was palpable, and I found myself equally intrigued by her. Conversation flowed easily between us, and I couldn't believe that someone as stunning as she wanted to spend time with me.

As the weeks turned into months, she never pestered me for details about my past or made me feel guilty for my quirks. Just let me be. Instead, she was a steady and reliable presence in my life, always there to offer support and encouragement as I worked through my fears. On weekday evenings, we would meet up at a local bar and bond over cold beers, sharing stories and laughing until our sides hurt. Slowly but surely, I began to let go of the pain that had been holding me back. Our schedules seemed to align perfectly, allowing us to spend even more time together. We just clicked, you know? We would hop in my work truck and explore the city and surrounding areas, discovering hidden gems and experiencing wild adventures together. With every passing moment, I could see the excitement on her face and feel her living life fully alongside me. Our connection was undeniable; it felt like we were meant to be together.

Each morning, I awoke just as the sun began to rise. I smiled as I recognised Zahra's rhythmic tap-tap-tap, a sound that had become synonymous with the start of each day since I moved into her small apartment. She entered with a tray in hand, the aroma of rich Ethiopian coffee and freshly made bread filling the air. I used to question her knocking. It was always her habit to knock before entering a room, even when it was her own. But I didn't mind—it was just another example of her thoughtfulness in everything she did.

"Good morning, Habte," she greeted me with a warm smile. "Your coffee is ready."

As I sipped on the rich, aromatic brew, I felt a sense of comfort and familiarity wash over me—Zahra's simple gesture meant everything to me during those difficult days of adjusting to a new country. Zahra and I spent our days wandering through the colourful exhibits of the National Museum of Ethiopia, marvelling at ancient artefacts, and discussing Amharic phrases. She also took me to her favourite nature spots, where we hiked and picnicked on delicious Ethiopian dishes like injera and wot. Zahra's kindness and empathy were like a fire, spreading warmth wherever she went—traits that seemed to run in her family. One evening, while staying with Zahra's family in Addis, I met her cousin Mita. Her beauty was striking, with high cheekbones and piercing dark eyes. She greeted me with a warm smile and a firm handshake. Throughout dinner, she captivated us with tales of Ethiopian history and folklore. In that moment, surrounded by strong, intelligent women, I couldn't help feeling content, a sense of belonging, for the first time in a long time. Mita exuded confidence and strength, sporting striking features reminiscent of a fearless Amazonian queen from Greek mythology, leading her troops on horseback into battle against the Greeks. Her presence was captivating and powerful, just like Zahra's.

The sun was setting, casting a golden glow through the window of our small apartment. Exhausted from another unfulfilling day of doing very little. I dragged myself inside and heard the faintest crying. I followed it to the bathroom, where Zahra sat on the tile floor, tears streaming down her cheeks. Despite her red eyes and runny nose, she was still the most beautiful person I had ever laid eyes on. Without a word, I kneeled beside her and pulled her into a tight hug. Our bodies seemed to meld together as we sat there, sharing our pain and fears without words. It didn't matter that our pasts were filled with trauma and struggles; in that moment, all we needed was each other. We spoke late into the night, opening up about our deepest wounds and insecurities. Looking at myself in the mirror, I could still see all the scars, revealing past demons. I experienced a sensation of weight being lifted off my shoulders. I didn't feel like a broken man; with Zahra by my side, I felt whole again. She listened to every word I spoke with genuine understanding and care. I felt like someone truly understood me and cared about what I had been through. It was like, I wasn't alone anymore. And that meant everything.

After that night, Zahra and I spent every moment together. We held hands on walks, exchanged secrets over coffee, and talked for hours until the sun rose. The more time we spent together, the more I wanted to share everything with her—my fears, insecurities, and past traumas. As our love deepened, I knew it was time to open up completely. With shaky hands and a racing heart, I sat on the edge of the bed. Zahra sat next to me, her hand resting gently on my back as she encouraged me to speak. Our eyes met, and I took a deep breath before finally telling her everything that had been weighing on me for so long. She listened attentively, never judging, or pressuring me for more than I was ready to share. At that moment, I knew our love was unbreakable.

Chapter 15

Taking a deep breath, I described the day that forever changed my life—the day of a violent attack. An abduction, and torture with no purpose. The words fell from my trembling lips, while Zahra listened intently, her face betraying no emotion. But when tears welled up in my eyes, she reached out and gently held my hand in hers, providing silent support and understanding. Through shaky breaths, I shared my struggles with PTSD and depression, as well as how they had affected not only me but also those closest to me. I shared my struggles with trusting others, stemming from past experiences of being let down by those closest to me. And throughout it all, Zahra remained attentive and empathetic. When I finished speaking, we sat in silence for what felt like an eternity. But then she wrapped her arms around me and whispered three simple words: "I love you." At that instant, all my worries and responsibilities seemed to disappear, and for the first time since the incident, I felt truly supported and understood. Still trembling, I continued talking. "You know," I said as I paused to take a deep breath. "I can remember every single detail of that day—every noise, every smell—it's all still there."

Zahra's small hand tightened around mine, offering comfort and support as I struggled to find the courage to speak. Her touch was a lifeline, grounding me in the present. We sat in silence; her presence spoke volumes—a safe space for me to open up. I desperately needed to do so. Through tears, I finally found the words to tell her everything. Her gentle voice reassured me, "You don't have to if you're not ready."

"I need to," I choked out. And with that, I spoke about the assault, the pain, and the fear. Zahra listened intently, never taking her eyes off mine. I could feel her empathy radiating towards me. "It's okay, take your time." And as I spoke, memories flooded my mind—their attacks on my body, their cruel words echoing in my ears. It felt like I was reliving it all over again, but this time with someone by my side who truly understood.

Zahra saw through my tough exterior and into the depths of emotion that I had buried deep inside. She held my hand tighter and urged me on with her voice, giving me the strength, I needed to push through the pain and anger that had been building up for so long. And in that moment, as we shared this dark part of my past, I knew that with Zahra by my side, I could face anything. My voice cracked with loathing and hurt as I relived the memory.

"They left me on the side of the road like I was nothing," I spat, my voice dripping with bitterness and betrayal. A single tear escaped down my cheek, hot and searing like a branding iron. Zahra's empathy was instinctive, almost suffocating in its intensity. It felt like she wanted to bear all of my pain for me. But even her powerful presence couldn't numb the raw ache in my heart.

"I'm so sorry you had to go through that," she said softly, her words heavy with sincerity. I shook my head, unable to hold back any longer, my voice shaking uncontrollably as I spoke. "Thanks," I managed to choke out.

Zahra reached out and took my hand in hers, offering silent support and understanding as she waited for me to continue. "I always blamed myself," the words came out in a whispered confession, heavy with guilt and self-loathing.

"But it wasn't your fault," Zahra insisted fiercely, shaking her head in disbelief. "You were just living your life." The gentle squeeze of her hand was a lifeline, giving me some sense of validation for the blame I had carried for so long. Her kind words brought more tears to my eyes. In a rush of emotion, I continued speaking. "Maybe if I had been stronger or not such an idiot, it would have turned out differently that night." My head hung low. "It's hard to shake off the guilt and shame," I admitted.

Zahra gently brushed away a tear that had escaped my eye, then wrapped her arms around me. "You are so strong," she whispered, her voice filled with admiration.

"Thank you for sharing this with me." And in that moment, I realised she loved me for who I was, scars and all. Her touch and words were like a soothing balm to my emotional wounds. Our relationship deepened as we became each other's pillars of support, holding each other up through the healing process. We learnt to communicate openly and deal with triggers together. Zahra's unwavering support and understanding became an anchor for me during some of my darkest moments. She took a deep breath, steeling herself for what she was about to reveal. She told me about her harrowing past in Addis Ababa—the challenges, the societal expectations, and the struggle against her own desires. Her words shook me to my core; it was like facing my own pain in a mirror. But strangely, hearing her story brought comfort.

"I fought for my dreams," she declared confidently.

As she spoke, I saw the fierce fire in her eyes and felt an overwhelming urge to protect her beyond my duty as a soldier. In that dimly lit room, with the sounds of the city below us serving as a backdrop, we bared our souls and saw each other in a new light. Both of us were survivors who had weathered storms and emerged stronger.

"I never knew," I declared, my voice quivering. "You've been through so much."

She gave me a bittersweet smile, reminding me that we all have our own struggles in life. I gazed into Zahra's eyes and saw a glimmer of pain but also a deep strength that I admired. She spoke about her struggles with a steady voice, pausing occasionally to wipe away tears. As she shared her story, I could feel the warmth of her body against mine and our heartbeats syncing in rhythm. "You've been through so much," I said, my voice trembling with emotion.

"But you're still standing," I added, marvelling at her resilience. Zahra gave me a small smile, her eyes reflecting a mix of sadness and determination. She told me about facing death and loss, and how hope had seemed like an impossible dream at times. I pulled her close to me, wanting to offer comfort and support.

"You're incredibly strong," I whispered in awe. Zahra met my gaze, her tears now flowing freely, but her resolve unshaken. "Love keeps me going," she said, her voice filled with conviction. And in that moment, I knew it was true love truly is one of the strongest forces in the world.

I didn't hesitate before saying it back to her. The words came easily to me like they were always meant to be said. "I love you." It was like the most natural thing in the world for me to say, and I knew it was true. I felt like this was the start of something special. We were sharing our deepest truths with each other, and in that moment, nothing else mattered.

As I stroked her hair, I couldn't help but feel a sense of connection between us. We both overcame obstacles and became stronger. "You know," I said softly, "we're not so different, you and I."

Zahra tilted her head in curiosity, her eyes glistening with emotion. "How so?" she asked.

"Fire has forged both of us," I responded, tracing the scars on her arm with my fingertips. "But it's what makes us who we are today."

She nodded in understanding and let out a soft chuckle. "I guess our scars aren't so different after all," she said. And in that moment, as we shared our deepest truths with each other, nothing else mattered except for the love and strength that bound us together. Her words spoke volumes about the bond growing between us, one that went beyond physical attraction. As the night wore on, my mind drifted to the duality of fire: its ability to destroy yet also purify. It reminded me of what Mike Tyson's trainer and mentor, Cus D'Amato, once told him about the connection between fire and fear.

"A boy comes to me with a spark of interest. I feed the spark, and it becomes a flame. I feed the flame, and it becomes a fire. I feed the fire, and it becomes a roaring blaze."

CHAPTER 16

"Where man is, disagreement follows."

Ethiopian Proverb

For three decades, my body has been a constant warzone of physical and mental traumas. Each morning, I wake up to an exhausting battle just to get out of bed and face the day. My limbs ache, my mind races with anxiety and fear, and every step feels like a Herculean effort. Doctors toss around labels like confetti - PTSD, bipolar disorder, chronic fatigue syndrome - offering hollow solutions while I am just another guinea pig in their experiments. Every visit, the doctors rattled off cryptic medical jargon that felt like a foreign language to me. I kept returning, desperate for a solution to my broken self. But with each X-ray and therapy session, I could see the puzzle pieces of my injuries scattered and jumbled, a reflection of my stormy past and internal struggles that have left me broken and scarred. On the days when my struggles consume me, I can't escape the memories. The flashbacks came in waves, each one bringing back graphic images of the kidnapping and the brutal violence that was inflicted upon me. A never-ending nightmare, crushing my spirits and leaving helpless. A cancer, gradually consuming, sapping away any remnants of happiness. Yet nothing could or will ever prepare to the horror that was yet to come - monstrous beasts that would make all prior suffering seem like child's play. Detachment became a coping mechanism. It felt like I was just a spectator watching my own life unfold from far away. Some days, the thought of getting out of bed was overwhelming. It felt like a constant, cruel joke. Even if there were fleeting moments of optimism, they never lasted long before fading into despair again. My scars were both a source of pride for what I had overcome. They were a map, tracing the journey I had taken to reach where I am today. My mind was messed up. I couldn't think straight. Everything's a blur. Can't focus. In my nightmares, I am confined to a mental ward. My hands are restrained, and I can't move them without feeling the tightness of the straps. My mind is clear, with no trace of madness. I struggle against the black polyester with all my strength, but I cannot break free. My back aches. A pool of saliva gathers in the back of my mouth. The personnel have left me alone.

My heart races and my eyes dart around, searching for any sign of help. But there is no one coming. The walls in my mind are not without sacrifice - they bring back intense flashbacks and moments of disorientation. I can feel my brain's cells battling to preserve those painful recollections, unwilling to let them slip away into obscurity. Trouble was coming, and it wasn't just about survival anymore. This was a battle against pure evil. I had to protect everything I held dear. The stakes were higher than ever, putting not only my world but the souls of my loved ones at risk. Failure wasn't an option. I would have done anything to keep them safe. My thoughts would always drift to our future, filled with uncertainty and fear. After ten years in the Royal Marines, people saw me as tough and invincible. But inside, I was just a hollow shell haunted by brutal memories. My scars may have healed, but the pain continues. I still avoid mirrors, not wanting to see that broken man staring back.

As we spent more time together, we got closer. Zahra showed me how to truly live. Her laughter was like medicine for my soul. She saw the world in a way I had never considered before, finding beauty and purpose in the simplest things. Her outlook challenged my narrow mindset and pushed me to break free from mundanity & embrace life. With her, every day was an adventure waiting to be discovered. Suddenly, just existing wasn't enough anymore, I wanted to experience life to the fullest. My time at the United Nations was defined by one thing above all else: the rapport that we formed. My colleagues and I developed a strong mutual respect, forged through our experiences in hostile environments. We faced it all: honing my commando skills during operations across the globe, keeping calm under fire, calling the shots without flinching, and navigating uncharted territories. But what really stuck with me? The true essence of safety. It wasn't just physical but also about protecting people's rights and dignity. This principle has stayed with me, guiding me in all aspects of my life.

Chapter 17

As soon as I climbed into my pickup truck, I rolled down the windows and inhaled the crisp air. It was my escape from the city. The noises faded behind me as I drove down the open road. This was the place where my thoughts were uninterrupted, and I could finally process all that had happened. I could at last take a deep breath and contemplate. The endless fields and sprawling countryside provided the perfect backdrop for contemplation. It was just me, the hum of the engine, and the crunch of gravel beneath my tyres. The solitude gave me time to reflect and ponder what could have been. I'd sit for hours watching the wind tell tales across the savanna, whispering to anyone who would listen. Here, life was devoid of all of its intensity. The natural world has prevailed over all of mankind's creations. On this particular outing, something out-of-the-ordinary happened—a deep-rooted connection with Mother Nature that left me awestruck. I could feel a natural vibrancy flowing through everything. The earth hummed beneath my feet, and the trees seemed to sway in rhythm. Suddenly, a rustle in the bushes caught my attention. Out of the dense foliage, a hyena emerged, its fur matted and scars visible on its face. It slinked forward with calculated movements, its sharp eyes scanning for any potential danger. Its black eyes locked onto mine, assessing me with caution and curiosity. I lowered my gaze, not wanting to appear threatening to the lone hyena in front of me. Its approach was stealthy, crouched low to the ground. Its sharp eyes scanned my body, sizing me up as its next potential meal. As we made eye contact, there was a moment of recognition. It continued its approach with fluid, calculated movements, ears perked, and nose twitching for any sign of danger. Despite being known as an ugly predator, it moved with a grace and fluidity that seemed almost otherworldly. Its fur was a blend of browns and blacks, spotted like a wildcat's coat, blending perfectly into the rocky terrain. The only other sounds were the distant caws of vultures fighting over scraps left by more successful predators on this unforgiving land.

As the beast drew near, I felt a strange sense of calm wash over me. Certainly, I was scared; however, my heart did not beat as rapidly as it should have. It was almost as if I somehow knew this creature wasn't going to harm me. The memory of that day is still clear: the sun's rays scorched my skin. The air was dense, filled with hyena stench, dirt, and my own sweat. Now that it was closer, I could see the blood and decaying flesh smeared on its face, a reminder of the hyena's role as a scavenger. Its breathing was calm and steady, and now, standing in front of me, a sound resembling laughter broke the tension. The creature's movements and low-slung profile were graceful, almost hypnotising. Its eyes remained fixed on mine, but more than that, it seemed to stare directly into my soul, as if reading my thoughts. Still today, I swear I heard it talking in my head—and that's when the real fear set in. This thing was huge—bigger than any Disney creature you could imagine. And yes, he was definitely a male. He sat down in front of me without a second thought, as if we had performed this dance at least once before. Our staring competition seemed to go on for minutes, yet I knew it had only been a matter of seconds. But as time went on and my fear faded, I felt linked to him in a strange way. We were both outcasts, misunderstood by the world. I always saw this creature with its spotted fur and crooked back as a villain, but today it was a force of nature, a vision of realism. When it was finally time for him to leave, he turned and moved away slowly, though he never took his eyes off mine, eventually returning to the place from where he had first appeared.

There was a moment of silent understanding between man and beast. If you stripped away all human complications, it was compelling. And I think that's what Zahra saw in me—someone who, despite everything, only wished for simplicity. She taught me how to look past the negative in people and see the potential within them. I remained seated on the bonnet of my truck, gazing into the void where the hyena had vanished. Remembering Zahra's words, 'nature has its own language, one that speaks through symbols and miracles if only we open ourselves up more to listen.' I started appreciating my self-discovery in Ethiopia, not just as a means of escape from my inner troubles but also as a chance to connect with nature. I had a nagging feeling that something was not quite right, which remained with me. It reminded me of the supernatural tales I had heard growing up, about creatures that lurk in the shadows and hunt unsuspecting victims. There was still a sense of agitation. I felt like the universe was trying to tell me something important through the hyena encounter. Taking a deep breath, I started the engine. I couldn't believe what had just happened back there on that dusty path. The journey back to the city was one of reflection. Zahra's presence felt stronger than it had in months. And with every mile I put between myself and the creature, I could hear her whisper encouragement. Though I had sensed her presence before, this felt like something else—a stronger connection—clear and almost telepathic.

As I entered the bustling chaos of Addis Ababa, the sun had just begun to set, and the sky was ablaze with rich colours. It was a stark contrast to the peaceful, open plains I had left behind just a few short hours ago. I took a deep breath, feeling the energy and chaos of the city pulsing around me. My mind raced back to earlier when the hyena, or whatever it was, stalked towards me. Surprisingly, instead of fear, I felt a strange sense of calm. Why was that? I was scared, sure, but for some reason, my heart didn't race like it should have. I could almost feel its hot, rancid breath on my skin, yet I couldn't bring myself to run. Why didn't I run? It was as if some instinctual part of me knew that this creature posed no real threat.

As I made my way back home, my mind was still buzzing with the events of the day. We spent hours breaking down each and every moment, from the encounter with the hyena to the intense emotions I felt. As midnight approached and our conversation drew to a close, she leaned in close and whispered, "Sometimes, when you're gone, I swear I can hear your voice calling out to me." A lump formed in my throat as her words resonated with me. I too had heard her call my name when we were apart.

Zahra's delicate fingers trailed along my neck. Her words were like a gentle caress, providing comfort and understanding.

"You know, occasionally life provides unexplained abilities, granting us a light to see into the darkest of places," she said, brushing a strand of hair out of her face.

I couldn't have agreed more; the hyena was unexplained, a symbol of nature's unpredictability and beauty. My mind was preoccupied, but Zahra's touch on my shoulder brought me back to the present. She spoke softly, "Tommy, I can see that you carry a heavy burden. I want to help you carry it." Her words brought tears to my eyes.

I voiced my fear, "But what if I can't do it? What if I'm not strong enough?"

She met my gaze with understanding and confidence, responding simply, "You are."

She was a quiet strength; it was as sturdy as the mountains that cradle her homeland—unchanging, unwavering, and eternal. Her concern for me was genuine, breaking down the walls I had built. I wondered if she dreamt of me—if I existed in her dream world the same way that she was in mine.

Chapter 18

"If relatives help each other, what evil can hurt them?"

Ethiopian Proverb

I wake to a sliver of light cutting through a gap in the curtains, a soft gold creeping over the edge of the bed. My eyes feel weighty like they're glued shut, but the light won't let me sleep any longer. It's too damn persistent. I shift, the sheets tangled around my legs, too hot under the blanket and too cold without it. It's always like this—somewhere between comfort and discomfort. The incessant chirping of the birds outside my window sounds like they are screaming for me to get up. I roll over and squint at the faint light seeping through. It's too early for this, I think as I bury my face in the pillow. But the birds are insistent, taunting me with their cheerful songs. I finally give in and sit up, wincing as my stiff muscles protest. My body feels like crap like I've been carrying a weight on my shoulders all night. I stretch, and every joint pops and cracks, "fuck", the only word that comes to mind.

Stepping into the kitchen, a musty smell hits my nose. The blinds here are drawn shut, keeping out the morning sun. I flick on the light switch, revealing a chaotic scene. Piles of dirty dishes fill the sink and cover every inch of counter space. The sunlight inevitably sneaks through the closed blinds, casting harsh beams on the mess. But as it reaches the centre of the room, it transforms into a soft, glowing haze. Dust particles dance in their path, creating a mesmerising display that turns the mundane kitchen into a dreamlike space. For a moment, I forget about the clutter and just stand there, lost in the beauty of it all. The pungent aroma of stale coffee mingled with the stench of unwashed dishes—remnants of a life that now seemed distant; today it was drowned in sorrow. The only sound is the steady hum of the refrigerator—a quiet nudge that life marches on despite our overwhelming grief. I stood in the doorway, observing Zahra as she moved about our shared space. She gathered crumpled tissues and arranged to throw pillows with delicate care, seemingly trying to mend the irreparable. It felt hopeless watching her attempt to fix something that had already shattered beyond repair. Yet, in her actions, I saw the desperate hope and intention to make our broken world whole again.

Her soft voice pierced the stillness, like a gentle breeze rustling through leaves, breaking the heavy silence. I turn to find her standing before me, her eyes searching mine for some kind of solace. I reached out and pulled her into a tight hug, her body fitting perfectly against mine. She felt like a sanctuary, a momentary escape from the pain. "I'm here," I whispered, trying to hold back my tears.

"And I'll always be here for you," she replied, her words full of understanding and love.

I whispered my gratitude into her ear, breathing in the scent of her shampoo that always brought me comfort. When we pulled apart, she looked at me with her wise brown eyes, taking in every detail of my face.

"I've got your back," she reassured me, but there was a hint of sadness in her smile.

But as she spoke about her upcoming trip to Ethiopia, frustration and disappointment flooded over me. No matter how hard we tried to make plans together, life always seemed to get in the way. Tears threaten to spill from my eyes as I cling to her, grateful for her unconditional love and support. She may not be able to take away my pain but having her by my side makes it more bearable.

I held onto the edge of the kitchen counter, my knuckles turning white with tension. Zahra stood across from me, her eyes set on a faraway place.

"Tommy, about Ethiopia," she started.

My heart clenched at the mention of her home country.

"I know," I interrupted, my words catching in my throat like broken glass. Our eyes met, and she could see the turmoil within me.

"Zahra," I said, my voice tinged with desperation I couldn't hide. "Why must you go now?" She sighed and turned away.

"Please, we've been over this," she said, her posture resolute. "I need to see my family."

"You, of all people, should understand the importance of family."

'Family,' The word bounced around in my head like a pinball.

A sense of darkness crept into my vision, threatening to unleash memories of my days in captivity. It was a feeling I knew all too well, one that could easily consume my mind.

"That's why you have to let me do this," she said, snapping me out of my reflections. Her hand reached out towards me, and I instinctively stepped back, as if her touch could burn me. A cold sweat broke out across my skin as I frantically searched for a way to escape her penetrating gaze.

A vivid flashback consumes me as I pull away from this world. *The ropes dig into my skin, leaving deep red welts that throb with pain. A knife presses against my throat, its sharp edge drawing droplets of blood. Death's icy grip tightens around me, suffocating me with its cold touch. A bone-chilling cold racked my entire body as if thousands of needles were piercing my flesh at once.*

I was aware that I was behaving in a selfish manner, but I was unable to control myself. I remember that moment clearly. I called her 'sweetheart' like I always did, but it felt foreign on my tongue. I could see the hurt and disappointment in her eyes, but I couldn't stop myself. The word 'sweetheart' felt like a lie, dripping with deception. She saw the turmoil within me, the constant struggle between my facade of a decent man and the demons of my past clawing at my mind.

"Darling." I could feel the warmth radiating from her body as she took my trembling hands in hers. Her voice, always gentle and reassuring, spoke the words I needed to hear. "You are more than your trauma," she said, her eyes locked on mine with unwavering strength. A flicker of doubt remained, but her words were like a shield against it. Slowly, I started to believe her.

"Am I?" Doubt crept in, threatening to shatter the fragile peace I had fought so hard for. Her grip tightened on my hands, and she nodded firmly.

"Yes," she said, her voice filled with conviction and belief in me.

Emotionally, I struggled to keep my composure as I gazed into her eyes, torn between my own desires and the inevitable farewell that awaited us. Love is not about clinging on to someone; it's about giving them the freedom they need. And I understand that she must go see her family; in fact, it's what's best for both of us. As she softly strokes my face, a familiar scent of lavender drifts towards me from her hair.

I hold her tightly, barely able to speak. "Please promise me you'll take good care of yourself," I plead.

She leans in and places a gentle kiss on my cheek, assuring me with her words, "Always." But then she turns the question back to me. "And what about you?"

I square my shoulders and lift my chin, attempting to appear confident despite the overwhelming uncertainty that clenches at my stomach. I try to nod confidently, but my trembling lips give me away.

"I'll manage," I say with a forced smile, knowing deep down that I will struggle without her by my side. I hold on tightly to her, trying to imprint every detail of her warmth and scent into my memory before she leaves for the days ahead, which will undoubtedly be filled with loneliness without her by my side. Together, we find strength in one another's composure and feel reassured as we hold tightly to each other.

The night before she left, I sat on her bed and watched as she neatly folded her clothes and packed them into a small suitcase. My heart clenched with dread as I thought about the long months ahead without her. When she finished packing, she came over to me and placed a hand on my shoulder, trying to offer reassurance. But the sadness and worry seeped through my defences, making it difficult for me to hold back tears.

I felt guilty for wanting her to stay, but I knew they needed to see her. As she held onto me tightly, I could sense her unease.

"I could always stay," she offered, but her lack of conviction gave away her true feelings.

"Your family has been looking forward to this, and so have you," I reminded her. "I was just being selfish. I'm sorry.

"Every part of me wanted to say 'no', but I knew pressing her to stay would only add to her troubles. I just wanted to protect her always. My mother told me love meant listening to their heart, too. For a while, I melted into her, savouring the scent of her hair and the way her body completed mine. But then unease crept in as I saw shadows watching us.

My eyelids sank, and I was transported back to the Philippines, reliving the chaos and cruelty that unfolded many years ago. It felt as though it were happening over and over again in the present. And then the voices came—menacing and determined to strip me of everything. They spoke lies and threatened ruin. Their false words and terrifying threats left me feeling trapped in an unending nightmare.

CHAPTER 19

The grey, early morning light filtered through the windshield as we drove towards Heathrow airport. I winced as the sun's rays hit my face, intensifying my already-pounding headache. Zahra sat next to me; her eyes fixed on the passing scenery.

"How are you holding up?" I asked, breaking the heavy silence in the car.

"Exhausted," she replied with a weary sigh.

"I'm sorry," I responded with concern.

The radio played a cheerful tune, but it only served to mock our sombre mood. For the remaining three-hour drive, we were both lost in our own thoughts. Zahra stared out at the rain while I kept my focus on the road ahead, pretending not to think about what awaited her in Addis Ababa.

As we approached the airport, Zahra suddenly reached for my hand and squeezed it tightly. "I'm going to miss you," she said quietly, trying to reassure me.

When we pulled into the crowded parking lot, she reached up to her neck and unclasped a small wooden cross. The intricate carvings and faded paint told a story of its own. She placed it gently in my palm, our fingers brushing against each other's skin.

Her voice was soft but steady as she said, "Take this with you." I could see the emotions swirling behind her eyes as we exchanged a bittersweet embrace, knowing that this moment of closeness was limited. I held onto the cross, feeling the weight of both its physical presence and the love it represented.

"To protect you while I'm gone," she spoke with a steady voice, but I could see the sadness swimming behind her eyes.

Passing the cross, her fingers were trembling, and tears welled in her eyes. A talisman of her culture and for me, it would represent a symbol of protection. I held onto it tightly, feeling its weight and significance. With a silent understanding, I put it in my pocket, unable to form any words as my throat tightened with emotion. This was it—the point when our love would be tested by distance and danger. I watched as she stepped out of the car to retrieve her luggage from the boot, her petite figure seemingly swallowed by the vastness of the airport. My warrior queen was about to embark on a journey without me by her side. Our hands intertwined one last time before we said goodbye, holding onto each other as if our lives depended on it.

"Take care of your mother," she said, as we stood before the baggage drop-off.

"Please don't worry; we will be fine. " I replied.

Amid the chaotic hustle and bustle of the airport, I felt her grip on my hand loosen with each step. The crowds, the signs, and the looming gates all blurred together as we made our way towards security. With every footfall, it felt like a piece of me was being left behind. When we reached the final barrier, I clung to her hand desperately, as if my touch could somehow stop time and keep us together. But as I looked up at the blinking departure board above, reality set in like a weight on my chest. Tears welled up in my eyes and I could see them mirrored in hers. "I don't want to go," she whispered, her voice cracking with emotion. And in that instant, my heart shattered into a million pieces.

The robotic voice echoed through the bustling airport terminal, announcing the last call for Flight 372 to Addis Ababa. Zahra's hand tightened around mine, her eyes searching my face with unspoken love and fear. Our arms wrapped around each other in a desperate embrace as we both struggled to hold back tears, knowing that our time was limited. "Stay safe," she began, and I gently placed a finger over her lips, silencing any words from escaping. We both knew what we wanted to say: Stay safe. Come back to me. I love you. But in that moment, our actions spoke louder than words ever could.

"Shh," I whispered.

She stood before me, her bag slung over one shoulder and a determined look on her face. I couldn't help but admire the warrior queen she had become. But as our eyes locked, I saw a glimmer of vulnerability that mirrored my own. We stood there in silence for a moment, both struggling to find the words to say. With a newfound confidence, I turned to her and spoke the words we had always lived by: "No distance can weaken us." Her eyes filled with a mix of purpose and sorrow.

"Stronger," she replied, her voice wavering slightly. It was clear that the weight of our fast-approaching farewell had taken its toll.

The flight attendant's voice crackled over the intercom, announcing the final boarding call for her flight. I tightened my arms around her, trying to hold on to every second we had left together. She gazed up at me with tear-filled eyes while the scent of jasmine and coconut lingered in the air between us. Reality set in. It was time. My throat tightened as I watched her gather her carry-on and turn to leave. I reached out and pulled her back into my arms, wanting to hold onto every last moment. The floral scent of jasmine and coconut lingered on her skin as she gazed up at me, tears welling in her eyes.

My voice shook as I whispered those three words, "I love you," my heart aching at the thought of not being able to say those words every day.

"I love you too," she replied, burying her face in my shoulder. We both knew this would be our last embrace for a while. Our conflicting emotions battled within us as we gripped each other, wanting to hold onto this moment just a little bit longer.

With a lump in my throat, I spoke to her in a hushed tone. "Please promise me you'll stay safe," I pleaded, trying to hide the tears in my eyes. "I'll be waiting for your call when you land."

Our eyes met, and I could see the unspoken goodbye and understanding in her gaze. We both knew this moment was coming—the inevitable "see you later" that we had been preparing ourselves for since she first mentioned this trip. I pulled her close, wanting to remember every detail of her embrace, knowing it would be the thing I missed most while she was gone. I felt her body shake slightly as we both held back tears. But I refused to let myself cry. Not here. Not now.

"Tommy," Zahra's voice was barely a whisper.

"I know," I replied softly, unsure if she really heard me.

She nodded, trembling as she reached up to trace my jawline with a tender touch that left me speechless.

"Take care of yourself, darling," she said with a gentle smile that didn't quite reach her eyes.

I gave her a nod in return, unable to find words. With one last look, Zahra turned and walked away, leaving me standing alone and bracing myself for the time apart.

Standing motionless, life in the airport drones—people flurry around me, their voices a distant hum. I am frozen in place, unable to move or speak as my heart tears itself apart. Everything seems to blur and fade as if I'm in a dream. The gate agent calls out again, final boarding for the flight to Ethiopia, and I take one last look at Zahra's retreating figure before she disappears. Time seemed to slow down until the gate agent slammed the door shut, jolting me back to reality. With heavy steps, I make my way to the large window and watch as the plane taxis down the runway. My tired reflection stares back at me, conveying the emotional toll of our goodbye. The plane's engines roared to life, and I pressed my hand against the cold glass window to watch as it continued down the runway. It is mainly white in colour, with the tail showing the Ethiopian flag's vibrant colours: green, yellow, and red. The airline's logo, written in both English and Amharic, is displayed on the forward section in red lettering. The aircraft gained speed, and my heart raced with each passing second, I silently prayed for a safe journey. It felt like I was right there with her, the aircraft shaking with increasing speed, mimicking the turmoil in my mind. I could feel the wheels gripping the tarmac as it propelled forward. I imagined her leaning back in her seat, taking deep breaths to calm her nerves. The roar of the engines filled the cabin, drowning out any other thoughts as the plane gained speed and lifted off into the sky. The plane climbed higher and higher, carrying Zahra away from me and into an uncertain future.

"Stay safe," I whisper, willing my words to reach her above the roar of the engines. I turn my attention away from the window. Home beckons, but my feet feel rooted to the spot, unwilling to leave this spot where we said our goodbyes. So, I linger a little while longer, trapped in the heaviness of our emotional goodbye.

With each step, the fog seemed to cling to me, mirroring my grief. My eyes stayed glued to the road ahead, as if afraid to look away for even a nanosecond. I gripped the steering wheel tightly, feeling the pattern of the leather leave deep imprints on my palms.

Finally, I arrived at our once-happy home, now just a shell filled with memories. As I walked through each room, it was like seeing them for the first time. The kitchen where her voice would fill the air with sweet melodies as she cooked...the sound still echoes in my mind and taunts me with its absence." God, how I miss her." I enter the living room, and it feels like a floodgate of memories has opened. I see us on the sofa, tangled up in each other's arms, our laughter blending with the sound of the TV in the background. In the bathroom, her hairbrush sits on the counter, bristles clogged with strands of her dark hair. My heart aches at her absence. But it's when I reach our bedroom that I feel my emotions truly overwhelm me. The warmth of her perfume still lingers, as if she just left moments ago. The unmade bed holds no trace of our lovemaking, just sheets and blankets now. Yet, this room...this was where we were free to be ourselves, stripped down to our most vulnerable selves. As I lay down on the bed, still clothed and exhausted from the weight of my grief, every whispered 'I love you' reverberates within these walls, etched into my memory forever.

I shifted in bed, reaching for Zahra's familiar form next to me. My fingers grazed the cold, empty sheets and I sighed. It had been a year since I slept alone in our bed, and the coldness of her absence stung. Tears prick at the corners of my eyes as I drift into a troubled sleep, the faint scent of her perfume remains, and I feel myself leave this world.

My eyes snapped open, but the world before me was unreal and distorted. It had to be a nightmare. My skin prickled with unease, the tension making me want to scream. Voices thundered around me, taunting and teasing with every word, as I struggled to make sense of it all. My heart hammered in my chest as I tried to separate reality from delusion. Shadows danced around me, looming and menacing, creeping me the hell out. And then, fucking agony as something sharp sank into my neck, tearing through my flesh like a wild animal. The pain was unbearable, but worse was the loss of control over my own body. A horrific scream tore from my throat as darkness eventually swallowed me.

CHAPTER 20

"A single stick may smoke, but it will not burn."

Ethiopian Proverb

The room's quiet, aside from the faint hum of the fridge in the kitchen down the hall. It's the only sound in the house now that the radiators are off. The air is cool, too cool. I notice the way the light spreads across the floor, how it catches the dust floating lazily in the air. Odd how you only ever see that in the morning, like the sun's giving you a glimpse into the stuff you'd rather ignore. I glance at the clock— 6:02. Too early, but late enough that staying in bed feels senseless. I sigh, long and deep, like maybe it'll make me feel better. It doesn't. The shadows on the walls shrink as the sun rises little by little, and I can't help but stare at them for a second, watching them retreat like they're afraid of the light. Eventually drawing my eye to the picture of Ethiopia on the opposite wall. It's quiet now, almost peaceful. Almost. Something about it makes me restless, though, like I should be doing more to find her, but I'm not. I'm lying on my bed, eyes closed, but all I get is that weird buzzing behind my eyelids, like my mind's still running at full speed. I shift, my body sinking deeper into the mattress, but my thoughts are lighter than air, slipping away. It starts slow, like a thread coming loose. My thoughts unravel, one by one, until the edges blur and I'm not here anymore, not really. My breathing slows, the mass of the bed weakens, and I'm drifting, but not into sleep—into something else. I'm not sure when the shift happens, but suddenly I'm somewhere else, somewhere better, or maybe just different.

My back and shoulders felt like they were being crushed, each breath a struggle against the weight pressing down on me. Sweat ran down my face, stinging my eyes, as I pushed through the pain. My body was screaming for rest, for water, but I ignored it, relying on the grit I'd learned over years of hard training. My knees buckled, my shins ached, and the blister burning between my shoulder blades burst, sending a shock of pain through me. But I gritted my teeth and kept going.

I was a Royal Marine again, strong, and unafraid. Wisdom? Well, that was a different story. I'd always been driven, and always pushed myself to the edge. Nothing had changed. Flashbacks of commando training flashed through my mind—bone-deep exhaustion, every step laced with pain. But we never stopped, not once. Bones snapped, muscles burned, but we pushed forward, determined to earn the green beret. When we finally passed out and those green berets were placed on our heads, we knew we were ready. Our first deployments were a blur of heat, cold, and adrenaline as we learned what it meant to be the elite. We went everywhere—from searing deserts to frozen wastelands—operating with precision and lethal skill. But amidst all the chaos, it was the brotherhood that defined us. Losing a comrade was like losing a part of myself, but it strengthened my resolve, and made me feel more deeply committed to those who were left standing. Sometimes, in the quiet, I felt their presence—the men we'd lost, like ghosts walking beside me. I could see their faces, hear their laughter, recall the nights we shared in cramped barracks or under starlit skies, waiting for whatever came next. Those memories are detailed, preserved in my mind like snapshots frozen in time. The Royal Marines were more than a unit; they were family. That bond has stayed with me, woven so deeply into my identity that I can't shake it, even here, surrounded by darkness.

Now, I found myself on a different mission, a rescue mission—to save Zahra. The landscape in my mind twisted, morphing between battlefields and unfamiliar places. The harsh sand suddenly became Ethiopia's lush green highlands, where she had been taken. I led a unit of spectres, men I knew well—comrades who had long since fallen. They didn't speak, but their eyes told me they were here with me. We moved as one, kicking up dust and memories as we advanced. This wasn't real—I knew that much. But if I couldn't save her in the waking world, I'd be her protector here, in this dream. The path ahead was familiar, despite the nightmare shifting around me. We moved through a maze of acacia trees, our steps in sync, a rhythm we knew well. The air was thick with the scent of eucalyptus, so different from the cold, empty room where I lay in reality. As we reached a clearing, an oasis appeared—a serene paradise, water shimmering under a blue sky. For a moment, it felt like a place of peace, a refuge. I let my men rest by the water's edge, watching as their ghostly forms relaxed, free from the burdens they'd carried. I started to join them when a distant cry shattered the calm. Zahra's voice. It cut through the dream, drawing me away from the oasis and filling me with a new sense of urgency. We pressed on, deeper into the heart of this surreal Ethiopia. Each step seemed to echo with Zahra's laughter, her voice growing louder, surrounding me like a guiding force. The land twisted around us, fragments of my memories blending into the horizon. We passed villages scarred by conflict, places that mirrored the scars within me. Children peeked out from behind tattered curtains, eyes wide and solemn, each gaze a reminder of Zahra's spirit. The sun was setting, painting the sky in reds and gold, adding an almost sacred beauty to this journey. Finally, we reached a mountain crest, overlooking a valley bathed in dusk. Nestled among the shadows lay a village, untouched and timeless. It was like a scene from a memory I hadn't known I had. Zahra would be here. I was sure of it. The men who had been my companions faded into the darkness, leaving me to continue alone. It was fitting— this journey had begun with a single heartache, and it would end with a single resolve.

As I walked through the village, each sense came alive. The clatter of pots, the scent of spices, and laughter drifting from doorways—all wrapped around me like a warm embrace. Somewhere in this maze of life and history, I felt Zahra's presence, as real and intense as ever. And then, under the ancient boughs of a massive tree, I saw her. Zahra. Her hair caught the moonlight, and her laughter, soft and bright, eased the ache in my chest. She looked exactly as I remembered, as if time and loss had never touched her. I froze, afraid that any movement would break the spell. She turned, her gaze locking onto mine, eyes filled with love and sadness.

"Tommy," her voice was a melody I'd forgotten, filling every hollow place inside me. "You can't change what fate has written."

I felt tears well up, and I couldn't hold them back. Here she was—my wife, my love, alive in this place beyond time. She gestured for me to sit, and when I did, the children around her scattered, leaving us alone beneath the tree. She reached out and took my hand, warmth flooding through me. It was as if I'd come home, if only for a moment.

"Shh," she whispered, her touch gentle as she placed a finger on my lips. "No need for words, my love. I know your heart."

We sat in silence, the kind that said everything we couldn't. Finally, she spoke, her voice soft and steady. "You've held onto so much pain, Tommy. So much guilt. But it's time to let go. I'm at peace. You need to find yours."

Her words sank into me, and for the first time, I felt the weight of my grief begin to shift. "How can I?" I managed to choke out. "Every day without you feels like a lifetime."

She cupped my cheek, her touch like a balm to my soul. "You've been so strong, Tommy. Stronger than anyone I know. Use that strength to heal—for yourself, and for others who need you."

Her gaze drifted to the village around us. "This place," she said, "is a reminder that life endures, that love carries on even when people are gone. It exists because people like you choose to remember, to keep dreaming."

I looked at the village, feeling its quiet resilience. The children gathered around us, curious and solemn, sensing the gravity of the moment. Zahra smiled, her eyes reflecting the starlight.

"Promise me, Tommy," she whispered, her voice both firm and gentle. "Promise you'll try to find joy again. For me. For you. For us."

I nodded, unable to speak as tears streamed down my face. Her words filled me with a quiet resolve, a glimmer of hope that maybe, just maybe, I could honour her memory by living fully. Zahra leaned in, pressing a gentle kiss to my forehead, and in that moment, I felt her forgiveness, her love, her strength.

"Remember," she murmured, her voice fading, "I'm always with you."

And then she was gone. I was left alone beneath the ancient tree, a weight pressing on my chest, but a new sense of purpose filled the empty spaces inside me. Zahra s memory would be my guide, her love my shield, as I made my way back to a world that needed me as much as I needed it.

CHAPTER 21

I jolted awake, my skin damp and chilled. The red digits on the clock glowed: 5:22 a.m. Another day had slipped by without any word from her. My heart pounded in my chest, each beat thundering in my ears as I gasped for air. Breathing was like pulling shards of glass into my lungs, sharp and jagged. I fought to calm myself, but panic wrapped itself around me, squeezing tighter. Or has something terrible happened? The thought alone terrified me. I've had recurring dreams, but this one felt... different. Vivid. Real. I needed answers. I needed to know what was happening to her. The dread in my gut refused to let go, despite every attempt to convince myself it was all just in my head. She still hadn't reached out, and my mind was spinning through every terrible possibility. My desperation turned to impulse, a frantic drive to do something, anything, to find her and not be alone again. I peeled myself out of bed, sheets sticking to my sweat-soaked skin, and stumbled to the bathroom. My head throbbed, the echoes of Zahra's presence in my dream still pulsing in my mind. My fingers shook as I touched my forehead where, just moments ago, I'd felt her lips press against my skin. I splashed cold water on my face, hoping to snap myself out of it, then checked my phone. No messages. The blank screen stared back, maybe thanks to the spotty Wi-Fi and constant power outages here in Ethiopia. But even that couldn't stop the hope gnawing at me—any minute, I thought, she'd get in touch. I couldn't stay inside, couldn't breathe in the close walls. I stepped out into the pre-dawn air, watching my breath cloud and dissolve into the dark. An owl hooted somewhere nearby, and the leaves under my feet whispered as I walked. I wandered through the streets, clinging to every memory of Zahra, every place we'd touched and laughed. Streetlights cast dim halos over the empty roads, but I felt lost, stumbling along with no real sense of where I was headed.

At the park, I found myself on the overgrown path we used to walk, tangled with weeds and tree roots. Each step was shaky, uncertain. Guilt weighed on me, a leaden ache in my chest—guilt for not fighting harder to keep her, for not going with her, for not being there to protect her. Each step felt like moving through a wasteland, a mirror of the emptiness I carried inside. The smell of freshly cut grass and roses hung in the air, familiar and almost comforting. My eyes roamed, looking for anything, any trace of her left here, a tether to hold onto. We'd spent hours here, swinging and talking, letting time drift away. The memory of the chains creaking filled my ears, and I could almost hear her laugh. I reached her favourite swing and sat down, the cold metal biting through my clothes. The sky lightened, shades of purple and orange washing over the horizon. I closed my eyes, letting the memories wash over me. Birds chirped in the trees, bright and alive against the emptiness that had taken over since she left.

Then, as I sat there, something clicked. Her love wasn't gone; it was here, surrounding me. I could feel her presence in the quiet, in the gentle sway of the swing. The wind stirred, carrying her voice, a soft whisper telling me to keep going, to find her. And in that moment, I knew I couldn't stop. I had to bring her home.

CHAPTER 22

"A home without a woman is like a barn without cattle."

Ethiopian Proverb

*P*romise me you'll call every day."* My last words to Zahra echo over and over in my mind.

'Every day," she'd whispered, her voice so soft I barely heard it. I could picture her nodding with that confident smile, the one I loved. Now, though, it feels like a mockery, taunting me in this empty apartment.

Home is silent, the kind of silence that gets under your skin. Every creak of the floorboards, every tick of the clock makes the space feel vast and hollow. I drift through memories, half listening for a sound—any sound—that might bring me hope. All around me, there are pieces of her: an unwashed coffee cup by the sink, her favourite throw blanket draped over the sofa, the faint scent of her perfume lingering in the air. I try to distract myself, throwing myself into small tasks, but my thoughts keep coming back to her, to the emptiness that's settled in since she left. I worry that the good memories will eventually fade, replaced only by the pain I've worked so hard to keep buried.

As the light fades to a deep orange, stretching shadows across the walls, the room feels too big, too empty. I'm exhausted, but my mind's running on a loop, chasing thoughts that lead nowhere. The sunset fades, leaving the room in that grey, uneasy twilight I hate, where everything feels off, like the world's holding its breath. Shadows stretch and creep across the room, and though I try not to notice, my eyes keep catching on things—the outline of the dresser, the shape of the chair, the curtains barely moving without a breeze. It's like the whole room is waiting for something, and I'm stuck in the middle of it. I turn over, pulling the blanket tight around me, trying to shut it all out. Another hour ticks by. The sunset's gone, and darkness settles over everything. I wish I could turn my mind off for a minute, just stop the constant churn. But the more I try, the louder it gets. I feel like I'm trapped, sinking in my own head. I know I need to sleep, but every time I close my eyes, *I see her again. Zahra. Her smile, her laugh, the way the sun bounced off her hair when we sat outside that little café in Addis Ababa. Her aunt Halima had just cracked a joke, and Zahra had laughed, that deep, warm laugh that made everything feel right.*

I miss her every day. But right now, I have to stay here for my mother. She's bedridden, too sick to be alone, and I can't leave her side, even though all I want is to be with Zahra. I glance at my phone, the silence stretching, filling me with a dread that's grown too familiar. My mind cycles through every terrible possibility. Is she safe? Is she even alive?

I scrub plates harder than I need to, splashing water everywhere, trying to distract myself from the silence pressing in, the ticking clock that feels like an eternity with no word from her. Images of her flash through my mind, her face, her voice. I can feel my hands shaking, the tears I've held back finally welling up. I can't shake the feeling that something awful has happened, that every passing minute means more danger. The hours tick by, and finally, I collapse in my cluttered office, surrounded by the stale smell of coffee and cold pizza. The flickering lamp casts dim light over the stacks of papers and reports that pile up around me, waiting for attention I can't give.

"I'll have to put work on hold. I can tell them later I'm not coming in," I mutter, half to myself. "Maybe I'll say it's Covid... No, Long Covid sounds more believable." I pause, nodding slightly as if convincing myself. "Yeah. That should buy me a little more time."

I scroll through social media, search the news, my eyes straining as I absorb every headline, every snippet of information about what's happening back there. When night falls, the weight of it settles over me like a shroud. The silence grows heavier, each minute without news twisting tighter in my chest. My mind spirals, each doubt, each fear piling on until I can't see a way out.

Another day passes with nothing. No call. No message. I refresh pages, scrolling obsessively, until I stumble on headlines that chill my blood. The reports are bleak, each one worse than the last stories of uprisings, violent clashes in the streets, armed men hunting civilians down like prey. I click on a video and watch in horror as familiar streets go up in flames, smoke billowing as explosions echoes in the distance. I recognise the places where Zahra and I walked together, places now lost in chaos and terror. My stomach twists, and my hands shake as I force myself to keep watching, absorbing the horrors.

One article catches my eye—a news piece that feels like a punch to the gut.

'Ethiopia has experienced a chilling wave of terror, leading the government to declare a state of emergency. This decision comes in response to brutal clashes in the Amhara Region, now torn apart by violent power struggles. The rebels, armed and unyielding, are battling the Ethiopian National Defence Force (ENDF) in a desperate fight for control, casting a shadow of fear and uncertainty over the country.'

My throat tightens. Dessie. I remember that town, the days I spent there with Zahra, her family. Now, it's in shambles, civilians caught in the crossfire, innocent lives torn apart. I stare at my phone, the silence a gnawing ache. I whisper to myself, "Stay alive," hoping somehow, she'll hear me, knowing how empty the words sound. I can't keep waiting, can't keep hoping. Sitting here, doing nothing, is tearing me apart. But right now, that's all I have.

CHAPTER 23

Leaving my mom's bedside felt like ripping out a piece of my own heart. I couldn't shake the worry that clung to me, gnawing at my insides, not only because of her frail state but also because of Zahra's sudden disappearance. Turning to my brother, John, who stood stoically by the door, I could see the glint of unshed tears in his eyes. He reached for me, and we held each other tightly, both of us shaking with the kind of grief words couldn't touch and praying for our mom's recovery and Zahra's safe return.

"We'll find her," I said, my voice barely above a whisper, more for myself than him. But inside, dread crawled up my spine, gripping me in a way I couldn't shake. The possibilities, all the terrible things that could have happened to her, twisted like shadows in my mind.

By the time night fell, those shadows felt alive, bending, and stretching with my darkest thoughts. The news didn't help—article after article flooding my phone, each headline worse than the last. It was surreal. One minute, she was here, and the next, this war, in a country I barely understood, swallowed her whole. The government blamed the TPLF for the violence; the TPLF blamed the government for oppression. But I didn't give a damn about the politics. All I knew was that I needed Zahra safe, home. I made a silent vow to protect her and the rest of my family, no matter the cost. As I made my way through the dark house, checking locks, double-checking every door and window, anxiety clawed at me, building with each step. This place used to be our safe haven. Now, it felt like a prison, a place where I was waiting for news that might never come. I was scared as hell, but I had to keep it together. I couldn't let myself break. If I did, I'd never find her.

Then, my phone blared, making me jump. Tigi's name lit up on the screen, and my hand trembled as I reached for it, desperate for answers. Did I have the courage to hear her news, though? Relief? Horror? My heart hammered as I answered, forcing my voice to stay steady.

"Hello?" My voice came out sharper than I intended.

"Tommy... it's Tigi," she said, her voice shaking. "Have you... heard anything?"

I paused, my throat tightening. "Nothing," I replied, swallowing down the frustration building in me. "I've been trying to reach everyone, every lead I can think of, and still nothing—fucking nothing!"

I heard a heavy sigh on the other end. "I need to talk to you. Can I come over?"

I cut her off, my tone biting. "Thanks for calling, Tigi, but I'm busy." The words were cold, and I regretted them the moment they left my mouth.

"Tommy, please…" she said, her voice breaking, but I ended the call, leaving her words hanging in the silence.

Tigi had always been there, had always shown up when others hadn't. She'd been like a sister to Zahra. I knew I'd need her support, but right now, all I could focus on was refreshing the news page, obsessively hitting reload, trying to pull up something, anything. I couldn't stop imagining her caught in the middle of it all—scared, alone. God, I hoped she wasn't scared. The scenarios played in my mind, but none of them ended the way I wanted.

CHAPTER 24

My fingers flew over the keyboard, scrolling frantically through endless articles, forums, anything that might offer a lead. Each click, each new tab, only fuelled my frustration until, finally, I slammed my fist onto the desk, hard. "This can't be all there is," I muttered, shaking my head, eyes burning from hours of staring at the screen. All I had were dead ends, each one landing like a punch, leaving me more drained and defeated. I hit the desk again, a raw, frustrated sound escaping my throat, filling the empty room and echoing back like mockery. The ache in my hand brought me back, grounding me just enough. I took a deep breath, forcing myself to calm down. The laptop's pale blue glow cast an eerie light around the room, highlighting my desperation as I tapped out yet another message. Zahra's name slipped from my lips, barely a whisper, like a prayer. I glanced at our wedding photo on the mantel—her radiant smile, eyes full of life— and quickly looked away, not ready to face it. Not yet.

"Come on, come on," I muttered, hitting refresh. The seconds ticked by, stretching painfully. Each minute without word from her felt like a punishment. A sharp buzz jolted me, and I snatched my phone, heart hammering, only to see another spam email. My stomach dropped. Disappointment twisted inside me as I started pacing, eyes flicking to the framed photos on the shelf—reminders of a life that felt close enough to touch, yet achingly far away. I froze at a noise outside the window, my pulse spiking. I rushed over, breath held, only to see the neighbour coming home late. "Calm down," I muttered through clenched teeth, but the words felt hollow. I forced myself back to the laptop, combing through every detail I had, praying for something—anything—that might lead me to her.

Then I saw it—a post from Mita Zegeye, Zahra's cousin. I'd only met her once, years ago, in Ethiopia. My hands shook as I typed out a message. *Mita, any news?* I waited, fingers drumming on the desk, my eyes flicking between my phone and the laptop. Nothing. I closed my eyes, picturing Zahra across from me, laughing in that soft pink sweater she loved. The image of her was so vivid, I could almost feel her warmth. But when I opened my eyes, the emptiness hit hard. She was gone. Just... gone.

A headline caught my eye: *Conflict Engulfs Ethiopian Towns.'* I clicked, heart sinking as images of destruction unfolded. It was Zahra's hometown. The once-quiet streets we'd walked together were now unrecognisable, shrouded in dust, stained with the life blood of the innocent. I couldn't breathe, my world narrowing to that horrific screen.

"Not there," I whispered, then louder, "Not fucking there!" My fingers hovered over a video, my heart pounding too hard to hit play. The clock on my laptop blinked back at me, every passing second a brutal reminder. Her last message sat open on the screen, her smiling face staring back at me from an old photo taken at Cardiff Castle. *Where is she?'* I thought, my mind too terrified to finish the question. My voice came out in a broken whisper, "Zahra, please... give me something."

A sudden knock shattered the silence. My heart leapt, wild hope flaring for a split second. I moved to the door, hands trembling. It came again—louder, more insistent. I took a deep breath and looked through the peephole. The hallway was empty, just a dim flicker of light casting shadows. Confusion washed over me as I stepped back, slumping to the ground, the familiar ache tightening around my chest. Time lost had lost all meaning— minutes? Hours? I didn't know. My mind blurred, the same empty room staring back at me when I finally looked up. And still, I couldn't shake the feeling that something, someone, was just out of sight. For a brief second, I could've sworn I saw a flicker of movement, but when I looked again, it was gone. I forced myself back to the computer, a single thought anchoring me: I had to find her. Then, as if summoned by my desperation, a message popped onto the screen: *Meet me. Addis Ababa. We need you. Urgent, Mita.'*

I stared, barely breathing. There it was—a direction, a lifeline. For the first time in days, a small spark of hope flared to life inside me.

CHAPTER 25

*"The one who is mistaken is the one who does
nothing."*

Ethiopian Proverb

Facing the mirror, I stare into eyes that don't feel like mine—hollow and lost, like they belong to someone else. Mita's message flashes in my mind, each word hitting like a punch: *Meet me. Addis Ababa. We need you. Urgent.'*

A surge of something fierce burns through me, pushing away the fog. I can feel my pulse pounding, a reminder that time is running out. No more waiting, no more hesitating. I've already lost too much time. This ends now. She's alive. I know it. And she's out there, waiting for me. I'm going to find her. I'll do whatever it takes—bribe, fight, crawl through hell if I have to. I'll kill if it comes to that. But I'm not coming back without her. Whatever's in my way—whoever's in my way—they're just obstacles. I'll get past them, one way or another. With one last glance at the stranger in the mirror, I turn.

I rush into the kitchen, feet slipping on the cool tiles, and practically smack the coffee machine on. As it whirs to life, I grab a mug, filling it with the strong, steaming brew that's my only chance at focus. The familiar scent jolts me awake, and I swing open my laptop, zeroing in on the airline website. My fingers fly over the keyboard, navigating the endless maze of flight options, searching for the one that'll bring me closer to her. Price doesn't matter. Time doesn't matter. All that matters is reaching Zahra, even if it means breaking both my bank and my sanity. I grit my teeth, wishing I could summon a plane out of thin air. Then, on the screen—tomorrow, a non-stop flight with just a few seats left. I hit "book" without a second thought. Another step toward finding her. In a flurry, I arrange a taxi, inform my colleagues, friends, anyone who needs to know that I'll be gone. But one call remains, the hardest one: my brother, John, and Mom. I save it for last, knowing it'll take every bit of composure I have left. Taking a deep breath, I brace myself for their reaction.

I head to the bedroom, throwing my black duffel onto the bed, its corners crisp against the rumpled sheets. With one swift motion, I unzip it, flipping open the top to reveal my meticulously organised gear. Each item has a place, each one essential. I methodically run through my mental checklist, repacking everything with practised precision—socks rolled and tucked into boots, rain jacket folded neatly at the top, water bottle secured on the side. Every piece fits perfectly. Years as a Marine trained me for this, and packing is muscle memory, a ritual that settles my nerves. I even slip a few leftover Ethiopian Birr into a hidden pocket for emergencies. I zip the bag with a final, satisfying click, feeling a surge of adrenaline course through my exhaustion. Whatever lies ahead, I'm ready. I heft the duffel, feeling the weight shift in my hands, and go through a mental roll call: snacks, an old compass, a worn map of Addis, my passport, and cash. Somehow, just knowing they're there bringing a sense of calm. I catch my reflection in the hallway mirror as I turn to leave—my eyes are dull with grief and exhaustion, my bald head slick with sweat. But beneath the fatigue, there's a fire, a quiet determination. By the mirror, a picture of Zahra catches my eye. I trace a finger over her smile, letting it stoke that flicker of hope inside me.

One more night. One more sleep, and I'll be on my way.

CHAPTER 26

Sitting by my mother's bedside, I glance at the photo on the table. It's of us at the beach from when I was a kid. She's got her arm wrapped tight around me, her smile bright enough to light up the whole ocean. That same smile is still there, but now deep lines crease her face—a map of all the years spent worrying over my brother and me. She was always the fierce one, our protector, shielding us from everything ugly in the world. Now, all I can do is sit here and watch her lying frail and thin, cancer tearing her apart. Her skin is pale, her breaths shallow, and the morphine barely takes the edge off her pain. I feel a pang of helplessness as her eyes meet mine, and her weak smile tells me something I don't want to hear—she's tired. Maybe she's ready to let go. After making sure she's resting, I walk down the hallway, the smell of antiseptic and chemotherapy clinging to the air. Her faint cough echoes from the bedroom, lingering even as I step into the living room. There, my brother John sits on the sofa, his face glowing in the light from his phone. I clear my throat, and he looks up, his brows pulling together in concern.

"You alright?" he asks, setting his phone aside.

I hesitate, my palms damp. "Can we talk?"

John straightens, his expression serious. "Of course. What's going on?"

I sit down across from him, taking a deep breath. The words I need to say sit heavy on my chest. "It's about Zahra. I... I need to find her, John."

His eyes widen. "Wait—what? Zahra? You mean..." He trails off, but his face says it all.

I nod, swallowing hard. "I have to. She's... she's out there somewhere, and I can't just sit here, not knowing." I take a deep breath and tell him the entire story, leaving no detail out. Then, I wait in silence for his response. He goes quiet, taking in the weight of my words.

"Are you sure about this?" There's worry in his voice, the same worry that's been wearing him down since Mom got sick.

"I am." My voice is steady, my mind already set. "I have to do this. For Zahra."

He looks at me, conflicted. "Then I'm coming with you."

A surge of gratitude swells in my chest, but I shake my head. "No, John. You're needed here, with Mom. She needs you. I couldn't go knowing she'd be alone."

He lets out a long breath, leaning back. "I don't like it," he says, finally. "But if you're going... I get it."

"Thank you." I mean it, every word. "I'll be back—with her."

We share a long, silent look, both of us aware of the risks, the sacrifice. Then he pulls me into a tight hug, and for a moment, it feels like everything's as it should be. But as he lets go, I feel the weight settle in—a tangled web of loyalties pulling me in different directions. My heart aches for Mom, for Zahra, for everything I'm leaving behind. But I know what I have to do.

That night, sleep eludes me, the enormity of what lies ahead an ever-present revenant. Restless thoughts churn, dark imaginings of what horrors Zahra might face while I remain here, a world away. Guilt eats at me, a relentless beast. How could I have let her go alone? In the thrum of silence, a voice whispers, slithering through my mind, insidious and taunting. *You failed her. You weren't there when she needed you most.*' I squeeze my eyes shut against the onslaught, but the voice only grows louder, feeding on my deepest fears. Zahra's face dances behind my eyelids, her absence a gaping wound that refuses to heal.

Chapter 27

The air thickened suddenly, heavy as if time itself had slowed. Every step felt like wading through water, yet I moved as if weightless, gliding deeper into this dark, twisted world. Shadows crawled and writhed around me, shifting into creatures with snarling faces and contorted limbs. Their talons clicked against the pavement as they closed in, driving me deeper into a maze of narrow alleyways. The dim, flickering streetlights cast only weak, trembling shadows, doing nothing to protect me from the nightmare lurking in every corner. Twisted faces emerged in the crowd, glaring with an intensity that made my skin crawl, their eyes filled with hunger, their hands clawing at me as I pushed past. The rough walls scraped against me, leaving trails of blood. I struggled to break free, their whispers hissing in my ears, taunting me, pushing me onward, a hunted animal with no escape. The buildings, structures of concrete and steel surround me on all sides, hemming me in. Every nerve was on fire, my heart pounding like it might burst, muscles burning as adrenaline coursed through me. Sweat poured down my face, stinging my eyes, blurring my vision. My boots thudded against the pavement, each step jarring, but I couldn't stop. Not now. Not with Zahra's life hanging in the balance.

"Zahra!" I shouted, my voice raw, desperate, carrying into the night like a lifeline.

With every ounce of strength left in me, I sprinted across the barren field toward her. But she seemed to slip away, fading into the shadows like a mirage. Her small frame shook as she looked around, trapped, danger closing in on all sides. Her eyes were wide with terror, breaths coming in short, panicked gasps. The crescent moon hung above us, casting a cold, accusing glow, as if we were pawns in some twisted game.

Tears filled Zahra's eyes, a choked sob escaping her lips. The stench of death clung to the air, thick and suffocating. Her hands trembled uncontrollably as she stood, frozen in fear, at the mercy of forces I couldn't see, forces that seemed to revel in her helplessness. And then, from somewhere behind me, a voice cut through the night, low and full of ruthless satisfaction.

"I've got her now." It was over. They had found her.

My eyes snapped open, and I bolted upright, gasping, my heart pounding against my ribs. The sheets were twisted around my legs, trapping me, and I clawed them off, desperate to move, to escape the lingering horror of whatever I'd just seen. My whole body shook, rigid with a fear that clung to me, seeping into my bones. The voice from the nightmare still echoed in my head, mocking me, dripping with threats I couldn't quite understand. I shivered, drenched in cold sweat, as the fragments of the dream faded, leaving me hollow and raw. It felt too real, like I'd been fighting for my life against something I couldn't see, something dark and relentless. And even now, awake and staring into the shadows, I couldn't shake the feeling that I was helpless against it. I forced myself to breathe, pushing back the panic clawing at my throat, but it was like wrestling with shadows—my chest felt tight, every breath shallow, like fear itself had wrapped its hands around my lungs. I didn't know what was coming after me, but I knew it was there, lurking, watching.

"Tommy, please!" Zahra's voice cut through the darkness, raw and desperate.

My throat tight with terror. "I'm coming, Zahra," I gasped, stumbling over my words. "Hold on."

CHAPTER 28

I rubbed my clammy cheeks, trying to shake off the fragments of last night's nightmare. I wiped the sleep from my eyes, glancing at the thin stream of sunlight sneaking through the flimsy curtains. Another long day. With a sigh, I pushed back the covers, swung my legs over the edge of the bed, and clenched my jaw, wincing as I tasted blood. I'd been grinding my teeth again, like always. Once, I'd tried wearing a mouthguard to stop it, but like every other attempt at self-care, it didn't stick. I dragged myself to the bathroom, spat blood into the sink, and brushed my teeth, the mint taste cutting through the metallic tang. Zahra's voice echoed in my mind, just like in last night's dream. Pleading for my help. I closed my eyes, took a deep breath, and fought to keep the fear at bay. I couldn't afford it—not now. Not when she needed me. With a final sweep of the room, I tossed the last of my things into the open bag, making sure I hadn't missed anything essential. Right on cue, the taxi honked impatiently outside, a sharp reminder that it was time. I grabbed my bag, headed out, and climbed into the backseat. My fingers fiddled with my passport as I tried to keep my face steady, calm. I smiled at the driver, hoping it looked confident.

"Terminal 2, please. Ethiopian Airlines," I said, my voice carrying a conviction I wished I felt.

As the taxi pulled away, I stared out the window, giving myself time to think, to really feel the weight of what I was about to do. I knew the risks. The country was on the brink of chaos, political turmoil at every turn. The language barrier, the sheer size of the place—it would be like trying to find her in a sea of millions. But Ethiopia? In the middle of a civil war? What was she thinking? I should've stopped her. Why didn't I stop her? I should've fought harder. Now...what if I never find her? What if she's just... gone? Lost in all of it? No. I can't think like that. I won't. The fear claws at me, but I won't let it win. Love pulls me toward her with a force stronger than any nightmare. She needs me. What if she's hurt? What if she's calling my name, expecting me to be there, and I'm not? I clench my fists, glancing at my reflection in the window. There I am, weathered, older—lines and scars marking the battles I've fought, the losses I've faced. But beneath it all, still a soldier. Still a marine. *'Once a marine, always a marine,'* they say. I hope they're right. I can do this. I am resilient. I am strong. Today isn't just another day; it's the beginning of something else—something bigger. Redemption, maybe. My own personal battle. This journey will test me, I know it will. I've proven myself in other countries, other wars, but now it's Africa's turn. Ethiopia—a land shaped by beauty and conflict, a place that will test me to the core. But I'm ready. I have to be.

Fragments of a dream flood my mind—images of Ethiopia, vibrant and overwhelming, a place where every sense is stretched to its limit. The sharp scent of spices and sweat stirs something raw inside me, pushing out any doubt. This memory—it doesn t let go, drives me forward even as unrest churns around me, the threat in the air as thick as the heat. I push through the crowd, deeper into this tangled world, each step a surge of pain that almost brings me to my knees. But I can't stop. Zahra s gone, and 1 d walk through fire to find her. It feels like dancing with death, a breath away from disaster. But I keep going. Courage is all 1 ve got left, and 1 ll hold onto it with both hands. A minefield awaits me as I step blindly into it. I am ready—or as ready as any man can be.

The taxi approaches the airport, and in the distance, I see it rise—a fortress of glass and steel, brimming with people reuniting, finding one another. My stomach tightens with a mix of dread and hope. I remember Mita's words, echoing in my mind like a promise. This is it. I'm ready to face whatever waits for me, to fight until I find her, to finish this journey I've started.

Chapter 29

"The skin reacts according to the country it is in."

Ethiopian Proverb

Why is it always me? Out of all the seats on this plane, why am I the one stuck next to this guy? I've barely sat down, and already I want to claw my way out. The stale sweat, the sour breath, and something else I can't even place... it's suffocating. I need to distract myself. Deep breaths. No—definitely not deep breaths. Shallow breaths. I just have to keep calm, keep it together. The hum of the plane is some comfort, at least, a thin barrier against the stench and the swarm of thoughts in my head. But no matter how much I try, I can't stop worrying about Zahra. A raw, metallic taste fills my mouth, and a shiver runs down my spine. I can't shake this feeling of something lurking, something dangerous. My skin prickles, and then I hear it—the voice again, the same one that's haunted me for days. It's everywhere and nowhere at once, a raspy whisper that digs right under my skin.

"You have arrived," it snarls, low and guttural, like it's coming from inside my head.

No. I'm not hearing this. It's in my mind, it has to be. I open my mouth to answer, but the words are locked inside me, trapped by fear. Where is it coming from? There's no one here... so why the hell can I hear it? The voice shifts, becoming softer, almost soothing.

"Don't be afraid. I'll be here when you're ready."

A chill crawl up my neck, and I rub it, half expecting to feel someone's breath on my skin. My heart is racing, the beats too loud, too fast. The voice stops, but the fear doesn't. Then the plane jolts, hard, and I grip the armrests, white-knuckled, until the seatbelt sign pings on. I look out the window and see Addis Ababa coming into view, its cityscape glinting under the sun, normal except for the plumes of smoke rising in the distance, tainting the otherwise clear sky.

I must've drifted off at some point. We're almost there, and I can finally breathe again. But the stench from the guy next to me has only grown stronger. Somehow, he's now deep in conversation with the guy across the aisle. They're chatting loudly about Ethiopia like they're seasoned experts, though it's clear they barely know what they're talking about. The guy across the aisle, tall and obnoxious even while seated, chimes in as if he's addressing the entire plane.

"You know the problem with Ethiopia? No one's got the guts to make the tough calls. You put me in charge for a week, and I'd have this place running smooth as hell."

"Yeah, they're soft," says my seatmate, nodding. "These leaders need to be tough. Show people who's boss."

It's obvious they're here on some vanity project, something they'll brag about online. Their arrogance is unbearable, each word they say dripping with condescension. My fingers itch with anger, and a dark voice inside me whispers, daring me to act. I imagine grabbing him by his greasy hair and smashing his head against the seat in front of us, again and again, until he's silent. I try to shake off the thought, but it only twists into something darker, more satisfying. I can almost feel the release, the surge of power. They think they know everything, but the way they toss around the name "Derg" makes my blood boil. They talk like they understand it, but they have no clue. I remember the day I walked into the Red Terror Museum in Addis, the shadowed halls lined with photographs and mementos, each carrying the weight of thousands of stories, thousands of lives. I can still feel that history pressing down, see the darkness that swallowed whole families, whole neighbourhoods. The memories claw their way back, sharper with each heartbeat. I squeeze my eyes shut, but they don't stop.

I remember Zahra telling me her family's stories, her hands trembling, voice cracking under the weight of what they endured. She told me of the Derg's raids, how they'd go door-to-door in the dead of night, civilians twisted into soldiers, armed and ready to strike down anyone who even looked like a political rival. Entire families vanished, children ripped from their homes, blood staining the streets. The death tolls. Staggering. Amnesty International estimated it at two hundred thousand lives lost. Addis was swallowed in a darkness so thick, so absolute, that it left a stain that never washed away.

My love for Ethiopia is bound to Zahra, woven with her family's history, her country's struggle. And now, with things on the edge again, the fear of watching it happen all over is almost too much to bear. But I know I'll do anything—*anything*—to protect this place that's become a second home. Just a few more minutes, and we'll land. I can make it. I just need to keep it together. "Deep breaths," I mutter, voice low, reminding myself to hold on a little longer.

Chapter 30

The plane dips sharply, and my stomach lurches up into my throat. Oh, God, I think I'm going to be sick. I glance out the window, and the ground is coming up way too fast—closer, closer. I shut my eyes, squeezing them tight as the engines roar, a sound that rattles through the whole plane and vibrates in my bones. It's like everything's about to come apart, like the fuselage itself is on the verge of giving in. Every jolt shakes me to my core, my teeth clattering as we drop lower and lower. Pressure builds in my ears, a deep ache that drowns out everything else. I reach for my water bottle, hoping for some relief, but it's empty. I can barely swallow; my throat so dry it feels like sandpaper. My hands are glued to the armrests, my knuckles white, the seatbelt biting into my waist as I brace myself. The landing gear drops with a heavy *clunk,'* and I hear a grinding noise beneath us that makes me question if the wheels are even still there. Then— *thud*—we hit the tarmac, hard. I'm thrown forward, my seatbelt yanking me back as the brakes scream, and the whole plane vibrates like it's shaking itself apart. People clap as we slow to a crawl, and I just shake my head. I'll never understand it—the applause. It's a routine flight, not a miracle, but maybe we all just need something to hold on to, a way to say, *We made it.'* All I can think about is getting off this damn plane, getting one step closer to Zahra. The aisle is packed, everyone desperate to stand, grab their bags, get moving. I squeeze out of my seat, stuck in the line of people slowly shuffling forward. When I finally step off the plane, the heat slams into me—thick and heavy, like stepping into a furnace. The air is filled with dust, and there's a faint hint of something burning. It's earthy, raw, nothing like the stale cabin air I've been trapped in. Sweat prickles along my neck and forehead as I take it all in—the blur of people, voices rising and falling, the scent of cooking fires somewhere in the distance. It's alive, so different from the stillness of the plane.

We funnel into the terminal, and it's a strange, almost surreal mix of urgency and calm. A mother shushing her crying baby. A businessman checking his watch, a look of irritation etched across his face. People are talking, lost in conversation, while the loudspeaker crackles with an announcement I can't quite catch. My legs feel wobbly from the flight, and anxiety thrums through me like a current. Somewhere in this city, Zahra is here. Whether she knows it or not, I'm coming for her. I get in line for visas, wiping the sweat off my brow as the nervousness gnaws at me. The terminal isn't what I expected—it's quieter, emptier. There's a kind of tension in the air, people moving with a weary sort of determination, as if they'd rather be anywhere but here. I shift my weight, inching forward with each step, each movement bringing me closer to whatever comes next, to Zahra or the next clue. The line inches forward, and I grip my passport, the weight of everything pressing down on me. The promises I've made, the hope that's driven me, and the persistent doubt that maybe - just maybe - I'm being a fool. Is this bravery, or is it desperation? At this point, I can't even tell the difference anymore. As I waited in line, my gaze drifted to the woman ahead of me. She clutched a crumpled document in her hands, fingers gripping it so tightly her knuckles were white. Her brows were furrowed in deep concentration. Suddenly, she seemed to sense my eyes on her. Her slender frame tensed, and she turned to meet my stare with piercing dark eyes. Exhaustion was etched across her face—the shadows under her eyes hinted at countless sleepless nights, and the slump of her shoulders spoke of a heavy burden. She gave a slight nod, a weary acknowledgment, before turning back to face the counter. It was clear that conversation was the last thing she wanted. And I get it. Right now, we're just trying to get through. Just trying to survive another day.

The woman behind the visa desk glanced up at me, her brow furrowed and eyes heavy, a look of someone who'd seen too many stories pass through her line. She wore a faded traditional Ethiopian dress, the fabric worn thin, her fingers moving expertly as she counted currency and shifted papers with a practised hand. I held steady, sliding my passport and cash toward her, fighting the urge to betray any hint of nerves. She spoke quickly in Amharic to her colleague, her words carrying authority, but they kept glancing my way, eyes shifting from my passport to my face, and then to the documents again, as if piecing something together. I had to appear calm, like I belonged here, like this was just another checkpoint on a familiar road. *Family is everything,'* Zahra had told me. Her words echoed in my head, steadying me as I waited.

Finally, just as I started to wonder if I'd be denied entry, she returned, her eyes softer, something almost understanding in her gaze. The loud thud of the stamp hitting my passport broke the silence. She handed it back, the new visa stark and final on the page.

I nodded, murmuring a quiet "thank you," my voice swallowed by the noise of the terminal.

My fists clenched as I walked away, feeling the tension still coiled tight in my hands. This was it. I'd come to Ethiopia for answers, and now there was no turning back. I pushed through the crowded arrival hall, eyes scanning faces as I walked, half-expecting—hoping— to find someone looking back with some glimmer of recognition, some sign they understood why I was here. The noise of the airport buzzed in the background, swallowed by the singular focus in my head: Zahra, and the truth about what happened to her. As I moved deeper into the crowd, I felt the weight of countless eyes—strangers watching me, suspicion written on their faces. I was a foreigner, an outsider here, but I couldn't let that stop me. I kept moving, head down, trying to navigate the crush of people. It was sweltering, sweat soaking through my shirt as I tugged at my collar, craving relief in the stifling heat. I tried to imagine Zahra's hand in mine, a phantom comfort keeping me grounded as I navigated the chaotic crowd. I tried to blend in, avoiding eye contact, walking with a sense of purpose, hoping I didn't stand out more than I already did. Everything here felt like a challenge, every step a test of my resolve. The blare of a taxi horn snapped me back as a driver yelled at a pedestrian blocking the road. People jostled past, voices loud and clashing. Yet, oddly, there was also a sense of familiarity, like this chaos was exactly where I needed to be.

The sun was sinking, casting long shadows across the city, and soon, night would fall over Addis. I knew what that meant. In a place like this, night held secrets and danger, a time when those looking for answers walked carefully. I'd spent too many nights alone in foreign cities, haunted by memories and the weight of old ghosts. But this felt different. A quiet confidence had settled over me, a feeling that somehow, no matter how rough the road, I'd see this through to the end.

CHAPTER 31

"When the webs of the spider join, they can trap
a lion."

Ethiopian Proverb

Outside the terminal, Addis Ababa greeted me with a wild embrace — the city's pulse pounding in the relentless honking of cars, the hawkers' voices slicing through the humid air, and that unmistakable scent of berbere wafting through the smog. I stood still, caught off guard by the rush of memories. It felt like being thrown back into a past life, one I had tucked away but never truly left behind. The heat, the dust, the earthy aroma — it was all here, just as I remembered, and yet everything felt different, like returning to a childhood home and finding the walls repainted. I took a long breath, letting the thick, spiced air settle deep into my lungs, almost as if I could absorb a piece of the city back into myself. How long had it been since I'd last stood here, since we'd packed up and moved, trading this chaos for the cool, grey calm of Cardiff? Too long. I realised I'd missed this more than I'd let myself admit. Instinctively, I reached into my pocket for my phone, even though I already knew what I'd find. The blank signal icon blinked up at me, indifferent and unchanging. No bars. No service. Just like it had been for weeks now, ever since the network had crumbled. The government said it was a "temporary measure," a way to maintain order, though we all knew what that really meant. The phone felt cold and useless in my hand, an artefact from another world. I'd only just managed to receive Mita's message before everything went dark — one last lifeline before we were cut off. The words had been brief, hastily typed, and I'd read them a dozen times by now, memorised each line. *'Meet me. Addis Ababa. We need you. Urgent, Mita.'* That was it. No details, no explanations. Just those six words. I let out a frustrated sigh and shoved the phone back into my bag, feeling the weight of it settle against me like a stone. It was a hollow sort of loneliness, standing here disconnected, surrounded by the relentless life of the city. This was home, and yet, without the means to reach her, I'd never felt further away. The city is a blend of worlds—new high-rises sprouting up beside humble tin-roofed stalls. I've been here countless times, but today, something feels different, heavier. There's an intensity in the air, like the city itself is holding its breath. Horns blared, and people called to each other in rapid Amharic, the language half-familiar but still slipping through my mind like water. I moved with slow, deliberate steps, trying to shake off the tangled thoughts storming through my head. The smell of exhaust and the heat clung to everything, mixing with the aroma of roasting coffee that drifted from a nearby stand. I weaved through the busy crowd, trying to spot a familiar face in the sea of strangers. Taxi drivers yelled out destinations, their cars worn and battered from endless battles on the road, while people streamed past, hurrying to their rides or welcoming loved ones with warm embraces. I tried to catch someone's eye, maybe exchange a friendly word, but they looked right through me—glances that were quick, detached, indifferent. They know I'm a foreigner without a second thought. Children darted past, their voices echoing, "Faranji! Faranji!" I'd been in Africa for years; this wasn't new. But today, it felt different, the curious stares replaced by something sharper, almost resentful. The looks lingered, reminding me that no matter how much time I spent here, I'd always be an outsider. I scanned the area anxiously, hoping Mita would arrive soon. Just then, a man shuffled up to me, dishevelled and weathered, his sunken eyes searching mine. His clothes were a patchwork of bright colours that seemed to clash in every possible way, and his hand was outstretched, holding a crumpled, faded map.

"Need a guide?" he asked. Politely, I declined and explained that I was waiting for a friend.

His reaction was unexpected, a strange noise escaped from his lips - a sharp inhale followed by a shrill sound like teeth kissing. His face twisted into an unsettling grin, and he let out a laugh that sounded straight out of some vintage horror flick. With every word I spoke, I felt as though I was throwing pebbles into a vast, empty canyon. The space between us stretched wider, and the sense of isolation grew, until a shock took hold, leaving me frozen in place. I scanned the crowd, and suddenly, bits of Zahra seemed to be everywhere. One woman's nose crinkled just like hers when she smiled; another had dimples that ran just as deep. The curve of a cheekbone here, the shape of an eyebrow there—pieces of her, scattered in every stranger's face. My heart raced, my gaze darting from person to person, as a light breeze swept across my face. I tried to shake off the strange illusion, but it lingered, keeping me on edge. I stopped, not sure what to do next, my mind spiralling with questions I couldn't answer. What should I do? How do I navigate this mess of memories and confusion? Then, a sinking feeling settled in my chest, thick and heavy. My breath hitched, and no matter how hard I tried to push the memories away, they pressed in, relentless and sharp.

Suddenly, the unmistakable scent of blood filled the air, even though there was none around. It was like a phantom smell from the past, but my senses couldn't tell the difference. Faces began to crowd my vision—terrified, pleading eyes, mouths open in silent screams. Then, out of nowhere, the blare of a horn shattered the illusion. A blue taxi screeched to a halt right in front of me, and the door flew open. I blinked, snapping back to reality, my eyes falling on the man stepping out. His face was weathered, and deeply lined, his eyes wild but sharp. His clothes were worn, and mismatched, hanging loosely on his thin frame—a man clearly at odds with life's harder edges. But as he walked toward me, his shoulders squared, and a fierce determination glinted in his gaze. Life may have been harsh, but he looked ready to stare it down, unyielding. Then it hit me—hard and sudden. This was Samuel Getachew. The man who had driven us on my wedding day. The man who, on that very day, became both my brother and one of my truest friends. A slow grin spread across my face, mischief creeping in, as if we were partners in some grand scheme. We stood there, face to face, like two kids who'd just pulled off the ultimate prank, bonded by a shared history and challenges we'd both survived. Our connection? Unbreakable.

"Dehina neh, Tommy, how's it going, my friend? Mita sent me." He declared this as he extended his hand to clasp mine.

"Dehina neh, Samuel, you're a sight for sore eyes," I said, exhaling a long breath I hadn't realised I'd been holding.

Samuel's face broke into a grin, and before I knew it, he'd pulled me into a tight, familiar hug, like we were brothers. It reminded me of my brother John, and for a moment, that familiar ache stirred in my chest. Here, in this city that felt vast and overwhelming, Samuel was the one steady anchor I had. His warm hand on my back grounded me, and I let myself feel a sliver of relief. The sounds of car horns, street vendors, and the city's endless hum faded a little as he took my bag and led us to the taxi, weaving through the bustling crowd like he'd done this a hundred times. I clung to his words as he spoke, navigating through the local dialect with an ease I envied. Each phrase was like a lifeline, reassuring me that I wasn't as lost as I felt.

As we settled into the taxi, the towering buildings and crowded streets felt less intimidating with Samuel beside me, guiding me closer to Mita—and hopefully, Zahra. The city seemed to shrink a little, the unfamiliar edges smoothing out, though a quiet unease still simmered under the surface. We were moving away, but something told me the real challenges lay just ahead.

Chapter 32

The city streaked past in a blur of neon lights and shadows. Samuel's hands gripped the wheel tightly, his knuckles pale against the dark interior, as he navigated us through the crowded streets. Every turn, every bump over the cobblestone streets brought me closer to my destination and deeper into my own anxiety. I exhaled slowly, trying to shake the tension from my shoulders, grateful Samuel was here. Through the window, glimpses of a familiar yet foreign world slid by, pieces of a life I used to know. A tightness clung to my chest; a dull ache that made each breath feel shallow. Everything felt fragile, like the whole city was teetering on the edge. One wrong step, and it could all come crashing down. I caught sight of soldiers ahead, setting up a roadblock. My stomach twisted. What the hell am I walking into? Rebels? Government forces? Honestly, I didn't care. All I knew was that I had to find her. The thought of her—her face, her smile—was the only thing keeping me going, keeping me from unravelling completely.

We came to a stop outside the hotel, and for a moment, I just sat there, not ready to leave the safety of the cab. I took a breath, steeled myself, and opened the door. The sun was dipping low, casting everything in a soft orange glow. I turned to Samuel, grasped his hand, and murmured my thanks. We shared a look, knowing we'd meet again tomorrow, and then he drove off, disappearing into the city's maze. As I approached the hotel entrance, I forced myself to calm down, to breathe. Mita held the key to everything we'd need for our next steps. Then, from the shadows just beyond the dim hotel lights, she appeared. A warm smile softened her strong, graceful features, her high cheekbones catching the glow of the streetlamps. Her eyes—sharp, dark, and knowing—met mine, grounding me. It was the same strength I'd admired when I first met her in this city, years ago. She wore a traditional shamma, dyed deep reds and browns, like she was prepared for something more than a meeting. As I took in her Amazonian presence, I couldn't help but feel out of place, like I should've come ready for combat. She pulled me into a tight embrace, one that held all the grief and strength we'd both been carrying. For a second, I let myself believe that maybe Zahra was somewhere close, waiting, safe. We walked into the lobby together, the plush carpet muffling our footsteps as Mita led the way, her stride purposeful. Beneath her calm demeanour, I could sense the weight she was carrying too, the same desperation and determination that fuelled me.

Inside the room, we stood in silence under the dim light of a single lamp. Mita's gaze was heavy with unspoken words, and a hint of something else—something that warned me this wasn't going to be easy. My heartbeat fast with a mix of dread and hope. She reached into her frayed leather bag and pulled out a folded bundle wrapped in dark fabric. Slowly, she unravelled it, revealing a hand-drawn map covered in symbols and lines I didn't understand. As I stared, the map seemed to come alive with an eerie energy, like a doorway to another world. The sharp, unfamiliar markings gave the room a strange, almost haunted feeling. This wasn't just a map. It was a piece of something ancient, something that held secrets and truths I wasn't sure I was ready to face. The silence thickened as Mita prepared to speak, and I braced myself for whatever would come next, knowing there was no turning back. Mita's voice was barely a whisper, but I felt the weight of each word.

"This is bigger than us, Tommy." Her fingers traced over the worn map, lingering over points with an urgency that made the air feel even heavier. "We need to start here," she said, her finger resting on a spot, "but it won't be easy. The price..."

I cut her off. "I don't care about the price, Mita. I'm going, with or without you. She's, my wife. My responsibility." I took a breath, forcing conviction into my voice. "She's alive. I'll find her. I'll bring her home."

Mita's eyes sharpened. "Listen to me, Tommy. She's my family too. And I have others missing, others who need answers." Her eyes locked onto mine. "You need me. We need each other."

I shifted uncomfortably under her gaze. "I know, it's just..."

She cut me off. "Don't apologise, Tommy. We're family. We're in this together."

I paced, adrenaline pushing me forward. "And if she's gone... if they took her life..." My words hung heavy in the air. "Then I'll take my vengeance." I shook my head, forcing myself back to reality. "I know how bad things are. People are dying every day. But not her, Mita. Not you, and not me. We'll make it."

Mita nodded, pressing her lips together, focused on the map laid out on the small hotel table. Her finger hovered over a faded line before dropping, her expression hardening. There was a distance in her eyes, a weight she carried, a shared grief etched into both of us from these brutal times. The hotel's old air conditioner droned to life, its rattling hum barely cooling the thick heat pressing through the walls. I stayed quiet, giving her space to gather herself, and then she spoke, her voice steady but laced with tension.

"We need to be strategic. Some areas are controlled by people who won't think twice about using us."

Her gaze flicked back to the map, running over territories like she was reading invisible warnings. The room felt colder suddenly, a draft slipping through the cracks in the walls, chilling us both. From somewhere below, a faint, haunting melody rose, hollow and mournful, tugging at our nerves. I couldn't help but wonder if it was Zahra's voice echoing through the halls. As the tune grew louder, the room seemed to close in, the walls pressing around us.

I leaned closer to Mita, trying to shake off the creeping unease. My voice was tight, barely a whisper. "Do you hear that?"

Mita's face froze, eyes wide. She didn't answer; she didn't have to. Then, without warning, the lights flickered, and everything went dark. The melody turned shrill, a twisted lullaby echoing in the blackness, clawing at something deep within me. I felt Mita's hand clamp onto mine, her grip fierce, a silent plea in the face of whatever was out there. We stood rooted in place, breaths shallow, hearts pounding together in the suffocating silence. In the dark, every sense sharpened, every sound amplified. I could feel something—someone— watching us from the shadows, lurking just beyond reach. Mita's grip tightened, almost painfully, as we stood frozen, her breaths barely audible in the thick stillness. The silence itself seemed to throb, alive, coiled around us, waiting. And then... everything went quiet. Utterly, oppressively quiet, as if time itself had slowed, dissolving into an endless void. Shapes began to swim in the blackness, drawing me deeper. I felt myself slipping, tumbling into the dark, caught in a current with no beginning or end. Time had lost all meaning—minutes stretched into hours, hours into eternity. My throat burned with the scream trapped inside me, a sound I couldn't make, as my sense of self drifted away, every thought a fading echo, every muscle paralyzed. Whispers slipped in and out of my mind, ghostly and intangible, leaving only a trace of dread. I felt myself floating in a void, an endless emptiness with no escape. Suddenly, bursts of colour shattered the black, flashing like lightning. But each flash only faded back into darkness. Just darkness. I was left with nothing but memories— haunting fragments clawing at my mind, tearing through reason, dragging me back to moments I'd tried to bury. *Each image is sharper than the last, each one slicing into me, locking me in a prison of my own history. I was desperate for answers but terrified of what I might find. The scenes replayed, frantic, vivid, each more nightmarish, each more vivid.*

CHAPTER 33

The memory hit me like a truck, sudden and brutal, leaving me breathless. Manila—the night I was taken, beaten, and left to die. That night burned into me, carved deep, a horror I could never shake. I remembered being crammed into the cramped footwell of a car, my body soaked in blood, spilling from wounds I couldn't even keep track of anymore. The layers of fat I once carried with pride had been no armour against the blows that seemed to go on forever. Blood filled my mouth, thick and metallic, mingling with snot and spit as I struggled to breathe through the pain stabbing at every inch of me. Each gasp tore at my ribs, raw and broken. I could still feel their kicks landing, the dull thud of their feet crushing into my bones, breaking whatever was left. Their faces were a blur, their features distorted by the fog of agony, the shock. I tried to scream, to beg, but my voice was lost in the sickening rhythm of their fists and feet, beating me down, one strike after another. I could barely remember anything before that night. Everything was just fragmenting now—half-formed memories of a life I'd never get back.

The beatings were endless, a brutal rhythm of fists and feet that left me numb. At some point, I felt myself slipping away, like my soul was trying to escape from this battered, broken body. The pain faded into a dull throb, replaced by a cold emptiness that sank deep into my bones. Was this it? Was I dying? I braced myself, desperate to survive, but the blows just kept coming, relentless. A voice broke through the chaos—a nasty mix of Tagalog and broken English, taunting me from every angle. Someone spat, his face just a shadow in the dark, his breath filled with cigarettes and alcohol. Another one shoved me harder, laughing as he did it. "Welcome to hell, my friend," he sneered, almost bored with his own cruelty.

"Let me out," I demanded, voice barely a rasp, but my words were met with another flurry of fists, each punch a deliberate reminder that I was theirs to hurt. The guy in the front even threw himself over the seat, landing a few blows, his face twisted in rage. I tried to speak, to plead, but they hit me harder, savouring each second. The car reeked, a thick stench of sweat and something worse, something rotten. I could barely remember how it started, only that I was trapped, drowning in agony. Suddenly, someone grabbed my hand, twisting two fingers back. I felt them snap, one by one, each break followed by sickening laughter. Three more fingers, gone. My body shook with each wave of pain, but their laughter rang in my ears, twisted and triumphant. I could barely keep my eyes open, but images flickered in my mind—memories, regrets, faces I wanted to see one last time. I gritted my teeth, forcing myself to stay conscious. They wouldn't break me. Not like this. I'd die fighting if I had to. Outside the car, the night was alive with noise—shouting, laughter, blaring music, the sounds of people who had no idea what was happening here. The air was hot and thick, the smell of sweat and alcohol clinging to everything. I could just make out lights through the cracked side window, dancing off the glass as if mocking me. The world beyond was dangerous, but I'd rather take my chances there than in this suffocating hell. Every sound, every flicker of light seemed to taunt me. I wasn't going anywhere. Suddenly, I felt my stomach lurch, a surge of fear and nausea hitting all at once. I could barely see through my swollen eyes, vision reduced to a narrow blur. I cursed myself, and my decisions. How did I end up here? I heard voices—women outside, laughing and shouting, oblivious to my suffering. Self-pity gnawed at me, but deep down, a twisted thrill surged in response. Maybe I'd walked into this mess, but I'd fight my way out. Driven by that last bit of reckless energy, I forced my muscles to move. I twisted, kicked, thrashed—anything to break free. The car rocked under the struggle. A fist cracked against my jaw, snapping my head back, and filling my mouth with blood. The taste was metallic, and bitter, but it fuelled me. Desperation took over, and I lunged forward, slamming my head against the nearest figure. There was a crunch, a howl, and in that split second of confusion, I yanked my arm free and clawed at the door handle. The door swung open, and rough hands yanked me out, dragging me onto the sharp gravel outside. I stumbled, feet bare, gravel cutting into my skin. The night air hit me, thick with smoke and dust, and I tried to focus, searching for a way out. Shadows circled around me, laughter and leering faces everywhere I turned. I could barely stand, but the adrenaline kept me upright. Then he appeared—the driver, grinning like he'd just won some twisted prize.

He stepped closer, his face inches from mine. "Welcome to Manila," he sneered, voice dripping with mockery. "Having fun?"

I forced my swollen eyes open, teeth gritted against the pain. His voice was like ice, taunting. "No heroes here, my friend. Just fools like you who don't know when to quit."

Blow after blow, they kept coming. I wanted to scream, but blood filled my throat, my bones cracking under each hit. Somehow, I fought back against the darkness closing in, against the pain and fear. I tried to speak, but all that came out was a broken whisper, the taste of copper thick on my tongue. The driver leaned in close, a cruel smile twisting his mouth.

"Oh, don't worry," he said, almost whispering. "We're just getting started."

CHAPTER 34

The lights flickered back on, jolting me. The single bulb above swayed, casting eerie shadows around the room, and a chill crawled over my skin. I blinked, adjusting to the harsh light, and the haunting tune that had filled the silence stopped—but the echo of it was still in my head, playing over and over. Mita's fingers loosened their grip on my arm, and she immediately started rummaging through her bag, her hands shaking. Our breaths came quick and shallow. We both knew, somehow, that we weren't alone in whatever was happening here. The shadows from the swinging bulb seemed alive, twisting into shapes that flickered at the edge of my vision. I squinted, trying to make out what was real and what was my imagination playing tricks. I stepped cautiously toward the corner of the room, each step creaking underfoot, as if the hotel itself was groaning under the weight of its secrets. The sound echoed, then faded into silence.

"We're being watched," Mita's voice was barely a whisper, but it sliced through the tension like a knife. Her eyes darted around the room as she muttered something else, so softly I barely caught it. '*Bouda.*" She bent forward, her breath coming in quick gasps, the scent of her fear stirring something in me—half terror, half something I couldn't name. That name. It sent a jolt through me, tugging at something deep, something I'd read in one of Zahra's books. I'd seen it before, in stories about ancient Ethiopian folklore, tales of the *evil eye'* and curses that could change lives with a glance. Legends whispered about in dark corners.

I shook my head, trying to push it away. "That's… impossible, Mita." I forced out a laugh, though it was empty, bitter.

But she didn't laugh. She just watched me, her face serious and pale. "You think it's ridiculous, I know. I don't want to believe it either. But… some people do believe," she whispered, almost to herself.

I wanted to dismiss it, to tell her this was all a bad joke, but her eyes were wide and darting around the room, finally settling on mine with a fierce intensity. "These protests—they're not just protests. Someone's controlling them, using them to push an agenda, to seize control. They want power. They want to drive us out, take everything, and silence anyone who resists."

Her words hung heavy in the air, and I could see the desperation in her eyes, as if she needed me to understand, to believe. That word— *Bouda* —conjured images of hooded figures lurking in the shadows, of secrets buried for centuries. My mind spun, and an icy dread settled in. Zahra's name flashed in my mind, and a sickening wave of fear washed over me. Could she be mixed up in this? What if she was just a pawn to them, tangled in something more sinister than anything I'd imagined? I glanced at Mita, whose eyes burned with a quiet fury. She nodded as if reading my thoughts.

"Zahra doesn't know what she's dealing with," she said. "To them, she's just a piece in their game."

My heart pounded, dread spreading through me. This was more than a threat. It was something ancient, something dark, and I wasn't sure either of us would get out unscathed. Mita's words were like venom, sharp and biting as she paced the room, her every move tense, like she was waiting for something to strike. She yanked back the tattered blinds, her face close to the cold glass as she scanned the street below, searching for any sign of movement. The room felt too quiet, too charged. I could feel my stomach knotting, and images of what Zahra might be going through flickered in my mind, each one worse than the last. But beneath the fear was something fiercer—a love for her that seemed to grow with every frantic word Mita let out.

"Look at me, Tommy," Mita's voice cut through my thoughts, steady and commanding. She had a map spread out, her finger pressing down on a point in the Wollo region, near Lake Hayak. I'd been there before; I knew the rugged terrain, the isolation. "This isn't some story," she said, her voice low and unyielding. "This group, they believe in their power. They think they can control hyenas and command them. To them, it's not superstition—it's real."

"Hyenas?" I tried to keep the disbelief out of my voice, but Mita heard it, her gaze hardening.

"I know how it sounds." Her hands were trembling as she folded the map, her face rigid with fear. "But you need to understand the kind of people we're dealing with. This isn't just dangerous—it's something darker, something that defies logic."

I swallowed, feeling the weight of her words settle like stones in my chest. Every part of me wanted to believe it was absurd, just wild tales. But something in her voice, the sheer urgency, made it impossible to dismiss. This was no ordinary search for Zahra—this was a descent into something I barely understood, where reality blurred with myth.

"Zahra…" Her name slipped out of my mouth, barely a whisper. Where was she? Was she safe? The questions haunted me, trailing me like shadows. I felt the darkness creeping closer, a traitorous voice whispering in my ear, urging me to let go of reason, to give in to whatever twisted strength lay waiting in that darkness. But I shoved it down. I couldn't surrender, not now. Not when she needed me most. Mita was watching me, her eyes intense, fixed on mine. She took a deep breath and continued, her voice steady but thick with something like reverence—or fear.

"They're more than just people, Tommy. These followers believe they're touched by something… other. They think they're guided, influenced by beings who've been among us all along, hiding in plain sight, bending reality to their will." Her hands moved with her words, almost like she was casting a spell, and I sat there, hanging onto every syllable. She leaned in close, her voice a low whisper. "These entities, Tommy… they're gaining power, pulling followers in, promising them things no one else can give. Wealth, power. Enough to make anyone desperate forget themselves."

I felt my stomach twist. "And the cost?" I asked, my voice tight.

Mita's eyes met mine, unflinching. "The cost is always the same. They take everything. And those who follow don't come back."

A cold shiver crept down my spine. I didn't need to hear the details to understand what she was saying. I'd seen what the lure of power could do. The way it seduced, corrupted, left nothing behind but an empty shell. And now, here I was, caught in a nightmare I never could have imagined.

I stood up, turned away from Mita, and began to pace the room with my fists clenched. I stared back at my reflection in the grimy window, a haunted shell of a man. The voices in my head grew louder, a sinister chorus urging me to embrace the darkness that threatened to consume me. I squeezed my eyes shut, trying to block out the whispers, but they only intensified, taunting me with visions of Zahra's fate. I had never experienced such intense guilt, which now manifested as anger, but I had nowhere to vent it, at least not just yet. My blood boiled. Frustrated and enraged. I clenched my fists, struggling to control the fury building inside.

"Those bastards!" I yelled, my voice echoing through the room.

She reached out to touch my shoulder, but I shrugged her off and slammed my fist against the wall. "We have to find her before it's too late!" I growled through gritted teeth, my whole-body trembling with anger.

Mita bit her lip as she whispered urgently to me, her eyes darting around the room. "They're coming for us," she said, fear etched in every syllable. "If we don't do something, they'll take over the country."

This new revelation only fuelled my panic. Time was running out; it was unbelievable, and it seemed far-fetched, but my gut told me there was truth to Mita's claims. But at the same time, everything was clicking into place.

"We have to fight back," I declared, my voice firm and resolute. "Fuck them all!"

Mita nodded fiercely, her expression hardened, and her fists clenched, a determination blazing in her eyes. I can't let fear stop me, not now. But God, I'm terrified.

Mita settles onto the floor, using her backpack as a makeshift pillow and wrapping a blanket around herself.

"Mita, please, take the bed. I'll be okay on the floor." I protest.

But she laughs and responds, "No need to be a gentleman here. I am happy here; But she laughs and responds, "No need to be a gentleman here. I am happy here, enjoy your last night of comfort.

"We'll be roughing it for a while after this." She rolled over onto her side and pulled a colourful scarf over her head, signalling the end of the conversation.

CHAPTER 35

"Evil enters like a needle and spreads like an oak tree."

Ethiopian proverb

When I step into the lobby, Samuel's already waiting outside, pacing. Mita had come down earlier to settle the room charge, gather some food, and pick up whatever essentials she could from the hotel kitchen. There's an intensity in the air, a tension as thick as in any Hitchcock thriller. She's dressed in faded khakis and worn boots, looking ready for whatever the day throws at her. As she walks toward me, I catch the set of her jaw, the stubborn determination etched into her expression. It's a look I've come to admire more and more.

"Morning," she says, her tone clipped, but there's warmth behind it. She seems more focused, and more determined than ever. Whatever cracks I'd seen in her armour last night have been mended overnight, replaced by that fierce resolve that always draws me in.

"You ready?" she asks, her voice steady, purposeful.

I nod, managing to keep my voice calm. "I am." But the doubts creep in anyway—what if we're too late? What if... No. Don't think like that. Not now.

The morning light is almost blinding as we step out together, the cool air a relief after the hotel's stale confinement. Mita's bag bounces against her back as she walks, her energy outpacing mine. I hesitate for a moment, gathering myself, then spot Samuel standing by his car, arms crossed, watching us approach. The car's as beat-up as they come, but it's got a ruggedness that makes it seem indestructible—just like Samuel. They're a pair, worn down but still going, with sheer grit holding them together.

As we move closer, that damn voice comes back, the same one that's followed me everywhere—on the plane, in my dreams, even here. *Tommy, who are these strangers?'* It hisses, low and mocking, wrapping around me like smoke. My chest tightens, my legs freeze, and I try to swallow, but my throat's gone dry. 'Stop. Just stop talking. Please.'

"Hey," Mita's voice breaks in, her face concerned as she glances back. "You alright?"

I'm about to answer when the voice comes again, digging deeper, insidious. *You've sealed your fate—and everyone else's.'*

I'm scanning the empty street, half-expecting to see someone whispering the words, but there's no one. My whole body's trembling by the time I reach Mita and Samuel, my limbs heavy, my throat dry. I give a stiff nod, not trusting my voice. Last night, Mita had told me why Samuel was joining us—how rebels had torn through his village, a quiet place near Dessie, and turned it into a nightmare. They'd left nothing but destruction behind: homes reduced to ashes, bodies of men, women, and children scattered like broken promises. But worst of all, young girls like Samuel's daughter were taken, and stolen away. They became the spoils of war, ripped from their families. Mita and I exchange a look, an understanding passing between us. We know loss; we know what it is to be driven by grief and revenge. In Samuel's eyes, I see the same sadness that stares back at me every morning— a raw, relentless mix of rage and helplessness. The three of us are bound together by sorrow, our different losses merging into a shared need for justice, even if it's misguided. I climb into the backseat, careful to avoid Samuel's eyes in the mirror. My hand clenches and unclenches on my lap, torn between wanting to reach out and share our grief and the need to protect myself from feeling his pain as well. We sit in silence, the car a capsule of unspoken suffering. With a final twist of the key, the engine sputters to life, shattering the quiet. As we pull away from the curb, a knot tightens in my stomach. This is it. I'm either coming back with Zahra, or I'm not coming back at all. The inside of the car surprises me. Unlike its worn exterior, it's clean and well-kept, a small pocket of order amidst the chaos outside. The leather seats shine, and a small Ethiopian cross dangles from the rearview mirror, catching the morning light Zahra had given me a similar one for protection. I couldn't stop thinking about her words as I tightly grasped the cross that now hung from my neck. *'It will keep you safe,'* she had said with tear-filled beautiful eyes. I squeezed it tight in my fist, finding comfort in its familiar touch against my skin. Now, as we rumble down the road, I hold onto that promise, letting its weight ground me. Little did I know just how much I'd come to depend on it in the days ahead.

CHAPTER 36

We left the chaotic streets of Addis Ababa behind, trading the blaring horns and exhaust for the crunch of gravel and the low rumble of the engine beneath us. The road stretched out rough and endless, flanked by mountains that seemed to rise out of nowhere, rugged and unforgiving. Lush greenery closed in on either side, dense enough to feel like a jungle pressing against us. I cracked the window, hoping for a breath of cool air, but as soon as I did, Mita and Samuel shot me a look from the front seats, disapproval written all over their faces. I sighed, giving in and rolling the window back up.

"Fine, fine," I muttered, feigning exasperation. I'll be happy to volunteer myself as a delicious lunch once we arrive. By then, I'll be perfectly cooked," I grinned, hoping to lighten the mood. After a pause, Mita and Samuel finally broke into laughter. But just as I relaxed, the car jolted hard to the left.

"Hold on!" Samuel shouted, yanking the wheel to avoid a toppled cart on the road. Mita and I were thrown sideways, gripping the seats as the tyres screamed against the rough terrain, leaving behind the acrid stench of burning rubber. Samuel's face was set, calm but focused, as he wrestled the car back under control. After what felt like an eternity of bouncing and rattling, we finally hit a stretch of smooth ground, and a collective sigh filled the car.

Samuel chuckled, wiping a bit of sweat off his brow. "Guess those years of off-roading paid off," he said, steering us back on track.

We pressed on, the road unpredictable, turning from smooth to rough without warning. The heat bore down on us, thick and relentless, and inside, it felt like we were roasting. I managed to crack the window just a bit, hoping they wouldn't notice—or maybe they'd just given up trying to stop me. Either way, it helped. Dust seeped in, coating my skin, and filling my lungs. Sweat glued my shirt to my back, and grit lined my teeth every time I swallowed. The hills around us looked half-dead under the blazing sun, twisted trees casting long shadows. Samuel kept sneaking glances at me in the rearview mirror, like he could read the mess of emotions I was barely holding together. Maybe he could. Maybe he knew what it was like to feel this anxious, this on edge. But he didn't say a word. I looked out the window, eyes drifting over the landscape as it blurred past, but my mind was anywhere but here. I couldn't stop thinking about her. Where was she? What were they doing to her? My memory of her face was slipping, her smile turning hazy and distant, replaced by flashes of her screaming, her eyes wide with terror. The thought gnawed at me with every mile, a dull ache in my gut that wouldn't let up. What if I was already too late? What if every bump in the road, every delay, was taking me further from her? I closed my eyes, trying to calm the storm inside, but in the darkness, all I saw was her, surrounded by faceless men, armed, shadows twisting into something monstrous. I gritted my teeth, cursing myself for letting her come here, for not keeping her safe. I should've been there. Should've stopped her. The car hit another bump, and I forced my eyes open, blinking against the glare. I didn't know what lay ahead, didn't know if we'd find her in time. But no matter what, I couldn't turn back now. I wouldn't.

Samuel's hands gripped the wheel tight as he navigated the pitted road, his eyes flicking to Mita with each sharp turn or sudden pothole. I caught the quick glances they exchanged, as if she were guiding him in some unspoken way. I could only imagine her murmuring instructions to watch for the next goat or donkey that might suddenly wander into our path, though I barely understood a word of their language. The sun climbed higher, beating down mercilessly, and beads of sweat trickled down my face. The taxi's air conditioning had given up miles ago, so we left the windows cracked—just enough to let in a hint of air but not the clouds of dust that seemed determined to coat every surface. Mita kept tracing her finger along an old, worn map, though it felt redundant. There was only one route north, and we were already on it. The landscape had shifted since we left Addis. Gone were the crowded streets and tall buildings, replaced by dry, dusty plains and sparse vegetation. Occasionally, we passed goats, a lone camel burdened with goods, and even a troop of baboons picking at the ground. I tried to keep my eyes on the road ahead, but I couldn't shake the feeling of being watched. Every so often, I glanced back, half expecting to see a shadow following us, but there was nothing—just an endless stretch of road and dry, empty land. It felt unsettling, as if we were the last people left in the world. Ahead, small villages emerged and disappeared in the dusty haze. Children stopped playing to watch us pass, their curious eyes following the car until we were out of sight. Mita looked back at me, her expression serious, and broke the silence.

"We're close now," she said, her voice barely above a whisper. "She was last seen near here."

A chill ran through me. Samuel's jaw was clenched, and the atmosphere shifted, a quiet tension settling over us. Every bump and jolt of the car seemed sharper, every ache in my body amplified. I hadn't even set foot on the ground, but this journey was already taking its toll. Samuel slowed, and I knew we were getting close to dangerous territory. The breeze had dropped a few degrees, cooler than it had been earlier, but it did little to settle my nerves. I stared out the window, searching the terrain for some sign of hope or reassurance. Instead, all I saw were shifting shapes in my peripheral vision, faces and figures that melted into shadows before I could make them out. Each glimpse only deepened the sense of isolation, the feeling that here, in this unfamiliar land, I was truly alone.

Then, the town appeared in the distance, like a mirage against the dusty landscape. Buildings rose from the earth, smoke from chimneys casting a haze over the scene. It would've looked peaceful if not for the gunfire crackling in the distance. My breath hitched. *The war's spreading.'* I clenched my fists, grounding myself. She has to be here. Alive. Waiting somewhere safe. I clung to the thought, but deep down, I felt the creeping fear that hope was all I had. Samuel suddenly hit the brakes, and we all lurched forward.

"What's wrong?" Mita asked, her voice tense.

"Roadblock," Samuel replied, pointing. A group of men stood ahead, their vehicles blocking the road. He didn't waste a second, steering the car off the main road and into the shade of a few scraggly trees.

"Time to walk," he said quietly, cutting the engine.

I exhaled, my hand resting on the door handle. Fear clawed at my insides, but there was no room for it now. I pushed the feeling down, my boots hitting the dirt as I stepped out, a cloud of dust rising around me.

CHAPTER 37

The village is small, encircled by simple homes, each one built with whatever the land could spare. As we step off the dusty path, I feel countless eyes on us, watching from behind curtains, around doorways, or through narrow, cracked windows. The air is thick, almost suffocating, as if everyone's holding their breath. My heart pounds as conversations hush, each adult halting their work to take in the stranger walking through their world. I keep my face neutral, steadying myself with a slow, deep breath. I'm here with good intentions, I remind myself, though they can't see that—all they see is a stranger. A group of children peeks out from behind an outhouse, wide-eyed and wary, their mouths slightly open as they take me in. I try a smile, something gentle and reassuring, but they scatter instantly, laughter and whispers echoing softly as they disappear behind a house. As I walk further into the village, I spot an elderly man shuffling down the road. His clothes look like they've been patched and re-patched over years, the fabric thinned to a dull grey. He's wearing a frayed rope as a belt, his bare feet calloused and tough from a lifetime on rough ground. He's like a snapshot from another era, a living piece of history, and I wonder if he, too, will watch me with suspicion. The place is alive with the quiet hum of daily life—women balancing baskets, men tending to livestock—but there's a charged tension in the air. The muted colours of the village blend together, from the brown earth to the greens of the grass, all softened by a haze of wood smoke. Spices and the aroma of cooking meat hanging in the air, both inviting and overpowering, like a world trying to welcome and warn me all at once. I feel as if I'm oceans away from home, yet closer than ever to what I came for.

We reach the market at the heart of the village, weaving through the crowd, and still, no one meets my eyes. They're absorbed in their own worlds, animated gestures and voices rising and falling as they barter. I can see grains and spices laid out in heaps on white cloths, flashes of bright reds and soft yellows. The people move around the stalls, their eyes quick and calculating, immersed in the rhythm of daily life. But for me, it's as if the world has slowed, each step bringing me closer to the question that's haunted me across thousands of miles. *Where is Zahra?'* I rehearse the words silently, the weight of them making my throat go dry. I approach a small cluster of villagers, trying to catch their attention as they laugh together, completely unaware of the storm inside me. I picture Zahra here, with these same people, her bright eyes and easy smile. Would they remember her? Would they hear the urgency in my voice? I swallow hard, my clothes clinging to me, soaked in sweat, every nerve on edge. The laughter fades as I approach, replaced by silence. Their eyes lock onto me, wary and guarded. My mouth goes dry, and my hands tremble slightly as I raise them, a silent plea for help. I muster the courage to speak, but my voice is barely a whisper against the heavy air. "Zahra," I say, the name slipping out like a fragile prayer. "My wife..."

The word hangs in the air between us, unanswered, met with guarded looks and narrowed eyes. Around me, people exchange glances, their voices low and cautious. Mita and Samuel stand beside me, silent and unreadable, as if waiting for a signal that everything is all right. But I can feel the weight of their stares, feel their reluctance to open up, to trust.

I take a shaky breath, my voice catching as I add, "Please, I just need to know if anyone has seen her."

Time slows as I wait, the silence stretching out, thick and stifling. I can feel the tension like a taut line, waiting to snap. I don't know if they'll answer, if they'll help, or if I'll be left to piece together the fragments on my own. But I stand there, heart pounding, waiting for the smallest glimmer of hope, the faintest spark that might lead me to her. Her name should have been enough to bridge the gap between us and these villagers. But instead, it was met with blank stares and a guarded silence. Mita introduced herself in Amharic, her words confident, her gestures deliberate as she explained why we were there. With a steely resolve, she maintained her composure, seemingly willing them to assist us. But they didn't budge, their faces like stone. The harder she tried, the more they shut down. My frustration simmered, growing with each non-answer, each disinterested look. I took a steadying breath, choosing my words carefully.

"Ebakih, please help us. She's my wife—she's, my world." I hadn't noticed the tears stinging my eyes or how much I must have stood out, with my weather-worn face and desperate expression.

Mita's voice suddenly cut through the tension, switching to a dialect that had the heads around us turning, drawing in more villagers to watch the scene unfold. I could hear them murmuring, pointing at me, and I could tell by the intensity of their voices that I was the topic of debate. It was as though we were knocking on the walls of a fortress they had no intention of opening. And yet, Mita didn't falter. She kept talking, her words firm but pleading, pushing against the resistance like she could break through if she only tried hard enough. I looked around, searching their faces for any sign of understanding, but they were unyielding, expressions as hard as the rugged mountain peaks looming in the background. One by one, they turned their backs, shoulders squared, jaws set. And with the last villager's retreat, a silence settled around us, heavy and final.

As the sun dipped lower, I sought shade under a dying tree, wondering if this was all worth it. Should I keep pushing, risking Zahra's safety in the process? Would it be smarter—safer—for her if I backed off, if I got out of the way? I scanned the marketplace like a chessboard, analysing every move, every risk. Could I outsmart the people hunting her? Could I beat them at their own game? From my shaded spot, I spotted a vendor seated on an old crate, surrounded by bundles of *khat* leaves, bargaining with customers over the leaves prized for their stimulant kick. Some chewed it all day, every day; I'd tried it once, but all it left me with was a gritty taste and green bits in my teeth. Above, colourful kites soared, watching like hawks for dropped scraps of food. Beneath their watchful gaze, a group of women sat on woven mats, quietly preparing coffee. But it wasn't the warm, communal scene I was used to. There was a tension there, a caution in their movements, as if the wrong word might spark something dangerous. They whispered among themselves, casting nervous glances over their shoulders, their voices barely audible. Despite their attempts to maintain a facade of normalcy, it was clear that something was amiss. It left me with a lingering unease, as if I were witnessing a hidden secret between them. Mita's arrival had clearly sent ripples through the village; her presence here made my purpose all too obvious. As the sun sank lower, I slumped against a rough acacia tree, exhausted. A wrinkled woman nearby worked on fabric, her eyes flicking up to watch a group of children playing. Her expression was tense, her movements more wary than joyful. The fading light threw long shadows across the square, making everything feel heavier and more ominous.

Whatever hung over this place, it was enough to silence these people, to keep them wary and guarded. Their daily rituals went on, but beneath the surface, there was fear—an awareness that one wrong word could bring danger. I understood their silence, I felt the threat pressing in on all sides. But the stakes were high, and I couldn't leave without answers.

Chapter 38

From my hidden spot, I spotted him: a young boy, maybe nine, with skin dark as night and hair wild and matted, standing alone at the edge of an alley. His clothes were torn and dusty, barely hanging on him, and his eyes—wide, wary, with a quiet wisdom that didn't match his age—stayed fixed on the busy market. He seemed so out of place among the guarded faces and hurried strangers. There was something about him, something fragile but unbreakable, a flicker of resilience that I couldn't look away from. Before I knew it, I was on my feet, moving toward him, pulled by some invisible thread. I tried to smile as I got closer, a soft, friendly smile, hoping he'd feel my intentions. Slowly, I extended my hand, palm up, showing I meant no harm. He held his ground but looked around, his eyes darting like he might bolt any second. Up close, I could see the sadness etched into his face—a sadness that made my own troubles feel small in comparison. We stood there, a quiet space between us, like an invisible wall made of everything we couldn't say. I wanted to tell him that I understood, but the truth was, I didn't. Whatever he'd been through, it was beyond anything I could imagine. The boy shifted, just a small step, kicking up a little cloud of dust as he inched closer. The noise of the market seemed to fade, and all I could focus on was him, this small, silent stranger, accepting my unspoken offer, a tentative, cautious trust. As the sun dipped lower, casting long shadows over us, we stood there, two strangers, letting a fragile connection settle between us in the fading light.

I leaned in close, lowering my voice to a murmur as I looked the young man in the eyes. "I'm looking for someone," I said, words heavy with the weight of it. "Someone important."

The name Zahra slipped out of my mouth, barely a breath, but it lit something in him. His gaze sharpened, and he glanced around, checking the crowd, making sure no one else had caught it. Recognition flickered across his face, followed by a slow, subtle nod. He swept his eyes over the street one last time before he reached out, his small hand slipping into mine. I felt the trust in that grip—fragile and precious. Without saying a word, we'd crossed a line, a silent understanding binding us. I nodded, keeping the moment delicate. Together, we drifted up the alleyway, slipping out of sight of the crowd's curious eyes and whispered chatter. He moved ahead, weaving through the narrow streets with a quick, quiet grace that

I struggled to keep up with. My shadow stretched alongside his, merging into the lengthening dusk. We were an odd pair, but in that instant, connected by something unspoken. He led me through a web of side streets, each narrower, darker, and more twisted than the last, like stepping deeper into a hidden world. Secrets felt alive in this place, pulsing behind every door, every barred window. The sun was sinking, casting longer shadows, and I could feel a chill creeping in as night approached. We didn't want to be out here in the dark; that much was clear to both of us. Every step seemed like a gamble, every corner hiding something unseen. I quickened my pace, nerves on edge, while he kept his head on a swivel, his eyes darting from shadow to shadow, alert for any threat. I couldn't shake the feeling of being watched, of unseen eyes tracking our every move as we slipped further into the maze.

After what felt like hours of wandering, we finally stopped in front of a crumbling building with sagging walls and cracked windows, its roof slanting at a precarious angle. The heat bore down on us, almost smothering us. Sweat drenched me, but my new companion looked unfazed, like he'd just taken a stroll. He caught my gaze, giving me a quick, reassuring nod before he disappeared into the shadows, leaving me alone to face whatever waited inside. I took a deep breath, trying to steady my hands as I reached for the warped wooden door. It creaked loudly, protesting as I pushed it open and stepped inside. The instant I crossed the threshold, a stench hit me—a sickening mix of rot and decay that forced bile up my throat. Tears stung my eyes as the foul smell engulfed me, curling into every inch of the crumbling room. My feet sank slightly as I took a cautious step forward, the rotten floorboards groaning under my weight. The place was littered with signs of life interrupted bits of fabric snagged on broken furniture, empty bags scattered like discarded memories. And then I saw it: a dark, viscous pool of liquid, half-illuminated by a thin sliver of light from a crack in the wall. My stomach twisted as I realised what I was looking at. This wasn't just an abandoned building; it was a place where horror had unfolded, where pleas for mercy had gone unanswered. The deep crimson stains on the floor seemed to pulse, almost alive, telling me a story I didn't want to hear. A whisper reached me through the suffocating silence, faint yet haunting.

Tommy.' Zahra's *voice.* It was like she was right there, calling out to me from across a chasm I couldn't see. My knees hit the floor, sharp stones biting into my skin, but I barely felt it. My heart hammered as I forced out the question that had burned in me since the beginning.

"Is this... is this where they took you?"

Yes.' Her voice was thick with pain, a single word that held the weight of a thousand horrors.

I couldn't hold back the tears any longer. They slipped down my face, warm and bitter. My throat was tight as I forced myself to ask the next question, even though I dreaded the answer.

"Did they... did they hurt you?"

A heavy silence followed before she answered, voice barely a whisper. 'I don t know. I can t remember.'

Her words sent a chill through me. The idea of Zahra suffering—of her enduring anything like this—was like a knife in my chest. My fists clenched, nails digging into my palms as I asked, teeth gritted.

"Did you call for me?"

'Tommy,' she said softly, 'I ll always call for you.'

The weight of her words hit me like a punch. How many times had she called for help, only to be met with silence? How many times had she waited, hoping I'd come, only to be left alone in the dark? And still, after everything, she believed in me. That faith felt like a heavy responsibility, fuelled by love and an ache that ran bone deep.

"Is this... is this the end?" I stammered, my voice breaking under the weight of it all.

Before despair could drag me under, her voice cut through with fierce determination. 'No!' she said sharply. 'This isn t over. Come find me.'

I closed my eyes, clutching onto her words like a lifeline. "Zahra," I whispered, my voice raw. "I promise—I'll find you. Just hold on a little longer."

The thought of her, wounded but holding on, ignited something in me, a fierce resolve that pushed away my fear. I couldn't fail her. Not now. I wiped the sweat from my face, feeling its sting in my eyes, and drew a steadying breath. I had to keep going. I had to get back to Mita and Samuel—they'd be panicking by now. With one last glance at the dark, haunted room, I turned sharply on my heels and headed out, my mind fixed on one thought: I would do whatever it took to bring her back.

CHAPTER 39

Ethiopian proverb

I hurried back to where we'd hidden the vehicle, my chest tight with worry, hoping I'd find them still there. As I got closer, I saw Samuel's silhouette crouched over a pile of supplies, his movements careful and precise as he sorted through the gear, packing everything with his usual efficiency. I thought about telling him about Zahra's voice in my head, and the mysterious boy who'd appeared out of nowhere, but I decided against it. It was too early for that. He'd only pepper me with questions I couldn't answer. Samuel looked up when he heard me approach, his face grim in the moonlight.

"The roads north are blocked—government forces and rebels. We'll have to camp here by the car tonight," he said. "And tomorrow, we go on foot. Only what we can carry. We need to stay off their radar."

I nodded, trying to ignore the unease tightening in my gut. While he continued to organise our supplies, Mita arrived, arms full of bags. She'd managed to gather food and water from the village. Samuel quickly took over, stowing away the supplies with the same steady hands. He placed the bundles of fragile injera bread carefully on top, protecting it from getting crushed. Watching him, I felt a rush of gratitude. Samuel had a way of making things feel almost... manageable. Like we might actually make it through this. As Mita sorted through what she'd brought, I couldn't help but notice how much she reminded me of Zahra. Her precise movements brought back memories of Zahra at the Cardiff market, picking through produce with the same focused care. Mita's determination showed in every movement; she'd done this before. As I watched her and Samuel work side by side, their movements so in sync, I felt a flicker of hope. Maybe we had a chance. I turned back to my own backpack, anxiety simmering as I repacked it. Each item I touched tugged at memories of a life I was leaving behind. My fingers lingered on a small, battered photograph of

Zahra—her bright eyes, her wide smile. She was the reason I was doing all this. Everything led back to her. And I knew I couldn't stop until I found a way back to her, no matter what it took.

Samuel's voice cut through my thoughts. "Hey, check this out," he said, holding out a small bag, a proud smile breaking through the tension on his face. The bag was coated in dust, and I crouched down to peer inside. A mix of nuts and dried fruits. My stomach growled, a sharp reminder that it had been far too long since we'd eaten.

"Nice work, Samuel," I said with a grin, grabbing a handful and munching down.

Mita's eyes lit up, and she nodded as she unpacked the rest. "Good find. We can't afford to waste a single thing."

As we divided up the provisions, the seriousness of our situation loomed over us, but there was also a strange comfort in it—in being together, fighting this fight as a team. I felt the weight of the nearly empty water bottles and a lump formed in my throat.

"What about water?" I asked, glancing between Mita and Samuel.

Mita's smile faded, and a shadow of worry flickered in her eyes. But she kept her voice steady. "Drink what you've got for now. There's a well we can reach in the morning, as long as no one's guarding it."

Samuel nodded; his brow furrowed. "And we'll keep an eye out for other water sources as we move. Just have to be careful, not waste a drop."

I took a deep breath and nodded, feeling the familiar weight of uncertainty settling in. But when I glanced at Samuel and Mita—my allies in this chaos—there was an unspoken resolve between us, a silent agreement that we'd face whatever came next together. With our packs ready, we settled in for the night, knowing that tomorrow would be a battle all its own.

Samuel's gaze drifted to my neck, and his eyes lit up with curiosity. "What's that?" he asked, pointing to the necklace peeking out from my collar.

Instinctively, I clutched the small wooden cross Zahra had pressed into my hand at the airport. "Just a keepsake," I said, trying to sound casual. "Something to bring me luck on this journey."

Samuel gave a small nod, his expression softening. "It's good to have something to hold onto. A reminder of what matters."

His words struck a chord, and I managed a small smile. "Yeah. It helps. Keeps me grounded."

A knowing look passed across Samuel's face. "I get it. I've got my own lucky charm—something my daughter made for me when she was just a kid. I carry it with me everywhere."

My curiosity got the better of me, and I leaned forward. "Do you have it with you now?"

"Of course," he said, not missing a beat. He reached into his pocket and pulled out a small, worn leather pouch attached to his belt by a frayed string. He carefully fished out a smooth pebble, cradling it in his palm. "It's one of two—my daughter has the other."

The pebble was small, but its deep, rich purple colour caught the faint light, hinting at countless journeys through rivers and streams. As I leaned closer, I noticed faint Amharic script etched into its surface—delicate lines that spoke of love and devotion. The details were hard to make out, but the meaning was clear: a connection that distance couldn't break, a bond that had endured. I traced a finger over its worn surface, feeling the years it had weathered.

I handed the pebble back to him, meeting his eyes. "It's more than just a charm, isn't it?"

Samuel's smile was wistful, a shadow of a memory passing across his face. "Yeah, it is."

Before the silence could stretch too long, Mita's voice cut through, steady and firm. "We should rest and start at first light, earlier if possible. We'll need every minute."

Her tone was serious but carried a warmth that kept the tension at bay. We exchanged a look, all of us aware that the night's calm wouldn't last, but ready to face what came next.

CHAPTER 40

Dawn was breaking, and with it came the risk of being spotted. I repacked my bag, double-checking each item like it might be our last line of defence. My hand brushed against Zahra's cross, its smooth edges worn from years of holding onto it. I tucked it into my shirt, feeling its familiar weight against my chest—a quiet comfort, hidden but always there. Zahra caught my eye, and for a moment, we just looked at each other. Then we shouldered our bags. They felt lighter now, stripped down to the essentials, but somehow heavier too loaded with purpose, with the weight of what we'd left behind and what we still carried inside. The sky was just starting to glow with the first hints of pink and orange, the air cool and fresh on our faces. It was a small mercy, knowing the heat would return soon enough to bake the earth beneath our feet. Ahead, hills rolled out endlessly, the wilderness stretching far beyond. There was no time to admire the view, though; time wasn't on our side. The mountains loomed in the distance, their jagged peaks scraping the sky, their shadows creeping down into the valleys below. A thin mist clung to the slopes, ghostly in the dawn light, while the wind rustled through the trees, carrying with it a sound like a bird's cry—a sharp, eerie wail.

Mita glanced up, listening. "It's just the eagles," she said, her voice steady. "They're common around here."

Samuel nodded. "Majestic creatures. They rule the skies out here. They've earned their place."

We moved on, our footsteps crunching in the dirt, leaving behind a trail that felt too fragile against the vastness around us. The night before, that voice had returned, taunting me, promising that I'd never escape. It said it would follow me, wherever I went. Was it just another hallucination? Or could it really track me down, even here in this emptiness?

Step by step, we changed. We were no longer just three people on a tough journey—we were survivors, stubborn and determined. The thorny undergrowth tore at our clothes and scratched our skin, but we kept going. There was a fierceness in us now, an unspoken pact to keep moving, no matter what. Zahra walked beside me, her face etched with lines of grief and love, a reminder of what we were fighting for. Samuel's voice echoed in my mind, grounding me with his quiet wisdom. And Mita, strong as iron, led the way, her focus unshakable. Together, we pressed on, knowing that whatever waited for us ahead, we'd face it side by side. The silence between us stretched out, our shadows long and thin in the morning light, each of us lost in our thoughts. As we pushed deeper into the Ethiopian wilderness, the ground beneath us grew harsher and more unpredictable. Scrub brush clung to rocky outcrops, the wind rustling their dry leaves. It was a land of stark beauty, remote and unyielding. Our boots crunched over loose stones, the sound blending with the distant cry of a bird, creating a steady rhythm that carried us forward. Every step felt precarious, like we were walking a tightrope between the past and the future. Mita moved ahead with an easy grace, her worn boots finding the path with a confidence that only came from experience. Her old canvas rucksack, faded and patched, swung against her back, still holding strong after years of use. Samuel followed close behind, his heavy boots grinding into the earth, his bag swaying at his side—a companion on too many journeys to count. And then there was me, struggling to keep up, my boots worn down to thin leather, every rock jabbing through the soles, reminding me of how far I still had to go. The pack was already rubbing my back raw, every step grinding against the tender skin beneath, the blisters growing and bursting with each jolt. But at least the distraction dulled the ache in my feet for a moment. Memories surged up, unbidden—back to my days as a commando, when we marched through hell and back, crossing unforgiving terrain with way too much gear strapped to us. Endless marches in searing heat or freezing rain, scaling jagged mountains while trying to ignore the burning pain from the webbing that cut into our shoulders. For a second, I almost smiled at the thought, but the pain snapped me back. I gritted my teeth, clinging to the lessons that had been drilled into me—push through, keep moving, don't think about the pain. As I lost myself in those memories, Mita's rough, calloused hands suddenly smeared a handful of warm, earthy mud across my face. The gritty paste filled every pore, masking my pale skin with a dark, slick layer that stuck like a second skin. It clung to my scalp and stubble, turning my features into something almost unrecognisable. With my head wrapped in a scarf and my body dressed in local clothes, I tried to disappear into the landscape, but I knew I was fooling myself. My pale skin, made for Scotland's grey skies, stood out here like a marshmallow in black coffee. We moved forward cautiously, eyes straining against the shadows gathering in front of us. The fading light blurred the landscape into a wash of browns and greens, broken only by the lone, sentinel trees rising like sentries. Haik loomed in the distance, but as the sun dipped lower, shadows swallowed the land, and a chill of unease crawled through my bones. I felt like a spectre drifting through this rugged terrain. The silence was unnerving, but underneath it, I caught hints of whispers, and faint rustling from creatures I couldn't see. The wind slid through the grass, cool against my skin, carrying with it a murmur that sounded like secrets. Just as I thought I might relax; I heard her voice. Saw her face. It cut through me like a blade. Torture, but it's all I have left. If I ever find her—no, when I find her—will she still be the same? Or will the woman I love be gone, replaced by a stranger?

Samuel moved ahead, his silhouette carving a path through the darkness that seemed ready to swallow us whole. He knew these trails like the back of his hand, and for now, I trusted him to lead us through. With the night came a coolness that eased the burn in my lungs, but every step left a trace I couldn't see, and every sound made my pulse jump. The faint rustle of grass, the shift of shadows—my mind twisted each one into something deadly lurking just beyond my sight. My heart pounded so hard I half-expected it to give me away to whatever might be out there, waiting. I turned to Samuel, breaking the thick silence that had settled between us.

"What about the wildlife here? I mean, there's just an endless parade of sharp-toothed creatures lurking about, right? Hyenas? Wolves? Snakes? Lions? I asked, trying to suppress the obvious edge in my voice but clearly failing. My eyes darted nervously around the shadows of the forest, scanning for any delightful little hint of danger just waiting to pounce. Samuel's deep chuckle sliced through the darkness like a knife, and the sound sent a delightful shiver down my spine. He stopped and leaned oh so casually against a tree, his voice dropping to a dramatic whisper."

""You see" he said, "it's not the hyenas or the snakes you should be afraid of It's the warehyenas—local legend you know just a twist on those oh-so-everyday werewolf myth" My heart picked up speed as I turned to face him, trying to read his expression in the dim light.

"Warehyenas? What the fuck are you talking about?" Zahra had mentioned these stories once, but I'd brushed them off, as just local legends. But now, out here in the dark, and with Mita telling me about the Bouda, a part of me wondered—what if there was some truth to it?

Samuel leaned in, his eyes practically glowing, a hint of something wild in them. "See, werewolves—they're still human underneath it all, right? At their core, there's still that human part. But warehyenas?" He shook his head, a grin tugging at his lips. "That's a whole different story. Some of them, yeah, they start off as human, and they get the power to shift into hyenas. But the others..." He paused, letting the words hang there, the grin widening. "They're hyenas first. Animals. And somehow, they figured out how to mimic our appearance to walk among us."

My mind spun with the thought, images flashing in my head that I didn't want to see. I tried to laugh it off, but it came out shaky. "You're messing with me, right?"

He didn't break eye contact, and for a moment, I couldn't tell if he was joking or dead serious. "They can mimic voices" he went on "calling your name in the dead of night trying to lure you into the darkness away from the safety of the others."

I forced a laugh, but a knot had already twisted in my stomach. Just last night, I could've sworn I heard voices calling my name—Zahra's voice, and others I couldn't quite place. I'd told myself it was just the wind, my mind playing tricks. Now, I wasn't so sure.

"Come on, man, don't tell me this now," I said, my voice a little too high, a little too raw.

Samuel gave me a sympathetic look, but there was seriousness in his eyes. "Next time you hear someone calling your name out here, make sure it's really them before you answer."

I rolled my eyes trying to mask the tremor in my hands "Oh that's just great Thanks for that real helpful" But underneath the sarcasm an unsettling chill crawled up my spine.

He let out a quiet laugh, shaking his head. "Tommy, you've been watching too many nature shows."

"I'm serious," I shot back, glancing around, feeling every rustle of the leaves like a threat.

Samuel's grin widened, but he kept his voice low, his Ethiopian accent giving his words a rhythm that made them sound even more like a warning. "Hyenas are scavengers, man. They'd rather eat what's already dead. They don't come after people unless they're desperate."

I frowned, not entirely convinced. "Okay, but what about the snakes?"

He gave a lazy shrug, barely glancing up. "Most of 'em won't bother you," he said. "But if you see one with a head like an arrow and a body thick as your leg…" He paused, his eyes locking onto mine, all humour gone. "Run."

I swallowed hard, glancing around the shadowed forest again. I wasn't sure if he was messing with me or giving me a genuine warning. But either way, I couldn't shake the unease that had settled deep in my bones.

CHAPTER 41

The moon cast a pale light as we trudged on, cutting through the darkness of the forest. The tension hung in the air like a storm waiting to break, but Samuel's easy humour provided some relief, lightening the weight of our anxiety. Still, as we moved deeper, a gnawing unease settled in my stomach. It felt like we were being watched, like a pair of unseen eyes tracked our every step. We'd only been walking for a few days, but it felt like weeks. My muscles screamed with every step, but I forced my face into something resembling calm. I didn't want to worry Mita or Solomon, even though it was obvious how uncomfortable I was. And then it hit me—pure, unfiltered panic, making my skin prickle. Almost at the same time, Mita's face shifted, her usual warmth replaced by sharp focus. Her eyes, once soft, were now hard as steel, and she raised a finger to her lips, signalling us to stay silent. Her movements were deliberate, her body tense as she led us forward, inch by careful inch, through the undergrowth. Watching her navigate the terrain, I realised just how much of a force she truly was—strong, calculating, capable. Every rustle of leaves, and every crack of a branch became a potential threat. Even Samuel had stopped making jokes. He might've laughed off my nerves before, but now the danger was real, and we all felt it. Mita's hand shot up, and we all froze. We dropped to the ground, disappearing into the tall grass, trying to make ourselves invisible. The moon peeked out from behind the clouds, casting its silvery light through the trees, painting the ground in strange, shifting patterns. I looked up at the stars, millions of them twinkling in the sky, and for a moment, everything felt dreamlike, like I was floating somewhere between reality and a nightmare. But the sound I heard next was all too real—my ears caught it first, the unmistakable, guttural chorus of laughter and growls. My eyes adjusted to the dark, and that's when I saw them.

Hyenas. A pack of them, tearing into a carcass in a small clearing. The moonlight glinted off their blood-stained fur as they feasted, the sickening sounds of flesh tearing and bones cracking filling the air. My stomach churned, fear clawing up my throat. They were wild, primal—nothing but raw muscle, sharp teeth, and an insatiable hunger. Despite my fear, I couldn't look away, horrified yet strangely fascinated by the brutality of it all. The hyenas moved with an eerie grace, their laughter echoing through the night. Mita's hand clamped onto my shoulder, her nails biting into my skin—a silent reminder to stay still, stay quiet. Her eyes caught mine, fierce and unblinking, and I knew she wouldn't let anything happen to us. My heart thundered in my chest, each beat reverberating through me, but I forced myself to breathe slowly, to stay calm. The night was unforgiving, the hyenas' cackling growing louder, and I could almost feel their gaze, hungry and calculating. We stayed low, hidden in the grass, watching the gruesome spectacle unfold. It felt like we were part of some twisted safari, too close to danger, without any of the safety. I watched as Samuel and Mita whispered to each other in Amharic, their voices too low for me to understand. Their faces were tense, their eyes darting between the pack and the path ahead, calculating our next move. I thought about telling them about my run-in with a hyena in Addis, but the words stayed stuck in my throat. Maybe another time.

Finally, after what felt like hours, Samuel gave a signal, and we began to move. We crawled slowly, inching away from the hyenas, the darkness around us thick and suffocating. I tried to keep my eyes on Mita's backpack, focusing on the path just ahead of me, each step a small victory. The ground beneath us was rough, uneven, and every step a potential misstep, but we moved carefully. Samuel led us with the confidence of someone who'd walked these paths for years. Before we changed direction, I couldn't help but glance back at the hyenas. They were still tearing at their meal, their muscular bodies shifting in the moonlight, their eyes reflecting something almost otherworldly. An unsettling thought crossed my mind—if there were creatures out there that were worse, more dangerous than these hyenas, what chance did we have? The memory of the creature in Addis flashed before my eyes, and I scanned the pack, but none of them matched the terrifying size of that beast. We kept moving, each step feeling like a gamble. Samuel's earlier warnings rang in my ears— rebels, predators, threats in every shadow. It felt like we were navigating a maze full of traps, one wrong turn away from disaster. But there was no other choice. We had to keep going. I found some comfort in Samuel's steady presence. There was a strength in the way he carried himself, something that said he wouldn't let anything happen to us. I'd learned a bit about his past—a soldier in the Ethiopian Guard, someone who'd once lived by the rules of war but had walked away, choosing a quieter life. But now, with his daughter in danger, he was back in the fight, and nothing—not men, not monsters—was going to stop him. I could see it in his eyes, the determination, the fire. He'd burn the world down to save her, and in this moment, that was exactly the kind of person we needed leading us.

CHAPTER 42

Haik's lights shimmered in the distance, just barely breaking through the thick tangle of vegetation. My breaths were short and sharp, each inhales matching the rhythm of my boots crunching softly over fallen leaves. I moved carefully, trying to avoid the brittle twigs that might betray our presence. Each step had to be deliberate—over branches, through thorny bushes, my ears straining for every rustle, every snap that might mean danger. The moon rose above the treetops, bathing everything in a silvery glow. Its cold light cast long shadows, stretching out over the forest floor, and I wondered if it knew my secret—if it could see that I was a man unravelling, coming apart at the seams. I closed my eyes for a moment, just long enough to hear her laughter again. Zahra's voice, echoed through the eucalyptus groves back in Addis, filling every corner of our small apartment. But now, that laughter was only a ghost, fading into the emptiness of the highlands. A sharp sound tore me out of my thoughts—a hoot, trilling through the darkness. An owl, maybe, calling out as if to remind me to stay alert. My training kicked in, and my eyes scanned the trees, and the undergrowth, searching for threats. It had been years since I wore the uniform, but the instincts were still there, buried just beneath the surface. I let out a quiet chuckle, more bitter than amused. I could still do this, even if my body protested with every step. My brothers-in-arms would've laughed, maybe called me crazy, but they'd understand. They always did. I rubbed my hands together, not for warmth but to keep my focus. The forest felt alive, shifting and breathing in the dark. The only light came from the slivers of the moon slipping through the canopy. The Ethiopian night wrapped around me, heavy and ancient, like it understood my sorrow better than I did. Maybe out here, in the quiet, I could find a way forward—a way to get Zahra back and to make those bastards pay for taking her from me. A bark echoed through the darkness, sharp and too close. I froze, my heart hammering as I turned to Samuel.

"What kind of dog is that?" I whispered.

Samuel's face tightened, his eyes scanning the shadows. "That's not a dog," he said. "It's a wolf. They sound like that when they're calling to each other."

I muttered a curse under my breath, dread settling deeper in my gut. Wolves. Just what we needed.

We pushed on, the smell of damp earth and rotting leaves filling my lungs. The uneven ground was treacherous—loose rocks, hidden edges that threatened to twist an ankle, to send me tumbling into the valleys below. Exhaustion crept in, making my steps clumsy, but I couldn't afford to slip. Not here, not now. We had to keep moving. The trees thinned, and suddenly we were out in the open, a wide plateau stretching before us, dotted with jagged peaks rising up to obscure the horizon. The wolf howled again, distant this time, and I let out a breath I didn't know I'd been holding. I pulled my clothes tighter against the chill, but it did little to keep the cold out. I knew threats were still out here, hidden in the dark. I took a cautious step, nodding to Samuel and Mita to stay vigilant. We were exposed now, moving through the moonlit openness, a small group of misfits who'd somehow become a family. We came to a stop, the skyline in the distance, illuminated by the faint glow of stars and moon. Mita stood beside me, her face half-lit, filled with awe.

"It's incredible," she said, her voice laced with something I couldn't quite place. "But it's heartbreaking too, isn't it?"

Samuel joined us, his lips curling into a forced smile. His eyes told a different story, one of pride mixed with pain. "This land has endured so much," he murmured. "Wars, famines, invaders... but it always rises again. Ethiopia is resilient."

Suddenly, I felt it—a presence lurking just beyond the edge of my vision. A voice, sharp and filled with malice, sliced through my thoughts like a knife.

'It's almost time... Do you feel it? The end is near," it hissed, the words slithering into my mind.

Panic froze me, my legs locked in place. I couldn't move, couldn't speak. It felt like I'd been swallowed by the darkness. Mita and Samuel turned to look at me, their brows furrowed in concern. My fists clenched, teeth grinding together until I tasted blood. I forced the words out, each one dripping with venom.

"Get out of my head," I spat, my voice low. The anger inside me was a seething mass, barely contained. Under my breath, I muttered, "You'll burn in hell," my voice trembling with rage.

The voice faded, but the sense of it lingered, like it was still there, waiting. Watching. It felt familiar, like it knew me better than I knew myself. Like it had always known how this story was going to end. And somewhere, deep down, I knew this wasn't over. They were here, waiting, whispering my name as if they already owned me. As if they were just waiting for me to break.

CHAPTER 43

We trekked deeper into the highlands, the landscape shifting around us into an endless stretch of ancient rock and sun-baked earth. The wind picked up suddenly, gusts strong enough to sting my eyes and kick up clouds of dust, making the air thick and hard to breathe. The silence was heavy, broken only by the occasional shriek of a bird of prey somewhere overhead. And I couldn't shake the feeling that something was watching us, hidden among the rocks and scrub, tracking every step we took. I was scared of what I'd find if I kept moving forward—but more scared of what it meant if I turned back. I took a step and heard a crunch. I froze, lifting up my foot. There, half buried in the dust was a flash of white. Bones. I knelt down, brushing the dirt away to reveal a pile—bleached, dried out, stripped clean. It was the ribcage of something big— maybe a cow, maybe a horse—sprawled out in the dirt like a shattered cage. The skull lay nearby, jaw opened in a silent, toothy grin. Whatever this was, it hadn't just died; it had been hunted, devoured, picked apart until nothing but the bones remained.

"We should keep moving," Mita said. Her voice was flat, serious, without a trace of humour. "Before we end up like that."

I stood and looked around, and that's when I noticed them—more bones scattered across the landscape, a trail of death that wound deeper into the wasteland. Some carcasses were in pieces, others intact but hollow, as if life itself had been drained from them. The faint scent of decay lingered in the air, even though most of the flesh was long gone, leaving only these stark, skeletal reminders behind. We kept moving, and eventually, the ground started to rise—a gentle slope that promised to lead us toward what they called the *Roof of Africa.*' The incline quickly steepened, turning into a brutal ascent. I looked up at the towering peak ahead, my heart pounding in my chest. I closed my eyes for a moment, took two deep breaths, and tried to steady myself. My legs ached with every step, my muscles screaming in protest, but I pushed on. The ground was treacherous—loose rocks, shifting dirt, everything conspiring to throw me off balance. But we kept going, driven by sheer determination. Samuel was ahead of us, moving like this was a casual stroll, his confidence maddening. Mita was right behind me, also unfazed by the rough terrain. It annoyed me, how easily they moved, how effortless they made it look. I used to be able to do this without a second thought. In a surge of frustration, I made a promise to myself to sneak some rocks into Samuel's backpack during our next break. Petty, I know—but the thought lifted my spirits.

My whole body was on fire, my limbs on the verge of collapse, but I couldn't stop. I thought of Zahra, her courage, her fire, and it kept me going, kept me from falling apart. My feet dragged, my eyes stung from the sweat, and still, I pushed forward. Mita and Samuel were there, their presence grounding me, their strength keeping me from giving in. We scrambled over rocks and navigated around sharp drop-offs. Every obstacle made us stronger; every challenge fuelled our determination. Sometimes I'd spot a mountain goat standing still, its eyes watching us, curious. This was their home, their sanctuary—a place to escape whatever hunted them below. Just as the moon dipped behind thick clouds, we found a spot to rest—a twisted old tree near the summit that offered some shelter from the wind. The night was eerily quiet, every rustle of the bushes, every whisper of wind seeming louder than it should. Goosebumps rose on my skin as I scanned the shadows. Sleep came slowly, as it always did. My limbs felt heavy, my eyelids drooping, and I let myself sink into the darkness, welcoming the escape. It was peaceful at first—a quiet, comforting emptiness. But then something shifted.

It started as a flicker, a sense that something was wrong, just on the edge of my awareness. The calm I'd been feeling vanished, replaced by something heavy and oppressive, like a fog pressing down on my chest. I tried to move, to shake myself awake, but it was like my body was locked in place, weighed down by something I couldn't see. The heaviness wasn't just holding me—it was trapping me. And I couldn't break free. Everything around me was sharp, vivid, and too real to be a dream. This was different—scary different. One moment, I was myself, and the next, it was like I'd woken up in someone else's body. Except it 'was' my body, just... wrong. I could feel my pulse behind my eyes, that familiar pounding that comes when fear sinks its teeth in, but this time there was something else. A hunger, raw and deep, gnawing at my insides. It almost swallowed me whole. The smell hit me—blood, flesh, dirt. A metallic tang filled my nose, thick and heavy. My jaw was moving, and suddenly I realised I was biting into something. Soft, warm, and wet. Blood filled my mouth, and instead of gagging, I wanted more. My teeth ground down on bone, ripping through muscle, and each bite sent a shiver through my body, something deep and primal vibrating in my spine. But underneath the hunger, there was fear—my fear. I was still in here, still me, but I had no control. I tried to pull back, to stop, to close my eyes, but I couldn't. My muscles weren't mine anymore. They belonged to something else, something feral and unyielding. The sounds around me were distorted crunching, tearing, and heavy breathing. I could feel them, the others. Bodies pressed against mine, their fur brushing my skin. They were like me, driven by the same hunger, jostling and shoving for a piece of the kill. It was chaos—pure, primal frenzy— and I was right in the middle of it. I tried to scream, but what came out was a low, guttural growl, vibrating through my throat, thick with power. It should've disgusted me. The scent of fear, of blood—it should've turned my stomach. But it didn't. It was all part of it, part of this twisted feast. My own thoughts felt small, human, intruding on the animal instinct that was drowning me out. And then it hit me again—the taste of marrow on my tongue, the scrape of bone against my teeth, the muscles in my jaw working as I tore into the kill. Every nerve in my body lit up, some twisted pleasure thrumming through me, but I wanted out. The terror was still there, but it was buried under the hunger, suffocating under it. I felt myself slipping away, piece by piece, losing the parts that made me 'me'. My thoughts were fading, replaced by the rhythm of feeding, the raw satisfaction of staying alive. I was drowning, gasping for air that wasn't there, and I was powerless to do anything but keep going.

Time twists and warps around me, like I'm caught in the claws of my nightmare. Then, without warning, it snaps, and I'm thrown back into the real world. Panic floods my senses, lighting up every nerve. I scramble backwards, my hands and feet slipping on the damp earth. There's a bitter, metallic taste in my mouth, like something foul had died there, and my entire body is soaked in cold sweat. My breath comes in ragged, shallow gasps as I try to remember where I am. It's like I can't find my way back to reality—everything is blurry, spinning. My chest feels tight, each breath harder than the last, but I force myself to suck in air, to quiet the screaming in my head. I wipe the sweat from my face with a shaky hand, trying to pull myself together. But it's still there—that sound, the growling, and echoing somewhere deep inside me. And I know the truth, even if I don't want to admit it. Some nightmares don't vanish when you wake up. They follow you, lingering, like the dampness clinging to my skin. I shake my head, trying to clear it, but it won't leave. My hands won't stop trembling. *'It's not real. It's not real.'* But why does it still *feel* real? I rub my eyes, trying to ground myself, and when I look up, I see a flash of white—a smile. Samuel, with his impossibly straight, white teeth. His smile makes something in me loosen, and I let out a long breath I didn't even realise I was holding.

"Rise and shine, sleeping beauty," he says, his voice playful, like he's talking to a kid.

"What the hell?" I groan, still feeling the edges of the nightmare clinging to me. "It's only been five minutes, man!"

He keeps smiling, amused at my irritation. "Actually, it's been almost two hours," he says, raising an eyebrow. "You weren't exactly having a peaceful nap, Tommy. Thought it was time to bring you back."

"Yeah?" I ask, still trying to fully wake up.

"Yeah," he nods. "You were muttering, even growling a bit. Whatever you were dreaming about, it didn't look like a good time. Figured I'd do you a favour."

"Thanks for that," I mutter, rubbing the back of my neck. "It wasn't... nice."

I look over to Mita. She just gives me a gentle smile, already reaching into her backpack, her eyes soft, like she's trying to say *'It's okay.'*

We move on in silence after that, each step careful, one foot in front of the other. I hear my mom's voice in my head, her words from when my dad died— *One step at a time, Tommy.*' I whisper it to myself now, just loud enough for me to hear, and I find a little comfort there. We push on, just silhouettes against the dark, the night swallowing us whole. The foliage crunches beneath our feet, and there's this heavy feeling in my bones—like a warning, primal and impossible to ignore. We're not alone. The air is thick with it, the feeling that something is out there. Suddenly, there's a rustling to my left, and I freeze, every muscle tensed, ready. Probably just some animal, a predator prowling through the undergrowth. But then, more sounds follow—low, unsettling, like whispers in the dark, and a shiver runs down my spine. The peace of the night is gone, replaced by something far more dangerous, something that feels like it's watching us. I can't shake the feeling that the night itself is playing with us, that Mother Nature has chosen this moment to test us, to make our fears real, to drag them out into the open. And as we move forward, all I can think is that this darkness, this fear—it's all too real.

CHAPTER 44

At this altitude, the air is cooler than when we set out—much cooler. I can feel it with every breath, the thinness of it making my chest work harder, and it only adds to the growing list of things I want to complain about. But I keep my mouth shut. There's no point. Up here, we're completely exposed—no trees, no buildings, nothing to give us even a hint of cover. Just the open expanse, stretching endlessly in every direction. Every step sends a new protest through my body. My shins are on fire, my feet ache from hours of trudging across uneven ground, and a sharp pain has settled in my right hip, reminding me I'm not as young as I used to be. I try to focus on my breathing, each inhale a reminder that I need to stay sharp. Out here, caution is our best weapon. With no cover, we're sitting ducks if anyone's watching. Every rustle of grass, every shift in the wind feels like a signal, a warning. But it's the silence that gets under my skin—the heavy, expectant quiet, like we're holding our breath, waiting for something to go wrong. The moon slips out from behind a cloud, casting everything in a pale, almost eerie light. And that's when I see it—the rift ahead, dark and jagged, cutting across the landscape. I stumble for a second, my foot catching on a loose rock, but Mita's hand is there, steadying me before I fall. She gives me a quick nod, and I force myself to keep going. Samuel moves ahead of us, surefooted, leading the way with the kind of confidence that only comes from knowing the land like it's a part of you. Watching them, I realised something I hadn't fully understood before. Mita, Samuel—they aren't just guides or strangers I've met along the way. They're the lifeblood of this place, part of what keeps Ethiopia alive and keeps it moving forward. And they're not alone. There are so many others like them—ordinary people doing extraordinary things, each playing a part in the country's survival and recovery. It's humbling, in a way that makes the complaints I've been holding onto feel small and pointless. They're carrying something much heavier, and they're doing it with a strength I can only admire. As the night surrenders to dawn, the first light stretches our shadows long and lean across the rugged terrain. My legs ache, my back screams for rest, and I can feel every one of my years weighing me down. But there's something else too—something deeper, a resilience that keeps me moving. I fix my eyes on the horizon, where the sky meets the earth, and force myself onward, one step at a time. The sun slowly rises behind us, casting a warm glow over the landscape, and the cool air fills my lungs, pushing back the exhaustion, even if just for a moment. We crest another ridge, and for a brief second, I pause to catch my breath. The sweat rolls down my forehead, dripping into my eyes, and I wipe it away, tasting salt on my lips. I glance at Mita, and despite everything, I can't help but feel a flicker of hope. The first light of dawn paints the world in a glow that almost makes it beautiful, despite the hardship, despite the pain. Every inch we've covered has been hard-earned, every ridge crossed a battle of sweat and willpower, but we keep moving. The reward that awaits us is worth it—we believe that we have to. I shut my eyes for an instant, letting everything fade, just feeling the stillness that lives inside me. When I open them again, there it is— Haik. Like a mirage on the horizon, the town appears, the very place we've fought to get to, and my heart clenches in my chest. The lights had guided us through the dark last night, leading us to this point. I turn to Mita, wanting to ask if we're really going to make it, but my voice catches, too tight in my throat to escape. I swallow the words and focus on the view—Haik, the town I know and love. Seeing it fuels me and drives me to keep going. We pick up the pace, and I can't shake this feeling—like we're heading towards something that's bigger than us, beyond our understanding. Why does the air feel heavy, like we're wading through a world thick with something unspeakable? Every now and then, I glance over my shoulder, half-expecting a shadow to rise behind us, something monstrous. There are days when my head just doesn't work, when focusing is like trying to swim upstream, and everything gets lost in the fog. Maybe it's some kind of self-defence, my mind's way of numbing the pain, dulling the trauma. But then there are moments of sharp clarity— moments where every detail cuts through, every feeling comes rushing back, and I see it all. This is one of those moments. There will be a future. I have to believe that. It's what keeps me going. Every step I take now is not just for me but for Zahra, for everyone who's been hurt, everyone who's been wronged. Each step is one closer to a future where maybe, just maybe, we can find peace. I have to believe that. I have to. A sudden, distant gunshot snaps me out of my thoughts. The sound is faint but sharp, echoing across the mountains like a crack of thunder. At first, it's just dull pops in the distance, barely noticeable against the wind whistling through the rocky valleys. But then it becomes clearer—the rhythm of shots, rapid bursts broken by long pauses, the tension of the air thickening with each round. The echoes bounce off the mountains, twisting, making it impossible to tell where they're coming from or how close they are. The silence between the shots grows heavier, and oppressive, like the mountains themselves are holding their breath. I strain to listen—the sharp crack of a rifle, the faint shouts carried by the wind, though the words are lost to me. My chest tightens, and I exchange a glance with Mita. We're getting close now. Too close. This just got real.

I stand there for a second, feeling the tension hanging in the air, wondering what waits for us beyond the mountains. The gunfire will fade soon, swallowed by the silence of the highlands. But right now, it's real, and we're heading straight for it. No turning back.

Chapter 45

"Where there is no shame, there cannot be any honour."

Ethiopian proverb

The winding path led us back down into the valley, and I let out a long breath of relief as the forest welcomed us once again. The crowded trees offered their cool shade, their leaves whispering softly overhead. Finally, we had cover—shielded from the glaring sun and from anyone who might be watching. The earth felt soft underfoot, muffling our steps as we moved deeper into the woods, and I tried to focus on that small comfort, one step at a time. We reached the edge of a village, pausing to scan the area for any signs of danger before pressing on. Something felt off, though—an itch along the back of my neck, a feeling that we weren't alone. I kept my eyes on the ground, the dust swirling around my ankles, coating my skin. The air was stifling, every breath thick with dust and tension. Mita moved silently beside me, her eyes darting from tree to tree, alert to every movement. The only sounds were the rustle of leaves underfoot, but even that seemed too loud in the stillness. Then, the sharp, acrid smell of gunpowder hit, cutting through the air, and everything seemed to happen at once. Gunfire erupted, shattering the quiet. I sucked in a breath, and it felt like my chest was being torn apart. I looked at Samuel, and the terror in his eyes matched my own. We both knew this was just the beginning, that there was no coming back from this. I glance over at Mita, my heart pounding. Just a few feet away, she had taken cover in a shallow trench, pressing herself against a tree. Her eyes were wide, fear written all over her face as she peeked out, assessing the chaos around us. The sounds were deafening—rifle fire, the heavy thud of grenades, screams cutting through the noise. My heart hammered as I crawled through the dirt, bullets slicing through the air like angry wasps. I finally reached Mita, pressing my back against the tree beside her, the bark rough against my skin. The smell of smoke and gunpowder was overwhelming, filling my lungs, and choking me.

"We have to move," I hissed, barely louder than a whisper. "We can't stay here."

I caught sight of Samuel and gestured for him to come over. He moved cautiously through the chaos, stepping over branches, and ducking beneath debris. But then I saw it—movement behind him, a dark figure closing in, and Samuel didn't see it. My heart lurched, and without thinking, I turned to Mita.

"Stay low. Don't move," I said, and then I was up, rushing toward Samuel.

My legs burned as I ran, my eyes locked on the lone baobab tree ahead. I reached Samuel, grabbing his arm and yanking him down beside me, trying to hide us behind the twisted trunk. We crouched, pressed together, and that's when I noticed it—an old handgun in his hand, gripped tightly. I hadn't seen it before, and it startled me. It looked worn, and unreliable, but I squeezed his arm, trying to keep him still. His wide eyes met mine, and he nodded, fear clear on his face. Before I could say anything, I heard them—footsteps, figures emerging from the shadows. There was no way out, no way to run. They came at us, knives glinting, guns raised, faces twisted with cruel intent. We had no choice but to fight.

Chaos erupted. A gunshot split the air, followed by a scream that made my blood run cold. I turned just in time to see Samuel fall, his hand still clutching the gun as he crumpled to the ground. My heart twisted, my mind struggling to catch up, to understand. One moment he was there, alive, and then he was down. I dropped to my knees beside him, cradling his head, my hands covered in his blood. His chest was still, his eyes half-open but also half-empty, and all I could think was how just moments ago we were laughing, we were planning, we were alive. Now, this. I dropped to my knees beside Samuel, pulling him into my arms, and holding him close as if I could bring him back. Everything else seemed to fade away, the world shrinking to just the two of us.

"Come on, Samuel," I whispered, my voice cracking. "Please, just open your eyes. Just… make this right." My fingers brushed against his face, and I waited—waited for him to move, to blink, to give me something.

But he stayed still, and the silence was unbearable. A faint gurgle escaped his lips, blood bubbling from his mouth, and I knew he was going, really going. I held him tighter, my vision blurring with tears, and everything else around me started to fade away. The gunfire, the chaos, the screams—all of it dulled into a distant roar. All that mattered now was Samuel. My friend. The one I had lost in an instant. It was like the world had slowed to a crawl, the weight of it pressing on my chest until I could hardly breathe. My fingers trembled as I gripped his shirt, tearing it with a frantic desperation. The fabric ripped easily, exposing the wound beneath—a horrible, gaping tear, dark blood spilling out, soaking into the dry earth beneath him. The smell of copper hit my nostrils, sharp and suffocating. I searched wildly for anything, anything to stop the bleeding. I pressed my hands against the wound, feeling his heartbeat flutter beneath my palms, erratic, weak. But the blood kept coming, slipping through my fingers, pooling on the parched ground.

"Stay with me!" I begged, my voice breaking as I pressed my hands harder against the wound. Blood seeped through my fingers, warm and unrelenting, slipping away from me like water. Samuel's face had gone pale, the colour draining from his skin, and the light in his eyes was fading fast. He was trying to speak, his jaw clenched in pain, his breath coming in short, strained gasps.

"Leave," he mouthed, no sound behind it, just the shape of the word. His eyes, filled with fear but also something else—determination—locked on mine. He was trying to protect me, even now, even like this. He struggled, his fingers trembling as he reached out and grabbed my arm, his skin cold. "Please," he whispered, barely audible. "Find my daughter."

I swallowed, a lump tightening in my throat. My heart twisted painfully in my chest, and I wanted to tell him something—anything—that would make it better, that would make it hurt less. But no words came. I could only hold his hand, feeling him slip away. His eyes lost focus, drifting past me, staring at something far away. Samuel—my friend, my brother—was leaving, and there wasn't a damn thing I could do about it. I thought about his daughter, about the life she'd have to live without him now, and it shattered something inside of me. I squeezed his hand, even as it grew cold, hoping it would somehow be enough to keep him here. But it wasn't. He was gone. The stench of death filled the air, smoke from the gunfire still hanging thick around us. Samuel's face, twisted in pain moments before, now seemed almost peaceful, like he'd accepted whatever was next. But there was no peace for me. I still had to find her. I had to find Mita. Panic clawed at my insides, driving me to my feet. I scanned the chaos around me—the faces blurring together, none of them familiar. The burning buildings, the screams—it all melted away. I had to find her. I had to keep my promise. Suddenly, hands grabbed me, rough and unforgiving, yanking me backwards. I spun, trying to fight them off, but there were too many. Laughter echoed around me, mocking, as they dragged me down. I kicked, and twisted, but they kept coming, their faces hidden in the shadows, eyes glinting. The first punch landed square on my jaw, and pain exploded through my head. I tasted blood, warm and metallic, but I pushed myself up. They weren't done. Another blow, harder this time, sent me sprawling. I felt their kicks, one after another, each one knocking the breath out of me. My ribs screamed in pain, but I refused to stay down. Why wouldn't they just kill me? Why were they toying with me like this? I forced myself up again, my breaths coming in ragged, my vision swimming. I could hear their taunts, their laughter. They were waiting for me to break. But I couldn't. I remembered what Samuel had asked me. I remembered Mita. I had to keep fighting, I had to survive. Another blow—this one to the back of my head—sent me crashing to the ground. For a second, I almost let go, almost let the darkness swallow me. Then I saw Samuel, lying just a few feet away, his empty eyes staring at me. Even in death, it was like he was urging me on. Telling me not to give up. Somewhere in the chaos, I heard Zahra's voice. *Fight!* It cut through everything, like a war cry. My body moved before my mind caught up, adrenaline flooding my veins. I rolled away from the next strike, pushing through the pain, using it to fuel me. I staggered to my feet, my muscles screaming, my vision blurring. But I was standing. *Fight back! Live! Please, live!* Zahra's voice echoed in my head, her love wrapping around me, holding me up. I threw myself at them, fists swinging, not caring if I got hurt. I just needed to hurt them back. The first one hesitated, surprised. They hadn't expected this. I could feel my blows landing, and hear the crunch of bone under my fists. *'Tommy! Fight!'* Zahra's voice roared through me, and I let out a cry, swinging harder, my fists connecting with flesh. Blood splattered, the metallic tang mixing with sweat on my tongue. I fought like I was fighting for everything—every life lost, every moment taken. I fought for Zahra, for Samuel, for Mita. But eventually, the adrenaline started to fade. My body felt heavy, each movement slower than the last. Rough hands grabbed me, and I was yanked off my feet, and thrown into the back of a car. My wrists were bound, the rope cutting into my skin. I winced, the sharp pain shooting up my arms. The engine roared to life, drowning out everything else. I caught the cold, dead-eyed stare of one of my captors as they turned away, focusing on the road. Every bump in the road sent pain jolting through me, the ropes digging deeper into my wrists. I tried to brace myself, but I was too tired, too hurt. Fear settled in my chest, gnawing at me—not just fear for my life, but fear that I'd never find Zahra. That I'd failed her, failed Samuel, failed Mita.

The car came to a sudden stop, the door swung open, and I was yanked out into the chaos. The night was alive with gunshots, screams, and the flicker of firelight. My feet stumbled over debris, broken glass crunching beneath me as they dragged me forward. My captors' grip was tight, as if they expected me to run. My head swam, memories flooding back—wars fought, lives lost. Faces flashed before me—women, children, their terrified screams echoing in my ears. Rage burned in my chest, grief tightening like a vice around my heart. The weight of everything was crushing, but I couldn't let it break me. Not now. Not when I still had something left to fight for. Every step was a reminder: I was still alive. I was still breathing. And as long as I was, I wasn't giving up.

CHAPTER 46

In an instant, I'm thrown into the cell, my body hitting the cold, hard ground with a force that knocks the breath out of me. The impact rattles my bones, and I let out a guttural cry, my voice lost in the stale, suffocating air. I try to inhale, but each breath is a struggle, scraping against my raw throat. Pain radiates through me, a searing wave that makes every movement agony. I squint, forcing my eyes to adjust to the dim light that filters through a small, dirty window high up on the wall. The walls around me are rough, covered in strange, scratched symbols, each marking a story of desperation or madness. The symbols seem to twist and writhe in the dimness, and it makes my skin crawl. The weak light casts shadows that flicker and stretch across the stone, creating an eerie, shifting landscape that leaves me feeling even more trapped. I am alone here, alone in a nightmare I can't escape. I try to breathe, my chest aching with every attempt. Each breath feels like a knife, sharp and unforgiving. The room is dark, except for a single flickering bulb that casts a weak, unreliable glow. Shadows dance on the walls, almost like something alive is moving around me, something unseen. I hear water dripping from somewhere above, each drop echoing through the cell. It's freezing, the cold seeping into my bones, draining what little strength I have left. Then they come. A fist slams into my face, and my head snaps back, my vision blurring from the impact. I can taste blood, metallic and thick, pooling in my mouth. Through the haze, I see them—a group of men, big, sneering, their eyes gleaming with cruel delight. They shout at me in a language I don't understand, but their intentions are clear enough. They're enjoying this. They want me to hurt.

One of them steps forward, grabs me by the collar, and hauls me up, his face inches from mine. "Why... you... here?" he spits in broken English, his breath hot and sour. I try to answer, but my lips are swollen, my jaw aching. The words come out garbled, barely a whisper.

"I know nothing. I only want my family!" The ringing in my head and the sensation of warm blood trickling from my ear drown out my stuttering, fear-stricken plea.

"Liar!" one of them hisses before his boot slams into my ribs, knocking the air out of me. I crumple, curling in on myself, my body a knot of pain. The blows keep coming, fists, boots, whatever they can hit me with. "Why are you here?" they shout again, over and over, louder each time, each word punctuated by another blow. My body spasms from the pain, my mind reeling, but I have nothing to give them. I don't know what they want. I don't know why I'm here.

Their laughter echoes in the small, dark space, a sound full of sick joy. One of them leans over me, his face twisted in a cruel smile. He shoves a grimy gas can in my face, the stench of gasoline hitting me hard.

"Drink," he growls, his eyes locking onto mine. There's no hesitation in his voice, no mercy. Just one order. Drink. I can barely think. My lips part, and I taste the bitter, burning liquid. There's no time to resist, no space to defy them. There's just submission. Just the overwhelming taste of gasoline, and the cold fear that this might be the end. Many hands grabbed me from behind, yanking me back, and forcing my jaw open. The sharp edge of a metal canister pressed against my lips, the gasoline spilling in before I could even struggle. I gasped, choking as the burning liquid poured down my throat, setting fire to my insides. The taste was unbearable—bitter, oily, like poison—and I could feel tears streaming down my cheeks. My stomach twisted, convulsing, trying to expel the vile stuff, but the hands held me steady. I gagged and coughed, bile rising, and I couldn't hold it back. I vomited, the gasoline mixing with the acid, splattering onto the cold floor. The stench filled my nose, thick and acrid, making my head swim. Through the haze of tears and burning pain, I managed to croak out a question.

"What... what is this?" I gasped, my voice barely coming out.

"Gasoline," one of them said, his lips curling into a sneer. His buddies laughed, sharp and cruel, their cackling echoing off the walls.

I lay there, trembling, my cheek pressed against the cold concrete. The world spun around me, the edges of everything blurring. Their voices faded in and out, muffled and distant, a chaotic drone that made no sense. I blinked, trying to focus, but my vision wouldn't clear. My head throbbed, each pulse sending a fresh wave of nausea through me. I saw one of them step forward, a shadow in the chaos, a rifle clenched tightly in his hands. He moved closer, the shape of the gun coming into focus, I barely had time to flinch before he swung it down. The butt of the rifle slammed into my head, and pain exploded—white-hot, blinding. The world crumbled into darkness, the sounds of their laughter swallowed by the void, until all that was left was silence, an endless, empty whirring in the back of my mind.

My eyes snap open, but there's nothing—just darkness. I'm floating, weightless, like I'm suspended in the middle of a void. I can't see a thing, no shadows, no shapes. Just black. I blink, then blink again, instinct kicking in to make sense of the nothingness. But it's like my eyes aren't working, or maybe they just don't want to. I keep blinking, willing myself to see something, anything. Suddenly, it reminds me of that trip to the old mine in Wales, the pitch-black tunnel where I couldn't see my hand right in front of my face. I remember the way the darkness seemed to swallow everything, how I strained to find even a flicker of light. That's how it feels now—just me and the dark, pushing at the edges, waiting for some break, some clue that I'm not alone in here. And then, slowly, it happens. The darkness cracks, and a blinding light floods in, so bright it hurts. I stumble forward, squinting as I try to shield my eyes. My hand comes up automatically, blocking out the glare, and I blink against the sudden explosion of brightness. The ground is beneath me again, solid, and I realise I've stumbled out of whatever dark pit I was in. I'm standing in an open field, and the sun is blazing overhead, too strong, making everything else fade. I feel disoriented, caught between relief and confusion, trying to shake off the darkness still clinging to my mind. As my vision cleared, I found myself standing in the middle of a vibrant green meadow. I looked down, surprised to see my body was intact—no cuts, no bruises, nothing to hint at whatever had happened before I woke up here. It was like I'd just been dropped into another world. To my left, a cluster of palm trees swayed gently, their leaves rustling in the breeze, while on my right stretched a sprawling garden, bursting with colour. Flowers of every shade and shape were in full bloom, petals shimmering under the sun. At the entrance to the garden, two large lion statues stood, their stone faces carved in a permanent snarl. It almost felt like they were watching me, those cold eyes tracking my every move. The sound of water pulled my gaze forward, and I saw a fountain at the garden's centre, sending streams high into the air. The water sparkled, catching the light in just the right way to create a rainbow, a dazzling arc that almost seemed too perfect. The scene was beautiful, surreal even—But there was a strange stillness to it all, like I wasn't supposed to be here, like I was an intruder in a place meant to be left untouched. Beyond all of this, a sandy beach sloped down towards the crystal-clear waters of the ocean. Gentle waves lapped against the shore, and I could feel the warmth of the sun on my skin as well as hear the distant cry of seagulls. It felt surreal, like a scene from a fantasy, but there was a disturbing sensation aching inside of me. Many years of watching movies have taught me that places like this often contain hidden dangers. My gut told me that I would not survive this place. A female appears on the shoreline, running toward me, her shouts carried on the wind. Shouts that I can barely make out. As she gets closer, their words become clear 'Run! Wake up! You have to get out of here—now!' There's panic in her voice, and I know that voice too well. It's Zahra Fear grips me, freezing me in place. I want to run to her, but my legs feel like they're made of lead. I can't move, can't even turn away. Tears burn down my cheeks, and I can feel the grief tearing me apart, but I can't find my voice to call out to her. My screams stay trapped inside my head. No one hears me. No one is coming. I glance back over my shoulder, and that's when I see it—the darkness creeping closer, a shadowy mist rolling across the sand, swallowing everything in its path. It's like a living void, thick and suffocating. And then I hear it, a voice buried in the darkness, barely more than a breath. It's not Zahra this time, but it's saying the same thing she is. 'Wake up.' The words scrape against my mind, pushing me toward a truth I don't want to face. I turn back to see Zahra, but she's gone, vanishing into thin air. The peaceful garden is transforming into a nightmare, and the lion statues have come alive and are walking away. The fountain runs red with dark blood, drenching the dying flowers and suffocating any remaining beauty. The oppressive blackness envelops me—a dense fog that overwhelms every thought and sensation. And now the scream to wake up is all I can hear. It s not Zahra this time, but it s saying the same thing she is. 'Wake up.'

CHAPTER 47

"Tommy, wake up." Mita's voice cut through my foggy mind, sharp and urgent, dragging me back from whatever darkness had a hold on me.

My eyes snapped open, and I realised she was shaking me, her grip tight. My heart hammered against my ribs, and I felt cold sweat mingling with dried blood on my skin. My breath came out in jagged gasps, each one struggling to fill my lungs. For a moment, I couldn't make sense of anything—the world around me twisted, like I'd dragged pieces of the nightmare into reality. I was sprawled on a cold concrete floor, my back aching against the hard surface. Somewhere in the distance, water dripped in a rhythmic pattern, echoing off the walls. As I forced myself to sit up, pain shot through every inch of my body, but I didn't have time to dwell on it. Mita's silhouette loomed above me, her finger pressed to her lips. Her eyes flashed a warning. I managed a nod, still fighting the disorientation, but adrenaline quickly sharpened my senses. I knew we had to move, and fast. The air reeked of gasoline, burning the back of my throat. Beneath it, I caught the sour tang of sweat and fear, mingling into a stench that clung to everything. We couldn't afford to stay here another second. Ignoring the fire in my muscles, I pushed myself to my feet and followed Mita as she navigated the maze-like corridors. Each step sent a jolt of pain through me, but I bit down hard and forced myself onward. We had to keep going. Mita moved like a shadow, slipping through the darkness with practised caution, as if each step could set off a trap. We managed to stay out of sight, our footsteps drowned out by the distant clatter of voices and heavy boots. The air was thick with tension, but we pressed on, skirting around corners and ducking behind rusted pipes whenever we heard someone coming. Finally, Mita paused in front of a narrow door hidden in the wall. She glanced back at me, then quickly worked the lock. The door swung open, and a rush of cold, fresh air hit me like a wave. Relief flooded through me.

I stepped out into the night, the darkness closing around us like a protective cloak. The cool air felt like a blessing on my face, washing away the stale, suffocating atmosphere of the place we'd just escaped. We moved quickly, slipping through the underbrush, the leaves whispering under our feet. We kept low, careful to avoid snapping branches that might give us away. Behind us, shouts echoed off the concrete walls, getting fainter with every step. My breath steadied, and my body fell into a rhythm, moving with Mita like we'd practised this a hundred times. And then, after what felt like an eternity, we broke through into an open clearing. Moonlight spilled over us, painting the scene in pale silver. I sucked in a deep breath, the crisp air filling my lungs, and looked back at the shadowy building behind us. For the first time in days, maybe weeks, I felt a small, defiant smile tug at my lips. We'd done it. We'd slipped through their grasp, at least for now. But we couldn't stop. We moved on, winding through paths hidden by overgrown trees and thorny bushes. The air was thick with the earthy smell of decay, leaves rotting underfoot. The forest felt like it was holding its breath, as if it, too, was waiting for whatever came next. Eventually, we reached a small hut, nearly swallowed by the overgrowth. Its paint had long since peeled away, leaving behind a patchwork of greys where bright colours once had been. We pushed our way through a tangled mess of vines until we reached the door. The place was a ruin, but it was shelter. It was hidden. Inside, nature had reclaimed everything. Vines crawled through cracks in the stone walls, and moss crept over the floor, softening the edges of what had once been someone's home. But for all its decay, the place had a strange sense of calm, like time had forgotten it here. I leaned against a wall, catching my breath, letting the cool, damp air fill my lungs.

Outside, the river murmured on, indifferent to everything we'd just been through. Its steady flow felt like the only constant in a world turned upside down, a reminder that no matter what we do, no matter what mess we make, the world keeps spinning. For now, it was just me and Mita, hidden away in this crumbling hut, a fragile sanctuary in the middle of chaos. The place was falling apart, but it was something—a place to catch our breath. A reminder that nature has always been here, and it would outlast us all. The door hung half-open, letting in a sliver of moonlight and the soft rustling of leaves outside. The air inside was thick with neglect—musty and damp—but it also smelled of the earth, like it had soaked up every storm that ever touched it. The undergrowth outside acted like a natural shield, keeping us out of sight, safe from whoever might be out there looking. I sat in the corner, listening to the scurrying of unseen creatures, holding my breath as we heard distant footsteps, and people searching. Mita stood near the door, the moonlight catching the dust swirling around her, her face half in shadow. Exhaustion eventually pulled me down, and I found myself lying beside her on the cold ground, my body aching, and bruised from the last few days. I took a deep breath, and suddenly, I was back in my childhood—those nights camping with Dad in the Scottish mountains. The cold creeping in through our sleeping bags, the rain pattering on the tent, never dampening our spirits. Wet earth, pine needles, distant thunder echoing through the glens. Those trips taught me how to stay strong, and how to embrace whatever nature threw my way. My eyes grew heavier, and I let myself drift, Zahra's face rising up behind my closed eyelids. Her deep brown eyes, always full of emotions never spoke out loud—sorrow, hope, a hint of defiance. My heart twisted at the thought of her, our time together replaying like an old film reel as I slipped into sleep. But it didn't last long. Something stirred me awake. I could hear Mita's breathing, slow and even beside me, and for a moment, it was enough. She'd saved me—more times than I could count by now. She was my safety net, the only stable thing I had left. A part of me craved for the comforts of home, but they felt so far away, like another lifetime. For now, Mita's steady breathing was enough to anchor me, the rhythm lulling me back towards sleep. Just before I slipped under, one last thought broke through—Samuel. The promise I'd made him, to find his daughter. He'd died looking for her, and now that promise rested with me. It was the last thing I thought of before sleep finally claimed me—whatever it took, I was going to see it through.

CHAPTER 48

The pale pinks and oranges of sunrise lit up the horizon, a new day breaking through the darkness, dragging with it all the harsh realities I couldn't escape. Samuel was dead, Zahra was missing, and my body felt like it had been through a meat grinder. But I was still here, somehow. Still breathing. Gritting my teeth, I pushed myself up off the ground, forcing myself to ignore the pain. I'd made promises, ones I couldn't afford to break. If I let myself think about what might happen—No. I can't go, there. I won't. Mita stirred beside me, her arm brushing mine as she woke. Her eyes landed on my face, and the sleepiness vanished, replaced by shock. Her hand reached out, tracing one of the deeper cuts on my cheek with a gentle touch that made me wince.

"Tommy..." she whispered; voice thick with worry. "What did they do to you?"

I turned away, unable to meet her eyes. The pity there was too much—too sharp, too real. A reminder of everything I'd failed at. I'd let Zahra down. I'd let Samuel die. What kind of man was I if I couldn't protect the people I loved? I shook my head, trying to push away the memories of last night, the way Samuel's screams still echoed in my mind, the feeling of his blood slick on my hands.

"We need to keep moving," I said, my voice rough. Every part of me ached, but I welcomed it. Pain was better than thinking, better than feeling the hollow ache where Zahra should be.

Mita grabbed my arm, forcing me to face her. "You're in a bad way," she said, not letting go. "Let me take a look."

I bit back a protest as she started tending to my wounds, using the few supplies we had left. Her hands were quick but gentle, and I thought of Zahra—how she always seemed to know when I was hurting, how she could soothe the worst of it with just a look. She's out there somewhere. I can feel it. And I'll find her. I have to. Mita finished, and we gathered up the few things we had. Each second felt like a lifetime, each delay another moment Zahra remained in the hands of those monsters. We couldn't afford to wait. We had to keep going.

"If something happens to me..." I started, but Mita cut me off with a fierce shake of her head.

"We're in this together," she asserted, refusing to entertain any of my thoughts.

I wanted to believe her, but I knew we had more challenges ahead. Yet seeing the certainty in Mita's eyes gave me hope. I nodded silently acknowledging that we were in this together, and we set off again into the wilderness. The landscape opened up in front of us, the tall juniper trees casting shadows that stretched like fingers across the ground. I always looked forward to reaching these clusters of trees, and the way their branches filtered the sunlight and cooled the air. The damp scent of earth and pine surrounded us, birds flitting through the canopy, flashes of yellow and turquoise against the green. Mita's voice broke through the quiet.

"Listen. It's like the forest has its own language." She glanced over at me, her expression softer. "Draw strength from it, Tommy. We'll find her."

I nodded, focusing on the path ahead. The Ethiopian Highlands rose in the distance, a patchwork of rust and green. Mita pointed towards the horizon, where the jagged peaks of the Simien Mountains cut into the sky.

"Those are the Simien Mountains," she said. Her voice carried a mix of awe and determination. "We'll be there soon."

The terrain was rough—steep cliffs and deep valleys that made every step a struggle. But the sight was breathtaking, a reminder of why I'd fallen in love with this place.

"We'll rest soon," I offered, hoping it might bring her a little comfort.

We finally found shelter beneath a group of trees, sinking to the ground and leaning back against their rough trunks. The shade was a relief, cool against my battered skin. Mita's eyes fluttered shut, exhaustion taking over, and I watched her for a moment. Dirt smudged her face, and sweat streaked her hair, but she was still beautiful, and fierce. I felt a responsibility to keep her safe, the same way I felt about Zahra.

"We'll take turns keeping watch," I murmured.

Mita cracked an eye open and managed a tired smile. "Always the soldier," she said softly, and there was no judgment in her voice, just understanding.

I managed a weak smile in return. But my eyes kept drifting back to the landscape around us—the rocky ridges and the cliffs that made me feel small. Mita's steady breathing beside me was the only thing keeping me anchored as I scanned the valley below. For a while, the world seemed to hold its breath with us, the wind quieting, the trees whispering among themselves. Then, a sharp crack split the air. Gunfire. My chest tightened, and I froze, listening. It came in sporadic bursts, each one like a knife through the silence. The wind carried the faint smell of gunpowder, mixing with the dust and dry earth. Out here, surrounded by jagged rock and open sky, I couldn't see where it came from, but I could feel the threat in the air, a shadow hovering over us. The sun dipped low, casting long shadows, and a sudden rustle made my heart jump. My hand reached instinctively for a weapon I no longer had, muscles tensing with a soldier's reflexes. But it was just a small creature, scurrying through the underbrush. Out here, every sound felt like a warning, every movement a potential threat. I found myself wishing for a home, where danger didn't lurk behind every tree.

Night fell slowly, the moon rising up to cast its silver light over the land. It was beautiful in a way that hurt to look at, the air cooling, mist forming with each breath. An owl called out, its voice echoing through the trees, and I couldn't help but wonder what secrets it kept in its nightly watch. I kept my gaze fixed on the darkness beyond, my senses straining for any hint of danger. The wind is picking up, whistling through the valleys like a mournful song. Mita shivered in her sleep, and I draped my spare shirt over her, trying to keep her warm. She curled up, drawing into herself against the cold. Just as I too began to relax, a distant, eerie laugh cut through the night—high and unnatural. It made my blood run cold. It felt like something mocking us, daring us to come closer. I held my breath, listening, every nerve on edge. The darkness seemed to press in, and for a moment, I thought I heard footsteps—a branch breaking, a faint shuffle in the shadows. A bird burst from the trees, wings flapping wildly, and I envied its freedom, the way it could just 'go.' But I couldn't run. I couldn't hide from my own mind. And I knew that eventually, morning would come, bringing with it the reality I couldn't escape.

CHAPTER 49

*"The same water never runs into the same
river."*

Ethiopian proverb

Dawn breaks, casting a soft pink glow on the horizon. We wake early, the last of the night's chill still clinging to the air, my breath visible in the cold morning light. Across the valley, the first rays of the sun kiss the mountain peaks, turning them gold. It would almost be beautiful, if not for the memories of last night—the sound of hyenas laughing somewhere in the dark, their eerie cackles carried on the wind like taunts from the shadows. And further off, echoing between the mountains, and the sharp cracks of gunfire cutting through the night. We didn't waste time. We packed quickly, moving before the light gave us away. The morning air is crisp, carrying the clean scent of wet grass and eucalyptus, a sharp contrast to the dusty, burned-out world we've been trudging through for weeks. The winding path takes us through rolling hills, dotted with trees that whisper in the breeze, like they remember a time before the violence. For a moment, it feels like stepping back in time, to a world that once was—and maybe, if we're lucky, could be again. We walk in silence, lost in our own thoughts, the landscape deceivingly calm around us. But we know better than to drop our guard. Danger could come at any moment, from anywhere. In this quiet place, it's easy to forget the reality of what waits in the shadows, but the memory of last night keeps my nerves sharp. The question gnaws at me: will I ever see her again? Is this how our story ends? And if I do find her, will she be the same person I once knew, or will the world we've lived through have changed her into a stranger? Keep telling myself she's out there somewhere, that I'll find her. But every day, that hope fades a little more, slipping just out of reach like the disappearing mist of morning.

We kept moving north, each step taking us further from the lush green I'd known, into a landscape that seemed to grow harsher by the mile. Mita had insisted we travel beyond Lake Hayek—territory I'd never ventured into on my previous trips. Now, the ground beneath our feet was all jagged rocks and dry, brittle shrubs that crunched underfoot. Mita's eyes were always scanning, darting from one shadow to the next, alert in that way she always was. I couldn't shake the feeling that something—or someone—might be watching us. It gnawed at me, making me glance over my shoulder every few steps. All I saw were twisted shadows from the trees swaying in the wind, but that didn't ease my nerves. I spat out the grit that had settled in the back of my throat and wiped the sweat from my brow with a dusty sleeve. The sky stretched endlessly above us, a perfect blue, not a cloud in sight. A flock of birds drifted on the breeze, carefree and effortless. Along the rugged slope to our right, a group of baboons watched us, their shaggy manes rippling like old men deep in thought. They sat together, grooming each other, muttering softly like a gathering of old friends gossiping. Their murmurs mixed with the dry rustle of grasses in the wind, a strange kind of music in the emptiness.

Suddenly, Mita froze, raising a fist—a signal we'd used countless times to stop. I halted immediately. Her gaze was fixed straight ahead, her expression tense. I strained to see what she had spotted, but all I could make out was the rocky landscape melting into the horizon, nothing out of place. The silence stretched, thickening the air with unease.

"Something's off," she muttered, her voice barely more than a breath. "We need to find shelter before nightfall."

We found a narrow trail leading into a shallow valley, where a clear stream wove through the rocks, its gentle flow calling to us. The plants around it thrived in the cool moisture, a splash of green and colour in the otherwise dry landscape. The sound of the water had a rhythm that pulled me back to another time, another place—sitting by the water with Zahra, her laughter ringing through the air, her face lit up by the sun. For a moment, I almost forgot where I was. But then Mita's hand gripped my shoulder, and the tightness returned to my chest, dragging me back to the present.

"We should rest here," she said, her voice steady, though her eyes still swept the landscape.

I nodded; words caught in my throat. We settled by the stream, the cool water offering a brief relief from the heat. Mita busied herself with purifying the water, her movements practised and precise. I sat nearby with my knees pulled up to my chest, my gaze fixed on the way the sunlight danced on the water's surface, trying to lose myself in the rhythm, even if just for a little while. Mita knelt by the stream, cupping her hands to scoop up the cold water. She splashed it over her face, letting it trickle down her cheeks and neck, washing away the day's sweat and grime. Her movements were fluid, like she'd done this a hundred times before. A sigh slipped from her lips as the water cooled her skin, and for a moment, she seemed lost in the rhythm of nature. I was deep in my own thoughts when she appeared beside me, holding out a cup of water.

"Here," she said, her voice calm but insistent. "You need to stay hydrated."

I took the cup and drained it in a couple of gulps, the cool water soothing my parched throat. I handed it back to her with a weak smile, trying to show some gratitude. She gave a small nod and settled down next to me. We sat in silence for a while, each of us wrapped up in our own thoughts.

Then Mita broke the quiet, her voice low and hesitant. "Is everything okay?" She glanced at me, concern shadowing her face.

I shifted uncomfortably, trying to hide the turmoil twisting inside me. "I'm fine," I lied, forcing the words out through clenched teeth. We both knew better—my voice lacked conviction, and the silence that followed felt heavy, like a weight pressing down on us.

Mita didn't buy it. She never did. Her gaze bore into me, seeing past my flimsy act. "You're not fine, Tommy. I can see it—the way you carry yourself, the way your shoulders slump like you're carrying something you can't put down. Is it about Zahra?"

I clenched my jaw, the muscles tightening painfully. How could I explain the depth of it all? The guilt gnawed at me, a constant ache I couldn't shake. I had failed Zahra when she needed me most, and now, out here in the wilderness, I feared I'd fail her again.

"It's my fault," I muttered, barely more than a whisper, the words tasting bitter on my tongue. "I should've been there for her. I should've—" My voice caught in my throat, choked by the emotions that welled up inside me.

Mita leaned closer, gripping my face with both hands, forcing me to look her in the eye. Her touch was firm, and grounding, and her eyes burned with intensity.

"Listen to me, Tommy," she said, her voice hard and unyielding. "This is not your fault. You couldn't have known. Blaming yourself is only going to eat you alive."

I tried to turn away, but her hands held me in place, the warmth of her touch cutting through the cold knot of guilt that twisted inside me. "But I'm her husband," I argued, my voice breaking. "I was supposed to protect her, to keep her safe. And I didn't."

Mita's expression softened, but she didn't let go. "You didn't fail, Tommy. You're here, aren't you? You're still searching for her, still fighting for her. That's not failure. That's love."

The lump in my throat grew, and I swallowed hard, trying to steady myself. She pulled me into a hug, her arms strong and unyielding, and for a moment, I let myself rest against her, letting out a shaky breath. We held each other until the weight of our emotions eased, just enough to keep going. We packed up our gear and pushed on, even though my muscles screamed for rest. The heat was relentless, beating down on us as we trudged forward. Sweat dripped into my eyes, burning them, and each breath felt like fire in my lungs. My feet ached with every step, but I couldn't stop. We didn't have time to stop. The sound of a stream teased me from a distance, but ahead, there was nothing but dry, dusty land. Mita's stride never faltered, her eyes fixed on a point I couldn't see, her determination pulling me along.

"Tommy," she called back to me, her voice carrying over the crunch of gravel underfoot. "Remember why we're doing this."

I did. It wasn't just about getting to some spot on a map. It was about finding a chance for redemption, a chance to make things right. For Mita, it was duty, maybe even loyalty. For me, it was the desperate hope of saving Zahra, of righting my wrongs, of delivering my own justice for what had happened to her. I draped my dusty *shamma* over my head, trying to protect my face from the sun's merciless glare. My skin was already burning; I could feel it on my nose, where the skin had peeled and burned again. I rubbed dirt over my nose as a makeshift sunscreen, knowing that even a little exposure would cost me later. The ground was rough beneath our feet, baked hard by the sun, carved by centuries of wind and rain. The ancient rocks made me feel small, like just another traveller passing through. But out here, surrounded by the vast emptiness, I also felt a strange connection to those rocks, to the history they held. They had seen it all—the rise and fall of empires, the echoes of long-forgotten battles. And in their shadow, I was reminded of how temporary everything was. But even in this place, I couldn't shake the memories gnawing at me. They pressed in with each step, each heartbeat, like a shadow I couldn't outrun. Mita kept her eyes forward, unwavering, but I clung to her grit like a lifeline, forcing myself to take one more step, then another, knowing that whatever lay ahead, I couldn't afford to give up now.

CHAPTER 50

An explosion echoed in the distance, rattling the skyline. Heat shimmered on the horizon, bending and warping the edges of the landscape. Dust swirled around my boots with every step, the air so dry it felt like breathing in sandpaper. Another explosion, followed by the rapid pop, pop, pop of gunfire. I stepped over a pile of bones, bleached white and neatly scattered reminders that everything here fought to survive, and when one fell, something else feasted. Life here was cheap, death a constant companion. The sun sank lower, stretching our shadows long across the cracked earth. A narrow, winding path emerged before us, worn smooth by decades of shepherds' feet. It cut through the harsh landscape, guiding us forward. Ahead, a shepherd appeared, his face weathered like the land itself, a long staff in hand. His clothes, traditional and earth-toned, made him blend into the terrain like he'd been carved from the mountains. He exchanged a few words with Mita in Amharic, pointing us toward a narrow path through the mountains—one known only to those who'd walked it countless times before.

"Thank you," I said, stumbling through my limited Amharic and giving him a thumbs up. He almost smiled, a small curve of the lips that felt like a nod to my effort.

We followed his directions onto a narrow, treacherous trail, the kind where one wrong step could send you tumbling into the ravine below. My legs felt unsteady, every rock underfoot threatening to throw me off balance. But Mita assured me it would save time, and as we climbed higher, the air turned cooler—a welcome relief after hours in the blistering sun. I couldn't help but think of that scene from *Lethal Weapon,*' when the older cop mutters, *'I m too old for this shit.'* At that moment, I felt it deep in my bones.

The mountains loomed around us, their peaks sharp and unyielding, reaching up like they wanted to touch the sky. They made me feel small, insignificant—a speck moving through an ancient landscape that would endure long after I was gone. But as we climbed, leaving the noise and chaos below, a strange sense of calm settled over me, like Zahra's spirit was guiding me through this place. The weight of my worries began to lift, the pain dulled by the raw beauty of the land. We crossed a stream, its clear water bubbling over smooth stones, weaving its own path down the mountainside. The sound was soothing, a gentle lullaby in this wild terrain. Our boots crunched over gravel as we wound our way up toward a distant waterfall that glimmered like silver against the rock. Above us, a few sheep perched on a ledge, grazing without a care in the world. One lifted its head and met my eyes, and for a second, I felt a strange kinship—two creatures navigating this rough landscape, each trying to find our way. As the sun dipped lower, the mountains cast long shadows over a small village tucked into the valley below, surrounded by terraced fields that seemed to cling to the steep slopes. Stone houses with round roofs dotted the landscape, their courtyards neatly fenced. Smoke drifted up from chimneys, curling into the evening sky as the light faded to a deep, glowing orange. Mita squeezed my arm, her voice steady.

"This is where we'll find our first answers," she said with a confidence that I envied.

The trail down into the village was narrow, unpaved, and treacherous. Each step was a careful negotiation with loose gravel and jagged rocks. My anxiety spiked as we descended, every shadow making me second-guess what might be waiting for us below. Would they welcome us? Would they even tell us anything? And most of all—would we finally find a trace of Zahra? Mita had heard from a contact that Zahra had passed through this village, heading north. As we neared the edge of the village, I brushed the dust off my clothes, trying to appear more composed than I felt. Children playing by a house froze when they saw us, their games forgotten, wide eyes tracking our every move. Their sudden silence drew the attention of the adults, who emerged from their homes, watching us with guarded curiosity. I didn't sense hostility, but there was wariness, especially toward me. While we walked through the village, Mita pointed out landmarks, explaining that this place was called Tebisi. But her voice held a hint of uncertainty; this was her first time here too, and I could tell she was worried about being understood. The sun's last rays painted everything gold, giving the scene an eerie, cinematic feel, like we'd wandered into a Western. Any moment, I half-expected a lone cowboy to round the corner. But as the shadows deepened and the sky darkened, Mita's expression grew tense. She pulled me aside, her grip firm on my arm.

"We need to move quickly," she said, urgency in her voice. "They're close."

She didn't have to say who they were. I felt my heart quicken as I looked back at the path we'd taken, wondering if our presence here had already drawn unwanted attention. We couldn't afford any mistakes. Not now. She told me this village had dealt with these people before, and I knew right then—we were walking into a hyena's den. My pulse quickened as we moved through the narrow, crowded streets, the villagers casting wary glances our way. Mita slipped away quietly, mingling with those willing to talk, gathering bits and pieces of information like a detective. Her goal was simple: earn their trust and hear their stories. I was grateful for the break. My old hip injury throbbed with every step, and the sun had baked my skin a deep, raw red. I probably looked as terrifying as the devil these villagers feared.

When Mita returned, her boots crunched on the dry, brittle earth. In one arm, she carried a heavy shotgun like a mother cradling a child, the other slung with an AK-47. She'd found allies in a nearby village—others searching for their missing loved ones. Without a word, she handed me a knife from her pack. Its blade gleamed under the moonlight, catching my reflection in its metal. As I twirled it, feeling the weight, I couldn't ignore the darkness staring back at me—the part of me capable of taking a life if it meant saving Zahra. We stood there, looking out at the distant huts, their lights flickering like fireflies against the black sky. I strained my eyes, searching for something familiar, but the shadows swallowed everything except those far-off glimmers, luring us toward whatever lay ahead. Mita leaned in close, her breath warm on my ear as she whispered.

Her voice was steady, full of conviction. "They're not just after control. They want to wipe out anyone who stands in their way."

I forced a smile, trying to hide the twist of anxiety in my gut, and gave her a quick nod. But my hands trembled as I gathered our gear, every movement deliberate. I slotted each round into the AK's curved magazine, the metallic clicks both familiar and unsettling. The weight of each 7.62mm round brought back memories—ones I'd buried deep. The battlefield smell of oil and metal flooded my senses, dredging up visions of camaraderie, now just faded ghosts. The AK-47 was a weapon I knew too well. It's held its place as a staple of war since the 1940s, and here, it was a reminder of everything I'd hoped to leave behind. But in this place, where loyalty was rare, Mita was the only person I could trust. She caught my eye, and then checked her weapon with the ease of someone who'd been doing this her whole life. There was no need for words; our pact was clear. We were in this together, and whatever came next, we'd face it side by side. I slid the magazine into the rifle and chambered the first round, the sound sharp and final in the night air. There was no going back. Zahra's face flashed in my mind, driving me forward. I'd do anything—anything—to bring her back. Mita unrolled a worn map between us, tracing routes with her fingers. She pointed out buildings, compounds, and possible hideouts. We planned every step, every fallback point, like surgeons plotting an incision. Every choice had to be precise. I had one mission: find Zahra, no matter the cost. And I was ready for whatever came next—life or death.

CHAPTER 51

From the shadows, a massive figure stepped forward. He reminded me of *John Coffey'* from *'The Green Mile,'* towering over everyone, radiating strength and an unyielding presence. I couldn't look away. He was unlike any other Ethiopian I'd met before. I thought about asking where he was from but knew better than to ask such a stupid question. Mita introduced him as Solomon, our newest comrade. His skin was a deep, rich brown, glistening with sweat in the humid air. Muscles rippled beneath the surface, shaped by years of hard work and hardship. Scars crossed his skin—some old and jagged, others fresh, pink, and angry. He wore a loose, dirt-stained tunic tied with a strip of fabric around his waist, his trousers rolled up at the ankles. His calloused feet stuck out from worn leather sandals, straps cracked but sturdy enough for the rough paths of the highlands. Something about him unsettled me. His silence felt as heavy as the humid night, and I couldn't shake the sense that he carried secrets, buried deep behind his stoic expression. But in his eyes, I caught a glimpse of something raw grief, the kind that lingers even after the tears have dried. Mita later confirmed what I already sensed: they had taken his wife. Mita trusted him implicitly, but I'd learned to be wary. Trust is fragile in this world.

The night had finally settled in, and it was nearly time to move. Solomon stepped closer, offering me a hand to help me up. His hand dwarfed mine, rough and scarred, each callus telling a story of struggle. I didn't ask him what he was fighting for. It didn't matter. I was just relieved he was on our side. His grip was strong, and steady—a comfort in this uncertain place. We were bound together by loss, our unspoken bond forged in pain and a shared need for justice. Another figure emerged from the shadows behind Solomon, unnoticed until now. He was younger, with an intense, focused look in his eyes. Mita introduced him as Abiy, a former tour guide turned fighter. He greeted me with a warm smile, one tinged with sadness. Abiy used to lead groups through the breathtaking landscapes of this region, sharing stories about the land and its people. Now, those memories seemed like a distant dream, the peaceful days swallowed by conflict. I remembered walking those same paths when things were simpler, when peace felt like a possibility. Solomon's voice broke through my thoughts. He held out a crumpled photograph, its edges worn from years of being folded and unfolded. He stared at the image of a smiling woman, his eyes softening with a pain that went deeper than words.

"This is why I fight," he said, his voice barely a whisper. "For her. For them. And now, for us."

I nodded, feeling the weight of his words. It was enough—a silent pact between us. Abiy placed a trembling hand on Solomon's shoulder. Unlike Solomon, who wore his pain like a badge, Abiy was more of a mystery, his sorrow hidden beneath layers of resilience. Watching them, I sensed the bond between them, forged in hardship. Their fluency in English surprised me—it was rare here. They'd both studied at Wollo University before everything went to shit. It felt strange to hear them speak in English, their words careful and deliberate, making sure I understood every detail of the plan.

Abiy's voice broke the silence. "The path ahead won't forgive hesitation," he said, his tone low but firm. "Every moment we wait, their hold tightens, and our loved ones drift further from us."

He was right. We couldn't afford to wait any longer. We were a ragtag team, not born into power but united in our determination to fight for a better future. Solomon tucked the photo back into his pocket like it was a talisman, something to keep him safe. I looked him in the eye, still unsure if I could fully trust him. But I saw something there—a flicker of understanding, a shared burden.

"I'm sorry about your wife," I said quietly. Solomon's jaw clenched, and he nodded, the muscles in his neck taut with barely contained rage.

"They will pay for what they've done," he muttered, his voice carrying a dangerous edge. "I won't rest until I have my revenge."

In that moment, I knew we were the same driven by a hunger for justice that bordered on desperation. With Solomon by our side, I felt a glimmer of hope for the first time since Zahra disappeared. Mita and the others stood around me, shadows outlined in the moonlight, our weapons gleaming as we whispered through the plan. They spoke in their native tongue, then switched to English for my benefit. I felt like a child among them, listening to their every word, trying to keep up. There was no room for mistakes.

We set off towards the village in the distance, our footsteps muted on the soft earth. The darkness pressed in on all sides, broken only by the flickering light from huts ahead. I gripped my AK-47 tightly, feeling the reassuring weight of a knife strapped to my leg. We moved like shadows, swift and silent, each of us aware of what was at stake. As we crouched behind a boulder, Solomon pointed to a ridge in the distance. "That's our mark," he whispered, his voice barely carrying above the wind. The moon cast a pale light over the rocky ground as we moved towards it, Abiy's warning about enemy patrols echoing in my head. From the ridge, we saw the faint glow of campfires in the valley below. We watched, tense, our hearts racing with anticipation. Then, with a nod from Solomon, we descended on the camp like ghosts. Our weapons were loaded, adrenaline pumping through our veins. We were ready to face whatever violence lay ahead, united in our desperate mission to save our loved ones—and ourselves.

Chapter 52

Mita and Abiy kept low, using the shadows to slip toward the compound. Solomon and I watched as they disappeared into the blackness, my chest tightening with every step they took further out of sight. I turned to Solomon, and he gave me a nod, the kind meant to steady my nerves, but my gut still churned. Out of nowhere, a shadow peeled away from the darkness, a figure illuminated by the flickering moonlight. I caught the glint of a blade. There was no time to warn Solomon—he moved before I could even react. It wasn't a clean fight, not like in the movies. It was raw and wild, a desperate clash of bodies and weapons. No precision, no calculation—just two men locked in a brutal struggle, willing to kill or die for their cause. I could only watch, heart in my throat, as Solomon fought like a man possessed. Then it happened—Solomon's blade found its mark, sinking into the attacker's chest. The man's breath hitched, his body going rigid before collapsing in a heap on the ground. The night fell silent, even the insects stopping their chorus as if they too were stunned by the violence. Solomon fell to his knees, clutching his leg, his face twisted in agony. Blood seeped from a gash in his inner thigh, spreading through the dirt. Panic jolted through me, and I rushed to his side, tearing a strip from my shirt to use as a tourniquet. My hands shook as I wrapped the cloth around his leg, pulling it tight. The fabric darkened with his blood, warm and sticky against my skin. Solomon gritted his teeth, stifling a groan as I tightened the makeshift bandage. He tried to push himself up, but when I moved to help him, he shot me a look that said it all:

"Don't touch me." He fought his way upright, the heat from his body mingling with the earthy smell of blood and sweat. Even through the pain, there was a look in his eyes—something defiant, almost heroic, like he was daring death to come closer. "Move!" Solomon growled, his voice tight with pain. "Find her. Find them." His eyes burned with a mix of urgency and frustration.

I shook my head, my chest tightening. "No way. We're in this together." Remembering Mita's words.

He gritted his teeth, forcing out the words. "Go. I'll be fine. This tourniquet's good. Top-notch, my friend. Now go—get moving!" It wasn't a request; it was an order. And I knew he was right. There was no time to argue.

With a final glance back, I tore myself away, sprinting toward the entrance. The guilt burned in my chest, the thought of leaving him behind twisting my insides. But I forced myself to keep moving, pushing back the weight in my heart. Mita and Abiy needed me. I could only hope they were faring better than we were. The night was thick with mist, swallowing the far end of the wall, and the guard we'd spotted earlier had disappeared. The air buzzed with the distant staccato of gunfire, each shot vibrating through the trees. Brief flashes lit up the sky, turning the shadows into a warped, flickering landscape. Without Solomon, the danger felt sharper, more immediate. My body was on edge, nerves pulled tight. In close-quarters combat, there's no time for second-guessing, only reaction. Every footfall seemed too loud; every breath too sharp. Adrenaline coursed through me, turning my fear into a hard edge, a determination to see this through. The door to the building swung open easily. It wasn't even locked. I slipped inside, and the stale air wrapped around me, thick with the smell of damp concrete and something sharper—maybe blood. I ran a hand over my side, feeling the cold metal of my knife, my other hand gripping the rifle. A round was already chambered, the weight of it steadying my racing mind. I kept low, sticking to the shadows, and moving deeper into the compound. The murmur of voices drifted from a nearby hallway—guards, bored and distracted. One of them laughed, a quick, anxious sound that echoed through the empty corridors. It mingled with the low hum of the generator, the noise filling the silence like a constant, oppressive heartbeat. A series of corridors stretched out before me, some exposed to the night air, others winding into darkness. I chose the shadowed path, slipping into the black where I knew I'd be harder to spot. The darkness felt like a second skin, cold and unforgiving, but it was my best shot. I moved forward, knowing I was one step closer to Mita, to Abiy, and whatever awaited us beyond that next turn. Moonlight seeped through the cracks in the narrow hallway, casting shifting patterns of light and shadow on the worn floor. Doors lined each side, like silent guardians, each one marked by scratches, dents, and the faded memory of paint. Some stood slightly ajar, others tightly closed, as if trying to keep something locked inside. I approached the first door on my left, easing my rifle to my shoulder as I pressed my ear against the rough wood. All I could hear was the dull thud of my own heartbeat. Nothing else. My hand, slick with sweat, hovered over the handle. I had one chance to get this right. I tightened my grip, twisted slowly, and pushed. The door groaned open, revealing a room frozen in disarray. Torn fabric fluttered in the draft from a shattered window. Splintered chair legs jutted out like broken bones, and a pile of debris—books, papers, things I couldn't make out—spilled into a corner. Moonlight sliced through the darkness, illuminating the dust that swirled in the air. I moved on, each door revealing more of the compound's story. In one room, a cracked mirror caught my reflection. My face stared back at me—swollen eyes, bruised cheeks, a new scar trailing along my jaw. Blood smeared the floor, a path leading to a pile of discarded medical instruments. Or maybe they were torture tools. I didn't want to know. Graffiti covered the walls, faded and barely legible, but the words still clung to the walls—scratched in by desperate hands. Messages of love, defiance, and despair. Room after room, the story became clearer, but no less haunting. One held a makeshift barricade—tables and chairs stacked high, a sign of a desperate final stand. Bullet holes riddled the walls like twisted constellations. I paused, letting the scene settle over me. What happened here? A battle, a siege, or something far worse? The air seemed to whisper, carrying echoes of fear and courage. The corridor narrowed around me, urging me forward into this place of forgotten suffering. But still, no answers. Just fragments—a torn map, a blood-stained journal, a single shoe left behind. I stumbled back into the dim hallway, my breath coming in short, sharp bursts. Another door. My fingers brushed against the cold metal knob, sending a chill down my spine. This one was different. Unmarked, unassuming. With a deep breath, I turned the handle and pushed. A wave of stench hit me—a sickening mix of iron and rot that clawed at my throat. I swallowed hard, fighting the urge to retch, and stepped inside. The room was a nightmare made real. Rusted chains dangled from the ceiling like twisted vines, and bolted-down chairs sat in a circle, their surfaces stained dark with dried blood. The floor, once concrete, was now a canvas of crimson smears, telling stories of suffering too horrible to imagine. This wasn't just evil—it was a monument to it. My skin crawled, my stomach twisted, but I couldn't look away. Suddenly, footsteps echoed down the corridor, growing closer. Panic surged through me, and I frantically scanned the room for a hiding spot. Trembling, I pressed myself into the shadows of a corner, trying to control my breathing. The footsteps drew nearer, each one dragging out the seconds into an eternity. My heart hammered in my chest, every beat a betrayal that threatened to give me away. I clutched my dagger, its handle slick with sweat, as thoughts of vengeance clawed at my mind.

Then, a door slammed down the hall, the sound reverberating through the chamber. A voice followed—muffled, high-pitched, pleading. Young girls, their cries piercing through the walls and cutting into my core. Rage surged through me, hot and blinding, but I stayed rooted, torn between the safety of staying hidden and the desperate need to intervene. But the cries grew louder, more frantic, and I knew there was no choice. I couldn't stand by. I couldn't let them suffer. Not again.

Zahra's voice repeated in my mind, urging me forward. I pushed myself off the grimy wall, my muscles coiled tight with fear and determination. I crept toward the source of the cries, measuring each step, my breath coming in short bursts. My rifle stayed tucked away in the shadows—I'd need something quieter. My fingers wrapped around the cold steel of my knife, its weight grounding me. I trailed my hand along the freezing walls as I reached the door, feeling the cool metal knob beneath my fingers. The cries on the other side were sharper now, mingling with the clatter of chains and low, taunting laughter. With a deep breath, I steadied myself, feeling the adrenaline coursing through my veins, turning fear into something sharper. I twisted the handle and pushed the door open, stepping into the darkness with a fortitude that burned hotter than any nightmare I'd faced.

CHAPTER 53

The air hits me like a punch to the gut as soon as I step inside, thick with the stench of sweat, decay, and something far worse—something that twists my stomach and makes me gag. It's like nothing I've ever smelled before, a nauseating mix of unwashed bodies, human waste, and God knows what else. I pull my shirt up over my nose, but it barely makes a difference. This place is beyond filthy, the kind of dirty that gets under your skin and clings to you. And then, I see it—something I wouldn't have imagined even in my worst nightmares. The scene before me is a nightmare come to life, a vision of horror that my mind can't fully process. I force myself to stay steady, to keep my face blank, but inside I'm unravelling, the sight searing itself into my memory. It's a brutality so raw, so beyond anything I've known, that I feel a part of me shatter, leaving behind a scar that will never heal. The air around me warps, time itself bending as past and present crash together in a hellish blur. And there, in the centre of it all, lies a young girl— naked, her body twisted in a way that no living thing should ever be. Her limbs are bent at impossible angles, her face frozen in a mask of terror, eyes open but unseeing. The cold floor beneath her is stained with a dark, spreading pool. Every nerve in my body is screaming at me to run, to get away from this place where humanity doesn't exist—where survival is a twisted game, played by monsters with no limits. But there's another door ahead, half open, shadows pooling beyond it. I don't know what's waiting on the other side, but I know one thing: whatever it is, it can't be any worse than this. Or maybe it can.

My eyes are immediately drawn to a solid-looking wooden table dominating the centre of the room like a throne. A man is perched atop it, his back turned to me, leaning on top of it with his bare lower half thrusting aggressively against a small girl pinned beneath him. Her once-white dress now twists and bunches around her neck, revealing her emaciated body and leaving her arms awkwardly suspended above her head, akin to a puppeteer's manipulation. As I move closer, I witness the true atrocity of the scene unfolding before me—the girl's eyes and nose caked in dark blood, her face contorted in agony and disbelief as she struggles against her attacker's merciless violation. I moved with feral precision, honed from years of hard-hearted combat. Every muscle in my body was taut and ready to unleash the full force of my uncontrollable rage. My entire being recoiled at the horrific sight before me, but I suppressed the primal scream threatening to escape my lips. There was no room for error, not when a fragile life hung in the balance, so cruelly disregarded. The beast atop the terror-stricken girl was too engrossed in his vile act to notice my presence until I stood right behind him, a warrior seeking revenge. By then, it was too late for him to flee his inevitable fate. In one quick and brutal motion, I plunged the blade into his skull with merciless force. The impact caused it to burst through bone and cartilage. The cold steel of my knife replaced his eye—a fitting end for someone who took pleasure in inflicting pain. The creature slumped back, lifeless, as if a bullet had struck its eye. A grotesque tapestry of pulsating crimson stained the ground beneath him—a fitting and merciless final chapter of a sadistic predator's story, written in brutal strokes of blood and vengeance.

My eyes sweep across the room, taking in the horrifying scene before me. The first young girl remained motionless and naked on the floor. I pray she is now at peace. The savagery was evident in the shredded and scattered bloodied clothes surrounding her. Broken objects and smashed furnishings litter the entire area. Blood stains are everywhere I look, and splatter across the walls like abstract art. As I take in the gruesome sight, memories of Samuel's daughter flash through my mind before vanishing as quickly as they came. I force myself to look away from her. There is nothing I could do for her now. But the other one... she might still have a chance. I tense, every muscle wound tight, ready for whatever comes next. She stirs, trying to push herself up from where she's slumped against the table. Her legs give out, and she crumples to the ground again. I dart forward, but before I can reach her, a man bursts out of the shadows in the corner, his face twisted in rage. I barely spot the glint of the blade in his hand before he lunges at me, aiming for my throat, his eyes blazing with vengeful fury for his fallen comrade. Instinct takes over. I drop low, sweeping his legs out from under him. He hits the ground hard but rolls back up like a wild animal, a growl tearing from his throat. Now we're circling each other, eyes locked, both of us waiting for the other to make a move. My gaze flicks to the injured girl, curled into a ball on the floor, her sobs barely more than gasps. I don't have time. I need to finish this before he brings more of them down on us. He charges again, swinging the machete like a madman. Behind me, the girl lets out a weak groan—she's running out of time. No time for hesitation. I have to end this. I have to kill this bastard. With a quick fake to the left, I draw him off balance, then pivot and drive my knee into his groin. He folds over, gagging, and I rush to his buddy's crumpled body to grab my knife. But it's jammed in his skull, stuck deep. I yank at it, straining, but the body jerks with each pull, the knife refusing to budge. I let go, letting the head drop back with a dull thud against the table. I turn just in time—his partner is coming at me again, the machete slicing through the air. I'm out of options, left with only my fists. I brace myself, every punch a fight for survival—not just mine, but hers too. My breath tastes like iron and dirt, thick with the scent of blood. The blade flashes in the dim light, coming for my face. I duck, barely avoiding the swing, then drive my fist into his jaw with everything I have. His head snaps back, but he doesn't drop. He spits blood and snarls like a wild dog, eyes crazed. We crash into each other, fists flying, kicks connecting, both of us desperate for control. His machete slashes at my side, and fire burns through my ribs. I hiss in pain, feeling the warm blood seep through my shirt, soaking into the fabric. But the pain sharpens my focus, and fuels my rage. Each blow I throw is a step closer to the end—there's no room for anything but raw, unrelenting violence. He thought he could take me. He was wrong. The fight doesn't last long. I grab his head and slam it against the concrete floor, again and again, blood splattering my face and arms. A sickening crack echoes through the room, and his body goes limp beneath my hands. I stop, my chest heaving, lungs burning, sweat and blood running down my face. My side throbs with every breath, but I can't think about that now. When the silence returns, all that's left is the girl, trembling and staring up at me, her eyes wide with terror. I look down at the carnage, my own hands shaking, wondering if she sees me as her saviour—or just another monster.

I crouch beside her, pulling down the tattered remains of her dress to cover her bruised, battered body. Her muffled sobs speak to horrors I can't fully comprehend, the ragged breaths and broken cries barely scratching the surface of what she's endured. Blood seeps from between her legs, and her skin is a patchwork of cuts and bruises. When she looks at me, her eyes are empty, as if something inside her has been shattered beyond repair. I tear a piece of fabric and gently wipe the blood and tears from her face, my calloused hands moving with a gentleness I didn't know I still possessed. She flinches at first, but eventually leans into the touch, as if hoping, just for a moment, that the nightmare is over. Her lips tremble, her gaze shifts, darting beneath the table, her lips moving frantically spitting out a jumble of subdued words and pleas. I follow her eyes and reach under the table, pulling out a small pebble with dark purple markings. My chest tightens as I recognise it—Samuel had shown me an identical one when we first met, a gift from his daughter that he cherished. Could this really be the same stone? And if so, does that mean this girl is... no, it can't be possible. I glance down at the talisman she clutches in her bloodied hand. There's no mistaking it. The pieces fit together too perfectly, like a cruel puzzle. A cold shiver runs through me as I realise who she is and what this means.

The small, lifeless body of the child I had observed on entering, must be no more than ten, maybe twelve years old, lies in front of me. Her eyes are wide and fixed on the grimy ceiling above; a sickly yellow hue taints her final moments. My heart aches at the thought of what happened here—the senseless loss of a young life. But I push the grief aside. Now isn't the time. If I'm going to save Samuel's daughter, I need to act fast. Taking a deep breath, I force my thoughts back into focus and turn to the shivering girl in front of me. Her shock mirrors that of the dead girl—a terror too deep for words. Despite my efforts to comfort her, she trembles uncontrollably, like a leaf caught in a storm. Time is running out. We have to move. Gazing down at this traumatised child, I can't help but think of Zahra, another innocent victim of this cruel world. Is this what she has suffered already? Am I too late to save her? Suddenly, the voice I've been dreading rings in my ears, cold and mocking.

"Oh, Tommy, your fate is far worse than anything these girls have suffered," it sneers, ending with a low, grating cackle.

I don't have time for this. I shake my head, trying to push the voice away, and focus on Samuel's daughter instead. Her eyes meet mine, wide and searching, full of questions I don't have answers for. Her father's intelligence is there, sharp and piercing, as if she expects me to know what to do, to say something that makes all of this make sense. But I'm empty. I never asked Samuel her name—not while he was still alive, anyway.

I swallow, my voice coming out softer than I expected. "What's your name?" I finally ask, feeling foolish for not knowing.

She looks at me, her face bruised and swollen, eyes bloodshot from tears. "Aster," she says, her voice surprisingly strong despite everything she's been through.

Panic rises in my chest. We have to move, now, if we're going to make it. I speak firmly, trying to keep my own fear from seeping into my words.

"Aster, listen to me. You need to stand up, okay? Can you do that?" I put my hands gently on her shoulders, my touch soft but urgent. Her eyes flit around the room, taking in the horror, her face twisting with fear. I know this place will haunt her forever—if we survive.

I try again, mimicking walking with my fingers. "Can you walk?" I ask, my voice strained, the urgency tightening around my chest. Her eyes meet mine again—scared, desperate—but there's something else there too. Trust.

I look around, the stench of blood and death heavy in the air, and I know we can't stay here. There's no more time. I don't give her a chance to respond. I wrap my arms around her, lifting up her, ignoring the white-hot pain that shoots through my side. Her breaths are shallow, but she's breathing. She's alive. I grit my teeth, feeling the weight of her against me, her small frame trembling.

"Hang in there, Aster," I whisper. "I'm going to get you out of here."

And I move, each step echoing in the dark, each heartbeat a reminder that every second counts. We need to find help, but we can't stop yet—not when danger is still lurking in every shadow of this place. I push through the darkness, feeling her weight in my arms, and the warmth of her blood soaking into my sleeves. Each step is agony, but I can't let myself slow down. Not when her life depends on it. She's bleeding heavily, and I know that every minute counts. I lay her down gently in a hidden spot, rummaging through my backpack, praying for something that could help. I rip fabric into makeshift bandages, pressing them against her torn flesh. The task feels impossible, like trying to plug a leaking dam with paper. But I have to try. She doesn't make a sound, her eyes distant, as if the pain is beyond her reach now. I pull her back into my arms and keep moving, ignoring the burning ache in my muscles. A sharp cry escapes my lips when she convulses against me, her body struggling against the trauma. I clench my jaw, biting back my own fear. We need to find shelter, medical help—something, anything. If we don't, she won't make it. And I refuse to let that happen. This is all so fucked up. But if I can keep moving, if I can stay strong just a little longer, maybe I can save her. Maybe I can give her a chance. I push through the dense, tangled paths of the forest, my senses on high alert, scanning for any sign of our pursuers. Her father's stone is still clutched tightly in her hand, a symbol of a life that might not survive the night. I shudder, forcing down the disgust and horror at what she's been through. All that matters now is getting her out alive.

CHAPTER 54

Pushing through the overgrown foliage, sweat pours down my face, stinging my eyes. The brush scratches at my skin, leaving red trails as I push forward, my heart hammering so hard I think it might burst. Each step feels like a fight against nature herself, branches clawing at my legs, roots twisting around my ankles, waiting for me to fall. I stumble over rocks, and scramble over fallen logs, forcing my way through until we reach a small clearing beneath a canopy of ancient trees. But even here, surrounded by shadows, I can feel the eyes of predators, always watching. I lower Aster gently onto the ground, my breath ragged, sweat dripping into my eyes. Somewhere in the distance, a howl splits the night, sending a shiver through me as the cold air bites at my skin. I'm on edge, scanning the darkness for any movement, any noise, knowing danger is always close. The forest is unnaturally quiet—just the occasional rustle of leaves, and the chirping of hidden insects. This place doesn't forgive weakness; it's a world where only the strongest survive. The howls grow louder, creeping closer, desperate. I reach for my knife, but my hand finds only an empty sheath. I remember too late—I left it in that bastard's skull.

Aster is still breathing—barely. She's so small, so fragile, but somehow, she's holding on. Her breaths are shallow, her body trembling with fever, but there's a fight left in her. I grip her hand, my voice breaking as I whisper to her, trying to keep her here with me. I take off my shirt and cover her, like it could somehow shield her from everything she's endured. Tears blur my vision, first from rage, then from grief, falling onto her feverish skin. She's slipping away, her breathing growing weaker, the warmth draining from her.

"Aster, stay with me," I mutter, my voice shaking.

I've seen death before, but not like this. Not with someone so young. My hands tremble as I try to stop the bleeding, pressing down on the wound, but there's too much blood. I blink back the tears, forcing myself to hold it together. But why did it have to be her? Just a kid. I feel useless, like I'm fighting against a force I can't beat. I want to scream at the unfairness of it all, to rage against a world this cruel. But all I can do is hold her closer, whispering lies I don't believe. She's slipping away, and I can't stop it. Moonlight slips through the branches, casting pale shadows on her face. In her features, I see Zahra—strong, and resilient, even through suffering. Something burns inside me, pushing back against the grief, and I look up at the stars, trying to get my bearings in this unfamiliar stretch of the Ethiopian Highlands. Desperation drives me as I arrange leaves into a makeshift bed for her, ignoring my own exhaustion, and my own pain. My hands, scarred and trembling, brush against her cold skin, searching for any sign of life. But deep down, I know the truth—I was too late. She's still clutching her father's pebble in her small hand, that tiny symbol of hope that now feels like a cruel joke. Grief rises in my chest, impossible to choke down, and a cry rips from me, raw and broken. I couldn't save her. Not out here. Not like this. Tears streak down my face, and the howls in the distance grow closer, the hyenas' laughter echoing through the trees. They're closing in, drawn to the scent of blood and distress. I'm not good at this—at being vulnerable, at feeling things. It's easier to push it all away. Yet, I can't.

With a heavy heart and trembling hands, my calloused fingers, rough from years of living and fighting, dig into the unforgiving earth, carving out a shallow grave for the young girl lying before me. Her face, once vibrant and full of life, is now still and peaceful in death. I whisper a prayer for her. Aster, a beautiful, innocent soul whose life was taken too soon. The earth is hard, and as I dig, my thoughts drift to the journey that led us here—a hardened soldier turned reluctant saviour, burying a stranger in a distant land. Undeterred by my fingers being raw from the earth, I push through because of a duty that trumps any pain. The grave is shallow; in this place where life and death are indifferent neighbours, nature does not allow for depth. As I gently lay her delicate body into the grave for her last goodnight, my hands cradled her fragile frame with a tenderness I never knew I possessed. With kind respect, I place her father's stone on her chest as a symbol of peace in eternal rest. And in a rasped voice, I say my final goodbye. Tears stream down my face, knowing I have broken the promise I made to her father—to keep her safe from harm. Rising slowly to my feet, I feel the weight of grief settles on my shoulders. I rise, my body aching, the weight of grief settling on my shoulders. The night is a silent witness, only broken by distant cries and the wind whispering through the trees. As I look up at the stars, I hope, somehow, that she's found peace, that she's with her father now. Under these ancient trees, she belongs to this land, a daughter of Ethiopia, a daughter of Solomon. But with her death, the weight of this place presses down even heavier on my soul. I turn away, knowing I have to keep moving. She was just a child, caught in the crossfire of a senseless war. But to me, she was everything I fought for—and failed to protect. The trees stand like sentinels, their branches reaching out like hands. I take one last look at her resting place, my chest tight with guilt, before forcing myself to move.

"I'm sorry," I whisper to the night. Aster's face fades into the faces of countless others, all lost and crying out for help. Their voices echo in my mind as I finally succumb to exhaustion and drift into an agitated slumber.

The shadows move like a dedication—a moving fusion of anguish and sorrow that has accompanied me throughout this conflict. Zahra appears bound and helpless; the image freezes me like a statue. She is standing in the middle of a battlefield, her white dress stained with dirt and blood. Her eyes widen with fear as she takes in the destruction before her. Her eyes meet mine, full of tears and pain. I watch her slowly disappear with her mouth open, desperately trying to unleash a scream, but silence rules her. Then I hear it as a desperate plea.

'Find me, Tommy.'

In the silence before daybreak, I feel nothing but emptiness. Blood has left a rusty taste in my mouth, and the damp, cold air surrounds me. As I try to sit up, a sharp pain surges through my side, evoking an involuntary groan from my throat that sounds foreign to me. Something warm spreads down my side. I reach down, and my fingers come back slick with blood. Panic begins to set in as I struggle to recall. To stifle it, I bite down on my lip. How did it come to this? How could I have let things escalate to this point? Despite the fear, there's a faint voice I hear, telling me to keep going. Zahra's voice cuts through the haze.

'Get up,' she commands.

I grit my teeth and push myself up, fighting against the pain with every breath. The air is thin and cold, and every movement sends a fresh wave of agony through my side. But I force myself to stand. There's no other choice but to keep going, to push through the pain. The rising sun casts a grim light over the blood-soaked ground, and the world feels eerily quiet around me. I glance back one last time at Aster's grave, offering a silent apology before turning away.

'Find me, Tommy.' Her voice is a whisper, but it cuts through the darkness, pulling me back to reality.

Every step is a struggle, every breath a battle against the pain, but I keep moving, because that's all I can do. I can't let her death be in vain. I can't let Zahra down. As the thorns of doubt claw at my mind, I cling to one thing—love. For Aster, for Zahra, for a place that's become a part of me. The shadows stretch long across the ground, but I push on, even as my strength wanes. Death might be waiting for me, but I refuse to meet it without a fight.

CHAPTER 55

*"The leopard's eye is on the goat, and the eye of
the goat is on the leaf."*

Ethiopian proverb

Once again, night has swallowed the landscape. Frustration gnaws at me—I haven't made much progress, not with this unforgiving terrain and my battered body. But at least it's cooler now, and I have more water. All day, I tracked a plume of smoke, following the distant rumble of war. But with the darkness, the smoke has vanished, leaving me without a guide. The sounds of battle still echo in the distance, though, a constant reminder that time is slipping away. My unease twists tighter with every moment, a knot forming in the pit of my stomach. In the distance, a faint light flickers—a single glow, like a lone firefly in the black. Despite my exhaustion, despite every muscle screaming, I push forward toward that tiny beacon. Each step feels like a small victory, however fleeting. The moon hangs low in the ink-black sky, casting shadows that stretch long across the rocky ground. My heart pounds in rhythm with my unsteady footsteps, each beat driving me toward that distant glow. It feels like it's waiting for me, mocking my struggle, almost anticipating my downfall. My thoughts drift to Zahra, to the last time I saw her smile, and heard her laughter. It feels like a lifetime ago, a memory from a different world. I'll find her. I'll bring her home. No mistakes. No hesitation. I've prepared myself for this, for whatever comes next. Fear is just another obstacle, like all the rest. I'll go through them, over them, around them—it doesn't matter how. I'll get to her. She's out there, and I'm not giving up. The trees rise like sentinels against the star-filled sky, no longer passive observers but imposing giants, their twisted branches reaching out like claws. Shadows shift and dance, blurring the line between what's real and what's not. I feel the weight of isolation, the vast emptiness of these highlands pressing down on me. Out here, I realise, you're truly alone. Nature is in charge, and humans are small, fragile intruders. Life moves on without me, and I struggle to keep up. My legs feel like lead, but I keep forcing them forward. Every rustle of leaves sends my nerves into overdrive. The silence is oppressive, broken only by my ragged breaths and the quiet mutter of desperate prayers that do little to calm my racing thoughts. A sharp pain lances through my side, a hot, searing burn, and the bitter taste of blood fills my mouth. I clench my jaw, but every step sends another stab of pain through my body. It's like a knife twisting deeper with each movement, my body struggling to repair itself even as I push it further. Agility is out of the question—I'm just trying to stay on my feet. The tiny pinprick of light still glimmers ahead, a promise of hope in the darkness. And that's enough. For now, it's enough. The flickering light grows closer, revealing the entrance to what looks like a cave. Moss and ferns cling to the damp stone, a splash of green against the grey and brown earth tones. The opening is wide enough for a small group to pass through side by side, but just beyond, it quickly narrows into shadow. I move slowly, careful to keep my steps light and quiet. The cave entrance is half-hidden by overgrown branches and brush, and I can hear voices beyond it—low, muffled, just out of reach. I strain to catch their words, but they slip through the cracks of my understanding. Who are they? Are they dangerous?

My heart pounds, a rapid drumbeat in my chest. I inch closer, stepping carefully over loose stones that threaten to betray me. As I get nearer, the voices start to sharpen, still speaking Amharic. I hold onto the hope that I might catch a phrase I can make sense of, but I can only pick out pieces.

"…yasegal…," one voice mutters.

"…mefiten alebin…," another responds.

I freeze, holding my breath. Are they talking about me? I can't be sure. I need to get closer, but if they see me, it's over. I catch movement out of the corner of my eye and duck behind a cluster of large rocks. Three men emerge from the cave, their faces hidden beneath layers of dusty fabric. They move off to the left, their voices fading as they disappear into trees. I remain perfectly still, straining to hear them until their words blend into the sounds of the forest. When the silence returns, I let out a long, shaky breath, forcing my muscles to unclench. Once the coast is clear, I edge toward the cave entrance. The ground here is uneven, scattered with gravel and larger rocks that crunch beneath my feet. I move slowly, feeling the cool air from within, a damp, musty scent carrying hints of earth and the faint drip of water somewhere deep inside. I step into the darkness, and the world around me disappears—no light, no shadows. Just black. I press myself against the rough, cold wall, the stone damp against my back. My fingers trace the jagged edges as I try to steady myself. I clear a spot on the floor, brushing away bits of debris until it's as comfortable as it's going to get. The night's chill creeps into my bones, and I wrap myself in a scrap of old fabric, taking a swig from my dwindling water supply as I tend to my cuts and bruises. Exhaustion pulls at me, and I sink onto the cold ground, finally free of the elements that have pounded me for days. *I'm too old for this shit.'* The thought drifts through my mind, a half-smile tugging at my lips. I hope that Zahra is safe somewhere, far from this mess. The image of a warm fire and a hot meal flicker through my mind, offering a momentary escape from my reality. Here in the cave, I feel safer, if only just a little. I let myself relax, loosening my grip on the fear that's been my constant companion. My eyes slide shut, and I let my mind drift. Thoughts carry me back to simpler days. I remember lying in the tall grass of the Scottish Highlands, staring up at the rare patches of blue sky, dreaming of flying. My parents always said I could do anything, but as I grew older, those words lost their power, worn down by time and struggle. Still, in those quiet moments, I imagined the feeling of soaring through the clouds, weightless and free. But now, I'm grounded. Here, with the ache in my bones and the shadows pressing in, that dream feels impossibly far away. The cold seeps into me, but the cave walls offer some comfort. I take a deep breath, letting myself sink deeper into memory.

Reality blurs, and 1 m a kid again, running wild through open fields. The air is crisp, my legs are strong, and the sky is endless.

Then, the darkness pulls me back, thick and suffocating. I gasp, lungs straining, feeling the cave closing in. I try to hold onto those fragments of freedom, but instead...

Chapter 56

I'm soaring, weightless, like a bird. I can feel my body—my arms outstretched, my legs loose beneath me. The wind presses against me, cool and sharp, carrying me higher, like invisible wings are lifting me. Below, I see a village, a cluster of small huts scattered like broken teeth across the earth. There's a peace to it, but it's fleeting. Suddenly, everything changes. A chill grips me, and the sky above twists from soft blue to an ominous black, swallowing the light. The sun that was once warm on my skin now feels harsh and deceitful, and the clouds shift from soft pillows to dark omens. A fierce gust of wind slams into me, shoving me sideways. I'm nothing against the vastness of the sky, just a speck caught in its chaos. I try to break free, to escape the dark clouds closing in, but they wrap around me, suffocating, heavy, like they want to swallow me whole. A sour taste coats my tongue, bile rising up with the fear clawing its way up my throat. My thoughts spiral, twisting into something dark and frantic. 'This isn't real,' I tell myself, but the whispers are there low at first, growing louder, turning cruel. Voices, inhuman, mocking, spitting venom. They gnaw at me, each insult cutting deeper, pushing me to the edge of sanity. 'No, this isn't real. It can't be.' I repeat it like a prayer, desperate. 'It's all in my head. Just in my head.' But the voices don't stop, and the darkness keeps closing in. The line between what was real and what wasn't had blurred so completely that I could no longer tell the difference. And then, suddenly, Zahra was there, materialising as if from thin air. A soft blue glow surrounded her, lighting her up like something holy, her face gentle and full of promise. I reached out to touch her, desperate for that sense of comfort—but as my fingers drew near, her expression twisted, morphing into something hateful and cold. Her beautiful face turned into a malicious scowl, and whatever sense of salvation I had hoped for was ripped away. I lost control, like I was free-falling into the abyss, weightless, directionless. What had started as a dream, a peaceful return to a simpler time had shifted into something monstrous. The wind lashed at me, turning sharp and biting, terror replacing any sense of calm. I looked down, and the earth seemed small, and insignificant beneath the vast darkness around me. My heart pounded, each beat making it harder to think straight. Panic tightened its grip, whispers in my mind urging me to give in, to let the fear take over. Looking into the horizon, desperate for any sign of help, but all I saw were looming shadows—threatening, unknown. With each passing second, everything felt more vivid, more real, until it was impossible to tell where the nightmare ended, and reality began. Below me, massive plumes of dark smoke rose, curling up from burning structures. The screams carried upward, *slicing through the air, sharp and full of pain. It was a chorus of terror—people s voices mixing in agony, rage, fear. I saw them, like tiny figures scattered below—people running, scrambling for safety under the dark sky. Mothers clutching their crying children, men desperately trying to defend them with whatever they could get their hands on—sticks, rocks, their own bare fists. The attackers were faceless shadows, barely illuminated by the orange glow of the flames, sweeping through the village like an unstoppable wave. It was chaos. My instinct was to look away, to shut it out, but I couldn t. I was glued to the scene, unable to turn away from the horror. The flames twisted and rose, consuming everything they touched, casting flickering shadows that made the village look like it was alive writhing, struggling, dying. Every gruesome detail was burned into my mind, and I was powerless to stop it, powerless to change anything. It was as if I were a prisoner in my own nightmare, forced to watch as everything unravelled.*

The ground is covered with bodies, twisted and motionless in the dirt. Too many to count. Some are still moving, trying to crawl, but I can tell they won t make it far. The smell hits me again, stronger this time—acrid, thick with smoke and blood. It coats my throat, and I gag, trying to keep the bile down. The smoke clings to my skin, sticky and choking. Gunshots snap through the air, sharp cracks that cut through the chaos. The screams are worse—high-pitched, raw, desperate. My head is held in place, as if some unseen force refuses to let me look away, forcing me to witness everything. And yet, there s something surreal about it too. Up here, above it all, there s this eerie kind of calm. The sounds drift up to me, muffled by distance, and for a split second, it almost feels unreal. But then the screams break through, and the smell, the heat—all of it—feeds on my fear, until it s all I can feel. The more I panic, the more intense it gets, a cycle I can't seem to break. I can't control my flight. I m just being pulled along, powerless to stop it. I drop closer, forced to watch it all unfold but unable to do anything about it. The village is burning, and I m just... watching. Helpless. There s an ache in my chest—something deeper than fear or grief, like I m losing a piece of myself. I don t even know who or what it is, but the loss is there, gnawing at me. Below, the clearing looks like an arena—a place purpose-built for this violence, trapping people with no way out. The innocent has nowhere to run, and it feels like the whole scene is being played out just for me, like a twisted performance. This isn't warfare; it's a massacre. And then I see them. Creatures I thought only existed in myths or nightmares—beasts that belong in movies, not here. They rip children from their mothers' arms, their laughter echoing through the clearing, mocking the agony around them. It s that laughter that makes it worse. It s high, almost gleeful, as if they find joy in it all. The mother's screams tear through me, but I m frozen, unable to help, unable to even look away. I watch as the monsters behead the children in front of their mothers, and all I can think is: 'Why are they laughing?'

Husbands, brothers, sons—all of them stand frozen, waiting for their turn, unable to fight back. They re just... there, forced to watch as their families are torn apart, as the monsters devour the flesh of the people they love. I hear the sound of bones cracking, the screams stretching into the night, and I know that sound will stay with me forever. The wind carries it, making it echo in my head, and I know no matter what happens next, I will never be free of it. The entire scene is painted in horror—blood and shadows mixing to create something from a nightmare. I watch as the creatures, twisted hybrids of hyena, wolf, and something almost human, rip into their victims. Their matted fur is slick with blood, and their claws dig deep into flesh. The air is thick, the metallic tang of blood coating my tongue, choking me. Screams echo, bouncing through the darkness, each one more hopeless than the last. The ground, once untouched, is now soaked in crimson, a grotesque canvas of carnage. This isn't just a nightmare. It's too vivid, too real. It's unbearable. Everything escalates. A larger beast, its form even more grotesque than the others, explodes forward, lunging at a woman. It grabs her with brutal force, its talons digging into her skin. A man—trying desperately to protect her—stands frozen, his face twisted with helplessness. The scene is dim, everything swallowed in the blackness except for the horrific spotlight on them. The monster's powerful jaws tear into her, and her scream cuts through me like a knife. The man cries out too—a raw, emotional wail that seems to come from the deepest place of agony. Their voices blend in a symphony of anguish. Something tugs at me. There's a connection to the man— a familiarity I can't shake. His desperation feels like mine, and the woman… There's something about her voice that rips through me. It hits me like a punch to the gut. The realisation comes, terrifying and illogical, but unmistakable. Is he, is it… actually me, or a version of me? Panic grips me as the truth starts to form. I realise who the woman is. Can it be her…it is. It's her.' Suddenly, darkness falls like a heavy shroud. I feel like I'm being buried alive, the air around me heavy and thick, pressing down on my chest, crushing the breath out of me. Then, cutting through the suffocating void, a voice. It's familiar, dripping with malice, the words echoing with a twisted sense of triumph.

'Tommy, are you enjoying the show?" A laugh follows, cruel and unsettling. 'Did you see your wife?"

'No. Shut up. Shut the fuck up!" I gasp, my breath coming in sharp bursts, my chest heaving. My body jerks violently, forcing me upright, desperate to escape. 'Where is it coming from?" My eyes dart around the darkness. There's no one here. The room is empty, but I can still hear, that mocking voice.

My eyes snap open, and I'm out of the nightmare, but the images are still there, raw and vivid. The smell of burning flesh lingers, making bile rise in my throat. I try to slow my breathing and remind myself that it was just a dream. But the screams—they won't stop. They echo in my head, relentless. 'Was Zahra there? How could it be her? How could I be there?' My skin feels clammy, wrong, like it doesn't belong to me anymore. I want to tear it off, escape it, but I know I can't. I'm trapped in this body, in this mind, and I can't break free. The air is cold against my skin, but I'm burning inside. My chest ached, tight and constricted. My throat felt raw, like I'd been screaming. As fingers of light filter into the dark cave, I know morning has arrived. However, there is no sense of beauty or comfort in its arrival - only a sense of urgency. My veins throb with adrenaline, barely numbing the intense agony that courses through me. I push myself off the ground and take a moment to hydrate before stepping out into the morning light.

Chapter 57

My muscles are on fire, and my knees feel ready to buckle, but I keep pushing forward. The branches above sway, scattering the pale light of dawn in shifting patterns that make me squint. I raise a hand to shield my eyes, my boots crunching over leaves and twigs as I move deeper into the wild. Something catches my eye—a flutter of wings. A bird, vivid and bright, lands on a branch ahead, its feathers catching the sunlight in flashes of red and blue. The forest is alive with sound—rustling leaves, and scurrying creatures going about their morning routine, blissfully unaware of the chaos inside me. Nature doesn't care about my fears, my desperation. The woods hum their gentle tune, indifferent to my frantic search. I stop when I see a patch of grass, the blades swaying gently, green and stubborn. My eyes drift to the bark of a nearby tree, tracing the intricate lines and swirls that tell of years spent standing guard over this land. I let myself lean back against it, the bark rough against my spine, and let my legs give out. I slump down, trying to catch my breath, the air ragged in my lungs. A sudden rustle snaps me out of my daze. My head jerks up, eyes darting through the woods. The early morning light filters through the branches, painting the world in soft gold. For a second, everything looks calm, and peaceful. But I can feel it—something's off. There's a tension in the air, a shift in the shadows. I'm not alone. Then I see him—a tall figure a few yards away, standing still. He's wearing a worn, off-white robe, and for a heartbeat, fear grips me before I realise—he's just a shepherd. A herd of goats' cluster around him, his right hand resting on a wooden staff. Bright patterns are stitched along the edges of his robe, and a turban sits on his head, shielding him from the sun that's only just beginning to rise. Our eyes meet, and I see his surprise. He stares at me, his gaze sharp and searching, like he's trying to figure out what I'm doing here. He recovers quickly, though, his expression softening. There's a wisdom in his eyes, something deep, as if he's seen more of the world than I can imagine.

"Dehna neh?" he calls out, his voice gentle but laced with curiosity.

I freeze, caught off guard by the unexpectedness of it—of him, of his words. It's been so long since anyone's spoken to me like that. There's a kindness in his voice, something that momentarily grounds me, pulling me out of my fear, if only for a moment.

My throat was dry, the words stuck somewhere between my mind and my lips, my thoughts racing too quickly to make sense of them. All I wanted was to say that I wasn't a threat, that I needed help, but everything came out in a rasping croak. I tried to get up from the grass, but my legs, shaky and weak, betrayed me, giving way beneath me. The world spun, and I collapsed back down. Around me, the goats bleated loudly, their wiry coats brushing against the tall grass. Among the blend of brown and white, there was one that stood out—a black sheep, its rectangular pupils locking onto mine, an almost eerie awareness in its gaze.

The shepherd approached slowly, murmuring softly to his herd, his voice low and comforting. He herded them away from me with gentle nudges, his deep eyes meeting mine with a mixture of curiosity and caution. His presence, the way he moved—so calm, so deliberate—seemed to chase away the fear that had been building inside me, and I felt a strange, unexpected sense of peace.

I raised my hands slowly, palms up, a gesture to show I meant no harm. My throat burned as I forced out the words. "I'm... I'm not dangerous." The shepherd studied me, the caution still there, but I could see his posture soften, his eyes losing their edge. There was a moment—just a brief instant—when something shifted between us. A silent understanding. A decision not to be afraid. The sunlight caught his face, revealing the deep lines etched into his weathered skin, each crease telling a story of years under the sun, of life out here in the open. He reached down, extending a hand to me. Despite his frail appearance, his grip was solid and unyielding, effortlessly pulling me to my feet.

"Amesegnalehu," I whispered, hoping my attempt at his language made sense.

The shepherd's eyes narrowed, studying me. Then, after a moment, he nodded slightly, signalling for me to follow. "Teketelegn," he said, motioning to the right. I nodded, swallowing hard, feeling a small surge of hope as I steadied myself. He seemed to understand, and that alone was enough.

He paused, his eyes narrowing again, and reached into his dusty bag. He pulled out a battered metal canteen, holding it out to me. The canteen's surface was warm from the sun, and I hesitated for a second before taking it. His nod was subtle but unmistakable, urging me to drink. I took a small sip, feeling the water soothe my raw throat, bringing a momentary relief to my parched lips.

"Thank you," I managed to rasp out, handing it back to him. Our fingers brushed briefly, and in that tiny gesture, I felt a connection—a quiet, simple understanding. "Mita," I said, struggling with the words, my voice cracking. "My friend... I've lost her."

The shepherd's eyes softened, a flicker of something—empathy, perhaps—crossing his face. He gestured again, urging me to come with him. I pushed myself to follow, even though every step was agony. My muscles screamed, each step on the rocky terrain a fresh jolt of pain. I kept my eyes locked on his tattered cloak as we moved forward under the punishing sun. Sweat ran down my face, stinging my eyes, but I kept going. My side throbbed, the warmth of blood seeping into my shirt, but I bit down against the pain. I couldn't show weakness. Not now. Not in front of him. With my fists clenched and teeth gritted, I pushed forward, step by step, refusing to fall behind. The landscape had changed— the once gentle path was now a jagged, treacherous terrain of sharp rocks jutting out like bones. Each step was a battle. Suddenly, a low rumble echoed through the canyon, making my guide freeze. He cocked his head toward the sky, eyes narrowing. The rumble grew louder, a deep vibration that shook the ground beneath us. Without a word, he motioned urgently for me to follow. He moved faster, shielding his eyes against the sun's glare.

"Tolobel! Tolobel!" he shouted, a command I knew meant 'move—now.'

I picked up my pace, struggling to match his strides as we headed toward a forested patch up ahead. I tried to regulate my breathing, taking deep, steady breaths, but my legs burned with every step. Sweat trickled down my forehead, and I could feel the exhaustion settling in, but I didn't have time to slow down. Then, in the distance, I heard it—the faint roar of a waterfall. It was enough to give me a burst of energy, my feet moving faster as the sound grew louder, until it drowned out everything else. The sunlight filtered through the thick canopy above, illuminating our path in golden patches. Birds chirped somewhere in the distance, their songs blending with the rustle of leaves underfoot. We wound through the trees, the air cooler here, thick with the smell of wet earth and greenery. And then, we broke through, and I found myself standing on the edge of a cliff, staring at the waterfall in awe. Water cascaded down, crashing into a brilliant blue pool below, mist rising up in a shimmering haze. The canyon walls towered on either side, jagged and sheer, cloaked in lush greenery that clung to every surface, vines spilling over the rocks in wild tangles. It was as if the forest had swallowed this place whole, cradling the waterfall in a dense embrace of moss and leaves. Above us, the canopy was so thick that the sky was just a narrow slit of light. The air was alive here, buzzing with ancient energy, like I had stumbled into another world, a hidden realm untouched by time. The scent of fresh water and wet earth filled my lungs, mingling with the rich, earthy aroma of the plants. It was almost overwhelming but in the best way. Everything here felt alive, and vibrant, as if even the rocks were breathing.

"It's beautiful," I said, my voice barely louder than a whisper.

The guide turned to me, a smile flickering across his face, and nodded. He didn't need to say anything. The beauty of the place spoke for itself, a breathtaking reminder of the power and mystery of nature—something words could never truly capture. The cool breeze swept over my skin, and I closed my eyes, savouring it, letting it ground me in this moment. I looked out over the vast landscape before me—rolling hills, jagged cliffs, the spray of mist catching the sunlight. I could've stayed here forever, felt the earth breathing beneath me, but I had a mission. I turned to the shepherd beside me. He pointed to a narrow path, almost invisible, hidden behind the curtain of rushing water. He nodded, reassuring me without words. He knew where I needed to go. I glanced at him, and for a second, this place reminded me of an old photograph I kept framed back home, perched next to the TV. Except being here now, the real thing was so much more vivid. Raw. I took a step forward, and we both paused. We shared a smile—a silent recognition, a mutual appreciation. No words were needed. But still, I spoke.

"Thank you... Amesegnalehu," I said, my voice cracking a little as I tried to put my gratitude into words, my English and his language mixing together in a way that felt right.

"Ciao," he replied, smiling gently.

I turned and began to make my way down the narrow path. The ground beneath me seemed alive, pulsing with energy, every step resonating up through my boots. Off to my right, I spotted a troop of baboons on a rocky ledge, their dark fur slick from the waterfall's mist. They moved effortlessly, their eyes tracking me, curious but wary. One of them stopped and stared, as if trying to decide if I belonged here. I held its gaze for a second before it turned away. Birds darted through the air, their wings silent against the roar of the falls. Bright flashes of colour—vivid blues and deep crimsons—cutting through the endless green of the canopy. The path wound down steeply, hugging the cliff's edge, and I reached out, brushing my fingers against the damp moss that clung to the stone. And then, just like that, my thoughts shifted. Zahra. Her face filled my mind, her smile, the way her eyes softened when she looked at me. What if I never got the chance to say I'm sorry? What if she never knows how much I need her? I should've told her more—how much I loved her. I should've said it every single day. Does she know now? Or did I leave her with too many doubts, too many unanswered questions?

Chapter 58

By the crystal pool, where the water gathers, I spot a lizard sprawled on a large sun-warmed rock, its eyes watchful, its tongue flicking in and out as if tasting the air. The pool sparkles under the sunlight, vibrant greens and blues swirling beneath the glassy surface. I dip my hand in, feeling the cold water run through my fingers, trying to ground myself in its coolness. And then I hear it—Zahra's laughter. Light, carefree, dancing across the water's ripples, stirring something deep inside me. I close my eyes and whisper her name, so softly it's carried away by the breeze before I can even hear it myself. God, what I wouldn't give to hold her again, even just once. But there's nothing I can do except stand here, letting the cool mist of the waterfall spray my face, surrounded by this wild, untamed beauty. It almost feels like the forest is speaking, the rustle of the leaves like a language just beyond my understanding. Up in the treetops, I notice a troop of monkeys, their black-and-white fur standing out against the thick greenery. They move effortlessly, swinging from branch to branch, their calls blending with the thunder of the falls. It's been a long, difficult day. The cave this morning, the exhaustion building. I feel it now, creeping into my bones. I spot a mossy boulder nearby and make my way over, grateful for somewhere to sit. My pack slips off my shoulder, practically empty, but I take a moment to check it anyway. Only a few drops of water left. I finish them off and remind myself to refill before I move on. I lean back against the rock. It's damp, rough, but somehow comforting. I close my eyes, letting the rhythmic roar of the waterfall steady my breathing. In, out. Constant, like the falls themselves. The air is thick with moisture, and my mind begins to drift, the weight of the day slowly lifting. It's strange how it happens—one moment I'm here, feeling every ache and every exhaustion, and the next I'm just... fading. My limbs feel heavy, sinking into the earth, and the sound of the waterfall grows distant, like I'm hearing it from far away. And then I'm not fighting anymore, not holding on. I let go. Images flicker behind my closed eyes—shapes, shadows, fragments that never fully form. I feel myself fading, and I don't fight it. For once, it's a relief. The ground beneath me is cool, but I don't feel it anymore. The noise blurs into a strange kind of silence, and then, there's nothing but the dark.

And there she is. Zahra, standing at the water s edge, her figure glowing in the late sunlight. I try to call her name, but my voice cracks, fading into nothing before it reaches her. My throat tightens, and I can t even draw a full breath. She starts to fade, her image dissolving as if blown away by the wind, leaving me alone. I stand there, paralyzed by the silence, the clearing empty, my chest tightening.

"Fuck it!" I shout, my voice hoarse. The wind carries away my desperate cries, and as they fade, so does her mirage. I rub my hands over my face, feeling the dirt and the dried blood, the tears cutting clean trails through the grime. But no tears can touch the ache inside. *'Get up.'* Her voice is sharp, cutting through the fog of exhaustion. Zahra. I push myself off the rocky ground without thinking, my legs shaky, tears still blurring my vision. I think of Mita and Abiy—where are they now? Are they safe? I need to find them. I need to be with them, to know they're alright. Yet, I'm lost. I have no idea which way to go. My boots leave deep imprints on the damp earth as I move away from the waterfall, away from its beauty. What time is it? I don't know how long I've been out. The canopy above blocks out most of the light. Late afternoon, maybe. Branches snag at my clothes, thorns scraping against my skin as I push through the undergrowth. The forest is still alive with sounds, though softer now—nature's whispers, maybe offering encouragement, maybe warnings. I can't tell. My pulse quickens, and a low, restless hum settles in my stomach, a tension that's not quite fear. More like anticipation, the sense that something could shift at any moment. Out here, surrounded by cliffs and dense forest, I can feel something—something I can't explain. The earthy smell of damp leaves fills the air as I pick my way through the tangled roots and branches that seem determined to slow me down. I have no idea where I'm going, no clue where to find them, but I keep moving. I have to. Every rustle in the leaves, every bird call makes me jump, my thoughts spiralling through possibilities. Mita and Abiy have to be out here, somewhere. Just like me, lost and searching. The forest, once so full of life, now feels like a dark maze. I can't shake the fear—the thought of what might have happened to them, what might happen to me if I don't find them soon. I pick up my pace, driven by fear, by hope, by the need to know they're still alive. The forest shattered around me. A thunderous explosion ripped through the trees, the roar of gunfire splitting the air. Each shot cracked closer than the last, pounding in my ears. The ground beneath me trembled, and suddenly, the once comforting scent of pine and moss was replaced by something sharp, acrid a burning stench that stung my nostrils. It smelled like devastation. Smoke and sulphur filled my lungs as I stumbled toward the outskirts of what used to be a village. My throat tightened, eyes burning, and I doubled over, coughing, trying to spit out the ash that had already found its way deep into my chest. I kept low, moving forward, blinking away tears. The world had gone grey clouds of dust and ash choked everything, turning the remains of homes and buildings into nothing but shadowy outlines. Once sturdy houses now lay in splintered heaps, broken glass glittering among the wreckage. Figures moved through the ruins—villagers, their faces hidden behind makeshift cloth masks, searching through the rubble for something, anything they could salvage. Their movements were frantic, desperate.

My heart twisted painfully. Why was this happening to them? Where was Zahra? Was she somewhere in this chaos, scared and alone, calling for me? I took a piece of rag from my shirt pocket, pressing it against my face as I moved through the darkness. It wasn't just the night that was pitch black—the smoke smothered every glimmer of light, swallowing the stars, and leaving nothing but shadows. If Zahra were here, if she saw this destruction ravaging her homeland, it would break her heart. No—she *was* 'here. She had to be. I must believe that. I had to believe she was alive. It was the only thing that kept me going. But still, the thought troubled me: how do you keep going when the best part of you might be gone? My eyes scanned desperately through the haze. Where were Mita and Abiy? Fear clawed at my gut, a sickening dread that they, too, were lost in this chaos. My thoughts were a frantic jumble when suddenly, cutting through the noise of gunfire and shouting, a small voice reached me—a child's voice, high and sharp with fear. I didn't hesitate to follow it, my feet moving on their own accord towards the sound. In the middle of the village square, a young girl stood alone, clutching a ragged doll to her chest. She couldn't have been more than seven or eight. Her eyes were wide, tears cutting paths through the soot on her cheeks as she scanned the faces rushing past her, searching. Our eyes locked, and for a second, everything else—smoke, fire, fear—fell away. I knelt in front of her, the weight of everything—soldier, protector, husband, human—settling heavily on my shoulders. Whatever I was searching for could wait. Right now, the only thing that mattered was her. I knelt down to her level, speaking as softly as I could, trying to sound like I was someone she could trust. "Hey there, are you okay?" I asked though the words felt useless. Her wide eyes met mine, scared but hopeful. "Do you know where your parents are?" She just stared at me, her little brow furrowed in confusion. I doubted she understood a word of what I was saying. Slowly, she shook her head, her grip tightening around the small, worn doll in her hands.

"Hede," she whimpered, her voice barely more than a breath.

The sight of her—this tiny, trembling girl in the middle of a warzone—made my chest clench. Flames licked at the building behind us, and the snap of gunfire echoed through the air. Soot smeared her clothes, and her cheeks were streaked with dirt and tears. She looked so fragile, so lost. I couldn't leave her here. I couldn't.

"Take my hand," I said, holding my hand out to her.

She hesitated, staring at me for a long moment, then slowly reached out, her small fingers wrapping tightly around mine. There was strength there, surprising and heartbreaking at the same time—a trust she shouldn't have to give a stranger. Not here. Not now. I pulled her closer, shielding her from the smoke and chaos around us, trying to move quickly, keeping her head down as we moved through the debris. The remains of her village lay scattered, walls collapsed into dust, and makeshift shelters reduced to nothing. My arm wrapped protectively around her, and she coughed against my shirt, the sound so small and weak that it broke something inside me.

"It's going to be okay," I whispered, though my own heart hammered against my ribs, the words more for me than for her.

I didn't know if it would be okay. I didn't know if we'd even make it out of here alive.

Suddenly, she tugged at my sleeve, her eyes wide as she pointed towards a cluster of smouldering ruins.

"Temelket," she said, her voice shaking. I followed her gaze and saw what she was pointing at—a group of people huddled together beside a collapsed wall, their shapes barely visible through the haze. She tugged harder, her voice rising up, desperate.

"Alright," I said, nodding. I tightened my hold on her hand, and we moved cautiously towards them, weaving through the shifting crowds, people searching for loved ones, calling out names that were lost in the roar of flames and cries. Faces blurred together—fear, confusion, anguish. I scanned each one, looking for anyone who might be waiting for her, praying that this would be over soon. Then I saw her. A woman, her traditional dress stained with soot and blood, her hair once neatly braided, now a mess of tangles. She held a small bundle to her chest, her eyes darting around wildly.

"Selam?" I called, the unfamiliar Amharic word clumsy on my tongue. Her head snapped towards me, eyes wide. When she saw the girl standing beside me, her face broke open with relief. She rushed forward, her arms opening, and I let go of the girl's hand, watching as she flung herself into the woman's embrace. The woman knelt, holding the child close, her voice a stream of comforting words that I couldn't understand. I stood back, giving them space, my chest loosening just a little. The look on their faces—the raw relief— it was enough for now. Enough to feel like I'd done something right in this hellhole.

Another explosion went off, closer this time, the shockwave rattling my bones. My legs nearly gave out, exhaustion turning my muscles to lead. I watched as the woman gathered the child into her arms, moving quickly with the rest of the villagers, disappearing into the darkness of the trees beyond the village. I stood there, watching until they were gone, until I was sure they were safe. I turned away, my eyes drawn towards the mountain beyond what was left of the village. Zahra. The thought of her, somewhere out here, kept me moving, and pushed me forward even though every part of my body screamed to stop. I picked my way through the rubble, the remains of people's lives scattered across the ground—clothes, broken furniture, pieces of what used to be homes. The noise of the battle grew louder as I moved—the rattle of gunfire, the cries and shouts, the crack of something exploding. It was chaos. It was hell. And I had to get out of here. Faster. My legs stumbled, the ground uneven, my breath ragged, each step a battle of its own. I wasn't young anymore—God, I could feel every year of my age at that moment—but I kept going, driven by the one thing that mattered. I had to find Zahra. I had to make sure Mita and Abiy were safe. I had to keep moving, because stopping meant dying, and I wasn't ready for that. Not yet. I climbed, my hands and knees digging into the dirt, slipping on loose rocks. My body was beyond exhaustion, but the fear was worse—the fear of what was coming behind me, of the soldiers shouting, of the gunfire closing in. I pushed myself up, forcing one foot in front of the other. I had to make it to the top of this hill. I had to find some place to hide, some place to rest, even if just for a moment. My vision blurred, my head swimming from exhaustion and smoke. Somewhere in the distance, I could hear them—the soldiers, their voices echoing, a reminder that they were still there, still coming. I had to move faster, even though every step felt like it might be my last. I had to find shelter. I had to survive. Just a little further. Just one more step.

CHAPTER 59

"When the heart is sad, tears will flow."

Ethiopian proverb

The sun crept over the horizon, its rays piercing through the canopy above, waking me with a warmth that felt almost out of place. I had collapsed here, beneath this acacia tree, last night—my body giving up after hours of running, hiding, surviving. It had been too dark to see clearly, and I had no choice but to drop wherever I could, hoping it would be enough to keep me hidden. I hadn't cared about comfort. All I needed was a moment to stop, a moment to breathe. I must have passed out instantly; I could've slept through a marching band thundering past. Now, everything around me seemed too quiet, too still—until my thoughts filled that silence with the face of the little girl from yesterday. She'd been crying, her cheeks streaked with dust and tears, her eyes wide and filled with something more than fear. I could still hear her trembling voice, and see her tiny hands shaking as she held onto me. It wasn't just her; there had been so many people, faces I couldn't forget. And I knew I couldn't let them go—because if I didn't remember them, then who would? Someone had to bear witness. I forced myself up, groaning as I shifted my weight, the damp ground beneath me cold and littered with fallen leaves that stuck to my clothes. The earthy scent filled my nostrils, making me sneeze, and pain shot through my ribs—sharp enough to make me suck in a breath and pause. I blinked, trying to ignore it, focusing on the space around me instead. There were birds, flitting between branches, calling out to each other. The distant sky was washed in soft greys, clouds drifting lazily over the ridge. I could see the slope I'd climbed last night—it looked impossible in the daylight, steep and unforgiving. How had I made it up there? Maybe the adrenaline had made me braver than I knew. The wind rustled the leaves above me, whispering a warning, and for a moment, I let myself pretend I was somewhere else— anywhere but here. But the distant rumble of an explosion shattered that illusion, a deep, echoing boom that rolled through the valley. Birds scattered from their roosts, and small creatures darted from the brush. I watched them disappear, wondering if any had slept beside me, wondering if I'd shared this place with a mole rat—or worse, a hyena. I'd been too exhausted to know, and that alone told me just how far I'd been pushed. I pulled myself up, my muscles screaming in protest. The ground seemed to sway under me, my vision blurring for a moment before settling. I wiped my eyes, my hand coming away damp—tears I hadn't noticed. I had to keep moving. There was no staying put. Somewhere ahead, there was a reason to keep going, a flicker of hope that whispered, you will survive. You will endure. You will find a way.

And then, like a mirage forming in the dawn light, I saw her. Standing in the distance, her face lit by the sun—Zahra. Her head held high, her gaze piercing right through me. I blinked, shook my head, tried to focus, and the image shifted. It wasn't Zahra—it was Mita. And beside her, Abiy. I exhaled, something between a sob and a laugh escaping me, my vision blurring again, but this time from pure relief. They were here. They'd found me. Mita ran to me, wrapping her arms around me, her warmth cutting through the coldness that had settled in my bones. Abiy was right behind her, his eyes bright, his grin wide, and I held onto them both as tightly as I could, as if letting go would mean losing them all over again. It felt like an eternity since I'd last seen them, though I knew it had only been days. Time had lost all meaning here—the days were just a blur of running, hiding, surviving, trying to hold onto something that felt like hope.

"Tommy!" Mita's voice cracked, thick with emotion. "We thought we'd lost you."

Abiy clapped me on the back, his relief palpable. "Thank God you're safe, man."

I pulled back, looking between them, my chest tight. "Where were you guys?" My voice came out rough, strained—too much silence had left it rusty.

Mita glanced at Abiy before meeting my eyes. "We found shelter in an old building for the night. We couldn't risk moving in the dark. And... there was this little girl. She told me a white man had helped her." She paused, her eyes searching my face. "She mentioned hyena-like creatures."

I shook my head, the memories still hazy. "I didn't see any hyenas. Thought I heard something, but... everything was jumbled. I couldn't tell what was real."

Mita's expression softened, and she reached for my hand, squeezing it. "Doesn't matter. You're here now. We're together again."

I nodded, swallowing hard. The relief was overwhelming, a flood that threatened to drown me if I let it. This place was taking everything from us—time, hope, sanity. It just kept taking. But here, with Mita and Abiy beside me, there was something to hold onto, something to fight for. Maybe—just maybe—we could start taking something back.

"We're going to make it," I whispered, my voice almost lost in the wind, but Mita smiled, and Abiy nodded.

"Damn right we are," Abiy said, his eyes fierce. "We're not done yet."

Mita's dark eyes glimmer, caught between wonder and worry as she gestures back toward the path they found me on. "The girl said she saw you heading this way. She'd never seen a white man before, so I figured it had to be you." She smiles, a warmth that reaches her eyes, softening the lines of her face. "How are you feeling?"

"Is she okay? Did she find her family?" I ask, my voice hurried, almost desperate. For a moment, Mita's expression falters. She looks away, her gaze drifting to the forest floor, and I already know the answer before she says a word.

"We left her with her aunt," she finally says, her voice barely above a whisper. "Her parents..." Her words trail off, leaving the rest unsaid. The silence hangs between us, heavy and raw. I feel a pang in my chest, a familiar sadness settling in, and I let myself sink back onto the soft grass, surrounded by the towering trees and the gentle, indifferent symphony of nature.

The silence stretches until I can't bear it. I force myself to speak. "Any updates?" I ask, though I'm not even sure I want the answer.

Mita glances at me, her expression weary but determined. "No changes," she says, her voice taking on that familiar tone—the one that tries to soften the harshness of reality. "We'll be yomping today, heading north." She grins slightly, her lips twitching upward. It's a term I'd taught her—one of those military words, foreign to her but now comfortably part of our strange little shared vocabulary. We sit together for what feels like hours, Mita and the others sharing their stories of being separated. Their voices rise and fall, weaving a tapestry of pain, loss, and small moments of hope. When I ask about Solomon, Mita's face goes still, her eyes clouding over. She takes a shaky breath.

"Solomon's at a clinic nearby," she says, her voice quivering, "with his family. It's makeshift, barely holding together. Supplies are thin. Insurgents have cut off most of the routes." She pauses, her hands trembling as she speaks, and I reach out, giving her fingers a gentle squeeze.

Mita's voice grows softer as she continues, recounting her escape from the compound—how she'd been separated from Abiy, how she found him in the woods later, exhausted and scared but alive. Her hands tremble as she talks, and I can hear the fear still in her voice, the way it hasn't quite left her, the way it's latched onto her bones. The sky darkens slowly, the day slipping into night. We huddle close, our bodies pressed together for warmth as the chill seeps into the air. Despite everything, despite the fear and the uncertainty, there's a strange comfort in being here, together. I close my eyes for a moment, letting myself feel it—the gratitude, the relief. We're still here. We still have each other. But even as we try to rest, a sense of unease lingers. The darkness feels heavy, the silence too deep, and I can't help but feel like danger is watching, waiting—hidden somewhere beyond the trees, in the shadows of the undergrowth, just out of sight. The kind of threat you can't see, but you know is there, lingering like a breath on the back of your neck.

CHAPTER 60

The sky was barely awake, and we were already on the move, scrambling to gather what little we had left. Mita and I exchanged a look—a silent reassurance that no matter what, we were in this together. Everything hurt; my body screamed at every step as I stumbled forward, dragging my feet over loose rocks. The thin cloth I'd wrapped around my head did almost nothing against the sun, which was already threatening to scorch us. Mita led us, agile as ever, while Abiy kept to the rear, his eyes constantly scanning the horizon, watching our backs. It was a rhythm we had fallen into—Mita leading, me in the middle, Abiy guarding us from behind. Every now and then, we'd come across a cluster of buildings—some small and crumbling, others more intact, as they'd only recently been left behind. It was clear people had fled, some of them in a hurry. We broke into the ones that looked abandoned, and took whatever we could find—food, water, even a proper head covering for me. I was still missing a pair of sunglasses, though. The brightness of the day felt like a hammer pounding into my skull, each pulse of light making my head throb. These empty homes felt heavy with their own stories, as if the walls were whispering the tragedies of the people who'd once lived there. It didn't take much imagination to know most of those stories didn't end well. We'd been moving since dawn, speaking little to conserve our energy. It wasn't just physical exhaustion that weighed me down, it was the mental drain—the endless walking, the aching muscles, the constant sense of danger hanging over us like a dark cloud. The sun beat down relentlessly, and the ground seemed to stretch forever in front of us, a vast wasteland of jagged rocks and dusty earth. My throat was parched, and sweat stung my eyes, blurring my vision. The air was thin, making every breath a struggle. We slid alongside the highway, ducking behind whatever cover we could find. There were armed checkpoints everywhere, men with guns blocking the way forward. We moved like shadows, avoiding detection. It felt like a twisted maze meant to break us, but I wasn't going to let it. Every challenge, and every obstacle we faced only hardened my resolve. I kept my eyes on the path ahead, gravel crunching beneath my boots, each step a reminder that I was still alive, still moving.

The village ahead was different. It was alive, bustling with movement. We approached cautiously, aware that any place with people could be dangerous. There were signs everywhere—walls riddled with bullet holes, homes reduced to rubble. The enemy had been here, and the damage spoke for itself. We moved silently, weaving through the ruins, our boots crunching over debris that had once been people's lives. Bloodstains marked some of the crumbling walls, dried and dark, reminders of the violence that had swept through. Abiy's eyes carried a weight of sadness as he took it all in, while Mita's gaze remained hard and focused, refusing to let emotion slow her down. Turning a corner, we were hit by the unmistakable stench of death. A body lay sprawled across our path, eyes staring vacantly, mouth open in a silent scream. My stomach churned, bile rising in my throat. I fought the urge to vomit, clenched my jaw, and forced myself to step over it. Keep moving. Always forward. To hesitate was to risk everything. Up ahead, the village faded into silence again— just the remains of what had once been, covered in dust and loss. We moved carefully, avoiding the places that looked unstable. Gunfire echoed somewhere in the distance, followed by silence, the kind that made your skin crawl.

"Just keep moving," I muttered, more to myself than to anyone else.

The stories we'd heard—the tales of what these people had endured—were beyond horror. It felt personal, like an attack on all of us, even though we hadn't been here. Zahra would never have stood for this kind of brutality. The thought of her brought me both comfort and fear. I kept seeing her in every shadow, hearing her voice in every whisper of wind. It made my chest tighten, a mix of grief and fury surging through me. My eyes stung, tears that I stubbornly refused to let fall. It wasn't just sadness—it was rage. A deep, blistering anger at the injustice of everything. My teeth ached from clenching them too hard, and as I spat out a mouthful of blood, I realised how close I was to completely unravelling.

"Forward," I whispered again, my voice barely audible

Mita's voice cut through the tension, firm and unwavering. "Watch your footing," she said, pointing at a pile of loose rocks hiding a steep drop-off. Her dark eyes never wavered, focused on the path ahead. She didn't need to turn around to know Abiy and I were right behind her.

I nodded in thanks, and Abiy did the same. My thoughts kept circling back to the men they called 'Bouda' or 'the Eye' or whatever the hell they were named. The ones that had taken Zahra—or maybe it was just my mind twisting the truth. I still wasn't sure if they even had her, if she was really out there, or if this was all just a delusion. It felt like their presence was choking me, a suffocating weight that I couldn't shake. The sun began to dip, casting long shadows over the landscape. We found a small clearing, a cluster of huts scattered around. Children played in the dirt, their laughter ringing out, blissfully unaware of the danger that lurked just beyond the trees. Adults stood on the edges, their eyes weary, their expressions guarded. Abiy flashed one of his rare smiles at a group of women drawing water from a well. They looked at him warily, their faces marked by fear and exhaustion. For a moment, I envied them—their innocence, their unawareness. But there was no room for envy now. Only survival.

"Smile," he said, a smirk tugging at the corner of his mouth, his voice dripping with smug confidence. "It disarms them."

His English was heavily accented, but the meaning came through clearly enough. I tried. I really did. My lips cracked painfully as they twisted into something like a smile. It must've looked more like a grimace, especially with my face caked in dust and my throat dry as sandpaper. Still, I reached out my hand, hoping to show them we came in peace—that we were allies, not enemies. But before I could make any real headway, Mita's sharp voice cut through the tense air.

"We need to keep moving," she snapped, her eyes darting left and right, scanning the tree line like an animal sensing danger. There was no room for hesitation, no time to try and make friends. The urgency in her voice jolted me back, and I could see it—a wildness in her eyes, the way they flicked from shadow to shadow. She wasn't just scared. She knew something was out there. We moved. Fast. The earth seemed to grab at our feet, each step sinking into the soft dirt, slowing us down, but we kept going, Mita in the lead. There was something wrong, a prickling sensation crawling up my spine. I felt exposed, like something—or someone—was watching us from the shadows, tracking our every movement as the sun sank behind the trees, leaving nothing but the dim glow of dusk. Mita picked up her pace, her breath coming in quick bursts.

"We'll rest when we find cover," she whispered, her voice tight.

The fear was unmistakable now, lacing every word. I pushed myself to keep up, my lungs burning, and my legs aching. I wanted to ask her what she saw—what she knew—but the look on her face told me better. Her gaze was a warning, and I didn't want to hear the answer. The last streaks of sunlight stretched across the sky as we left the village behind us. My mind betrayed me then, showing me flashes of Zahra's face—her smile, once so bright, replaced with a hollow emptiness. She stood, shackled to that tree, her eyes dark and vacant. They'd placed two stones in her palms—one for Samuel, the other for his daughter. I felt the bile rise in my throat and shook my head, trying to force the image away. My foot caught on something, and I stumbled, nearly falling face-first into the dirt.

"Keep moving!" Mita hissed, her grip like iron as she grabbed my arm, yanking me back upright. Her eyes met mine, and for a second, I could see past the fear. There was something else there, something desperate. "Don't look back," she said, her voice breaking slightly. "Just keep moving."

I nodded, swallowing hard, and forced myself forward. The memory of Zahra faded into the background, replaced by the immediate need to survive. To keep moving. To find cover before whatever it was—whatever was out there—found us first.

CHAPTER 61

Our path was anything but predictable, shifting beneath our feet as if the devil himself was at work, laying traps at every turn. The villages were no safe haven; they felt like a spider's web waiting to ensnare us, each stranger a potential threat. We had to be sharp, fast, and invisible.

"Over here," Abiy whispered, pointing to a shaded spot off the road. "Less visible."

I nodded, urgency thrumming in my veins. We pushed through the thick brush, brambles clawing at our clothes. "We're running out of time," I muttered, my voice tight with anxiety. Mita caught my eye, her expression unwavering, her eyes blazing with determination.

"For Zahra," she said, her voice steady. "We need to be smart and quick."

"Smart and quick it is," I shot back, swallowing down my fear. Every second slipping away was another lost chance to find her.

We reached the edge of the market, and Mita shot me a warning look. "Stick close," she said. "We're outsiders here, and information isn't something people are willing to share."

I gave a quick nod, my eyes scanning the chaotic market scene. Stalls filled with trinkets, dusty produce, and worn faces; everyone moved with purpose, no one sparing a second glance at us. We spread out, asking questions, probing for any news of the missing girls, for any hint of Zahra. Mita took the lead, her voice cutting through the chatter, demanding answers with a force that made people pay attention—if only for a moment. But the responses were the same: blank stares, dismissive shrugs, eyes that turned away.

"No luck," she said, her face etched with frustration as she regrouped with us. There was a flicker of something else there—disappointment, maybe even fear.

"We can't give up," Abiy urged, his dark eyes filled with a fierce resolve.

I nodded, wiping sweat from my forehead. We moved on, each rejection a punch to the gut, but we pressed forward, our resolve as unwavering as the relentless sun above us. The tension was suffocating, every moment a countdown we couldn't afford to ignore.

"The Bouda has everyone scared," Mita said grimly, her jaw tight.

"Then we fight them," I snapped, memories rising unbidden—violent, dark memories. The kind that twisted something deep inside me. I wanted to believe there was another way, but each second we lost chipped away at that hope. Zahra needed me. If I had to be a monster to save her, then so be it.

The day slipped into dusk, and the heat gave way to a biting chill. I found myself whispering her name, "Zahra," like a prayer.

"Zahra," Mita and Abiy echoed softly, their voices filled with the same mix of desperation and determination.

The village faded behind us, swallowed by the dark. The road ahead was a mystery—full of dangers seen and unseen, but we had no choice but to keep moving forward.

"Watch your step," Mita said sharply, grabbing my arm as I stumbled over a loose stone. I managed a weak smile, a silent thanks, but my mind was elsewhere, tangled up in fear and hope.

We huddled beneath a jagged boulder, seeking warmth, shelter—anything that might make the night more bearable. The cries of unseen animals echoed in the distance, and I tried to sleep, but Zahra's face haunted me. Her laughter, her smile, her small hand in mine—all of it just out of reach.

"Tomorrow," I whispered, barely audible. "Tomorrow, we'll find answers."

No one responded, but the question hung in the air anyway—Would we find her in time, or would it already be too late? Sleep eventually came, dragging me under, though it offered no comfort.

Dreams danced behind my closed eyelids—half-formed images of reunion, torn apart by flashes of despair. A voice echoed, haunting and taunting: It's too late; she's already in the beast's belly!

I woke with a start, gasping, my skin slick with sweat. Dawn had just begun to creep in, the sky tinged with pale light. Mita and Abiy were already awake, their faces serious, shadows etched beneath their eyes. The sun's first rays spilled over the horizon, painting everything in gold. Time to move. My body protested, sore and tired, but I pushed it aside. Pain didn't matter—not today. We walked for what felt like forever, though it could've only been an hour. Just like I had done countless times before, I ignored the ache in my legs and focused on the mission. The Marines had taught me that much—keep moving, no matter what.

"Akum," Abiy hissed, his hand shooting up, signalling us to stop.

We froze, breath clouding in the cold morning air. A low rumble echoed in the distance, growing louder with every passing second. I turned just in time to see a truck barrelling down the dirt road, kicking up a storm of dust. My heart leapt into my throat—friend or foe? We didn't have time to decide. The truck screeched to a stop, so close I could feel the heat off the engine. Men jumped out, rifles slung over their shoulders, their eyes cold and calculating. A tall man stepped forward, a scar running the length of his left cheek.

"Where are you going?" he demanded in heavily accented English, his gaze unflinching.

I swallowed, forcing calm into my voice. "We're looking for someone," I said. "A girl. Zahra Abete."

The name hung between us, and for a heartbeat, everything was still. I watched their faces, searching for any flicker of recognition. There was a shared look between them—brief, but enough to twist my gut. They knew her.

"Get in," one of them ordered, gesturing to the back of the truck. His voice was low, but there was no mistaking the command.

Mita's hand tightened around my arm, a silent question. But what choice did we have? I nodded, and we climbed into the truck bed. The vehicle roared to life, and soon we were bouncing over the uneven terrain, clinging to whatever we could to stay upright. Abiy held tight to the side rail, a flicker of defiance in his eyes. I could tell he was contemplating something reckless, but we had no cards to play—not yet.

"Where are you taking us?" I yelled over the noise, my voice nearly lost to the wind.

"Aticheneku," the driver shouted back, smirking. His expression gave away nothing.

The truck threw us around like ragdolls, each jolt sending pain shooting through my back. My mind spun, running through possibilities—where were they taking us? Would we find her, or were we heading straight into a trap? Anxiety clawed at me, gnawing at my resolve with every mile that passed. Suddenly, the truck jerked to a stop, the sudden momentum flinging us forward. I squinted through the dust, spotting a makeshift barricade of rusted oil drums and barbed wire. My heart hammered in my chest—this was it. Was this where we'd find answers, or was this the end of the line?

"Wuto!" someone barked, and I jumped down from the truck. My senses sharpened— the glint of sunlight off the barbed wire, the hard set of the men's faces, their eyes empty of emotion.

"Tolobel!" they grunted, shoving us towards a battered building scarred with bullet holes.

"Zahra?" I called, my voice cracking with desperation. Silence. Only the wind in reply. "Zahra!" I tried again, but no one answered.

"Bezih Bekul," one of them muttered, and I didn't understand the words, but the meaning was clear enough—keep moving.

I took a deep breath, steadying myself. The darkness of the building loomed ahead, and I stepped into it, my heart pounding. I had to find her. I had to know. The silence inside was heavy, and oppressive, and my voice came out as a whisper this time.

"Zahra," I called, but there was no response, only emptiness. It felt like we were caught between two worlds—the hope that she was still out there and the creeping dread that we were too late.

We were in limbo, teetering between hope and despair, and all I could do was keep moving, one step at a time.

CHAPTER 62

*"When one walks carefully, thorns hurt only
lightly."*

Ethiopian proverb

The building was unremarkable, just another crumbling structure in a city that had seen far too much. But the smell—roasted meat mingled with the sharp scent of incense—drifted toward us, making my stomach twist. Above us, the starry sky stretched endlessly, tiny beacons in the dark, a reminder of something bigger, something hopeful. I tried to focus on that as Mita moved ahead, her slim frame cutting through the shadows with practised ease. I stayed close, my steps echoing off the cracked concrete walls. Every creak, every whisper of sound put my senses on high alert—footsteps, distant barking, the murmur of low conversations—each one a potential threat. As we passed through darkened halls and locked doors, Zahra's face flashed in my mind—her radiant smile, her laugh that could light up the darkest of days. Those memories kept me moving and kept me from drowning in fear. I had to keep going for her. Nure appeared from the shadows, a tall figure with a worn face and eyes like dark pools, deep and unreadable.

He extended a hand, his grip firm. "Welcome," he said, his voice low and rumbling.

He motioned for us to follow him, and I did, my eyes scanning the room—taking in the worn faces, and the tattered uniforms. These weren't soldiers in the traditional sense; they were people who had been through hell and back, their eyes carrying stories of exhaustion and resolve. Mita translated his words as Nure pointed to a map spread across a makeshift table. Her voice was quick and strained, and I could see her knuckles turning white as she gripped the edge of the table. Soldiers were gathered around, their uniforms patched and frayed. There was something in their eyes that broke my heart—the fatigue, the haunted look of people who had seen too much. I couldn't help but notice the women among them, fierce and unyielding, rifles slung over their shoulders. They reminded me of the stories I had heard about the female warriors of Ethiopia—women who would defend their land to their last breath. Zahra was like that. I remembered the first time she stepped foot in Cardiff, how she shoved a man away from me at the bar without hesitation. She was always ready to protect those she loved. Mita's voice trembled as she translated the next part—Zahra's captivity. My fists clenched, and I struggled to keep my breathing steady. Her laughter, her smile, her eyes—they played in my mind, one after the other, until I thought I'd break. I stared at the map, tracing the lines and symbols with a finger, trying to keep my focus on the task. The air was thick with tension, filled with overlapping voices and frantic movement as people exchanged hurried information.

"Over there," a young man stepped forward, pointing to a wrinkled map. His eyes were burning with determination. "Past the crumbling mill, east of the river. That's where they'll keep her, along with the others."

His conviction cut through the chaos, and I could see my own desperation mirrored in his eyes. I turned to Mita, my hand trembling as I gripped her arm. "What about the families?" I asked, my voice almost a whisper, afraid of the answer.

Mita met my eyes, and I could see the pain etched into her expression. "No survivors," she said quietly, her voice hollow. "They slaughtered them all. Right here. In front of their families." She gestured to the ground beneath our feet, her face blank, like she had nothing left to give. The words hung in the air, heavy, suffocating. I looked down, trying to imagine the horror that had unfolded here, and it left me feeling hollow, like a piece of me had been ripped away.

I couldn't stand it any longer. "Zahra," I cut in, my voice trembling. "We focus on Zahra."

Mita paused, then nodded. I could see the tears glistening in her eyes, but she wiped them away, straightening her back. There was no time for sorrow, no time for anything but action. We needed to bring Zahra home, and I wasn't going to let anything stand in my way.

"We need to concentrate on Zahra," I repeated, louder this time, my voice cutting through the chatter.

Heads turned, and the room quieted, a dozen eyes now fixed on me. It wasn't just about Zahra—although, God knows, she was everything that drove me. It was about justice, about righting a terrible wrong. It was about taking down the people who had brought us to this moment, who had inflicted so much pain and suffering.

Nure nodded solemnly, his finger tracing lines on the map. "This is the plan," he said, and everyone leaned in. We began to mark checkpoints, and map out enemy activity—every detail critical, every moment precious. I soaked in every word, every directive, my focus sharp.

After the meeting, I stood back, watching the people around me—my new allies. They were huddled together, sharing warmth, a jug of honey wine being passed among them. Some chewed on khat leaves, their eyes wide and weary, looking for some escape, some momentary peace. They were strong, but I feared for them. I could see the pain in their eyes—the not knowing, the hollow, endless wait for loved ones who might never return. It broke my heart to see it, but it also made me want to fight harder, to make sure no one else suffered like this. And then there was Zahra—always Zahra—alone somewhere out there, fighting her own battle. The thought of her in pain, and scared, made my chest ache, but it also fuelled me. I couldn't let fear win. We broke into our teams—Mita and I would take reconnaissance. It wouldn't be easy, but nothing worth fighting for ever was. Zahra's safety gave us purpose, something to hold onto in the chaos.

CHAPTER 63

Under the cover of night, we move cautiously, the brush clawing at our clothes, and mosquitoes biting at any bare skin they find. We keep going, step by careful step, knowing we have to reach the compound before sunrise. The darkness is our friend, but it also hides threats, every rustle or snapped twig sending my nerves on edge. It feels like hours before we finally make it to the hill, crouching low behind the foliage. Below us, the compound sprawls out—a large building at the centre, surrounded by smaller huts, all encircled by a barbed fence. We watch in silence, tracking the movement of guards, the dim light catching the glint of their rifles. We memorise the rotations, and the gaps, looking for weak points, any place where we could slip through. The air is thick, and my stomach churns with tension, but we hold our ground until, we're sure. Then we retreat, making our way back to camp, exhaustion hanging heavy on our shoulders. The camp is barely more than a collection of scrappy tents. We sit together, too tired to care about the sweat or grime or the ever-present stink of oil and gunpowder. Nure hands me a compact semi-automatic, his eyes bloodshot and hollow. He takes a long breath before speaking, his voice low and rough.

"Be quick, be quiet," he says. He glances down at the gun, then back at me, his shoulders slumping as if the weight of everything we were about to do was resting on him alone. "Look, we're stretched thin here. We can't spare anyone else for this mission." He pauses, his gaze softening as it meets mine. "But we can at least give you some weapons, something to help keep you alive."

I nod, trying to keep the disappointment off my face, but it's hard. We risked everything to get here, and now it feels like we're alone again, with nothing to show for it.

"However," Nure says, rubbing a hand over the stubble on his chin. He looks exhausted, his voice barely a rasp. "We'll set up a diversion. The far side of the compound. It might give you the window you need."

I take a deep breath, letting the words sink in. A diversion. A chance. I focus, mapping out the plan in my head—using the chaos to slip in, to find Zahra. Mita nods beside me, her lips pressed into a thin line, a small flicker of hope in her eyes. Nure starts laying out the details, his voice still thick with fatigue, and I repeat the words in my mind like a mantra: Timing is everything. Timing is everything. The images of Zahra flash in my mind—her smile, her laugh—and I feel something tighten in my chest. She's out there, somewhere, waiting for me, and every part of me wants to rush in, to break down whatever walls separate us. But I know better. One wrong move, one hesitation, could cost me everything. Could cost us everything. The three of us—me, Mita, and Abiy—sit huddled around the small, flickering oil lamp. The map is spread out between us, its edges worn and stained, the ink smudged from years of use.

"If Bouda has Zahra, she'll be here," Abiy says, pressing a finger onto the cluster of buildings marked on the map. His voice is steady, but I can hear the tension underneath. He cares about Zahra too—we all do.

"We need a solid plan," Mita says, her eyes meeting mine, dark and determined.

I trace my finger over the map, my eyes narrowing as I think. "The rear entrance," I say. "It's less guarded at night. Fewer watchers." I look up at them. "It's our best chance."

Mita nods, her expression unflinching. Abiy leans forward, studying the routes. "Once we're inside, we stick to the shadows," I continue, swallowing hard. "Move silently, swiftly. We don't get caught. We don't stop."

"And if something goes wrong?" Mita asks.

"Three short whistles," Abiy suggests. "It'll cut through the silence without drawing too much attention."

I nod. "That works." I glance at them, one by one, letting the weight of what we're about to do settle in. We're all part of this, all pieces of a fragile plan. "We bring her home. That's all that matters."

We lean over the map again, fingers tracing the lines, debating the best route in and out. "The eastern wall is crumbling," Mita says, her finger running along the edge. "We could climb it, get inside that way."

Abiy shakes his head. "Too exposed. We'd be sitting ducks. The northern route's longer, but we'll have more cover."

I consider both options, Zahra's face flashing in my mind, and I know what I have to choose. "We go north. We take the extra time and stay concealed."

Mita nods, folding the map carefully. "Then it's settled."

We finalise the details, every word and plan weighed against the risk of what we're about to do. My heart pounds, but there's a strange calmness in the air as we prepare. I check my weapons—the second AK slung across my back, the dagger strapped to my side. My hands shake as I fold the map, tucking it into my pocket. That piece of paper holds everything we're fighting for.

"We should rest," I say, though the word feels strange. Rest is the last thing on my mind, but I know we need it.

The others nod, exhaustion written across their faces. I settle down, my mind drifting to Zahra. I imagine her beside me, her hand slipping into mine, her smile telling me that we'll make it, that we'll see each other again. I hold onto that thought. I have to. Without her, I wouldn't survive. I can't lose her. Not now. Not ever.

CHAPTER 64

I'm going in, and I'm coming back with her. Simple as that. People die here every day fine. But not her. Not me. We'll make it out. I have to. Come on, Tommy, remember your training! You've done this before, and you can do it again. Sure, I'm not as young as I used to be, but I've got enough left for one more fight. One last time. The cold night air stung my lungs as I took a deep breath, trying to steady the tremor in my hands. Time had taken its toll—I wasn't the same as I used to be. My knees ached, and my joints protested with every movement. I was asking my body to do things only a younger version of myself could accomplish. But I had to give it my all. This is my final chance; please, let me succeed one last time. My finger tightened on the trigger, seeking reassurance in the cold steel beneath my fingertips. I focus on that feeling, trying to calm the chaos in my mind. But it was Zahra who truly gave me strength. The thought of her, trapped somewhere in that compound, pushed me onward. I follow Mita's steps, mirroring her movements as she slips through the shadows ahead. She's swift and steady. The compound rises ahead, a hulking shadow against the night, born out of desperation—a prison that shouldn't exist. No room for fear now. No room for error. We wait, huddled in the shadows, crouching low, adrenaline pumping through every vein. My breath fogs in the freezing air, though the darkness swallows any mist before it can rise. The stars are hidden behind clouds; there is only blackness, thick and suffocating. Our plan is simple: wait for Nure's distraction, then slip in through the side. Crouching in the cold mud, my heart pounds in time with the distant explosions. The air reeks of sweat and gunpowder, the ground trembling beneath us. But then, that fucking voice, slithers into my mind—a sinister whisper that digs in, unsettling and sharp. I bite back the urge to scream at it, to tell it to fuck off. Focus, Tommy. One wrong step and it's over. For all of us. Suddenly, a blinding flare lights up the sky, and the compound shudders with a nearby explosion. Dirt and debris rain down, turning the night into a whirl of chaos. Gunfire crackles in the distance, each shot like a knife edge slicing through the dark. I flinch, pressing closer to the earth, the ground vibrating with the violence. Mita signals, her hand cutting through the smoke. She's all sharp edges and tension, but her face is set with resolve. I follow, edging closer to the breach point. In the chaos, guards scatter like panicked animals, chasing shadows in the dark. This is our moment. Mita slips through, moving like a ghost, taking down two men before they even realise she's there. Her knife flashes, then disappears, leaving only a brief, choked gasp behind. I catch up to her just as a guard lunges out of the shadows, too close. Without thinking, I closed the distance, my knife flashing in the dim light. I drove it into his throat, feeling the resistance as the blade went in, the warmth of his blood spurting over my hand. He gargled, eyes wide with shock, then collapsed. My stomach churned at the sight, but there was no time for hesitation. A twisted satisfaction burns in my chest, but Abiy's voice snaps me back.

"Enhid!" he hisses, dragging me back to the present.

I nodded, swallowing hard. Focus. Zahra was the goal. Nothing else mattered. We reached the wall of the compound, pressing ourselves against it. Mita gestured towards the entrance—just a few feet away. We waited, watching the guards run towards the distraction. Now.

"Mita, with me," I said, my voice low but firm. "Abiy, secure our exit."

Abiy gave a curt nod. "Got it." His eyes met mine, a silent promise passing between us. We had come this far, and we weren't leaving without her.

I watch guards stumbling through the dark. Mita and Abiy flank me, breathing low and steady, like we're all part of the same machine.

"Standby," I whisper, my voice a thread in the darkness. "We move when they're gone."

Mita gives a short nod, her eyes darting over the landscape. "Just a little longer."

I exhale, barely daring to blink as the guards disappear around a corner. "Now," I mutter, more to myself than anyone else, "let's move."

Mita stays close, her steps mirroring mine as we slip through the shadows into Zahra's prison. She's my shadow, the one who keeps me tethered to reality. Abiy lingers behind, keeping watch. When we reach the door, I grasp the handle, feeling the cool metal seep into my skin. The door creaks as I push it open. The room beyond was dim, the air thick with dust and the acrid stench of old smoke. My heart pounded as I scanned the shadows. There—in the centre of the room, bound and gagged, was Zahra. Her eyes widened when she saw us, tears glistening, a mix of fear and disbelief. Relief floods through me, so fierce it nearly drops me to my knees.

"Zahra," I whispered, my throat tightening. I rushed forward, but before I could reach her, a figure stepped out from the darkness—a tall, gaunt man, with a cruel smile on his lips. He raises a machete, but I didn't give him the chance. I squeezed the trigger, and he crumpled, the sound of the shots deafening in the small room. I raise my rifle and fire, the shots punching through the air. He crumples, but then two more emerge, knives flashing. I didn't have time to think, I barely had time to react. I threw myself forward, fists swinging. The world narrowed to the struggle—the grunts, the blows, the sharp sting of a knife grazing my arm. Mita fired, her shotgun barking out death, the blasts echoing like thunder. She finishes one off with a swift slash of her knife. I throw my weight into the last attacker, feeling the crack of bone under my fist, and the heat of blood on my hands. The room smells of sweat, blood, and gunpowder—too thick to breathe.

Finally, it's over. The bodies lie still, shadows stretched out on the floor. I turn to Zahra, her face bruised, with streaks of dirt and blood. I dropped to my knees, my hands trembling as I untied her bindings. She looked up at me, her eyes filled with both fear and relief. How did I let this happen? I swallow hard, the taste of iron and ash bitter on my tongue.

"Zahra," I murmur, barely more than a breath.

"Tommy," she whispered, her voice cracking. She lifts her head, meeting my gaze. Her chestnut hair hangs in matted tangles, her face a map of pain.

"We're getting you out of here," I said, my voice breaking. I pulled her into my arms, her body trembling against mine. "We're going home."

She manages a faint nod, and I help her to her feet, her weight pressing into me as we move. "Let's go home," I add, trying to inject hope into my voice, even though the word feels like a lie. I squeeze her hand, clinging to the warmth of her grip like it's the only thing keeping me tethered to this moment.

"Home," she echoes, the word catching in her throat like a question she's too afraid to ask. She leans against me, wincing at the contact, but her steps are steady.

"We need to move," Mita said, her voice urgent. "They're regrouping."

"Right," I said, supporting Zahra as we made our way towards the exit. "Stay close. I've got you."

The hallway was dark, the air cold and filled with the distant sounds of gunfire and shouts. We moved as quickly as we could, Zahra leaning heavily on me. My heart pounded, every creak of the floorboards making me flinch. But then, voices echo through the hall—men closing in on us. We have to change direction, slipping through a side passage.

"Dammit," I mutter under my breath, and Zahra gives me a small, pained smile. We turn another corner, only to find our escape route blocked by a locked door. Mita's eyes dart over the room, desperate for another way. Abiy was there, working at the lock, his fingers moving deftly.

"Almost... got it," he muttered, sweat beading on his forehead.

A shout from behind. A guard. He raised his rifle, and I moved without thinking, throwing myself between Zahra and the threat. The gunshot rang out, pain exploding in my side. I gritted my teeth, refusing to let go of Zahra.

"Tommy!" Mita screamed, her shotgun blasting the guard away.

"Abiy, the lock," I urge.

He nodded, pulling out his tools. His fingers moved deftly, but time was running out. Footsteps thundered behind us. A guard appeared at the end of the hallway, his weapon raised. There's no time to think—only to act. I reacted on instinct, lunging at the man. We collided with a bone-crunching impact, falling to the ground in a tangle of limbs. I fought like an animal, using every ounce of strength left in my body. I drive my fist into his jaw, feeling bone shatter under the impact. I hit him again and again. My hands are shaking, covered in his blood. With a fierce cry, I landed a swift and satisfying strike, sending him crashing against the wall with a deafening thud. He slid down the wall slowly, crumpling to the ground in a heap. The victorious rush in my chest was immense, almost overwhelming. I stood over him, chest heaving, every breath as ragged as if I'd just emerged from deep water. His body lay twisted, his limbs splayed awkwardly, a grotesque testament to the chaos of our confrontation. This wasn't about revenge—it was about survival. About Zahra. I could still see her terrified face in my mind and hear her desperate cry. The thought propelled me, forcing me to block out the searing pain from my bruises and focus on what mattered: getting her to safety. I glanced down at the weapon lying near his outstretched hand. My fingers wrapped around its hilt, the cold metal familiar, almost comforting. My knuckles whitened, and my pulse roared in my ears. I stared at the man on the floor—not a man, not anymore—a monster who had threatened everything I held dear. He looked up at me, his eyes glassy and unfocused, but there was something there—a flicker of fear. He knew it was over. His lips parted, and a broken sound came out, like he was trying to speak. I didn't care what he had to say.

"Fuck you," I whispered, my voice a ragged snarl. The words came out almost involuntarily, a release of everything bottled up inside—fear, anger, the bone-deep determination to protect Zahra. I couldn't let him hurt anyone else. Not ever again. Then I released a primal roar that echoed off the walls, I drove the blade into his chest. The impact reverberated up my arm, flesh and bone giving way beneath the force. His eyes widened, a gasp escaping his lips, a final pitiful sound that quickly faded to silence. The flicker of life in his eyes dulled as they rolled back, and then—nothing. I held the blade there for a moment, my breaths coming in shallow, uneven bursts. The room was silent now, save for my own breathing and the distant echoes of the chaos outside. Slowly, I pulled the knife free, my arm trembling from the effort. His body slumped lifelessly, the last remnants of tension gone. I swallowed hard, blinking against the sting of tears. The satisfying weight of the weapon in my hand was now heavy with the realisation of what I'd done. I glanced towards the door, towards Zahra, knowing I had to move. There was no time to dwell. No time to process. She needed me, and I wasn't about to let her down. I turned on my heel, leaving the body behind without a second glance. I had to protect her. At any cost.

"Move," I bark, my voice rough, desperate. We don't have time.

CHAPTER 65

Abiy's hands trembled as he fumbled with the rusty lock, his sweat dripping onto the metal. I could hear the rasp of his breath and see the anxiety in his eyes as he twisted the key. With a final desperate jolt, the lock gave way, and we pushed the heavy door open, slipping into the cool night. The air felt like a relief, wrapping around us as if to say, *'You're almost free.'* But then, the sound of a scuffle reached my ears. My heart lurched as I turned to see a shadow emerge from the dark—a rebel, his face twisted with rage. He lunged at Abiy, grabbing him by the neck and pulling him back with terrifying strength. The twisted smile on his face as he raised his bloodstained machete made my stomach plummet. My hands went numb, and my body froze as I saw the blade arc downward. The sickening crunch of metal on bone echoed in the night, the spray of blood painting my face in a warm mist. Abiy crumpled to the ground, his eyes wide open but unseeing. The world felt like it narrowed to a pinpoint—just the sight of his lifeless body, his blood pooling dark and thick beneath him. I wanted to scream, but the air caught in my throat, every breath a struggle against the grief clawing at my chest.

"No!" The word tore itself from me, a cry lost in the chaos.

My heart pounded in my ears as I raised my rifle, barely aware of my own movements. I fired, two shots ringing out in quick succession, and the rebel fell. His body hit the ground with a hollow thud, eyes staring vacantly at nothing. I dropped to my knees beside Abiy, my shaking hands hovering over him. But he was gone—he'd been gone the moment that blade came down. I felt the weight of it—a senseless loss in a place that had taken too many lives already. There was no time to mourn; Zahra and Mita's frantic shouts broke through the fog in my mind. I forced myself up, each movement heavy, as if I was underwater. I glanced down at Abiy one last time, swallowing back the bile that rose in my throat. I wanted to promise him something—that I wouldn't let this be in vain—but the words wouldn't come. There was only one truth here: we had to survive.

"Tommy! Come on, we have to move!" Zahra's voice was frantic, her eyes wide with terror.

Suddenly, the sharp rattle of gunfire erupted around us. Bullets whipped past, thumping into the earth. We threw ourselves to the ground, scrambling behind a boulder. My breath came in ragged gasps, and I dared a glance over the top. Figures moved through the shadows, angry shouts carrying through the night. They didn't know where we were, not exactly, but they were coming intent on making sure none of us left this place alive. I looked at Mita, her eyes locking with mine. There was fear there, yes, but also determination. We had no choice. I nodded, and together, we emerged from cover, firing back at the approaching men. The muzzle flashes lit the darkness, each shot a desperate plea for survival. I felt the rifle kick against my shoulder, and smelled the acrid tang of gunpowder. The men fell, one by one, their bodies crumpling into the dirt. It wasn't victory—it was survival, nothing more. The night went quiet again, the echoes of gunfire fading into the dark. My chest burned, each breath searing my lungs. Zahra was beside me, her face pale but her eyes steady. She looked at me, and for a moment, we understood each other without words—we were still here. We were still alive.

"We have to keep moving," I managed to say, my voice hoarse.

We moved silently, slipping away from the compound. The night air chilled the sweat on my skin, the adrenaline slowly ebbing away, leaving only exhaustion. We paused under a tree, the compound just a shadow in the distance now. Mita let out a shaky breath, her eyes wet with unshed tears. Zahra closed her eyes, whispering a prayer under her breath, her hands clasped tightly together. I listened to her words, feeling the weight of them—a plea for forgiveness, for Abiy, for what we'd had to do to survive.

We moved on, each step heavy with everything we'd seen, everything we'd lost. Abiy's face flashed in my mind, his laughter, his hope. It wasn't supposed to end like this. But as I looked at Zahra, her eyes filled with determination, I knew we couldn't stop. Not yet.

"Home," Zahra whispered, her voice barely audible.

"Home," I repeated, the word feeling like both a promise and a hope—something to hold onto, even in the midst of all this darkness.

CHAPTER 66

I tried to locate the source of the gunfire, but the thick undergrowth and dense trees seemed to echo the sounds from every direction, leaving me disoriented. We had stumbled into what remained of a nearby village—a place half-devoured by violence. There were still people here. Why hadn't they left? Why? We huddled behind a crumbling wall, my rifle clutched in trembling hands. My heart dropped when I realised the magazine was empty. Bullets tore through the air, and explosions shook the ground beneath us, filling my nostrils with the harsh stench of burning. But it was the screams that hurt the most—screams of agony that seared into my soul, drowning out everything else. I was powerless to help them. Helpless. This was hell—the violence erupting not just here but everywhere, the gunfire relentless. I pressed myself against the wall, willing the rough surface to swallow me whole, to make me invisible. My chest heaved, struggling for control. The rifle slipped from my grasp, falling to the ground, useless without ammo. All I had left was a small blade, the only thing standing between us and death. The crunch of approaching footsteps on the gravel made my blood run cold. I raised a trembling finger to my lips, silently begging Mita and Zahra to stay quiet. We couldn't be found, not now. Memories of my family flashed in my mind—their faces etched in fear, as if they were looking down on me from above. I squeezed my eyes shut, tears blurring my vision. We had to survive, for them. My fingers curled around Zahra's hand, clinging to life. I braced myself, knowing we might have seconds left. But the footsteps faded, leaving behind only the distant roar of gunfire. We stayed frozen, barely breathing, until silence settled over us. Slowly, I raised my head to peek over the wall, scanning for movement. The village was quieter now, but it was a silence filled with pain—the sobs of survivors, the crackle of flames licking at what was left of their homes. I gave Mita a nod, and we inched out of our hiding spot, bodies aching and battered from the strain.

It wasn't over. The war still raged on, the bloodshed far from done. But for now, in this brief lull, we were still alive. We moved cautiously, sticking close to the shadows, creeping through the rubble-strewn streets. Every sound, every shifting shadow, kept my heart in my throat. I turned to Mita and Zahra, their faces pale, eyes wide—they looked like frightened children waiting for reassurance. I swallowed hard, knowing they depended on me.

"Stay close. Stay quiet," I whispered, the words barely audible over the distant gunfire.

Mita nodded, her jaw set, her eyes filled with determination. We moved, using debris to shield ourselves, crouching low. My knees scraped against the jagged rubble, pain radiating through my body. Zahra stumbled beside me, her breath coming in sharp, shallow gasps. I gripped her arm, helping her stay steady. Suddenly, we heard a cry—a gut-wrenching scream of pain piercing through the darkness. Mita and I exchanged a glance. I shook my head, silently urging her to move on. We couldn't do anything for them. Not now. We had to survive. We reached the end of an alley, crouching behind a damaged wall. The moon hung above us, casting a pale, eerie glow over the devastation. My eyes darted from one potential danger to another—a collapsed building that could hide an ambush, a darkened doorway that might conceal the enemy. Mita took the lead again, her steps careful and deliberate. I felt Zahra's breath against my neck—a reminder of the fragile life I was trying to protect. Our goal was simple: make it to the outskirts of the village. Find somewhere safe. Regroup. Plan our next move. Every step forward felt like a victory. Every breath we took was borrowed time. The crunch of boots on the gravel returned, louder this time, and my heart pounded in my ears. We dropped to our knees, pressing ourselves against a pile of rubble, trying to disappear into the debris. I could feel Zahra trembling beside me. My hand found hers, squeezing it in reassurance. I nodded at Mita, who had her knife ready, her eyes wide but resolute.

"We just need to get out of here," I whispered, my voice cracking. "We have to keep moving."

Mita nodded. Her gaze shifted to a door nearby—plain, unassuming, our only chance. She motioned for us to move. We crawled across the street, keeping our bodies low, and our breaths shallow. We reached the door, and Mita pushed it open carefully. The room inside was dark, the air thick and stale. We slipped in, closing the door behind us. Safe, at least for now. I sank to the floor, exhaustion hitting me all at once. Zahra slumped against me, her head resting on my shoulder. I kept my knife within arm's reach, my gaze fixed on the door, watching for any sign of movement outside. Mita stood near the window, staring out into the moonlit chaos beyond. The weight of my choices, of every decision that had led us here, bore down on me. My hand found the top of my head, the rough stubble of my shaved scalp beneath my fingers. I let out a shaky breath, refusing to cry. Not here. Not now. We had made it this far. We would keep going. We had to. For our families, for each other, for a future that still seemed possible, even in the midst of all this carnage. The war wasn't over. But for tonight, we were alive. And that was enough.

Chapter 67

Mita interrupted my thoughts, her face lined with worry. "Tommy," she said, her voice barely above a whisper.

I let out a tired sigh, rubbing my temples as the weight of exhaustion settled over me. "Tomorrow," I murmured, the word feeling heavy on my tongue. "Tonight, we rest."

We huddled close, battered but determined. My mind kept drifting to the Boudas—their strength, their brutal revenge. We needed to be quicker, smarter, more strategic. Surviving wasn't enough anymore; we had to find the source of this toxin that threatened everything we held dear.

I looked at both of them, Mita and Zahra, meeting their eyes with what little resolve I had left. "We've come this far," I said, my voice a rasp. "But we've pissed them off good. They're not done with us. We have to be ready for whatever comes next."

Mita's hand found mine and Zahra's, her grip firm, her gaze unflinching. The memory of Abiy, Samuel, and those innocent girls flashed across my mind. A fear settled in the pit of my stomach—the kind that lingered even when you were too tired to think. I was scared to close my eyes, scared of what I'd see if I did. Scared they'd be there, waiting for me. The silence of the room pressed down on me, too still, too empty. Sleep wasn't coming, no matter how hard I tried. I shut my eyes, hoping maybe this time would be different, but instead, that familiar buzzing filled my head—like my mind was running full speed, refusing to rest. In the dark, I whispered her name. Zahra turned her head, her eyes meeting mine—glistening, the tears barely held back. She radiated a deep sorrow, but even then, the corner of her mouth lifted, just a little, like a flicker of light in the darkness. I squeezed her hand, trying to offer whatever comfort I could.

"We've endured the worst humanity has to offer," I said, my voice low, a whisper between us. "But look at us now—together."

She gave me a sad smile, her voice soft. "I love you, Tommy." Her gaze never wavered.

"I love you too," I answered, a warmth spreading through me despite everything. "I wouldn't have come all this way if I didn't."

Outside, the wind screamed through the branches, a chorus of howls that slipped through the cracks, stealing whatever warmth remained. I wrapped my arms tighter around Zahra, trying to share whatever heat we had left. Our makeshift shelter groaned under the force of the wind, the branches above creaking like they might splinter at any moment. The moonlight filtered through the gaps in the walls, casting faint, silvery beams onto the dirt floor. My breath left me in small, frosty puffs, barely visible in the dark. Even with Zahra's body pressed close to mine, the cold crept in, chilling me to the bone. The echoes of the fight were still in my ears, drowning out the quiet—but her steady breathing, the warmth of her beside me, it helped. It calmed the storm inside me, if only for a moment. I thought of the innocent people still out there, fighting just to survive on their own land. They weren't just fighting with weapons—they fought with their hearts, with everything they had left. We needed allies. We needed to trust strangers, and that kind of trust—born of desperation—was fragile. It could shatter at any moment. The line between friend and foe was always blurred. Around us, the dark was alive, magnifying every sound. A sudden cry from a nightbird startled me, echoing in the emptiness. And somewhere in the distance, wolves called out to each other, their howls haunting as they cut through the night.

I whispered Mita's name, seeing her silhouette by the window, her form outlined against the faint moonlight. She looked over her shoulder at me, her eyes weary but alert.

"We leave at dawn," I said, my voice barely carrying over the wind. "It's not safe here." She gave a curt nod and disappeared back into the shadows, ever watchful.

I turned to Zahra. Her eyes were wide, reflecting the fear I felt in my own chest. I gave her a small, reassuring smile—though I wasn't sure who I was trying to comfort more, her or myself.

"Are you ready for what comes next?" I asked, my voice a hushed murmur against the storm outside.

She nodded, her hand tightening around mine. "As ready as I'll ever be."

CHAPTER 68

"When the hyena is gone, that is when the dog barks."

Ethiopian proverb

The sun crested over the horizon, spilling light across the Ethiopian Highlands, and I gripped Zahra's hand, the tension between us almost unbearable. Our eyes locked, and I knew she could see everything I felt—fear, desperation, and the faintest glimmer of hope. Her eyes held mine, and she squeezed back, fiercely. It was a promise: we would find a way out of this together. The early hours had dragged on, sleepless and suffocating, the three of us unable to do anything but listen to the guttural cries of our pursuers echoing across the highlands. We huddled together, sharing sips of water and tending to each other's wounds. Zahra's tangled hair clung to her face, matted with blood and dirt, while Mita stood leaning against a wall, her eyes hollow from exhaustion and pain. It was almost surreal, like a scene from a horror film. But there was no director calling cut—no script to save us. Zahra's body pressed against mine for warmth and comfort. Mita watched me, her eyes filled with hope but also fear—an expectation that I might have a solution to get us out of this nightmare. I took a shaky breath. It wasn't the best plan, but it was all we had.

"Remember the lions?" I whispered, my voice barely audible over the rustling leaves.

Zahra's eyes widened. She knew what I meant. The lions—our special place—a secluded spot we'd visited once near her hometown. Mita stiffened beside us, realising what I had in mind. When the realisation sank in, fear washed over their faces. I hated seeing it there, hated that this was what we had to do. But we had no other choice.

"You two need to hide there," I said, my voice trembling. "Stay hidden until I come back. I'll draw them away."

Zahra shook her head, her lips trembling. "No, stop. Don't say that…" Her voice cracked, and she swallowed, trying to keep the tears at bay. "We'll wait for you. You'll make it back."

My heart twisted painfully. I forced myself to meet her gaze, my thumb brushing the back of her hand. "I'll do everything I can to be there. But if I'm not… you keep going. Understand?"

She closed her eyes for a moment, fighting the tears, then nodded. Mita's expression was hardened, her resolve forming like armour over her fear. I turned away, the last thing I saw being Zahra's tear-streaked face, and ran, branches whipping at my clothes as I disappeared into the forest. I moved fast, ducking under branches, and leaping over roots. Each step was fuelled by the terror that if I slowed, even for a second, they'd catch up. I had to make enough noise, create enough chaos, to keep them focused on me—not on Zahra, not on Mita. The forest closed in around me, the thick green canopy above hiding me from view. It was good; it would slow them down too. My breath burned in my chest, and I screamed into the forest, my voice raw and desperate. I wanted them to know where I was. I wanted them to come for me. I heard movement—the crack of a branch, and muffled footsteps. They were close. I kept running, dodging trees, slipping through narrow gaps where the underbrush was thickest. Anything to slow them down.

A man's voice echoed through the forest, sharp and commanding. "Tesebsebu! Eyashofebin new!" Another responded, even closer. "Hulunim bota fetishu!" I had no idea what they were saying, but I could guess well enough—they were hunting me, and they weren't giving up.

I stumbled forward, my foot catching on an exposed root, and I nearly went down. I caught myself just in time, my heart pounding. If I tripped, it was over. Keep moving. Keep going. I had to believe Zahra was safe. I couldn't think otherwise. I wouldn't. The forest swallowed me, the echoes of their pursuit fading. My lungs screamed for air, my legs feeling heavier with each step, but I couldn't stop. The memory of Zahra's face flashed in my mind—the way she'd looked at me when I'd whispered our plan. I clung to it, letting it drive me forward. Suddenly, the trees opened up, and I found myself at the edge of a village. It was eerily empty, the narrow alleys lined with weathered brick buildings. A poster flapped against the wall, its edges curling in the breeze. I ducked into one of the alleys, my footsteps echoing against the cobblestones. Where was everyone? My heart pounded in my ears, the adrenaline keeping me going as I moved blindly, searching for any way out. A goat bleated nearby, the sound startling me. I bit back a curse, forcing myself to stay focused. The voices of my pursuers were distant now, scattered through the forest, but they'd be here soon. I pressed myself against a wall, feeling its cold surface against my back, my torn clothes sticking to my skin. Gunfire cracked in the distance, and I flinched. What were they shooting at? Had they found Zahra? No. They had to be safe. I had to believe that.

"Tommy!" The voice cut through my thoughts, clear and mocking. It was in my head—it had to be. I clenched my jaw, pushing the panic down. No time for that. No time for fear. I needed to get to the river—to the lions.

I moved again, slipping between the alleys, the dust kicking up beneath my feet. The streets seemed endless, twisting and turning until I felt completely disoriented. I pushed forward, stumbling through the underbrush until I heard it—the rushing of water. The river. Relief flooded through me, and I headed toward it, the sound growing louder with every step. My legs ached, my muscles screaming for rest, but I couldn't stop now. I broke through the trees, the river glistening under the moonlight. I could almost see it—our spot—where Zahra would be waiting. I had to believe she was there. That she was safe. I stumbled down the slope, my breath ragged, my vision blurring with exhaustion. Somewhere behind me, the distant cries of my pursuers faded into nothing. The forest swallowed their voices, leaving only the sound of the river and the whisper of the wind through the leaves.

"Move," I muttered to myself, my voice hoarse. "Keep going. She's waiting."

Zahra's face filled my mind—her smile, her laugh, the way her eyes shone when she looked at me. She was my reason for everything. For every step I took, every breath I forced into my lungs. I couldn't let her down. Not now. I pushed forward, the river beside me, the path ahead leading to our meeting spot. I had to make it. For her. For us.

CHAPTER 69

I scrambled down the steep gully, slipping on loose gravel, my body moving faster than my fear. I couldn't feel the pain in my hip anymore—I wasn't sure if that was a good sign or a bad one. The only thing that mattered was reaching the clearing. When I finally saw the two familiar lion statues standing sentinel, their weathered faces bearing old scars, I ducked behind a tree, grateful for its cover. My breath was ragged, every exhale amplified by the silence. I tried to control it, pressing my back against the rough bark. It was just about waiting now. They should have been here by now. I kept repeating that it was no time for panic, that they might have been forced to hide—and that they were just waiting for the right moment to slip away undetected.

I closed my eyes, muttering under my breath, "They'll be here. They'll be here." But I couldn't ignore the gnawing pit of doubt in my stomach.

The forest felt alive, almost conscious. The rustling leaves and shrill bird songs made it hard to tell what was real and what was just my anxiety playing tricks on me. Insects buzzed around, their high-pitched hum adding another layer to the dissonant symphony. I tried to focus, my body trembling uncontrollably, but the effort was exhausting.

"Fuck," I whispered, my voice barely audible. "Where are they?"

The moon was beginning to fade as dawn approached, its dim light casting everything in muted shades of grey. The shadows seemed to have their own intentions, whispering threats to both hunter and hunted. And I knew—deep down, I knew—I was the prey tonight. My side throbbed with a deep, sharp pain. I looked down; the bleeding had stopped, but it still looked bad. I couldn't afford to think about it. Not now.

"Come on, Zahra," I whispered, staring at the path that led into the clearing. Every second stretched into eternity. I fidgeted, unable to stay still, my eyes scanning every inch of the darkness. "Please, just be safe. Please." I rubbed my eyes, trying to keep focused, but my belief was cracking, my fear growing stronger with each tick of the clock.

Suddenly, a rustle from the treeline. My eyes snapped to the source of the noise, and I squinted, trying to make out the figures. It wasn't Zahra or Mita. Two pairs of eyes stared back at me, unblinking, glowing faintly in the moonlight. My heart pounded as I crouched lower. "Hyenas?" I muttered, but the thought felt wrong. One of them stood up—almost upright—its chilling gaze fixed on me. Whatever they were, they weren't human. I reached for the knife strapped to my thigh, my hand trembling. I blinked hard, trying to convince myself it was all in my head, a figment of exhaustion and fear.

Then, out of the shadows, a figure emerged stumbling, battered. Zahra. She was limping, her face streaked with dirt and blood, but it was her. Mita was with her, equally bloodied but alive. Relief washed over me like a wave, my entire body sagging against the tree. The knife slipped from my hand and fell to the ground. "Zahra!" I gasped, breaking cover and running toward her, my eyes fixed on her and nothing else.

The hyenas—or whatever they were—had vanished. I didn't care where they went. All that mattered was Zahra. The moonlight caught her features, highlighting every bruise, every cut. She looked up, her eyes searching, and then she saw me.

"Tommy!" she called, her voice cracking. It was faint, nearly lost among the forest's sounds, but it reached me.

And then something moved. A flash in the corner of my vision—something rushing towards her from the underbrush. "Run!" I screamed, my legs propelling me forward, every muscle straining as adrenaline surged. She turned, eyes wide with terror, Mita right behind her. The creature closed in, its movements fast, unnaturally fluid. My heart pounded in my ears, my pain forgotten. I had to reach her before it did.

"Zahra, move!" I roared. My knife—shit, I had dropped it. I pushed myself harder, watching the gap between Zahra and the creature narrow. Ten feet. Five. With nothing but rage and desperation, I launched myself at the thing, my fists slamming into its body.

The impact sent us both sprawling, and I didn't stop. I hit it again and again, my knuckles cracking against bone, my vision blurred by tears and fury. It wasn't human. Its face twisted, its colours dark and unnatural. I snarled, unrelenting, my fists pounding until it was nothing but a mess of black and red beneath me. I couldn't stop. I wouldn't. Not until I knew she was safe. I rained down merciless strikes on the anonymity. Blood spattered, and oozed everywhere—on the ground, in my hands, arms, and body. I keep striking, each hit satisfying in its own way. It was a brutal place I found myself, driving me to such violence. This is fucked up. So fucked up. But if I can't stop, if I do, she's dead. I can't let that happen. I won't. Mita's silhouette lurked at the edges of my vision, poised to intervene if required. My pulse thundered, a savage rhythm in my veins drowning out any doubt. Any fear was gone, transformed into rage. A primal energy surged through me, pushing me on. The world melted into a crimson blur - hatred burned, passion ignited, everything mattered, nothing mattered. Nothing else existed.

The shadows concealed our fierce brawl. Even as life seeped from the body beneath me, I persisted in delivering punch after brutal punch. Blood coated us like paint, blending us together as if we were one being. My movements were becoming sluggish, everything burning and heavy, I tried to keep going. I wanted to keep going.

"Tommy!" Zahra's voice broke through the haze, her hands on my shoulders, pulling me back. I froze, my breath coming in ragged gasps, my body shaking. Blood dripped from my hands, and my arms. It was everywhere covering us both, soaking the ground. My stomach turned as I looked down at what was left of the creature. I felt sick.

"It's over," Zahra whispered, her voice gentle, trembling. She touched my cheek, her eyes full of tears. "It's over, Tommy. Please, come with me."

I looked at her, my vision swimming. She was right here, alive. Mita was beside her, her eyes wide, her face streaked with her own tears. They both reached for me, pulling me into their arms. I clung to them, my body wracked with sobs—the fear, the pain, the grief all pouring out in a broken, guttural cry. We held each other, three broken people trying to find some kind of solace in the chaos.

After what felt like an eternity, I pulled back, wiping my face with my sleeve. My breath was still shaky, but I nodded, meeting Zahra's eyes. "We have to keep moving," I said, my voice raw. "They'll be coming."

Zahra nodded, her hand finding mine, her grip tight. "Then let's go," she whispered, and together, we turned away from the clearing, stepping into the shadows of the forest, leaving the horror behind.

Chapter 70

I clutched Zahra's hand as if it were the last anchor keeping me grounded. The shouting grew closer, their voices harsh and jagged, like serrated edges cutting through the night. Zahra's grip tightened, her breaths quick and shallow as her eyes darted, searching for a way out. Panic flickered across her face, mingling with exhaustion. Every inhale scorched my lungs, a reminder of the skirmish that had almost broken me. In the dim light, I caught a glimpse of Zahra's fear, raw and palpable, reflecting back at me. This was our life now—a perpetual nightmare of running, hiding, fighting to survive. Mita's sudden, sharp intake of breath snapped me back to the present. She had stopped, her body rigid, eyes locked on something deeper in the shadows.

"There are more," she hissed, voice barely more than a breath.

My stomach knotted. "Shit. Move!" I gestured frantically, pulling Zahra closer as I met Mita's intense gaze. "We have to move. Now."

We bolted, weaving through the crumbling labyrinth of abandoned buildings, our footsteps masked by the shrill cries of the night. Zahra's hand was my lifeline in the darkness—trembling but unyielding. Mita led the way, her movements quick but uncertain, as if she had no clear direction, just an instinct to keep putting distance between us and them. Those bastards, they were always right behind us, like shadows. A wild part of me wanted to turn around, face them, and make them pay. Enough of the running, the fear. My hands itched for a weapon, for something that would end this once and for all. But I was torn, my thoughts pulling in a thousand directions. I heard their voices—closer now, too close—the crunch of twigs underfoot, the low rumble of orders exchanged. I forced myself to think, to focus, but it felt like trying to hold back a flood. How the hell do you stay calm when you're being hunted? They're not human, not really. Or at least, that's what I kept telling myself. But maybe I was just trying to justify the terror. I clamped my mouth shut before I could spill my thoughts out loud, teeth grinding against each other. 'They're not human,' I argued with myself, 'They're monsters.' Yet another voice in my head whispered back, 'They're just men—sick, twisted men.'

"They're tracking us. They can smell us," I muttered under my breath, feeling like I was coming apart at the seams. Hyenas and men—two predators, one and the same.

Mita's voice cut through my thoughts, urgent but controlled. "We can't keep running. We have to find shelter."

She was right. Damn it, she was right. I could barely hear my own thoughts over the pounding in my chest. My legs trembled, threatening to give out beneath me. But there was no way I'd stop now—not when stopping meant death. I clenched my jaw, forcing down the rising tide of exhaustion, clinging to a bitter determination. I swore to myself—I'd kill every last one of them before I let them take me. We stumbled into the skeletal remains of a building, its walls crumbling like the rest of this godforsaken place. Mita shoved us through the doorway, quickly pulling the door shut behind us. The air inside was thick with mildew and dust, suffocating. I leaned against the cold, rough wall, trying to steady my breaths, my pulse thundering in my ears. The place reeked of decay, but it was shelter. For now. Mita scanned the room, her mind already working through the next steps, but I saw the tension in her jaw, and the flicker of doubt in her eyes. I tried to match her composure, but my legs shook uncontrollably, threatening to collapse beneath me. Every sound outside felt amplified, as if the night itself had a heartbeat.

"We can't stay here long," I rasped, my voice barely more than a whisper. It sounded foreign, strange to my own ears. "They'll find us."

"We need a plan," Mita replied, eyes sweeping the shadows for any hint of a way out. "This is just to buy us time."

I nodded, swallowing hard, though my mouth was dry as ash. My gut twisted at the thought of lingering in this decaying tomb. But I knew she was right. We couldn't keep running—sooner or later, exhaustion would catch up, and they'd find us sprawled out in the dirt like prey. We edged deeper into the building, our steps barely making a sound against the rotting floorboards. I prayed they wouldn't creak beneath our weight.

Zahra's voice broke through the darkness, fragile and frayed. "They're getting closer."

I crouched beside her, trying to steady her shaking hands. Her arms wrapped around her knees, her body curled into itself like a wounded animal. I wanted to offer her some kind of comfort, but what could I say that wouldn't be a lie?

"They want blood," she whispered, voice cracking. "I can feel it."

I could feel it too—an anger that seemed to seep through the air, so thick I could almost taste it. I squeezed her shoulder, the gesture was hollow but desperate. "They'll pass us by," I whispered, as much to convince myself as to comfort her. "We just need time."

We pressed ourselves into the shadows as the noises outside grew louder, the hunters' footsteps crunching on the gravel, voices a murmur of rough syllables. Mita's eyes flashed, and she put a finger to her lips. Every muscle in my body went rigid, my breath held tight in my chest as if one exhale could betray our presence. Zahra's breath hitched, her wide eyes glinting with barely contained terror. I wrapped an arm around her shoulders, pulling her close, but the tension in her body didn't ease. My mind raced back to the days when I'd fought beside soldiers who never cracked, who held their ground even under fire. But I wasn't one of them anymore. And neither was she. They split up outside, voices drifting apart. My chest tightened. They're getting smarter, spreading out. Jesus, how many of them are there? And then—silence. Deafening silence. I held my breath, willing my heart to quiet its frantic pounding. My gaze darted to Mita's, the unspoken question passing between us. Was it over? Or was this just another game, another trap? Her expression remained unreadable, eyes scanning the shadows like she could see the future hidden in them. The darkness pressed in around us, heavy with unspoken thoughts, and for a moment, I dared to hope that they'd moved on. But hope was a dangerous thing, and I could feel it slipping through my fingers, as fragile as Zahra's trembling form beside me. Mita's hand brushed my shoulder, a gesture as grounding as it was painful, reminding me how close we stood to the edge of a knife.

"Rest, Tommy," she murmured, her voice low and steady, like she'd seen this all before. "I'll keep watch."

I wanted to argue, to insist I could keep going, but my body betrayed me. My limbs felt like lead, my thoughts splintering in every direction. I managed a nod, sinking against the cold stone, and letting Zahra lean into me. My eyelids fell shut, heavy with the weight of exhaustion. The darkness swallowed me whole, dragging me down into a dreamless void.

Chapter 71

"The cow knows the shepherd but not the owner."

Ethiopian proverb

My hands trembled as I hoisted Zahra onto my shoulders, urging her to grip the crumbling wooden frame of the window. The wood creaked, and a few splinters rained down as she scrabbled for purchase. Her breath came in quick bursts, each one filled with desperation. She strained, pulling herself up while I pushed from below, muscles burning. Finally, she disappeared through the opening with a grunt.

"Hurry, Mita!" I hissed, glancing back over my shoulder at the shadows flickering in the hallway.

Without a word, she clambered up, using my interlocked hands as makeshift rungs, her boots digging into my shoulders. A rush of cool air flowed in from the open window, carrying the crisp scent of pine and damp earth. Freedom. She reached for the edge, pulling herself through. Her head reappeared, backlit by the sliver of moonlight.

"Come on," she whispered urgently, her arm outstretched.

I grasped her hand, then Zahra's, their combined strength pulling me up and out into the night. My body hit the ground with a thud, sending a jolt of pain through my side. The chill of the night air stung my lungs as I gasped for breath, chest heaving. I forced myself to my feet, my mind screaming at me to keep moving. Mita was already pulling Zahra to her feet, eyes darting to the shadows that stretched like claws across the forest floor.

"They're close," I muttered, my voice barely more than a breath. The question circled in my mind like a vulture: how do they always find us? It's like they're always one step ahead, no matter how far we run. My jaw clenched. They want to break me. But I won't let them. I can't.

The forest closed in around us, branches clawing at our clothes, trying to drag us back. Zahra clung to my hand, her grip firm despite the terror in her eyes. I glanced at her, heart tightening. I'm doing this for her. She has to make it. Our footsteps pounded against the forest floor, every sound amplified in the silence. My legs burned, muscles turning to lead as the adrenaline faded. Time blurred, every step merging with the next until I couldn't tell how far we'd come. But the shouts behind us kept growing louder, and closer.

Suddenly, Mita stumbled with a cry of pain, crashing to the ground. Zahra was at her side in an instant, her hands fumbling to lift her. "Mita, can you stand?" she asked, her voice breaking.

I knelt beside her, feeling the cold sweat on Mita's brow as I pulled her up. "Come on, we have to keep moving," I urged, trying to keep my voice steady. Mita nodded, her lips pressed into a thin line, but her legs trembled beneath her, barely able to support her weight.

She stumbled again after just a few paces, collapsing with a choked sob. "Go," she gasped, clutching my arm with a grip that left bruises. "I'm slowing you down. Just—go."

"Shut up," I snapped, my voice rough with desperation. My mind was at war with itself. Every second we lingered, the sound of pursuit grew louder, the bootsteps crunching on the dry leaves like a countdown to doom. But how could I leave her? Mita wasn't just a burden—she was family. I looked at her pale face, then at Zahra, whose eyes glistened with unshed tears, pleading silently.

"We can't leave her," Zahra said, voice trembling. "She's family."

I swallowed hard, the weight of the choice crushing me. But survival clawed at my mind, urging me to run, to save Zahra and myself.

Mita's grip tightened on my hand, her fingers icy. "Please," she begged, her voice breaking. "You have to go."

As much as I wanted to deny it, a part of me knew Mita was right. But the thought of leaving her was unbearable, like tearing out a piece of my own heart. "No," I said, forcing steel into my voice. "We're not leaving you. Zahra, help me." Together, we pulled Mita to her feet again, her arm slung over my shoulder as we trudged forward through the underbrush, each step an agony. Zahra's breaths were ragged as she half-dragged, half-carried her sister, her face twisted with pain and determination. I pointed to a cluster of thick trees ahead, the shadows beneath them offering a brief promise of safety.

"There!" I whispered urgently. "We can hide there."

We slid down a steep hill, rocks scraping against our shins, and collapsed at the bottom, hidden beneath the canopy. Mita let out a whimper of pain as she clutched her injured leg, but she managed to stifle the sound, biting down on her knuckles.

"Are they still following us?" Zahra's voice trembled, barely audible over her gasping breaths.

I strained to hear beyond the pounding of my own heart. The forest seemed to hold its breath. "I think... I think we've lost them for now," I said, but doubt gnawed at my words. Zahra exhaled shakily, her hands moving to check Mita's injuries with a tenderness that brought a lump to my throat.

Mita clutched my sleeve, her fingers trembling as she pointed into the darkness. "There's a place... up ahead," she whispered, her face contorted with pain. "Homes... maybe a mile past those trees. We might find help there." She glanced back anxiously at our surroundings. "Maybe there's someone there who can help us."

I looked between her and the shadows where danger still lurked. The fear of being caught pulled at me, but so did the hope flickering in Mita's eyes. "We'll wait until nightfall," I said, trying to sound more confident than I felt. "Then we'll go. Just hold on, Mita. We're not leaving you behind."

CHAPTER 72

The evening sun dipped below the horizon, casting a warm amber glow over our huddled bodies. The dying light slipped through the gaps in the trees, leaving trails of gold across the blood-streaked earth. Our clothes clung to us, torn and heavy with sweat and blood—stark reminders of the brutal fight we had barely survived. As the final rays faded, a cold, creeping chill took over. It wasn't the kind that could be shaken off with warmth; it burrowed deep, stoking the quiet fear that lingered in the shadows. I glanced at Zahra and Mita, their forms hunched together in the long grass. Mita's face twisted in pain as she clutched her leg, a low groan escaping her clenched teeth.

Zahra, her hands steady despite the tremor in her voice, tried to comfort her. "Hold on, Mita. Just a little longer, okay?" Her words were soft, but a crack ran through them, like a thread barely holding together.

With a deep breath, I crouched beside them, slinging Mita's arm over my shoulder, feeling the weight of her exhaustion as she leaned into me.

"We need to move," I said, my voice barely above a whisper. The forest swallowed sound too easily out here. "I know it hurts, but we have to keep going. Just a bit further." Mita nodded, the movement slight, her eyes half-closed against the pain. I swallowed the lump in my throat as we staggered to our feet, each step feeling like an eternity.

Ahead, hidden among the dense foliage, I spotted the structures Mita had mentioned. They looked like part of the forest at first glance—weathered wood and makeshift walls blending into the landscape. It was a clinic, or at least something that had been transformed into one. Inside, the air was thick with the scent of antiseptic, sweat, and the unmistakable iron tang of blood. The atmosphere was heavy, a constant reminder that hope was as fragile as the wounded souls filling the room. Mita led us to meet Fatima Yusuf. Her eyes, deep and knowing, swept over us without flinching at our battered state. There was no pity in her gaze, only a quiet, unyielding compassion.

"Come, this way" she urged, guiding us into the dimly lit room. Her hands moved deftly, applying pressure to Mita's wound, her touch firm but gentle. "You've been through hell, but you're not alone anymore."

The clinic was little more than a converted classroom, with cots lining the walls where children might have once learned. Now, those walls seemed to absorb the groans and cries of the wounded, like ghosts refusing to leave. Whose kind gaze took in our bruised and battered bodies without any hint of shock or criticism? The sound of distant gunfire filtered through the cracked windows, a stark reminder that the forest was no sanctuary. At each shot, the room tensed—Fatima's hands would still for a second, as if listening for danger creeping closer. Mita clung to me, her breaths ragged, her eyes darting to the door with every noise. She looked like a lioness, trapped and restless, her survival instincts sharp and raw.

"Rest," I urged her softly, easing her onto a cot. Her eyes were already fluttering shut, but her grip on my arm tightened. I nodded, understanding the unspoken message: Don't let your guard down. Not even for a moment.

Fatima's presence was like a lotion, but it couldn't drown out the relentless tension that clung to every breath. The air was filled with the bitter notes of exhaustion and the sour tang of fear. Yet, even amid the suffering, there were glimmers of resilience—hands reaching out to comfort one another, whispers of hope exchanged like a secret language. Zahra sat across the room, her face turned away, but I saw the tension in her shoulders. She let a nurse tend to her wounds without protest, but her eyes kept drifting to the door, to the darkness beyond. I made my way over to her, my own legs heavy with the ache of days on the run.

"You, okay?" I asked, the question hollow in my mouth. She didn't answer, just gave a small, tight smile that failed to reach her eyes.

Fatima appeared beside me, a steaming cup of something that smelled vaguely of herbs in her hands. "Drink," she said, offering it to me. "It's not much, but it'll help with the pain."

I took the cup, feeling the warmth seep through my fingers, a brief comfort in the midst of chaos. "Thank you," I managed, though my voice came out rough. She gave me a look that saw through the gratitude, saw the fear lingering beneath it.

"You're not alone in this," she repeated softly, pressing a hand to my shoulder before moving on to the next patient. Her presence was like a thread tying us all together in this fragile, makeshift sanctuary.

I sipped the drink, the earthy taste grounding me for a moment. My mind drifted back over the past few days—a blur of desperate, breathless fleeing, of fear chasing us through every waking moment. The memory of screams echoed in my ears, too vivid to be ghosts. Yet Zahra's presence beside me, steady even in her silence, was a lifeline. A reminder that we were still here. That we still had a chance. Mita stirred in her sleep, a low whimper escaping her lips, and I draped a blanket over her, smoothing it down over her shoulders. She looked smaller like this, vulnerable, and it twisted something deep inside my chest. I couldn't shake the feeling that we were running out of time. I glanced around the room, my eyes falling on the faces of those who'd been here for days, their sunken eyes empty. Trapped in this in-between place—halfway between life and death. Beds—more cots than beds—line the room. Their sheets are threadbare, stained with blood and sweat. Fatima moved through the room like a shadow, her dark hair pulled back in a bun, her face a mask of calm determination. But there were moments—when she thought no one was watching—when her expression faltered, a flicker of grief crossing her features before she buried it again. I wondered what memories she carried, what losses had brought her to this forest, offering kindness to strangers in a world that seemed to have forgotten it. I glanced back at Zahra. She had finally drifted into a fitful sleep, her fingers curled into the thin blanket like she might slip away if she let go. I wanted to believe we could make it through this—that the clinic walls could keep out the horrors beyond. But I knew better than to trust in walls. We were all just waiting, holding our breath, hoping that the world outside wouldn't find us here. Steeling myself, I crossed to a man on a nearby cot, his leg mangled and bloody beneath a hasty bandage. His eyes were glassy, and unfocused, and I knelt beside him, my voice low.

"Breathe, just keep breathing. We're going to help you."

I knew he didn't understand my words, but he clung to the sound of my voice, and I kept talking, offering what comfort I could. Each word felt like a lie, but I whispered them anyway, hoping they might hold back the darkness, if only for a little while longer. The night deepened, and the forest outside seemed to close in around us, but inside, we fought to keep the fragile flame of hope alive. Fatima's words, Zahra's quiet strength, Mita's stubborn will—they were small, precious things. But they were enough to keep us moving forward, one painful, uncertain step at a time. I lie here, patched up but powerless, my body a dull ache beneath the bandages. Useless. Around me, the air buzzes with pain, mingling with the sharp scent of antiseptic and blood. The casualties blur together—farmers, children, soldiers—all reduced to broken bodies and haunted eyes. War had stripped us down to this. The faces around me are like open wounds, etched with the kind of suffering that never heals. Innocence meant nothing when bullets tore through the air, when shrapnel found its mark. In the corner, an elderly man clings to life, his breath a shallow rasp. He clutches the hand of a woman who kneels beside him, her voice a low murmur as she tries to comfort him, though I can't make out the words. Her eyes are dark with exhaustion, but there's a fierce tenderness in the way she brushes a hand over his grizzled cheek, as if willing him to stay. His lips move, forming words I can't hear, but I imagine he's pleading, bargaining with whatever gods might still be listening. Nearby, a small group crowds around a man with a leg mangled beyond recognition. Blood seeps through makeshift bandages—strips of sheets and shirts torn in desperation. They work quickly, their hands steady but strained, eyes hard with the determination of those who have done this too many times before. The man gasps, his face pale as they tighten a tourniquet, and someone whispers a prayer under their breath. The rhythm of their movements is practised, almost mechanical, as if they've trained themselves not to hesitate, even when hope is thin. I study their faces—tight with focus but shadowed with a weariness that runs deep. They've seen too much, and endured too much. And yet, they keep moving, keep fighting for one more heartbeat, one more chance. I wonder how long they can hold on. How long any of us can? As Fatima stitched the gash on my side, her hands steady and precise, I watched the clinic come alive around us. Outside, the wind howled, carrying distant shouts and the low rumble of danger. But inside, for a moment, there was a fragile peace. We had managed to find clean water—a rare blessing these days—and as I took a sip, the cold purity of it struck me, like a promise that maybe, just maybe, we had a chance.

"You can't let the darkness take hold," Fatima murmured, her voice barely rising above the muted chaos. Her accent thickened when she was focused, each word carrying weight. "This path... it's cruel. But you have each other. That's more than most have left." Her dark eyes flicked to mine, searching for some hint that I believed her. "You must rest now, while you can."

I nodded, though the anxiety gnawed at my gut like a hungry animal. Every breath felt too loud in the silence that followed her words. Across the room, Zahra sat on a worn wooden stool, her face swollen and lips split. One of Fatima's colleagues dabbed at the cuts with a gentleness that felt out of place in this broken world. Zahra winced but didn't pull away. Her eyes met mine, and I saw the flicker of fear she tried so hard to hide. But there was something else, too—a stubbornness, a refusal to surrender. Mita had already curled up on a thin mat in the corner. Her breaths came slow and even, her small body finally giving in to the exhaustion that had dogged her for days. She looked fragile like that, her face softened by sleep, free for a moment from the terror that had chased us here. I envied her for that escape, even if it was just temporary. The clinic was no fortress, but for now, within these walls, there was warmth. A small ember of hope, flickering but not yet snuffed out. And I clung to it with everything I had, praying it would be enough to carry us through the night. The last few days replayed in my mind like a looped nightmare, each scene more harrowing than the last. The air was thick with the cries of the wounded, and their pain seemed to echo inside my chest. Fatima moved like a shadow among them, her dark hair pulled back in a tight bun that accentuated the determined set of her jaw. She bent over each person with a blend of urgency and tenderness, hands steady as she dressed wounds and murmured words meant to soothe. Occasionally, she glanced our way, her dark eyes catching the dim light, holding a depth I couldn't quite read—part empathy, part something heavier that I didn't dare to name. The faint scent of jasmine drifted through the air, a strange comfort amid the chaos, but it only made the knot in my stomach tighter. How could I feel at ease when everything we knew was unravelling around us? Yet, when I looked at Zahra— her face pale but resolute—I felt a surge of strength. I clung to it, needing it more than I could admit. These people—these strangers—were risking everything to keep us safe. But why? What did they see in us worth saving? A sudden sting of pain drew my attention back to the too-tight bandage around my midriff. At least the bleeding had stopped, a small mercy in this waking hell. I winced, shifting, and that's when Fatima's voice cut through the low murmur of agony around us. She appeared beside me, holding out a chipped porcelain cup, steam curling from its rim like a lifeline. The earthy scent of the coffee mingled with the jasmine, filling my senses.

CHAPTER 73

The words, *You can't let the darkness take hold,'* echoed in my mind—hollow, meaningless. But I clung to them like a lifeline, hoping they might hold some fragment of comfort, even as the weight of the night pressed in. Shadows crept along the boarded-up windows, the wood scrounged from whatever wreckage we could find, casting jagged slivers of moonlight across the room. The lanterns sputtered, casting a weak, unsteady glow that barely cut through the gloom, illuminating rows of makeshift cots— torn mattresses, threadbare blankets, even bundles of leaves. It was a poor excuse for a refuge, but it was all we had. The air was thick with the stench of sweat, blood, and fear. Cracks splintered through the concrete walls, crisscrossed by graffiti in a language I couldn't understand. Bullet holes peppered the plaster, a stark reminder of the chaos outside. The senseless violence raged on beyond these thin walls—barbaric, mindless, inescapably cruel. There was no hiding from it, no pretending it wasn't there. I moved among the bodies, my boots sticking to the blood-soaked dirt beneath. Each step felt like a betrayal. I could feel the delicate balance of this place, teetering on the edge of collapse. We weren't trained for this—just ordinary people, dragged into a war we never asked for, trying to hold onto a sliver of hope in the darkness. I'd never thought of myself as squeamish, but nothing prepares you for the sight of blood pooling around a hasty bandage or a limb twisted at a sickening angle. This wasn't a scene from a movie—there was no art to the chaos, no poetic last words. Death didn't come with dignity here. It was ugly and brutal, a raw and unflinching end. The first time I watched someone die, I felt something in my chest cave in. It's not the kind of thing you can explain—it's like a part of you shatters, knowing that this person will never take another breath. Their life snuffed out in front of you, slipping away no matter how much you wish you could hold onto it. That emptiness—that helplessness—it's impossible to forget. I knelt beside a man whose face was twisted with pain, his breaths coming in sharp, shallow gasps. My hands were slick with his blood as I pressed down on the wound, feeling the warmth seep through my fingers.

"Stay with me," I muttered, but I didn't know if he could hear me over the rasp of his own breathing. "Just hold on a little longer."

Apply pressure. Keep him here. It's all I could think, all I could do. My arms ached, trembling from the strain, and a part of me knew that I wasn't stopping the bleeding—just delaying the inevitable. But I kept pressing down, harder, as if sheer force could keep his heart beating.

"Please," I whispered, my voice cracking. "Don't go. Don't..."

He shuddered beneath my hands, and I felt the moment he slipped away, like a thread snapping in my grasp. The silence that followed was a crushing weight, as if the room itself had exhaled. I stayed there, pressing down on empty skin, refusing to let go even when it no longer mattered. The words rang in my head again, mocking me now. *You can t let the darkness take hold.'* But it was too late for that—darkness was all that was left.

I wrapped my arms around a sobbing mother, her cries muffled against my shoulder. My words were empty—soft reassurances that felt like lies even as I spoke to them, flimsy attempts to cover the harsh reality surrounding us. Across the dim room, Zahra's gaze found mine. Her eyes, dark and weary, held a mirror to my own fears. It was a bond forged in suffering, but one that tethered us to each other. I inhaled sharply, trying to draw in her steadiness, willing it to settle my fraying nerves. I moved beside Zahra, the weight of everything unsaid hanging between us. Her bruised hand trembled slightly in mine, and I traced the scars that marred her wrists, remnants of the ropes that had once held her. My chest tightened at the sight—each mark a testament to the suffering she had endured, and the part of her that would never fully heal. I hesitated, words catching in my throat, knowing I could never ask her about what she had lived through in that place. The pain in her eyes told me enough. Instead, I let my thumb brush across her knuckles, hoping she would feel what I couldn't bring myself to say—that I was here, that I understood the unspoken weight she carried, that she wasn't alone. All we had was each other, but in the darkness, I feared that even that might not be enough.

I moved through the room once more, my steps careful among the crowded bodies, offering water and what little comfort I could. The air was thick, choking—filled with the stench of untreated wounds, infection, and something worse. The acrid smell of human waste mingled with the searing odour of scorched flesh, a nauseating mix that clung to my lungs. It felt like cruelty itself had taken root here, saturating the space, leaving no breath untouched. The moans and cries of suffering never stopped, a relentless hum that drilled into my skull, and I could feel each one like a stab beneath my ribs. Fatima was a blur of motion, tending to the wounded, and the dying with a focus that bordered on desperate. Her helpers moved alongside her, but even their combined efforts couldn't keep up. There were too many people, too many wounds. I admired their resilience, but a gnawing dread grew inside me, wondering how long any of us could keep up this struggle, how long before we were the ones lying on the ground, too weak to move. Mita, despite her own injuries, was up and moving through the room, her hands shaky as she fetched water from the well, handing out meagre portions of food. We murmured hollow reassurances to those too far gone to hope for anything more than a quiet end. An elderly woman, skin-like paper stretched over bones, reached out and clutched my arm with surprising strength. Her fingers dug into my skin, a desperate act.

She rasped, her voice cracked and broken, struggling to piece together the English she knew. "Did you…daughter, find?" Her lips quivered, tears spilling from eyes that seemed to have already seen too much.

I swallowed hard, forcing myself to hold her gaze, even as my own vision blurred with tears. "I'm sorry," I managed, my voice barely more than a breath.

She let out a sound, halfway between a sob and a sigh, releasing my arm, her hand dropping limply into her lap. I turned away, my throat burning, tears slipping down my cheeks despite myself. I was ashamed—ashamed that there was nothing I could do, ashamed that I couldn't even hold back my own useless tears. The weight of her sorrow followed me, heavy as a stone, pressing into my chest with every step I took.

The patients' cries and heart-wrenching stories crash over me, one after another, as Fatima translates their words. Husbands disappearing without a trace, mothers violated in front of their children—each account twists my insides tighter. My gaze drifts to Zahra, who sits motionless against the clinic wall, her arms wrapped tightly around herself. Her silence is like a scream, a haunting reminder of the things she's seen, the things she's endured. What happened to her? The question coils inside me, gnawing at my thoughts until they spill into my own dark memories—the pain, the shame, the way my own identity shattered beneath the hands of those who hurt me. A wave of nausea sweeps over me, and I press my eyes shut, fighting to keep the emotions from breaking through the thin veneer of control I'm clinging to. I have to stay strong, for Zahra's sake, for Mita's. But the fear keeps clawing at my chest— what if I can't protect them? What if something happens to Zahra, and I'm left with the blame?

A gentle pressure on my shoulder makes me jump, and I open my eyes to see Fatima's hand there, her expression soft but firm.

"They need hope as much as medicine," she murmurs, her breath warm against my ear. "We have to believe that better days are coming, that God hasn't forgotten them."

She guides me outside, where the air, though thick with dust and heat, feels a touch less oppressive than inside. Leaning against the crumbling wall of the clinic, she draws a deep, shuddering breath, like she's trying to summon the strength for what she has to say.

"I've seen Zahra and Mita before," she says, her voice barely more than a rasp. "Their families... I saw them about a week ago."

There's a weariness in her eyes, a sorrow so deep it makes my chest ache. Her words hit me like a jolt, cutting through the fog in my mind. I step closer, my hands trembling slightly, searching her face for any scrap of hope, any sign of something good.

"You saw them?" My voice cracks, and I don't bother trying to steady it. The answer feels like it could tip the world one way or another. Fatima glances away, her jaw tight as she seems to wrestle with what to say next. The silence between us grows thick, and all I can hear is the pounding of my own heart, waiting for the truth she's about to deliver.

"They were alive when I saw them last," she says, her voice cracking slightly as she meets my gaze, her eyes glimmering with a mixture of empathy and exhaustion. " The journey... it broke many of us. Not everyone was strong enough to make it."

My throat tightened as I absorbed her words, each one hitting like a stone in my chest. I watched her, waiting for more, but she hesitated, the weight of uncertainty hanging between us. When she finally spoke again, her voice was barely more than a whisper.

"I can't give you certainty, only hope," she murmured, reaching out to rest a trembling hand on mine. "Sometimes, in times like these, it's all we have left."

Her touch was gentle but carried something, not sure what, but something. The words surged through me, leaving my thoughts spinning. Our families were alive. The thought churned my insides. I glanced over at Zahra, curled into herself on the makeshift bed, her face pale and drawn. Her breath was shallow, with uneven patterns, as if even in sleep, she couldn't fully escape the torment. She looked so fragile, like she might shatter at the slightest touch. How could I break this news to her? Did she have the strength left to bear it, or would it crush whatever hope she clung to? Fatima's eyes searched mine, reading the turmoil I couldn't mask, her expression softening with a deep, weary understanding.

"Let her rest, for now," she urged gently, her voice like a lifeline in my storm of thoughts. "There'll be time for truth-telling once she's healed a little more. She needs that, at least."

I nodded, my gratitude unspoken but evident, clinging to her words like a fragile promise. I turned my gaze back to Zahra back inside, watching her chest rise and fall, each breath a quiet reminder that she was still here, still fighting. It was a small comfort, but I clung to it, desperate to believe that somewhere, our families were doing the same surviving, enduring. Fatima's voice grew rougher as she recounted their escape. Her hands twisted together, knuckles white, as she described the relentless fear that drove them from their homes.

"We ran for miles, not knowing if the next breath would be our last. There was gunfire, screams..." Her voice faltered, eyes clouded with memory. "We found children along the way, injured, lost. Some of them... they were barely more than babies. We couldn't leave them behind. We brought them here, kept them safe as best we could."

She stopped, breath shuddering, and for a moment, the only sound was the wind outside, howling through the trees. The weight of what we had seen, what we had lost, settled between us, heavy and unspoken. My mind raced with flashes of faces and voices, of places we could never go back to. In that moment, I felt closer to Fatima than I had to anyone in years—a kinship born of shared suffering. After what felt like an eternity, she looked out towards the horizon, where the first traces of dawn began to creep into the sky, painting it with muted colours. Her voice softened, a faint spark of awe threading through the exhaustion.

"Their resilience... it's incredible, isn't it? After everything, they keep going." Fatima's voice wavered, her words like a fragile thread holding us together. Her gaze lingered on the wounded, on the makeshift bandages stained with too much blood, and I could hear the unsteady hope catching in my own chest.

I swallowed hard, nodding, but the lump in my throat kept me silent. The word "resilience" echoed in my mind, tasting bitter and raw. It didn't feel like strength right now; it felt like desperation. I thought of Zahra, and how she fought against the shadows in her mind as fiercely as any enemy out there. Her strength was the only thing keeping me moving, dragging me forward even when my legs ached, and my spirit felt hollow. Tears burned my eyes, blurring the harsh lines of our reality. I turned to Fatima, wanting to tell her—thank you, I'm scared, I don't know if I can keep doing this—but the words stuck in my throat. She met my gaze, and her lips curled into a small, understanding smile, one that felt like a promise, or maybe just an unspoken pact between survivors. Then her expression hardened again as she took in the bodies around us, and we both fell silent, feeling the weight of our shared burden.

I shifted closer to Zahra, sitting by her side as she lay unconscious, her breaths slow but steady. My mind drifted, unbidden, to the days before everything fell apart—before we had to measure time by each heartbeat that wasn't silenced by violence. Zahra had been my constant in a world that never stopped shifting. Now, her face was gaunt, her body marked with scars from battles she never asked for.

"We'll reach Addis soon," I whispered, more to myself than to her, as if saying it aloud might make it true. But I could feel the monsters out there—the ones with guns, with hatred, the ones that took our homes and our peace. They were closing in, and every second we stayed here it felt like tempting fate. Still, I couldn't bring myself to move. Not yet. I held Zahra's hand, feeling the warmth of her palm against mine, a fragile connection that made time slow down. Around us, the sobs and prayers became a dull murmur, blending with the pounding in my head. My mind drifted in and out of the present, slipping into a space where time lost its grip. I wasn't sure how long I stayed like that—minutes, hours, it all blurred together. It didn't matter. My body was there beside Zahra, but my mind floated, unmoored, drifting to a different place. Faint images flickered behind my closed eyes, growing sharper until I was somewhere else, somewhere better, or at least less broken.

I saw my old apartment—the creaky floorboards, the photograph of the waterfall that always reminded me of quieter days, and the view of the city twinkling at night. I could almost hear the hum of the traffic below, the comforting sound of life going on. For a moment, the scent of jasmine from the plant on my windowsill filled my senses, and I was miles away from the smoke and the blood.

But then, like a rubber band snapping back, reality pulled me back to this place, this night, where the only warmth came from the fading grip of Zahra's hand and the unsteady hope in Fatima's eyes. And I knew, even as I loitered in that memory, I'd have to let go. Soon, we'd have to rise and keep moving.

CHAPTER 74

*"A hyena will enter through open spaces left by a
dog."*

Ethiopian proverb

We grabbed our bags and gear, the rising sun casting a mournful orange glow over the clinic's crumbling walls. Under the sagging canopy, the light barely reached through, leaving much of the place draped in shadows. The air was heavy with sadness and uncertainty, weighing down every step as we prepared to leave behind what little sanctuary the clinic had provided. We had spent a day here, resting, stitching wounds, offering what little aid we could. And now, it was time to go. Zahra clung to Fatima, her voice raw and breaking. I caught a word of thanks, but the rest blurred into the rapid rhythm of Zahra's Amharic. I had tried learning a few phrases, but she spoke so quickly it was like trying to catch rain with my hands. Her grip on Fatima was tight, desperate—knuckles pale against her dark skin, as she might never let go. Fatima's arms held steady around her, a solid pillar in the storm. But her eyes gave her away. They darted between Zahra and me, flickering with a worry she tried to hide behind a practised calm. She whispered something else, her voice soft and soothing, giving Zahra's back one last gentle pat before she turned to face me. Her expression shifted, her mask slipping back into place, but the edges were fraying. I felt my hand instinctively drift to the bandage on my side, feeling the ache beneath it. Fatima's eyes followed the movement, checking her work, and then she pressed a small bag into my hand—water, a few pieces of bread, and a bit of dried fruit. She took a step back, surveying us with a steely expression that didn't quite mask the sadness beneath. The morning air tugged at the hem of her dress, the cool breeze ruffling its edges. I made a final promise we would send help and supplies as soon as possible. Her eyes turned to Mita, who gave a solemn nod, her lips tight with the words she couldn't bring herself to say. They exchanged hushed words—something too private to intrude on. Then, Mita pulled her into a fierce embrace, her shoulders trembling with silent sobs. She turned away quickly, as if afraid that looking back might undo her resolve. Fatima stood in the doorway, her silhouette dark against the dim light inside the clinic. The distance between us grew with every step, until she was just a figure swallowed by shadows.

We moved south, feet sore, muscles aching, but the thought of giving up never crossed my mind. The path was brutal—sharp stones tore at our boots, and the uneven ground punished each step. Zahra stumbled once, catching herself against my arm, trying to disguise the pain with a tight smile. Her lips were cracked, her skin pale under the grime.

"I'm okay," she whispered, but I could hear the exhaustion creeping into her voice.

"Just a little further," I said, more to myself than to her, my eyes fixed on the harsh landscape ahead.

Each step felt like lifting lead. The promises I had made to Fatima twisted inside me—could I even keep them? Or had I offered hope I couldn't deliver? The questions churned in my mind like a storm, but there was no time for uncertainties. A sudden explosion shattered the air, tearing through the fragile morning calm. My instincts took over—I shoved Zahra down, throwing myself over her as a shield. Dust filled the air, stinging my eyes, and clogging my throat. The world around us went silent except for the ringing in my ears. I could feel Zahra's frantic breaths against my chest, her heart pounding like mine. Mita's face appeared through the dust, her eyes wide, darting from shadow to shadow.

"Get to cover!" Mita's voice cracked through the haze, her arm pointing to a narrow path between jagged rocks.

Without a second thought, we scrambled for it, knees scraping on stone, fear pumping through our veins. The scent of gunpowder hung in the air, sharp and biting. Was that aimed at us? Not sure, but they were close.

"Which way?!" I shouted, trying to keep the panic from my voice.

Mita scanned the path ahead, her breaths coming in sharp bursts. "Give me a second." She steadied herself, then gestured forward. "This way, follow me."

We moved as fast as our battered bodies could manage, slipping between rocks and staying low. Minutes stretched into agonisingly long breaths, each one filled with the fear that this step might be our last.

Finally, Mita's hand shot up, signalling a halt. "Water!" she whispered, pointing to a hidden pool under the thick canopy of trees. Relief flickered through me at the sight—a chance to catch our breath, if only for a moment.

We dropped to the ground, each of us gulping down water like it was life itself. Zahra's hands shook as she held the canteen, her eyes reflecting a thousand unspoken fears. I watched her, feeling the exhaustion settle. Mita crouched beside me, her hand gripping my shoulder with surprising strength.

"You need rest, too, Tommy. We'll take shifts."

I nodded, though my mind still buzzed with the adrenaline. I took a sip of the tepid water, feeling the grit of dust in my throat. The world around us seemed to hold its breath, the forest absorbing our presence as if we might vanish if we sat too still. Zahra leaned against me, her head heavy on my shoulder, her breaths coming slow and deep. I wrapped my arm around her, holding her closer, trying to offer comfort even as my own fears gnawed at me.

"We'll make it through this," I whispered to her, trying to believe my own words.

Zahra's voice was barely a murmur, her breath warm against my neck. "Can you promise that?" Her question lingered, fragile and raw.

"Yes," I replied, forcing the word past my dry lips. But even as I said it, doubt coiled tight in my chest, squeezing the air from my lungs. I stared into the shadows of the forest, feeling the weight of memories pressing in, unrelenting. Blood, fear, the cries of those I couldn't save—it all came flooding back, dragging me under like a riptide. But I had to keep moving. We all did.

CHAPTER 75

My feet ached with each step, the soles raw from the unrelenting terrain, while the sun bore down on us, turning the air to fire in my lungs. We moved on, scrambling and slipping across rocks, each stumble a reminder of how fragile our strength had become. The sharp pain in my side was my only comfort—it kept me tethered to the present, to the fact that I was still breathing, still fighting. But frustration simmered beneath the surface, building with every moment of silence between us. When we finally reached a cluster of trees with enough coverage to hide us, we collapsed in the thin shade. The air was cooler here, but not by much. As I looked over at Zahra, her face barely visible in the dimming light, a sense of dread settled in my chest. She turned to me, her eyes searching mine.

"I see you watching me," she said quietly, her voice frayed like the threads of her shirt. "You don't have to worry. I'm not going anywhere."

Her words were meant to be reassuring, but they only made my fear more tangible. I kept my gaze locked on her, afraid that if I looked away, she might vanish like a mirage. "I can't bear to lose you," I admitted, my voice breaking as I scratched at the dried sweat on my neck. "Not again."

She reached out, her fingers wrapping around mine with surprising strength, and for a moment, the warmth of her touch pushed back the darkness. "I'm right here," she said, her voice firmer now, as if she were trying to convince herself as much as me.

But how much longer could we keep this up? We'd been trained for situations like this, to evade and endure, but that was a lifetime ago. Now, my body felt heavy, and slow—every step was a reminder of the years that had passed since those days. As we moved south, we crossed paths with others, fellow escapees whose hollow eyes and sunken cheeks mirrored our own desperation. There was a wordless understanding between us, a shared knowledge of the fear and hunger that stalked us all. Mita, always bold, would break from our path to speak with strangers, gleaning scraps of information.

When she returned, I cornered her. "What did you find out?" I questioned, my voice sharper than I intended.

"They're still searching," she murmured, fingers combing through her tangled hair. The lines around her eyes deepened, betraying her exhaustion.

I nodded, feeling the weight of every decision pressing down on me. My bones ached with fatigue, but there was no room for rest. Mita softened as she glanced at Zahra, reaching out to place a hand on her shoulder.

"I have news," she said, her voice barely more than a breath. "Our family. They reached a refuge south, close to here. They're safe."

Zahra's breath hitched, and she whispered, many thanks, her arms encircling me in a hug that was tight but shook with weakness.

Mita's face hardened. "We need to focus on getting there ourselves," she said, her eyes scanning the distance.

Ahead of us, the road wound like a scar through the landscape, crowded with people trudging toward Addis Ababa. Mothers balanced bundles on their heads, children clung to their fathers' hands, and fear etched deep lines into every face. Zahra clutched my hand as we moved with the tide, our eyes darting from shadow to shadow, wary of every unfamiliar movement. The setting sun stained the sky with a burnt-orange glow, and I couldn't help but think of another exodus, another time—Cambodia, the 1970s, when millions fled tyranny. Memories bled into the present, and I gripped Zahra's hand tighter, feeling a fear I thought I'd buried long ago. I lifted a hand to brush the dust from her tear-streaked cheek, the touch as much for me as it was for her. Her body trembles, her breaths shallow and rapid.

"Are you okay?" I asked, knowing the futility of the question even as it left my mouth.

She forced a smile, the corners of her lips twitching upward, but her eyes betrayed the pain. "I've had better days," she replied, her voice brittle like dried leaves.

"We need to rest," I said, my chest tightening at the sight of her wounds. But she shook her head, her jaw set with grim determination.

"No time," Mita snapped, her gaze fixed on the horizon. "We have to keep moving."

The sun's heat clung to my skin, burning into my back, making me stand out among the dark faces in the crowd like a beacon. I craved the cool touch of shade, but the anguish in Zahra's eyes kept me moving. We couldn't stop—not when her family was within reach. Our bodies were wrecked, our spirits threadbare, and still, we pushed on through fields scorched by the sun and buildings shattered by violence. The screams of the dead and dying echoed in my mind, the price of failure. But hope clung to us, even if by the thinnest thread, the hope that we might find some semblance of peace. Mita walked beside me, a new rifle slung over her shoulder, her posture taut with vigilance. We stumbled upon another thicket of trees, just dense enough to hide us from prying eyes. We collapsed against the roots, panting.

"Ten minutes?" Mita's voice was rough, barely hiding her urgency.

"Ten minutes," I agreed, though I knew it wasn't enough. But there was no choice.

We sat in the shadows, every muscle tensed, ears straining for any sound that might betray a threat. My mind refused to rest, spinning through possibilities. We were so close, but the closer we got, the more I feared that it might all slip away again.

CHAPTER 76

I leaned closer to Zahra, our hands clasped tightly, my voice barely more than a whisper. "How are you holding up?"

She drew in a shaky breath, eyes bloodshot and swollen, her whole frame shivering. "Exhausted," she confessed, her voice frayed like a wire pulled too tight.

"We'll find them," I vowed, forcing my voice steady, even as emotion thickened my throat. I held her gaze, searching the depths of her despair. "Together."

She leaned in, her breath warm against my ear, the sound of it intimate and urgent. Her voice was a hushed, desperate plea as she whispered my name—so fragile, it nearly broke me. I had never heard her like this before.

"Zahra," I cut in, my own desperation surfacing, trying to be the man she needed. "We'll make it through this." But her grip tightened, nails—chipped and broken—digging into my skin, holding on as if she might disappear.

"Just promise me," she whispered, her words trembling as they left her lips, carrying a weight I wasn't sure I could bear.

I hesitated, knowing exactly what she was asking for. I wanted to lie, to give her something easier, but I couldn't deny her.

"Yes," I said finally, the word coming out stronger than I felt. I squeezed her hand in return, willing her to believe it. "But you have to promise me the same."

A faint, fragile smile tugged at her lips, a shared understanding passing between us. But before we could fully absorb the moment, Mita stepped in, her presence a sharp reminder of reality.

"Wait here; stay out of sight. I'll go check what's happening up ahead," she said, gesturing toward a distant group huddled near a slope. Gravel crunched beneath her boots as she moved away, each step deliberate despite the limp that she carried without complaint.

Zahra and I huddled behind the rocks, our bodies slumped with exhaustion, sweat soaking into our filthy clothes. I wiped the grime from her back, my hand lingering over each scar, each mark, and she did the same for me. Our eyes met, weary yet resolute, a shared history passing between us without a word. The sun began its slow descent, casting a burnt-orange glow across the scarred land. In a different life, this moment might have been beautiful—maybe even romantic.

The quiet stretched until Mita returned, her pace urgent, face shadowed with worry. Her breath came in quick bursts as she rejoined us. "Zahra, Tommy," she rasped out.

Fear knotted in my gut as I leaned forward. "What is it?"

Mita crouched beside us, catching her breath. Her words came out like a rush, her tone edged with urgency, and she switched to English for my sake. "They're nearby, held in a compound. Just like we heard." Her expression remained stony, but her eyes flickered with something darker. "But conditions are bad. Really bad."

Zahra's voice cracked, her fear slicing through the night air. "Are they safe?" Her eyes brimmed with tears.

Mita's face hardened. "As far as I know," she said, but the weight of her words pressed down on all of us. "But the guards are unpredictable—young kids, some of them, filled with twisted ideas and no discipline. It's a powder keg."

My mind reeled, my heart slamming in my chest. "We have to act, now," I said, barely managing to keep the fear from my voice. "I'll do whatever it takes to protect them." Mita's gaze lingered on me, a warning in her eyes.

"Stay hidden," she commanded, voice firm, thick with her accent, but the plea in her gaze softened her words. "I'll take Zahra to the compound, then come back for you."

A surge of protectiveness ripped through me, cutting through the fear. I couldn't let them face that danger alone. "No," I snapped, my voice unsteady. "I'm going with you. I won't just sit back while my wife risks her life." My hands clenched into fists, the resolve in my chest as hard as stone.

Zahra reached out, her fingers brushing my face, her touch grounding me against the chill creeping into the evening air. Her grip tightened, the weight of our past and everything we'd lost threaded into her words.

"Tommy," she said, each syllable heavy, deliberate. "Sometimes, the hardest thing is to trust. Trust Mita to lead us. Trust me to be strong. We need you here, clear-headed, so when we come back, you'll be ready."

Her words pierced through the fog of my panic, and I saw the truth in her eyes, the strength she was trying to show me. It felt like standing at the edge of a cliff, the wind pulling at my back. I fought the urge to pull her close, to refuse her plan. But then, I felt something thaw in my chest—trust, real and raw. I took a breath, tasting the dust in the air, and nodded. My voice came out rough, barely more than a growl.

"All right," I managed. "Stay safe—both of you."

She leaned in, her lips pressing against mine, soft and warm against the coolness of the air. A shiver ran through me, but her touch steadied me. "I will," she whispered, her voice carrying a fragile hope. "I'll see you soon."

I watched as she and Mita gathered their few belongings, slipping into the shadows. The tall grass swayed around them, the setting sun casting long shadows over their retreating figures. I pressed my back against the rough bark of a nearby tree, the ridges digging into my skin through my thin shirt, a grounding pain that told me I was still here, still breathing. The air was damp, and heavy with the scent of earth and rain that hadn't yet fallen. Shadows stretched long, twisting into shapes that made my breath catch in my throat. The darkness pressed in, a living thing, swallowing the night. Time became something slippery, each minute stretching and bending, bleeding into the next until they all felt like one endless moment. I squeezed my eyes shut, hoping it might pass faster that way, but the darkness behind my lids felt just as suffocating. A branch snapped somewhere nearby, and my heart lurched, its thudding the only sound in my ears.

"Focus," I whispered to myself, voice cracking in the cold. My breath came out in short, frantic bursts, visible puffs in the chilly air. *I can t fall apart now.'*

Gunshots rang out in the distance, piercing the otherwise still air, and sending my head spinning. I clung to the sound of the rustling leaves, of the small creatures stirring in the underbrush, hoping to drown out the fear. But the silence that settled in the wake of those echoes was even worse, like the universe was holding its breath. Traumas bled into the present, dragging me back to darker times—to places where the air was dense with the taste of blood, where I couldn't forget the faces of those who never made it. Zahra's voice words came to me, *Promise me.'* But the promise felt like a weight around my neck. My mind raged with everything I couldn't change, everything I feared, but somewhere in that storm, I clung to one certainty: I wouldn't let her down, not again.

CHAPTER 77

*"While men fear danger, women only fear the
sight of it."*

Ethiopian proverb

My eyes burn, each blink scaring as I struggle to keep them open. They sting with exhaustion, and my vision blurs from the strain of hours spent staring into the darkness. Fatigue weighs on me, pressing me into the hard ground. The earth beneath is cold, numbing my limbs, but I welcome its chill—it's better than the drowsiness trying to pull me under. Somewhere in the distance, a cricket chirps, its rhythm hypnotic, while an owl hoots, the sound haunting and lonely. Their calls blend into a strange lullaby, one that tugs at my heavy eyelids. My body is sinking deeper, each breath growing slower. I tell myself to stay alert, to fight this, but my thoughts slip through my fingers like sand, each one scattering into the night. Time stretches, and warps; seconds stretch into minutes, minutes bleed into hours. My mind drifts, and it's harder to remember why I was waiting in the first place. A part of me is screaming, desperate to hold on, but that voice is distant, muffled by the weight pressing down on me. I feel myself giving in, my head dipping lower, my limbs growing numb. My breath hitches, then slows, unnaturally—this isn't the peaceful slide into sleep. It's a cold, creeping feeling, like ice wrapping around my chest, squeezing. My heart pounds louder in my ears, but even that seems to grow faint, as if the world is receding, leaving me behind. I try to draw in a deeper breath, but I cannot, and panic flares through the fog clouding my mind. Something is wrong—terribly wrong.

Zahra wandered through the ruins of her childhood home, her movements slow, as though each step threatened to shatter her completely. The walls, blackened and brittle, bore the scars of a battle that had taken everything from her. The air was thick with the smell of ash and decay. Beneath her boots, pieces of shattered pottery and glass crunched, relics of a life that no longer existed. Her breath came in ragged gasps, mingling with quiet sobs, as her fingers traced the broken edges of a family portrait, now charred beyond recognition. She knelt beside a scorched wooden beam, brushing away a layer of soot, as if she might unearth something familiar beneath the wreckage. Her face was streaked with tears and smeared with blood, cuts and bruises marking her skin—souvenirs of a struggle she had barely survived. But there was no anger in her eyes now, only a hollow, aching sorrow as she sifted through the debris of a world that had collapsed. I stood a few paces away, transfixed, as a rush of memories assaulted me—images of the life we once shared, distorted into grotesque mockeries by the violence that had torn it apart. Each memory clawed at my mind, leaving me dizzy, and struggling to catch my breath. And then, among the twisted visions, I saw Zahra cradling a lifeless body in her arms. Her shoulders heaved with grief, her fingers digging into the fabric of a torn shirt. I stumbled forward, my legs trembling beneath me. But as I drew closer, a jolt of horror ripped through me—the body she held was mine. My own face, pale and bloodied, stared back at me, eyes wide and empty, mouth frozen in a silent scream. I tried to speak, to shout her name, but the words died in my throat, swallowed by an unnatural stillness that pressed in from all sides. And then came the whisper. It crept into my mind like a thread of ice, winding around my thoughts and squeezing. It was my own voice, distorted and distant, like a cold echo from the other side. 'You can t save her. You re already dead.' Panic flared inside me. I reached out a hand, desperate to touch Zahra s shoulder, to pull her away from my corpse and that awful, empty scene. But I was frozen, trapped in a body that refused to move, a mute witness to a nightmare I couldn t escape. Then, behind Zahra, the darkness shifted. At first, it was just a trick of the light, a blur in the corner of my vision. But as it coalesced, a shadowy figure emerged from the gloom, its form fluid and shifting, like smoke twisted into the shape of a man. My heart pounded as its presence filled the space, a deep, unnatural cold seeping through the air. I tried to scream, to warn her, but nothing came out—my voice, my will, swallowed by the terror that gripped me. Zahra remained oblivious, her eyes fixed on the body she cradled, the last remnant of the life she had lost. The figure moved closer, its edges solidifying into something more grotesque—a monstrous silhouette with clawed hands that gleamed in the dim, flickering light. It reached out, one long, gnarled finger brushing against Zahra s hair. And then, two glowing red eyes blinked open, glaring directly at me with a malice that burned like coals. Its mouth split into a jagged grin, revealing rows of teeth that glittered like knives. My mind screamed at her to move, to run, but my body remained rigid, useless, trapped in the grip of my own fear. Zahra's breath stopped, as if she sensed something, her head turning slightly, but the figure s arm moved faster, its claws inches from her throat. And all I could do was watch as the shadow closed in, my own blood turning to ice in my veins, the horror of my powerlessness strangling me as surely as that monstrous hand would soon strangle her.

My eyes snap open, my body jerking upright as if I've been hit. The ground beneath me is cold— rough. The mountain forest looms in the darkness, unnaturally quiet. The night sky, endless and unchanging, presses down on me, an indifferent witness. That nightmare... God, it's still clinging to the edges of my mind, slipping away like smoke but leaving behind a worrying void. My chest heaves, my skin slick with sweat, lungs burn as I gasp for air, like I've just surfaced from drowning. Fear controls me with icy fingers, squeezing tighter with each second. I glance around frantically, trying to find something, anything, that feels real. But the forest offers no comfort. My heart thrashes in my chest, like a wild animal trapped in a cage. *Get a grip. Get a grip.'* My thoughts tumble over each other, disjointed and anxious. It wasn't real. *It wasn t real.'* But it's hard to convince myself when my pulse is drowning out all reasoning. 'Zahra.' Where is she? Why the hell did I let her out of my sight? I choke back a sob, the pain swelling in my throat like a wound. I need to focus. If I fall apart now, I'm dead, and so is she. I swipe at my face, scrubbing away the dampness that clings to my skin. I can't afford to cry. Not here. I fumble for my water bottle, my hands shaking as I take a few desperate gulps, trying to wash the bitter taste of anxiety from my mouth. The water is lukewarm, but it steadies me, if only for a moment. I stuff it back into my bag, my movements jerky, and clumsy. I force myself to my feet, stretching stiff, sore muscles. My clothes cling to me, soaked through with sweat and cold from the night air. I glance around, scanning the darkness, each shadow a potential threat, every rustle a predator's whisper. My mind buzzes, and I can't shut it off. Zahra. Is she out there somewhere, breathing the same cold air, hearing the same distant gunshots? Is she safe? The memory of her eyes, wide with terror, flashes before me, and I want to scream at myself. *Why did I let her go alone?'* Now, every thought of her cuts deeper than any wound. I think of the way she looked when we last parted—bruised, exhausted, but still defiant. I clench my fists, the nails biting into my palms, trying to hold onto that image, to keep myself from crumbling. But the frustration roars in my chest, a wild, maddening thing that I can't silence.

A crack—something stepping on a twig—snaps through the silence, as sharp as a gunshot. My body goes rigid, instincts kicking in, every nerve lighting up like a flare. I draw in a breath, trying to steady the trembling in my hands. The cold and the terror that had held me in its grip a moment ago faded to a numb, focused clarity. Whoever—or whatever—is out there doesn't realise it yet, but they've just stumbled into their end.

"Tommy." The voice cut through the dark, sharp and urgent, yanking me out of the fog in my head. It was Mita. Her silhouette emerged from the shadows, blending into the night's deeper black. Her eyes held something new—something urgent. She moved with a kind of determination that tightened my chest. I spoke before I could stop myself, my voice rough and louder than it should have been.

"Where's Zahra? Is she okay? Tell me she's okay!" The panic clawed at my throat as my eyes darted around wildly, searching the dark for her. Thoughts spiralled—was she hurt? Dead? Lost somewhere out there?

"She's fine," Mita snapped, her breath coming in quick bursts, sweat glistening on her brow despite the cold. She glanced behind her, like she expected something—or someone. "But we have to go. Now. She's waiting at the camp's edge."

"What?" I cut in, too desperate for small talk. My mind was on the brink—fraying edges, slipping control. It all felt like a sick game I couldn't win. One nightmare after another.

"It's safer there, I promise you," she insisted, shoving what little she had left into her bag. Her hands trembled, but her voice was firm.

"How? How is it even possible?" I shot back, frustration bubbling over, my voice breaking with the edge of a childish plea. I knew I sounded unhinged, but I couldn't help it.

Mita stopped, turning on me with a ferocity I hadn't seen in her before. "Tommy, do you really think I could drag her away from her family just to make it back up this fucking hill?" Her words came out in a hiss, and I flinched at the raw anger there. I'd never heard her curse like that—especially not in English.

She was right, and we both knew it. I swallowed the knot in my throat. "Sorry... You're right," I muttered, but she was already moving, her focus back on the path down the hill.

"We don't have time for this," she said, her voice clipped as she pushed through the underbrush. "It'll take an hour, maybe more."

I matched her pace, feeling the weight of each step as my boots sank into the marshy ground. We slipped through the night like shadows. The darkness felt alive—both a refuge and a threat, hiding us while also hiding whatever might be out there. In the distance, a hyena's laughter echoed, or maybe it was just the wind twisting through the trees. My mind latched onto a Bible verse I'd heard in too many war movies—*'Even though I walk through the darkest valley, I will fear no evil, for you are with me.'* But out here, in this real-life valley of death, I feared everything. Every. Damn. Thing. I kept walking, kept hoping, and kept following Mita into the unknown.

CHAPTER 78

The trees thinned out, their shadows retreating like nervous ghosts, revealing a clearing. The first thing that struck me was the smell—a sharp blend of wood smoke, sweat, and something sour beneath it, a scent that clung to the air like a memory of decay and desperation. Ahead, the camp sprawled before us, a sea of sagging canvas and patched plastic tarps, fluttering like wounded wings in the cold breeze. Thin streams of smoke wound into the night, disappearing into the endless black sky, as though the earth was exhaling a deep, weary sigh. We crouched at the edge of the forest, Mita whispering our route in, her finger tracing the path to where Zahra was. The chill brushed against my skin, but it did nothing to cool the feverish pulse beneath it. The camp lived, but it was a muted, restless kind of life—like a heart struggling to beat. Voices murmured through the night, carried by the wind, blending with the rustle of makeshift shelters and the occasional cough or distant sob. Lanterns flickered in the dark, their light casting trembling shadows that stretched across the dirt paths. Figures drifted in and out of the glow, their faces indistinct, hollowed out by the lack of sleep, hunger, and hope. They moved like they were wading through water, each step a labour they could barely afford. A few gathered around small, feeble fires, their faces gaunt and sunken, turned inward toward the fading warmth. Children clung to their mothers, wide-eyed, their gazes darting around as if they expected some answer to emerge from the night itself. But there was nothing—only the endless wait. We held still, taking it all in. This wasn't just a place; it was a wound, raw and festering in the darkness, seeping its pain into the air. The trees behind us rustled, but the camp stayed indifferent, a hollow-eyed witness to its own suffering. It had seen too much to care about one more person stepping out of the shadows. A baby's wail pierced the silence, sharp and haunting, cutting through the murmur like a blade. My chest tightened as I looked over the sea of tents, counting the lives crammed into this broken place, each one clinging desperately to the fraying threads of hope. Zahra was somewhere in that tangle of faces, and we were going to find her, and take her south to Addis. But the camp looked less like a refuge and more like the re-education camps of the Khmer Rouge—places where hope went to die. Dawn began to creep across the horizon, staining the sky in muted reds and purples. The camp stirred, its inhabitants emerging from ragged shelters, brushing off another sleepless night like dust from their clothes. I followed Mita along the fence line, my breath fogging in the chill, the ground turning to slick mud beneath my boots. As we moved, I saw the faces that had become grimly familiar eyes hollowed by fear, bodies worn thin by hunger. Some glanced at us as we passed, their expressions resigned, already dead in some way. Others remained buried in their own misery, too trapped in their thoughts to notice us slipping by. We stuck to the shadows, keeping low, the harsh lights of the camp flickering across our path like searchlights. Ahead, children played around a dying fire, their laughter brittle and fleeting. I paused for a moment, watching them chase sparks like fireflies. A knot twisted in my chest, envy and sorrow mingling bitterly. How could they still find joy in a place like this?

Mita gestured to a gap in the fence, and beyond it, a small crowd jostled around a truck delivering water, shoving and elbowing to fill their containers. The fence barely resisted as we squeezed through, its wires snagging on my shirt. I felt it tear but kept moving. On the other side, I scanned the faces, frantic and half-crazed, desperate for a glimpse of her. Mita pushed forward, cutting through the narrow paths between tents, where the morning fires were just being stoked, and the smells of boiling rice mixed with the char of burning wood. I thought I saw her more than once—ghosts conjured from hope. But when I reached out, it was never her. Then, like a mirage, Zahra appeared, and everything else blurred away. We collided in a fierce embrace, arms tightening around each other as if we could shield ourselves from the chaos around us. I pressed my face into her shoulder, feeling the familiar warmth, the scent of her hair grounding me in a way nothing else could.

"I couldn't stop thinking about what could've happened to you," I whispered, my voice breaking. I felt the tremor in my own words, a raw edge that I couldn't hide.

Zahra pulled back slightly, just enough for our eyes to meet. Despite everything, there was still a softness in her gaze, a strength that defied the darkness around us.

"You'll never lose me again," she said, her voice quiet but steady.

A small smile touched her lips, one that reached her eyes. Even here, surrounded by despair, she had a way of making me believe that maybe, just maybe, there was still a chance. I couldn't shake the feeling that our reunion was bittersweet. Zahra's introduction to her extended family was brief, a blur of faces with hollow eyes and weary smiles. More people had joined us than I'd anticipated, but that hardly mattered. Reaching Addis was all that counted now. The sun's first rays pierced the dusty horizon as we gathered our few remaining belongings and slipped out of the camp. Beyond the tree line lay uncertainty, maybe even death. But our bond, forged through hardship, felt unbreakable. We leaned on each other as we made our way back toward the fence, our breaths mingling in the cool morning air. Whatever waited for us in the forest, I knew we'd face it together. Yet doubt gnawed at me. Were we right to drag these people with us, risking their lives? The fear that followed us seemed as relentless as the shadows beneath the trees. Zahra had insisted on bringing them— she needed their support, and maybe I did too. But were they safer in the camp, where rebels prowled the outskirts and worse things lurked beyond the fences? We'd seen firsthand the devastation those creatures could cause.

We pressed on through the day, stopping only for brief sips of water, forcing dry bread down our throats. The light bled out of the sky, and a chill set in. We needed to find a place to rest before darkness swallowed everything. The others huddled close, faces streaked with dried tears, bodies trembling with fatigue. I saw the fear in their eyes—a reflection of my own. Mita scanned the horizon, her jaw tight as she watched the clouds gathering, dark and menacing.

"We've got a long way to go," she muttered, her voice thick with worry. Her words settled over us like the growing night. Zahra nodded, lips pressed into a thin line. They both knew that whatever semblance of safety awaited us in Addis, we weren't there yet.

The night was thick with shadows, every branch and rustle seeming to whisper secrets. Then I saw something—a hulking form, moving close, keeping pace with us through the undergrowth. Whatever it was, it was big. I could see the mist of its breath, clouds of steam rising in the cold night air, mingling with the damp earth. My pulse quickened, each heartbeat a drum in my chest.

"Did you see any hyenas?" The words burst out of me before I could stop them, my voice cracking—sharp with fear, but tinged with something more desperate, a plea for validation.

Zahra's brow furrowed, her eyes narrowing as she glanced toward Mita, a silent question passing between them. Confusion rippled across her face, but there was something harder behind it too—an edge, like she was bracing herself for something she didn't want to name.

"You mean rebels, Tommy?" she asked, her voice uncertain, low, as if she didn't want the darkness to hear.

"No, hyenas," I snapped back, a flare of irritation breaking through the fear. Couldn't she see the danger right in front of us? Couldn't she feel the weight of those eyes in the shadows?

Mita glanced at me, then turned her gaze toward the distant lights of Addis, faintly visible through the darkening sky. "We're safe from the rebels this far south," she said, trying to sound confident. "Government patrols watch the outskirts of the city. The rebels wouldn't dare come near."

But something in me twisted, as if my mind had snapped a thread that held me together. Was I losing it? I could feel my pulse in my temples, a drumbeat that made the shadows dance. I could see eyes glinting from the underbrush and hear whispers in a language that slipped through my grasp like sand. Zahra's concerned gaze burned into me, but I forced a smile, or thought I did. My face felt foreign, and numb, as if I no longer had control over it. I tried to ignore the creeping dread that clawed at my insides, the certainty that something hunted us. The hyenas—they were real. I could hear them out there, stalking us, mocking me with their low, rumbling laughter. Every snap of a twig or rustle of leaves sent a jolt through my body, muscles coiling, ready to unleash violence if it came to that. But it wasn't just the physical tension that tore at me; it was the memories that churned beneath the surface, the trauma that wrapped around my thoughts like barbed wire.

"The hyenas are here!" I shouted suddenly, the words ripped from my chest. My voice echoed through the trees, sending a shudder through the group. "I can hear them!"

Confusion rippled through the others, their faces turning toward me, eyes wide with uncertainty. They didn't understand the words, but they recognised the fear. Zahra exchanged a worried glance with Mita before stepping closer, her hand finding mine, her grip firm yet gentle.

"Tommy, calm down," she murmured, her voice barely more than a breath. "You're scaring them."

She was right. I could see it in their faces—fear twisting into panic. I took a deep breath, trying to steady myself, to push the madness back. I couldn't afford to break, not now. Zahra squeezed my hand again, her touch anchoring me, and I nodded, though my heart still hammered in my chest.

"Let's keep moving," she said, guiding me back to the group. Her voice was gentle but firm, a lifeline pulling me out of my fear. And so, I followed, trying to shake the feeling that something waited just beyond the shadows, something that would devour us all if I let my guard down for even a second.

CHAPTER 79

The dense underbrush resisted us with every step, the thick vegetation snagging at our clothes and slowing our progress. The kids lagged behind, their murmured complaints barely masking their fear. They stuck close, more out of terror than obedience. The adults moved in grim silence, their faces drawn and hollow. I kept scanning the horizon, the distant glow of Addis Ababa a faint promise of safety—or an end to it all. The ground was treacherous, every footfall a gamble with hidden roots or loose rocks. When the way got too rough, the elders hoisted children onto their backs or cradled them in their arms. The strain showed in their stiff movements and clenched jaws. I reached for a small boy, hoping to give him a break on my shoulders. He shrank away, clinging to Mita's leg, his eyes wide with distrust. My own wounds and scars marked me as an outsider—someone strange, even monstrous, in their eyes. Continued existence was all that mattered. With each step further from the compound, my heartbeat slowed, but the tension never left. Every noise—the snap of a twig, the rustle of leaves—sent my pulse racing again. The sun beat down and sweat mingled with the dried blood on my side where the bandage clung stubbornly to my skin. I winced as I peeled my shirt away, mindful not to reopen the wound. Despite the steady rhythm of our march, I couldn't shake the feeling that we were being watched. Zahra must have sensed my unease; she squeezed my hand, offering a fleeting comfort in her touch. We pressed on, knowing that this trek was more than a fight for survival—it was a test, a trial that demanded everything we had left.

"It's going to be okay, isn't it?" Zahra's voice barely rose above a whisper, her words laced with doubt. "Tommy?"

I turned to her, but the words caught in my throat. I'd seen horrors that words couldn't touch, places that used to pulse with life, now empty shells. When I tried to smile, it felt like my face was cracking under the strain. All I could manage was a nod, but fear clawed at me from the inside. It wasn't just the threat of hyenas that haunted us. Something larger lurked in the shadows—something that troubled all of us, especially Mita, whose silence told me she understood too well. We navigated past crumbling structures, shielding the children's eyes from the worst of what lay scattered among the ruins. The soft earth muffled our steps, but the stench of decay was inescapable, pulling us back into memories of other places, and other battles. A sudden crack split the air, freezing us in place. My hand found Zahra's shoulder, trembling, as I scanned the others. Fear twisted their features into masks of misery.

I forced my voice into steadiness. "Stay calm," I whispered, though the words tasted of my own fear. "We keep moving. It's nothing." I pointed towards a distant grove, urging them forward.

We crossed the brittle ground toward the sparse cover of the trees, their branches like skeletal hands reaching out. Time blurred into the rhythm of movement and silence. Each sound felt amplified in the stillness—my heartbeat, the crunch of dry leaves underfoot, the breathless hush of the group as we huddled among the shadows. Night descended swiftly, wrapping the world in a shroud of uncertainty. I wiped my forehead with a blood-streaked sleeve, dragging Zahra with me through the thick underbrush until we found a hollow where we could disappear into the tall grass. The dried riverbed offered some cover, but it was also a trap. The quiet was oppressive, broken only by the chirp of distant crickets. From our vantage point, the ghostly outlines of abandoned huts glimmered under the moonlight— empty, lifeless. Beyond them, open ground stretched wide, a glaring invitation for danger under the silver glow of the moon. Should we wait here until dawn, when the light would reveal the hidden dangers, or push on through the darkness? The decision hung over me like a guillotine. Alone, I would press forward without hesitation, but the others needed rest— especially the children, who staggered with exhaustion. The group settled in, weary bodies sinking into the cold ground. Zahra and Mita nestled close to the tree line, their shoulders touching as if to ward off the night together. I watched them, my mind full of thoughts I could barely sort through. The shrill hoot of an owl cut through the stillness, a small comfort amidst the unknown. But other sounds lingered—rustling leaves, faint growls on the edge of hearing. I froze, muscles tensing as I strained to see through the darkness. The night swallowed every detail, transforming harmless shadows into potential threats. We stayed motionless, our breath barely stirring the night air. A sudden stumble, a small cry from one of the children—my hand shot up, demanding silence. Fear rippled through the group. Zahra moved to comfort the child, murmuring soft reassurances. No one moved. Eyes darted to me, waiting for direction. I pressed a finger to my lips, holding each gaze in turn until they understood the unspoken command: quiet, stillness. In that fragile pause, I found myself gripping Zahra's hand again. Her fingers twined with mine, and though the words remained unspoken, the message was clear: I'm with you. Whatever comes, we face it together. She glanced up, managing a tired smile, and I felt a flicker of warmth in my chest. We crouched there, holding our breath as the night deepened around us. The moonlit clearing beyond seemed to taunt us with its openness, a pale stage where anything could emerge from the shadows. The children, huddled close, had lost their innocence too early, their eyes haunted by things they shouldn't have seen. Mita took up a watchful position near the edge, her gaze never wavering from the darkness. My own thoughts twisted, a tangled knot of fear and determination. We were so close to safety, yet a part of me couldn't shake the sense that danger hovered just beyond the tree line. Maybe it was the fatigue, or maybe I truly sensed something out there—eyes that burned with more than the hunger of beasts. Whatever waited beyond this night, I knew we had to face it together, no matter how desperate the odds. And so, we clung to the shadows, bracing ourselves for whatever the darkness might bring.

CHAPTER 80

*"He who conceals his disease cannot expect to
be cured."*

Ethiopian Proverb

I drifted in and out of consciousness, suspended in a thick, disorienting fog that seemed to swallow time and space. My mind clawed for something solid, but the world around me wavered, elusive. Then, through the haze, a voice sliced in—low and commanding, each word laced with a quiet menace. It tugged at a memory buried deep, but the details stayed just out of reach.

"Tommy Thompson," the voice snapped, cold and unyielding. *"Get up."*

That bastard again, but this time the familiarity of my own name jolted me like a live wire. My pulse quickened as I fought to open my eyes, squinting against the pale fingers of dawn stretching across the sky. A headache pounded between my temples, but I forced myself upright, gripping the ground until the dizziness began to fade. The air was sharp with the scent of wet earth, carrying a chill that gnawed at my bones.

"Now, Tommy." The voice grew sharper, a finality in its tone. *"It's time to end this."*

A fire ignited deep within, a fury that had been simmering for too long. Memories of murder and loss surge forward—faces, broken promises, blood-soaked nights. The silence felt unnatural, thickening the air with a tension that caused a tightening pain. It was as if the whole world held its breath, waiting for something. Something in me to snap. My skin prickled, every hair on edge. I scanned our crude camp. The others had woken before me— sitting quietly, their gazes sharp, uneasy, watching my every move. Their fear mirrored my own, a reflection that sent a chill deeper than the cold ever could. I crouched next to Mita and Zahra, their small bodies tucked close together against the harsh bite of the early morning. They looked so fragile, faces pale against the dark of their hoods. I gave Mita's shoulder a gentle shake, leaning in close enough that my breath brushed her ear.

"We need to move," I whispered, my voice barely a thread in the thick air. Zahra stirred, her eyes blinking open in confusion, but she quickly caught on—fear sharpening her expression as she clung tighter to Mita's side. I felt sick, something was coming. It had just spoken to me. He said it was time. Time for what? End what? What is about to happen? But I know what is going to happen, I think have always known, that this could only end in one way.

I straightened up, rubbing the grit from my eyes, and winced as the ache in my legs flared to life. I hadn't slept, not really—none of us had. The cold had settled deep in our bones, and the fog, thick as soup, seemed to seep right into my skin, turning the air into a clammy weight that pressed down on everything. It clung to us, muffling even the sounds of our breaths, swirling in ghostly eddies that twisted through the trees at the edge of the clearing. I scanned the shadowy outlines of trunks, barely visible where the dense fog swallowed the treeline, erasing the boundary between forest and open ground. Out there, somewhere beyond the veil of mist, they were waiting. Hunting. I could feel it, sense it, a low, persistent hum in the back of my mind, a primal awareness that danger was out there. Somewhere. My chest tightened, my breath coming in short, frosted puffs that quickly vanished into the chill. I looked back at the others, crouched low in the shadows, wrapped in threadbare blankets, faces hollowed by exhaustion and fear. Their eyes flitted between the fog and me, wide and unsteady, as if they might bolt at the first sign of movement. The kids huddled closer to the adults, seeking warmth, seeking safety in arms that no longer had the strength to promise. They didn't know what was out there, not really. I wished it could stay that way. If they understood—if they truly understood what hunted us—they'd lose what little hope they had left. And hope, as thin and fragile as it was, was the only thing keeping any of us from breaking apart. "We need to move," I whisper, though I'm not sure anyone can hear me over the silence of the fog. It feels like we're the last people on earth; everything else is swallowed by the mist. I glance around, the world around us painted in shades of grey, the light just barely piercing through.

"Listen up," I say, my voice low and urgent. "Stay quiet. Stay sharp." I catch Mita's gaze, holding her eyes for a beat longer, trying to convey the severity of what we're about to do. "You take the point," I tell her. "I'll watch our backs." My words are calm, but beneath them is the heavy weight of what this means. We're walking into uncertainty, and every single one of us knows it. I turn to Zahra, her eyes wide and tired, the kind of exhaustion that doesn't come from lack of sleep but from carrying too many burdens. "Stay with the children," I murmur. "Keep them quiet."

She gives me a small nod, her lips curling into a half-smile that doesn't reach her eyes. There's a heaviness in her expression, a mix of defiance, terror and hopelessness. I want to say something else, something that might reassure her—reassure all of us—but the words stick in my throat. But what could I say? Good luck, we needed a miracle. There is nothing I could say, that wouldn't sound like a lie. I take in the people gathered around me. Fourteen of us, give or take. Mothers clutching their children. Grandmothers with eyes as old as the earth. Fathers, brothers, sisters, and orphans—people who were once part of happy families, are now forced into a fragile unit by circumstance. Each face reflects the same fear, the same raw purpose. They took everything from us, and scattered our families like leaves in the wind, but we're still here, together on the edge of this clearing, one last obstacle before the safety of Addis. The air is biting cold, curling around us, and I pull my clothing tighter. The clearing is bathed in pale, ghostly light. Trees loom on the edges, their dark silhouettes standing watch, as they are spectators at the coliseum, waiting for the bloodshed to start. Their leaves whisper secrets to each other, as though they know what's coming. I shiver, not just from the cold. Mita moves first, her steps careful and deliberate. I can see the tension in her shoulders, and the way her fingers twitch slightly as she scans the shadows. The rest of us follow, moving like ghosts, keeping low, each footfall a believed promise to stay unnoticed. The silence is intimidating, a vast vacuum that feels like it might crush us if we let it. A child's soft whimper cuts through the stillness, a sound so small yet so impossibly loud in this delicate quiet. Zahra's hand moves quickly, muffling the cry before it can develop. An elder shuffled beside me, his steps heavy, as if each one carried the weight of his years and fears. His face, etched with deep lines, twisted slightly when our eyes met—a silent exchange of understanding. His eyes were tired, resigned, as though he had already come to terms with whatever was waiting for us. My chest tightened in response. I wasn't ready for resignation, not yet. The desperation clawed at me, urging me to fight. I was not ready to accept anything. Yet I knew, every noise, every careless step, could be the end.

We continue, inching forward, moving as one. The group huddles too close, almost stepping on each other's heels. I want to tell them to spread out, to give themselves room, to give them a chance, but I know why they stay nearby. There's a feeling of safety in closeness, in knowing that if something were to happen, someone's hand is right there to hold, someone's breath nearby to remind you you're not alone. The mist thickens, and I strain my eyes, searching for movement, for any hint of danger lurking in the grey. My heart thuds in my ears, but I force myself to stay focused. We have to get through this. For them. For the children. For all that's been lost and for whatever fragile hope remains. With cautious steps, we push deeper into the clearing, the damp fog curling around our clothes like cold fingers. The sun—a pale, struggling orb barely visible through the mist—hinted at dawn but gave no warmth, only more uncertainty. Each step felt heavy, and hesitant, as if the very earth were trying to keep us from going farther. The wind shifted suddenly, a chill slicing through the air, and a fresh wave of mist rose from the grass. It was the kind of scene that shouldn't exist outside of nightmares. Slowly, silhouettes began to form within the haze. They seem to drift out of the fog, ghostlike, their movements unnervingly synchronised. My breath caught as they emerged, figures cloaked in darkness, too precise, too deliberate. A nightmare comes alive.

"What the…" Zahra's voice trembled, barely a whisper.

We stopped, our group shrinking together in instinctive fear, bodies pressing close as though that closeness could somehow protect us. I moved to the front next to Mita. They moved with calculated precision in a chilling display of unity. A parade of creatures that seemed to be a manifestation of my worst visions. There must have been at least a dozen. Strange beams of light flickered through the fog, catching still pictures, of terror-stricken faces, eyes wide and mouths slightly open in shock. A collective silence followed, the kind of silence that formed just before a scream broke loose. Silence was no longer needed; pure terror had taken over, leaving us unable to even form words. Then it happened. The screams. Shrill, desperate cries as the figures moved closer, ending any pretence of bravery, we might have had. As the figures of what at first appeared to be men drew closer, I instinctively moved closer to Mita. My heart hammered painfully against my ribs, and I felt Mita grab my arm, her fingers digging in so hard it hurt. I glanced at her; her eyes were wide, terrified. It wasn't just fear—it was the primal knowledge that we were powerless. The figures emerged fully from the mist, and at first, they seemed human—two arms, two legs, and a head. But something was wrong. Their shapes twisted as they moved, their outlines warping as though reality itself couldn't decide what they were. An electric charge filled the air, raising the hair on my arms. I stumbled, my boots sinking into the dew-soaked grass, and the sharp scent of eucalyptus mixed with something else—something metallic and wrong. Fear. I blinked, trying to clear my vision. The shapes were sharpening, and I wished they weren't. These weren't people. They weren't animals. They were something else, their limbs were swelling, and they had eyes that glowed with a malevolent intelligence. Voices filled my head, whispering dark things, impossible things. My thoughts twisted in confusion, every word like a blade against my mind. I clutched my head, trying to push them out.

"No," I muttered, shaking my head. "No, I won't. I... I can't." The whispers grew louder, more insistent, a cacophony of malicious intent. They wanted me to listen, to obey. My breathing quickened, panic bubbling up inside me. Jesus Christ... I'm not seeing this. This isn't real. It can't be real.

But it was. The creatures moved with a sickening gait, stepping closer, their inhuman features becoming clearer. Skin hung off them in loose, rotting folds, stretched tight over bones that jutted out at impossible angles. Their eyes blazed with hunger, something ancient and evil. These were not of this world. What the hell am I supposed to do against... that? They're bigger, faster... stronger. But I have to kill them. I have to. I can't believe this shit. This is fucking insane! As they circle closer, I catch the putrid scent of death radiating from their rotting bodies. My hand tightened around the knife at my side—a knife that suddenly felt more like a toy than a weapon. No backup. No plan. Just me, Mita, and a fucking dagger against these... things.

"Mita," I whispered, my voice cracking. "We have to..." I didn't even know what I was going to say. Run? Fight? It all felt pointless. There was nothing I could say now.

The creatures flexed, their forms warping grotesquely, bones cracking and muscles bulging in ways that defied logic. It was like watching humanity being peeled away, their true forms bursting forth—jagged claws, fangs that gleamed in the weak light, eyes that glowed with a predator's malice. Some of them dropped onto all fours, a sickening hybrid of man and beast, their fur matted and bodies shaking with barely restrained aggression. Their forms continued to stretch and morph, bones cracking and muscles bulging in a truly horrific spectacle. It was a gruesome display of flesh bursting free from their human confines. Their features twisted against the icy light. When they exhaled, steam rose from their bodies and breaths, creating a chilling smog. And I watched in disbelief an eruption of sharp, curved claws from the space previously occupied by their hands, I could feel their wicked intellect radiating from their gazes. Hyenas. The realisation hit me, and I almost laughed at the absurdity. Not wolves. Of course, not wolves. The ferocity, the cunning—these were hyena-men, monstrous, with twisted human faces hiding behind snarling muzzles. Their laughter—oh God, their laughter—echoed around us, high-pitched and mocking, the sound drilling into my ears and setting my nerves on edge. Before I had a chance to react, Mita's blood-curdling scream pierced through my bones as I watched a creature lunge at her, its eyes alight with a sick joy, jaws snapping open to reveal rows of filthy, broken teeth. Those claws. What the fuck am I even up against? Monsters? Real fucking monsters? This can't be happening. Another creature lunged, and I swung wildly, the blade of my dagger glinting in the weak light. It wasn't enough. It was never going to be enough. But I couldn't just stand there and let it end like this. The world around me was being torn apart—screams, snarls, the sound of bones snapping and bodies thumping the ground. The fog seemed to pulse, and I could barely see, barely think. But through it all, one thought burned clear and bright: I had to keep fighting. For Mita. For Zahra. For all of us. Even if it was hopeless.

CHAPTER 81

Suddenly, an icy chill seized my entire body, locking my muscles in place. I couldn't move, couldn't even draw a breath. My limbs felt heavy, like they were encased in stone, and a suffocating cold radiated from within. Panic throbbed in my temples. It felt like I was drowning in my own skin, buried under an avalanche of fear. A sudden warmth—alien and revolting—breathed against the back of my neck. Goosebumps erupted across my skin, and my heart stuttered. The hairs on my neck stood on end, every nerve tensed, alert, dreading what I knew was coming.

'Watch, Tommy,' a voice murmured, low and venomous. It seemed to vibrate through the air, I squeezed my eyes shut, trying to ignore it, but the words dug in like claws. *'You've seen this before. Remember?'* I couldn't make it stop. God, why wouldn't it stop? I looked around, desperate to find whoever—or whatever—was behind that voice, but there was no one.

'You'll never stop this. You can't. You're powerless.' The words filled the room, cold and certain, each one sinking deeper. I clenched my fists, trying to drown it out. Trying not to listen. But it was like the voice was inside me, clawing at my thoughts, digging in. My body wouldn't respond. I tried to move—anything, just a twitch—but every muscle stayed locked, like something heavy and invisible had pinned me down. Helpless, I could feel my own panic rising, a quiet horror at the thought that maybe this time, I couldn't fight back. I tried to scream, but only a faint whimper came out. My thoughts scrambled, slipping away before I could hold onto a single one.

"No… please, no," I whispered, the words barely audible, strangled by a fear that felt like it might suffocate me.

A scream built up inside my chest, desperate to break free, but all that came out was a shaky, stifled gasp. A thick, heavy silence pressed in around me, shutting me off from everything familiar, every point of safety. The noise hit me first—a low, rising rumble of screams and snarls, raw and savage, clawing at the edges of my sanity. They came from all sides, pressing in on me, leaving no escape. I knew this place. The clearing was exactly as I remembered it—not from a distant dream but from the raw fragments of memory my mind tried to bury. I could almost see the aftermath of the violence, the ground still echoing with what had happened here. Faces I couldn't fully recognise flickered through my mind, and then Zahra's face appeared, right there, like she'd been waiting. Her eyes were wide, full of fear, locking onto mine as if we were both back in that moment. The screams around us swelled, but all I could see was her, her terrified stare mirroring my own. It felt like my body had frozen in place, held up by an invisible force I couldn't fight. My breath came in shallow gasps as I struggled to take control. If I didn't move now, they'd kill her. I knew it with a sick, gut-wrenching certainty. And then, in a heartbeat, she was gone. My eyes searched the clearing, scanning the chaos. Where was she? All around me, claws and fangs tore into flesh, bodies ripped apart with no mercy, no pause. The creatures didn't look like animals anymore; they moved with precision, a dark intelligence that defied reason. Their snarling jaws and blood-matted fur filled the air with the thick, metallic smell of death. They didn't just kill—they tore, and shredded, making sure every scream lingered.

Somewhere in the blur, I caught sight of Mita. One of those things had her, its claws buried in her thigh and arm as she kicked and thrashed. Blood soaked the ground beneath her, and her eyes locked on mine, pleading. I opened my mouth to scream, but the sound was strangled by horror. The creature's dead eyes met mine as it ripped Mita's body apart and hurled it into the trees. Blood sprayed through the air, painting the branches in a grotesque display of violence. My mind reeled, but my body stayed frozen, rooted to the spot. The clearing lay open, the full horror exposed. These things didn't just kill for survival; they killed for the sheer pleasure of it, tearing through my family like nothing. Bloodcurdling cries filled the night, then fell silent, one by one, until only the sounds of tearing and snarling remained. My chest felt hollow, and empty, like my insides had been scooped out and left to rot. My thoughts twisted in desperation— 'Where's Zahra?'

I stood in a cage of mist, trapped in a ring of blood-soaked ground. And then, as if summoned by my own horror, the biggest of them all prowled out from the fog, its fur slick with gore, fragments of bone clinging to its body. It lifted its head, sniffing the air, locking its black, empty eyes on me. My heart thundered, my lungs tight as I struggled to breathe. A voice crawled into my head, dark and mocking.

'You cannot escape, Tommy. Here, your fears become real.'

I tried to scream, but no sound came. Then I saw her—Zahra, struggling in the creature's grip, her face streaked with blood but fierce, defiant. She was thrashing, clawing, her voice hoarse as she fought with everything she had left.

"Help me, Tommy. Please." Her voice trembled, her hand reaching toward me, eyes filled with panic, with a glint of hope that was slipping away. I reached out, but my feet stayed glued to the ground, helpless as the monster's claws tightened around her.

CHAPTER 82

Blood dripped from its bared, jagged teeth as it fixed me with a twisted grin. The creature's talons tore through Zahra's body, ripping into flesh and bone. She gasped, a sound so faint I barely heard it, and a spray of red splattered across the ground, pooling at her feet. I stood there, helpless, my body rooted in terror as it dragged her closer, one clawed hand clawing through the dirt, the other tangled in her hair. I wanted to scream, to fight back, but my legs wouldn't move, and my voice was frozen.

"Stay with me," I whispered, the words barely a breath. My voice cracked, the useless plea hanging in the air between us. Her eyes opened for a second, cloudy and dim, lips moving with no sound, just a faint rasp that broke whatever shred of courage I had left.

Then the creature's grip tightened, and it laughed—a guttural, mocking sound. Its body was a twisted combination of claws and bone, human hands mixed with talons and paws. Its eyes were too human, filled with sick pleasure, watching me watch her die. Zahra's hand reached toward me, her gaze fixed on mine, filled with silent pleading. It was a look I'd never seen before. Her hand fell to her side, fingers curling into the blood-soaked earth as the beast leaned in, its jaws opening wide, teeth gleaming as it tore into her. A scream, deeper and louder than anything I'd ever heard, filled the air. It was her, crying out one last time, so raw and desperate that even the creature flinched. The beast snarled in response, its serrated teeth glistening with saliva and blood. It shook her like a ragdoll, tossing her body aside when it was done, a dull thud marking her lifeless form on the ground. Blood seeped from her, pooling around her in the pale, cold light, her body empty, gone.

I sank to my knees beside her, feeling the weight of everything crash down, hollow and cold. Her name slipped out of me, barely a whisper, breaking as I spoke. My hands hovered over her, useless, shaking with the things I should have done but didn't. I couldn't fix this. I'd let her down. I'd let all of them down. Each breath clawed against my throat, the horror suffocating, endless. My body shook, not with fear anymore, but with rage, a rage so deep it made me shake as I cradled what was left of her. Around me, the creatures prowled, their laughter echoing like taunts. I closed my eyes, shutting them out, but their voices were there, their twisted faces and mocking gazes pressed into my mind. I could hear her voice somewhere in the haze, the words a low whisper.

'*Do what you must. Find a way,*' *she urged, her voice barely more than a memory.* '*Come find me. I'll be waiting.*' *Zhara called to me.*

The words burned through the haze, sharpening my focus. I stood up, a pulse of purpose beating with each heartbeat. The creature looked at me, eyes glinting, amused by my defiance. The mocking laughter grew louder, the snarls echoing. I clenched my fists, a single thought cutting through the terror: this was not the end. With every step, the ground beneath me felt heavier, soaked in blood and the weight of all I had lost. The beast's gaze met mine, taunting, daring me to fight, its claws ready, its fangs bared. And this time, I ran at it, my heart pounding, my fists clenched, my voice ripping out in a roar that drowned out the laughter.

CHAPTER 83

"One is born, one dies, but the land continues to flourish."

Ethiopian Proverb

My screams are lodged in my throat, any sound coming out is silent. I gasp for air, lungs burning, panic growing. Are these screams mine? I am alive, but am I truly awake, or trapped in a continual nightmare? What the fuck is this? My heart's pounding so hard I can feel it in my temples. I gasp, feeling as though I haven't breathed in a while. My chest feels heavy, as if someone's sitting on it, pressing down with the weight of the world. It takes a second to remember—the bloody clearing. Shit! I am no longer there. Zahra! What happened? No! It can't be real. A mercy as my memory's fog evaporates—I was torn from there, that hell, the blood, but where am I now? And where is Zahra? Is she still there? No, she can't be. She was killed, right? Or was she? I lay motionless, but my mind was a vortex of blunt voices and thoughts. My eyelids feel heavy. It's almost like they've forgotten how to open. I try to open them, but it's like they've been glued shut. I try to make sense of it all. Panic and reasoning rush in and out as blood pulses in my head. The words whirling around in my mind were like scattered pieces of a puzzle, making me even more frustrated about my true identity. That couldn't have happened. That didn't happen! Did it? My head throbs with the intensity of my thoughts. I try to swallow, but it's like swallowing razors. My throat burns, raw and swollen. The taste of metal— copper, blood maybe—on my tongue, mixing with the bitterness of chemicals, bile. My mouth is dry, my tongue scraping against the roof of my mouth like rough sandpaper. It's stuck up there, held in place by something that feels or tastes like plastic or rubber. There is a steady buzzing in my ears, leaving me deaf to the outside world. Silhouettes twist and contort, their images glitching in and out of focus. A loud bang, a door slamming shut. I think it's a door; it jars me back to the present time. I hear a voice. Voices, maybe? Distant, muffled. Too many sounds. Machines whirring, footsteps echoing down long halls. However, everything blends together, as if filtered through layers of dense, oppressive fog. I

271

can't make out words. Just noise. Dull, thudding sound. I shove them aside, but the physical pain is too intense. Sharp, shooting pains lace through my legs and arms, akin to electric shocks. I attempt to move, but my limbs are... useless. Hopeless lumps of flesh. My arms, my legs—they're heavy, unresponsive. I try to lift them, but there's nothing. No strength. Just pain. Every muscle in my body feels like it's on fire, as if it's lost its ability to function. An unusual pressure, as if forced open, surrounds the outside of my mouth. A searing sensation radiates through my left arm, increasing with every second. At the same time, a sharp pain shoots through my inner thigh. Once again, my eyelids resist my attempts to pry them open. But slowly, I manage. The light is painfully bright and blurry. I struggle to adjust to the light and focus, making everything appear blurry and shapeless without clear edges. I don't feel safe. My thoughts are still focused on the slaughter. How can something so tangible and barbaric be real? It all feels so real, but a part of me can't believe it actually happened. I am torn between accepting the reality and clinging to the hope that it was all just a terrible nightmare. Sounds filter in slowly, like water seeping through cracks. A rhythmic beeping. The soft hum of machines. It's oddly comforting. The pain in my arm intensifies until it is all-consuming. I clench my jaw and attempt to concentrate on my breath.

"Mr Thompson? Can you hear me?"

The voice is friendly but muffled. A nurse? A friend? I can't quite place it. The room around me begins to come into focus. There's a sterile white, clinical smell, an unmistakable presence of disinfectant mixed with something else I can't quite identify. This clinical smell can only mean one thing: this is a hospital. I attempt to move my hand to see if I can, but it feels as though concrete encases it, as if it's not even mine. A foreign object with a rubbery taste, likely a ventilator, obstructs my mouth, preventing me from speaking. Slowly I manage to turn my head towards the voice, but it feels like I am fighting against invisible restraints. The beeping speeds up. I can feel panic crawling up my spine and tightening in my chest. I want to scream, but I can't. I just can't. It hurts. Why can't I move? Why does everything hurt so much? What the hell is going on? It's like I have woken up in someone else's body. A body that's been smashed, hollowed out, and filled with suffering.

"Relax, stay calm," a new voice interjects.

I squinted at the blurry figure in front of me, leaning in closer, their arms stretched out towards my face. Then a pressure. A restricting weight in my throat, it's as though that object still is lodged. I can't draw in a full breath, my chest heaves with quick and panicked gasps. The sensation is sharp and uncomfortable, akin to someone scraping my insides.

Then, I hear the first lady again, "Okay, we are removing it now. Try to relax and breathe."

Relax? How the fuck am I supposed to relax when there's a tube shoved down my throat? She tells me to exhale, and as I do, I feel the tube moving, sliding up and out, and it's the strangest, most uncomfortable feeling—like I'm being pulled inside out. From my throat to my chest, I can feel it. It is a slow, deliberate drag, as if something is being peeled free. It's not painful—more like a burning irritation and a feeling of being choked, which is making me gag. As soon as it leaves my mouth, I start coughing up some phlegm. The air hits my lungs, and I cough again, my throat convulsing. It feels like I've swallowed sand, and each breath that follows is a struggle—shallow, ragged, like I'm relearning how to use my own lungs. I try to speak, but my voice doesn't come out right. It's just a hoarse whisper, broken and weak. My throat feels shredded and raw from the inside, and the taste in my mouth is metallic and bitter. My chest heaves as I suck in the air, trying to calm down, but each breath feels rough and shaky, like I might choke all over again.

A hand rested on my shoulder, followed by a soft voice. "Take it slow. You're doing great."

I nod, but I don't feel like I'm doing great. It feels like I've just fought my way out of something I wasn't supposed to survive. The memories of what did or did not occur continue to haunt my mind. Every breath hurt, and my throat felt inflamed as if I'd been screaming for hours. Thankfully, the tube is gone now. I can finally breathe on my own once more, although it feels like I have to relearn how.

"Water..." I mouth the words, but they are not audible.

I heard rustling next to me, then someone's shadow over me. "Here, take it slow." A straw touches my lips, and I gratefully sip the cool liquid.

Her features are clearer as my vision becomes sharper. She leans towards me with a smile on her face, which is slightly unsettling. But in her eyes, there is a look of pure wonder. She wore a crisp white coat and an apron adorned with two large bulky pockets at the front; she was quite pretty and exuded a Filipino charm. A small crease formed between her eyebrows as she concentrated intently on her tasks. She touches my hand, and I instantly feel the warmth radiate from hers. 'Where am I? What happened?' No sound comes out; it's all in my head. With my internal voice unheard, I focus on the room—soft beeps, a faint whirring, distant voices, all so muffled, like someone stuffed my ears with wool. I blink slowly, trying to focus and understand. Where the fuck is this? I quickly scan the room, hoping for any indication of safety. Is there someone I recognise? A window to see the outside world? Nothing. The image of Zahra's violent death flashes to mind. The memories play on a loop—unending and unbearable. Everything feels wrong. Tears prick at the corners of my eyes. I try to speak again, but my words are still failing me. There's so much to understand— so much to catch up on. My body feels foreign, weak, and uncooperative. My joints are stiff and resistant, as though they've rusted over time. A dull ache everywhere is accompanied by grinding pain. When I move my body, the skin on my back becomes especially sensitive, causing a stinging sensation. How long have I been here? Why can't I remember? My heart is pounding, and the beeping machines mirror my anxiety. I take it all in—the sterile walls—

the IV pumping fluids into my arm, the heart monitor beeping loudly. I'm stuck in this damn bed. Every cord and plug on the wall seem to connect to me, beeping and flashing constantly. Meanwhile, two or three nurses are bustling around, all of whom seem to avoid eye contact. The scent of detergent, the chilling temperature in the room, and the tape holding the IV needle in my vein were all familiar. It was all familiar. They have access to every part of me, including my thoughts. I can't help but feel exposed and vulnerable, like prey left out for the taking. These walls are already suffocating me. The sharp scent of bleach makes my head spin. And the machines... they're like a second heartbeat, telling me I'm trapped here. Ow! A sharp needle punctured my skin, jolting me back to the reality of my isolation. The memories surge back, each one piercing me like a blade. Zahra's face is burned into my mind, her presence haunting me even in death. Was it real? It had to be. The creature's breath and the taste of blood were all too vivid. 'Zahra!' I cried out, hoping for a response, but nothing escaped my mouth. 'Zahra, please!' I begged for a response that I knew would never come. I return to a world devoid of meaning without her by my side. Her name is all I have left. What will I do? What's the point anymore? My voice is choking. I desperately cling to her memory, but all I find are my own demons clawing and snarling. How do I even begin to forget? How can I seek justice when my heart is shattered beyond repair?

CHAPTER 84

I find myself in an alien environment, yet it feels oddly familiar—a place visited countless times. The air is still and stifling, offering no comfort. I feel cornered, no way out. All I want to do is wake up, but I don t think I can. The trees press in around me, forming a living wall that seems to stretch up into the sky, reaching heights that make me feel insignificant. Above, the swollen moon loiters in the dark sky, its silver orb casting a glow over the land. Zahra stands before me, her breaths steady and lungs filled with air; she is alive. How? I watched her murdered. I can t remove the images seared into my mind—a vortex of carnage. Blood, viscera, and terror grip me as I witness again and again, her body being torn to pieces. The monsters, dark and cruel, still cackle in the fog, mocking me as I relive the terror, and the screams that are still clear in my mind. This is the last memory I have of her—the final time I saw her face, heard her voice, felt her touch. I shudder, as I realise where I stand: the clearing where cruelty feasted upon her. Surprisingly, this horror-plagued ground appears unharmed. On the far side, there are huts and homes with enclosures holding goats and other livestock. It s just me, with Zahra standing about fifty feet away, a sense of fear hangs in the air. With each step I took, she raised her hand to stop my advance. Her lips curl into a smile like I've never seen before. Despite her undeniable beauty, there was something distinctly different about her—a dark and troubling difference that cast a shadow on her memory. Restless, she paces, muttering to herself as if possessed. She suddenly grabs her head, her face contorting in unspeakable agony. Her eyes locked with mine momentarily, pleading for help, but I was completely powerless to intervene. Her body began to convulse violently; the sickening crack of her bones echoed through into the night, making me recoil in horror. The once lovely skin covering her frame stretched and bulged grotesquely as some monstrous entity clawed its way to the surface from within her very core. In a crazed and torturous act, she feverishly tore the elegant shamma from her shoulders. Her hands, once delicate and gentle, now elongated into horrifying forms, with blackened nails twisting into sharp talons. The sight of her once-soft flesh rippling and tearing apart was an abomination of nature—enough to send even the most fearless soul into hysterics. Her spine bent out of shape like some repulsive deformity as she doubled over in pain, all the while snarling and screeching like a creature dredged up from mankind's darkest nightmares. Her jaw unhinged with an appalling snap, opening far wider than should be humanly possible. Smooth teeth shifted grotesquely into jagged fangs capable of rending flesh from bone. Hair, fur, or something sprouted rapidly across her body, thick and matted, like some dark outbreak overtaking her once flawless skin. I could hear the guttural growl rumbling deep within her throat as her bones cracked and reformed, muscles bulging unnaturally beneath the deformed flesh. It was as if this once radiant woman was being torn apart and rebuilt into the very monstrous abomination that killed her. Yet above all else, what haunted me most was the sheer terror in her eyes—those beautiful eyes that had once been so full of warmth and love, now trapped and terrified. The beast within her took over, consuming her very being along with the woman I loved. And just as suddenly as it started, it stopped, and her features were no longer visible. She had vanished completely, leaving behind only this freakish form. What stood before me was no longer human. This creature—this unholy beast in the form of a hyena—now towered over me, its breath heavy with saliva and bloodlust. There was no trace of my beloved Zahra within its malevolent glare. It remained there, wild, and aggressive, poised to rip through anything in the vicinity. The darkness closed in around us, swallowing any remaining fragment of hope as I stared into the evil eyes of unspeakable horror. A living nightmare imprisons me, leaving me alone with what used to be Zahra. Now, she transforms into a blood-soaked, savage creature, snarling in the same clearing that claimed her. She is the one person I cannot imagine my life without. And now… I m nothing. She draws near, her eyes glowing, and a tremendous growl resonates from her mouth, spewing saliva and other toxins all over my face…

I woke up, gasping for breath. Sweat-damp sheets tangled around my legs. I could feel the mattress underneath me, but it didn't feel like a bed—it felt like a cage, like I'd been locked in place. I remind myself to breathe and focus on the simple in and out. I need to ground myself, to find an anchor in this surreal reality. There is a lot to understand, much to remember and relearn, but for now, I'm here—I'm awake.

"He's awake," "call Dr Harris." A voice pushed through the images. I'm having trouble focusing on the words. "I'm Emily, the nurse assigned to your care here," she says abruptly. Just as I open my mouth to ask where the fuck here is, she continues. "You were already informed of this, and the doctor is on his way," she adds turning away. I watch her walk through the double swinging doors, disappearing from view, but not before giving me a stony look over her clipboard. She was a nurse I hadn't seen before, and I didn't like her or her attitude.

A man's voice interrupts me. "Mr Thompson?" he says, his voice calm and professional. "We need to conduct some tests, and this nurse will address any questions you may have." Taking a breath, he scans the room for something or someone. "We will schedule private sessions in the near future to discuss any further questions or concerns you may have," he added before turning to talk to someone. I can't make out what they are saying, but judging by the side glances in my direction, it's telling me all I need to know. I want to demand answers—to know why—or just scream. I quickly scan the room and see three doctors and a couple of nurses, including the Filipino nurse from yesterday. They are attentively working around me, their hands firm, their instruments probing and analysing. It's an intrusion, but probably a necessary one. My gaze falls on my trembling hands, along with the muscles and skin that have failed to protect everything I love. I was nothing but a useless shell, with tubes and needles going in and lines coming out.

'The hideous creatures keep returning to me, their murderous intent burning my heart. I tussled to look away, but powerful paws held me in place.'

"Mr Thompson, how are you feeling today?" A Filipino nurse brings me out of my awful visions. I have no idea how much time has passed, but judging by the condition of my body, I've been here for quite some time. Now, I have the opportunity to ask questions. She seems trustworthy, but I suspect she will follow a pre-planned script.

"Hi there, I'm Marie," she introduces herself with a smile. "We can chat while they check on your condition today." She pauses, then adds, "I heard you have some questions. Please fire away."

"How long have I been here?" I croak, a quiver evident in my voice.

Marie responds softly. "You've been in a coma, Mr Thompson." In a coma? The words take me completely by surprise. How much time has passed? Days? Weeks?

"A... year," Marie answers, almost as if she can read my thoughts. "You've been asleep for an entire year."

A year? My head swirls with disbelief. "It's Tommy," I murmur under my breath as I struggle to comprehend what she has just told me. A thousand questions flood my mind. What happened to Zahra? Is she safe? Are my mother and brother, okay? Where the hell am I? How did I end up here? I open my mouth to speak, but my voice fails me. I take a deep breath and try again, but still no words come out.

Marie places a hand on mine. "One step at a time, Tommy." My mom's past words are a small comfort, but I need more answers. Am I the only one who made it? Are we still in Ethiopia? Wait, what's happening to me? I am slurring my words, and my vision is becoming hazy. The room starts to spin, and I feel like I'm going to pass out. I try to speak…

"Take slow, deep breaths, Tommy. Rest now," she says softly. And with those words, my vision fades to black.

CHAPTER 85

*Monsters are real, and ghosts are real too. They
live inside us, and sometimes, they win.*

Stephen King

The dagger, it's right there in front of me. I'm back in the forest. Fuck! This has to be a dream. It has to be, because the same dagger I used to kill is now hovering in the air, about two feet away from me. What does this mean? I reach out and take hold of it, relishing the satisfying weight in my hand as it fits perfectly into my palm. It seems almost custom-made for me. I test its movements, swishing it through the air like a scythe. A loud rumbling in the distance startles me, and a blinding light forces me to cover my eyes tightly. Once the light dims, I cautiously open my eyes and examine the dagger in my hand. It begins to tingle, and before I know it, the dagger starts to disintegrate into grains of sand. The particles are slipping through my fingers and cascading to the ground below. As the grains of sand touch the ground, it also undergoes a transformation into sand. The ground shifts beneath my feet. I take a step back, battling to maintain my footing on the altering land. My body doesn't move fast enough to respond. I slip and fall backwards landing on the soft, warm sand. The trees around me also begin to crumble like fountains of sand, collapsing one by one, until all there is left are miles and miles of sand dunes, as far as my eyes can see. The sun approaches closer than I have ever experienced, its surface is a turbulent inferno of heat and light. Boiling waves of fire dance across its fiery surface, with bursts of explosive energy radiating outward. Despite its intensity, all I can feel is a comforting warmth radiating from it. I look around aimlessly and realise I am standing in the middle of an unending desert, the sand shifting beneath my feet like molten gold. The sky above is a deep, unnatural shade of purple. As the sun moves further away, it creates stretched-out shadows that distort the landscape. I rise to my feet and the sand dunes seem to relocate and morph around me, forming fascinating patterns that appear almost alive. Then, in the distance, a figure is running towards me, his form growing larger with each passing second. It's Samuel, I recognise him immediately. Without hesitation, I start running towards him, calling out his name and waving my arms to get his attention. He runs faster but the gap between us seems to be widening *as he becomes smaller in the distance. I pick up speed, my feet pounding against the dunes. But with each step, I feel myself sinking deeper into the sand. Soon, it's up to my waist, then my chest, and finally reaches my neck. I struggle to move, I'm stuck, only my head above the sand. I can no longer see Samuel, who has disappeared behind a nearby sand dune. The air is warm and still, and my mirror image stares back at me from every angle in the sky, each one diverse, as if mocking my every move. When I begin to study them, they abruptly shatter like broken glass, revealing Samuel standing nearby. His face is expressionless, barefoot, and almost naked. His body is glistening with sweat. He falls to his knees in front of me, tears pouring down his cheeks as he weeps uncontrollably. His voice is low and filled with grief as he speaks, ' Why didn't you save my daughter? She could have been spared. Why!"*

Sobs wrack my body, my eyes overflow with tears as I reply, "I'm sorry, I tried. Really, I did." Before I could ask for forgiveness… Samuel opens his hand to reveal his daughter's precious pebble. It's the same one that I placed in her tiny hand when I buried her. My head drops in shame, fully aware that I have failed both him and his daughter. When I lift my head once more, he has vanished. In a moment of despair, I release a heart-wrenching shriek. "SORRYYYY...!"

I bolt upright, gasping for air, "SORRYYYY...!" still tearing from my throat as my eyes shoot open. The dream bleeds into reality, my voice ricocheting off the walls of the room. My chest heaved, and for a second, I didn't know if I was still dreaming. The scream was stuck there, caught somewhere between sleep, and waking, eventually trailing off into gravelly, breathless gasps.

From behind me, a male voice spoke. "You're safe now, it was only a dream, Mr Thompson. Please be calm."

How the fuck can I be calm. Safe, fucking joking, isn't he? There was no sense of safety in anything. How could there be, when every time I shut my eyes, a never-ending parade of terrifying thoughts flashes through my mind? I consider asking for a phone call, but who would I even call? My brother? My Mum? Even if I could remember their numbers, I have no idea what I would say to them. I don't know, where I am, no one is willing to talk. I sigh in dismay and tug a small device off of my right index finger. Heart monitor or something.

As the days passed, it dawned on me that I was confined in this place. I didn't see any other patients; there were no other patients to be seen, only the same nurses and doctors making their rounds each day. Everyone in this place actively avoids me, as if I am carrying the plague. No, it's more like they were forbidden from speaking to me. And every time I felt myself drifting off, I knew it was because of the drugs they constantly pumped into my body. Their words I suppose were meant to comfort and give me an impression of security. But the fact is I felt isolated from the world in this hospital that was anything but ordinary. Dr Harris was always nearby, quietly observing and taking notes while I drifted in and out of consciousness. He was young, maybe early thirties, but there was something in his eyes that made him seem older—like he'd seen too much too soon. His dark hair was cropped short, clean, almost military style, with not a strand out of place. He had that neatly groomed beard that some men grow to look more distinguished, though on him it felt a little too precise, like he measured it every morning. He wore the usual doctor's coat, stark white, buttoned up. Underneath, a pale blue dress shirt with a navy tie, both of which seemed far too formal for a place like this. The kind of tie you'd expect in a law office, not a hospital. No wrinkles anywhere on him. He was spotless. The creases in his pants were sharp enough to cut glass, and his lace-up shoes—polished brown leather—looked like they'd never touched the ground outside.

Days and nights blurred together, yet he was never far away. They monitored my every move and dissected my every word. Therapy sessions felt like combat where I had to confront my emotions, exposing the events, and the nightmares that were ripping me apart internally. I squeeze my eyes shut, but that just makes it worse because all I can see is the nightmare flashing back, playing on a loop like some sick movie I can't turn off. I force my eyes open, only to find Dr Harris sitting at my bedside. I look down and see that one of my wrists has been restrained.

"Mr Thompson," he began, his voice relaxing and calm despite the weight of his words. "You've been through quite an ordeal. Your body has healed from the physical trauma, but your mind... that's where the true fight begins." He tilts his head to the side, his intense blue eyes zeroing in on something or someone behind me. He directed a small, almost unnoticeable nod over my shoulder. I couldn't see who or what he was nodding at, but a feeling of unease washed over me.

"The restraints," he says, noticing me looking at the band around my left wrist. "For your safety, as well as ours. We can't have you wandering around, can we?"

I frantically blurted out my questions to Dr Harris, desperate for answers. "What's happening? How did I escape from Ethiopia? Are those creatures dead? And where is Zahra's body? Did anyone else make it out alive?"

But then Dr Harris raised his hand to silence me, his voice calm and measured as he spoke. Despite the babel in my mind, I forced myself to take a deep breath and focus on what he had to say. Let's tackle this one item at a time," he said.

"Tommy, pay attention. You didn't leave Cardiff," Dr Harris stated firmly. I struggled to focus, my mind still reeling from the memories of Zahra's execution. "You were hurting after Zahra's death."

"So, you know it was real? Do you understand how she was killed? The monsters? The murders? Abductions. The fucking Rapes?" I paused to catch my breath, before realising what he had just said. "What do you mean I never left Cardiff? Are you taking the piss? He moves nervously on his chair, pushing back a fraction away from me. "You need to stay calm Tommy."

My thoughts were in a frenzy, trying to make sense of it all. "Stay Calm? How could I possibly stay calm? I was in Ethiopia. I was there. Zahra had been taken, friends were killed helping me. Stay calm? Fuck off!" I yelled directly into his face, spraying him with spittle.

He rises to his feet, wiping his face before turning to a nurse standing behind my bed. He nods slightly and gestures towards my IV line. Then, he turns to me with a serious expression. "Let's pick up this conversation later when you've had a chance to rest and gather your thoughts."

CHAPTER 86

My eyelids blink open, and I slowly wake, only to find myself in the same room, with its distinct scents and sights. The beep, beep, beep of the machines, telling me what I already know. My fingers are ice cold, but the rest of me is burning up. I'm sweating profusely, a regular experience on waking. My throat feels rough and scratchy, as if I had been shouting all night long. As my senses come back to me, I take inventory of my body. My chest rises and falls, confirming that I can still breathe. I look around and see clearly—no blurry vision or double vision. The sound of faint beeps and hums fills my ears, indicating that my hearing is working. But even though all my physical functions seem to be intact, my mind is a mess, struggling to hold onto any shred of sanity. There's a dull ache in my head and tightness in my chest, but at least I can feel something—better than the numbness I've been feeling for days now. I shift slightly in my bed, wincing as I feel the IV needle tug against my skin.

Marie leaned forward, her fingers twisting the edge of her sweater, a faint tremor in her voice. "Tommy," she murmured, her tone gentle yet carrying a tension I hadn't noticed before. "You're safe now. They put you to sleep because you were... well, you were in a state. They said you were becoming... agitated." She glanced around the room, her gaze skittering over the sterile walls, her discomfort plain.

"Agitated?" I echoed, struggling to piece together her words. I could still feel the foggy remnants of sedation dulling the edges of my thoughts, leaving me raw and frayed. I tried to meet her eyes, but she looked away, pressing her lips together as if preparing herself.

Her voice dropped, soft and hesitant, like she was breaking bad news. "You're here because of... an attempt," she said carefully. "They told me it was... a suicide attempt." She hesitated, the words almost stumbling out, her voice wrapped in apology.

I froze, a wave of disbelief crashing over me, tightening my throat. "No," I croaked, shaking my head. "That can't be. I went to Ethiopia. I went to find my wife." My voice wavered, the painful truth of her loss stinging behind my eyes, as vivid as if it had happened hours ago. I could feel the disbelief crawling up my spine as I studied Marie's sympathetic expression, the way she was looking at me like I was some fragile thing. But her face didn't change; only the pity there deepened.

"No," I repeated, more desperately. "I *know*' what happened. And I had to go. I had to." The memory of my wife was sharp and solid, something real I could hold onto, unlike this place with its stale air and harsh fluorescent lights. And yet, the doctor's words rattled back through my head, cutting through the confusion: *You never left Cardiff.*'

If I'd never left Cardiff, then where was I now? And why would they say I tried to—' *no,*' I thought, clinging to the last pieces of clarity. "Marie," I whispered, searching her face for some hint that she believed me, that she knew something I didn't. "Where... where am I?"

Marie shook her head and trailed off, looking around nervously as if afraid of being caught. She met my gaze, her lips pressed together in a tight line, but the fear lingered in her eyes, making them shine. Her gaze flitted back toward the door again, and I felt the tension ripple through her as if she expected someone to burst in at any second. Her fingers clenched and unclenched at her sides. She inhaled sharply, then nodded back, swallowing hard. As she turned to leave, I could see her visibly trying to shake off the drawn-out tension. Just as her hand touched the handle, the door swung open, and Dr Harris stepped in, his presence cutting through the room like a blade. His gaze fell on Marie, cold and dissecting. Marie froze. She looked down quickly, her shoulders hunching instinctively, then squeezed past him through the doorway, her footsteps fading down the hall before I had the chance to call her back. Dr Harris watched her go, his expression unreadable, though the slight twitch of his jaw betrayed some unspoken disapproval. With a sigh, he turned back to me and took the seat beside my bed, his gaze now fixed on me with the same relentless scrutiny he had just given her. For a moment, we just stared at each other, and I couldn't shake the feeling that he was looking right through me, sizing up every inch of what he thought he knew.

"Shall we continue?" His voice was steady, but it was his eyes that unsettled me. An odd shade of hazel, they caught the light differently—pale in places, almost golden in others, and completely devoid of warmth. They had the detached chill of a surgeon about to cut, watching but not really seeing. As he looked at me, I felt like a specimen under his gaze, sliced open, categorised, and diagnosed before I could say a word.

"Your injuries were severe, Mr Thompson," he said, with a tilt of his head that I suppose was meant to convey sympathy. "Frankly, it's remarkable you survived." Survived. What did that word even mean? There was no "surviving" in this, not in the way people thought. It was just a slow, forced existence in a body that felt alien and broken.

Harris's stare hardened, more insistent. "When you arrived here in October 2015, you were already teetering between life and death, Mr Thompson." He stepped closer, gaze pinned to mine, as though he could somehow force me to accept it. My mind started to spin, and in the dark haze of memories, Zahra's face surfaced—the raw pain of seeing her mutilated body, the way her eyes had looked when they...

I forced myself to speak, my voice breaking. "What about Zahra?"

He hesitated, and for a moment, I thought I saw something crack in his facade. "I'm sorry, Tommy," he said, his voice soft but clinical. "Zahra didn't survive."

She was dead. Gone. The image was vivid, and undeniable. I'd seen her die. They must think I'm insane, but they're the ones lying, aren't they? My fists clenched, and I forced myself to breathe slowly. If I made a scene, they'd just sedate me again.

"I need to see her," I managed, each word strained. "To know where she is. To find her grave."

He paused, gaze flickering as if calculating something, before finally nodding. But his expression held something back—a hint of evasion. "I'll... I'll look into that," he said, and then, as if to escape the moment, he rose and walked toward the door. But just as he reached it, he turned back, his expression almost paternal, with a sincerity that felt rehearsed. "You've endured significant trauma, Mr Thompson. Healing takes time, and it's important not to push yourself too fast. Give your mind the space it needs."

Give my mind space? How could I lie here and do nothing while my whole life was erased from beneath me? There had to be someone out there who knew I was alive. My brother, my mother, her family... anyone. But they were all out of reach, and all I had was this stranger with his hollow sympathy. As if sensing my desperation, he adjusted his tie, glancing down, shuffling his feet in that way of his that always gave me the impression he was uncomfortable with the weight of his own words.

"For someone with severe post-traumatic stress disorder, it's not uncommon to experience persistent delusions," he explained, his tone almost apologetic. "The mind creates vivid stories as a defence mechanism."

A bitter laugh rose in my throat, and I bit it down, a flicker of something dark and searing rising in my chest. I wanted to burn everything around me, to see what remained when it was all ashes. If I ever got the chance, maybe—just maybe—that's exactly what I'd do.

CHAPTER 87

I think back to those warm evenings with Zahra in Addis, her laughter mingling with the smoky aroma of roasting coffee. We'd sit for hours, trading stories about our homes—my Scotland, her Ethiopia. I remember one night when I told her about the Loch Ness Monster, painting a picture of the misty lochs, the ancient castles, and the soft, rolling hills of my homeland. Her eyes, wide and full of that bright curiosity, held me captive as I spun tales of an elusive creature lurking in the waters, half-myth, half-dream. I promised to take her there someday, to show her the places I cherished, to let her walk those hills with me. We'd see it all together. But I never kept that promise. It's strange, to think in past tense now. The memories ache, like a half-forgotten song I can almost hear if I focus hard enough. God, I miss her. They tell me it's been over a year since I last saw her, but that doesn't feel right. Memories blur, splintering like fragments of shattered glass. There's a lingering taste of sedation, of memories stripped bare, stolen in that stillness between consciousness and sleep. And I'm left clawing through the emptiness, trying to grasp at what they took, trying to piece her back together. She had laughed so easily that night, teased me about the madness of tourists flocking to see a myth. And then, she'd shared her own stories, the legends whispered in Ethiopia—the shape-shifting warehyenas. It wasn't like the werewolves in our Western tales, who howl at the full moon and change in an instant. No, the warehyenas slipped in and out of their monstrous forms, concealing themselves in plain sight, like predators who'd learned to hunt in broad daylight. Some called it magic; others whispered it was the scent of human flesh that drew out their true selves. I'd half-laughed it off back then, but now? I'm a believer. I remember hearing their screams, those gut-wrenching howls that crawled up my spine and lodged themselves deep in my chest, impossible to shake. In Addis, those sounds were believed to carry a prophecy. Two cries meant death for children, five or six for women, and seven marked a man's end. I can't count how many times I heard them in my nightmares, their echoes scraping against my sanity. Worse still were the voices they stole, imitating the people we loved, Zahra and Mita included. They morphed and fed on innocence, devouring from the inside. And I watched.

The weeks passed in a haze here, and in Dr Harris's office, I wrestle with my memories, holding them tight as he tries to strip them from me, piece by piece. He denies my stories, my pain, dismissing them like the ravings of a fractured mind. He thinks he's helping, that by dragging the truth from my dreams he's healing me, but it feels like he's stealing something essential, robbing me of the parts of myself that I need to hold onto. I remember Ethiopia, and no amount of his steady insistence can take that from me. The pain is real, a visceral ache that doesn't just bring tears but a hollowing out, a kind of slow, merciless erasure.

But I will remember her.

CHAPTER 88

I slowly open my eyes, and a musty, almost damp scent fills my nostrils. My eyes shift around the room, searching for shadows, for something lurking in the dark, but it's just me. Just the quiet. The room is unremarkable—a single window with bars. My whole environment has changed. What is this place? And what are they going to do to me now? These sensations are accompanied by disorientation and exposure. The last thing I remember is Harris telling me to rest and confirming we would continue our discussion later. And then, as standard, I drifted into a dreamless sleep. Does this mean anything? Have my dreams been stolen? Or have I stopped dreaming altogether? Perhaps it's simply because I can't remember them anymore. They have confined me to this space. It's essentially a cell, similar to a prison. But it's more than that; it feels like a creation of my imagination—a realisation of a dream. It's just a damn room. But for some reason, it feels vaguely familiar, like a distant memory I can't quite seize. I search my mind as I look around my new haunt. Fuck; I recognise everything here. The small, white-walled room had only the bare essentials: a metal-framed bed with a thin mattress, a scratchy wool blanket, a tiny sink with a leaky tap, and a miniature toilet. In one corner was a sturdy chair, and in the other sat a small round table covered in scratches and stains. I have a strange feeling of familiarity in this place, as if I've been here before. But that's impossible, isn't it? It must be déjà vu.

Over the next few days, I watch the constant stream of people in scrubs and lab coats going in and out of the room. Some strangers, while others trigger deep emotions, reminding me of friends and foes from different chapters of my life. The parade of personnel blurs together, a kaleidoscope of faces that I struggle to place. Each one drags me back to the past. The young Filipino nurse with kind eyes and a gentle touch awakens a flicker of hope, reminding me of Zahra's compassion. But in the next breath, a stern-faced doctor with a clipped accent makes me shiver, bringing back flashbacks of my torturers in the Philippines. I fight the impulse to panic, to demand answers from these ghosts of my past. The rational part of my brain understands that they are here to help me piece together the shattered fragments of my mind. Yet my wounds are deep, and I cannot shake the feeling that their probing whispers and troubled glances are just another form of humiliation. Every single thing that's happened in my life, or the ones I can recall at least, makes me question. I have to wrap my head around the fact that the decisions I've made to end up where I am now aren't as clear-cut as they seem. I'm lost, the line between right and wrong blurring before my eyes. Have I been living a lie? Have I really been fighting for justice, or have I simply been running from my own demons? The doubts are an incessant whisper that grows louder and louder as my time here goes on.

I catch glimpses of Zahra—the curve of a smile, the glint of an eye—but each time, the illusion shatters, leaving me hollow and aching. I want to scream, but my voice stays trapped, a silent plea unheeded. Mita also visits in the dark hours; her presence is a welcome relief from the endless train of strangers. She speaks in quiet tones; her words are from the past. *"We'll find her, Tommy,"* she promises. Her hand moves towards my arm but hovers just inches away. *"We won't give up."* And just like that, she's gone again, disappearing as quickly as she appeared. The only thing left behind is an overwhelming silence and tears trickling down my face.

She entered the room, a slim, tall figure in a white coat that flowed behind her slender frame. Wire-rimmed glasses obscured her eyes. She scrutinised me from head to toe, clearly trying to intimidate me. I mimic her movements and glance at her from head to toe. She has the vibe of a shrink. Dr Langley is another member of Harris's team. She introduces herself as Dr Langley, the primary headshrinker for Harris. She is undeniably more attractive than the man himself. It was evident that he chose her due to her striking appearance. I'll play along with their games. I will be the perfect patient. Perhaps if I give them what they desire, I might be able to find a way out of here. I only wish I knew their true motivations for constantly feeding me lies and their plan to keep me imprisoned in this terrible place.

"Tommy," she said softly, her voice impressively matching her looks, pulling up a chair beside my bed. All the normal pleasantries didn't last very long. I appreciated her directness.

"How are you feeling?" She started, straight to it, no fucking about.

I simply gave her a look. I gave her the kind of look you give someone who's just said something stupid and blatantly obvious. She continued with the usual doctor spiel. She then proceeds to repeat the story she wants—no, expects—me to believe. It's a story I've heard countless times before.

Do you remember Tommy? Do you remember what happened?" she asks.

I stare at her while sick images flash through my mind like a newsreel of carnage. Not the ones they want me to see. No, these are the true, terrifying ones. Where monsters killed my wife. However, I have come to realise that I must participate in their games and accept the stories they want me to believe.

I recollected what Dr Harris had shared with me before and asked, "I... attempted to kill myself, right?"

Langley's face turned serious. "Yes, you wrapped a wire around your neck and jumped from your balcony. The impact was brutal."

"And why the fuck would I do that?"

"You were a mess, and you had been hitting the bottle hard." Her gaze shifted to my arms, her voice softening but not losing its intensity. "And the scars on your body...you had been cutting and mutilating yourself, Tommy."

"What about Zahra?" I asked, wondering how they were going to explain this.

Langley's voice was quiet as she placed a hand on my arm. "Rebels killed Zahra and her family in their village in Ethiopia." The cold grip of despair seized hold of me; why would they tell me this?

I couldn't believe it. "No," I protested, shaking my head vigorously. "That's impossible. I was there in Ethiopia with her when she died." I struggled to steady my breathing as she continued her version of my past. Everything felt so real, but could her words hold any truth? Is my entire life just a figment of my imagination? No! It's them; I know what happened. I remember the truth; they're trying to manipulate my memories. They're messing with my head, changing the narrative. She is lying to me. They are all fucking lying. Aren't they? My fists clenched tightly as Langley tried to reason with me.

"Everyone is lying to me," I growled, feeling a surge of resentment.

"You're wrong, Tommy. Your memories are distorted. Your mind has created a false narrative due to the trauma you experienced. You never went to Ethiopia, and your feelings for Zahra were real but nothing more. " Your passion to protect her—those feelings were, and still are, genuine."

Could all of these individuals be conspiring against me? And what about Marie? Is she involved in this deception as well? Heat rose to my face as I squeezed my eyes shut, trying to silence Langley's words. I was denying the truth that was right in front of me. How could I have been so blind? I forced myself to look at her, despite the pain and guilt that surged through me. She sat calmly, her posture impeccable, and her voice steady as she spoke about the consequences of my actions. "These scars you've inflicted on yourself are a direct result of the immense tragedy you experienced."

Langley gestured towards my arms and spoke softly, "When you harmed yourself, you were only reiterating the pain of your past." A pile of crumpled tissues sat on the table, separating us.

"Your neighbours heard loud bangs and screams coming from your apartment," she stated with a heavy sigh. "They saved your life."

Tears fill my eyes as I glance down at my arms, marked with the scars of my stupidity. These scars are the marks of the torture I endured in the highlands of Ethiopia. Even now, the wound on my side and the scars across my body still remain. It's difficult to believe that jumping from a balcony could have caused this much damage. It couldn't have. Could it? I just didn't know anything anymore. The memory is still very graphic; every detail is clear in my mind. I would have given my life for her without hesitation; I thought I already had. The memories of the day the monsters came are so clear; I can feel the screams, the bloodcurdling cries of Zahra and Mita, and the children's innocent voices joining in. Their piercing wails still haunt me to this day. All I can do is scream with them. How could I have thought it was over? I don't recall being afraid, nor do I remember feeling brave or caring for anything. What stands out in my memory is my hatred toward them and my need to kill every last one of them. It felt natural to rid the world of their presence. It was a part of who I was, and I didn't care. The recent images or memories from the balcony are still uncertain. However, they become increasingly clearer with each passing day I spend in this place. Still, they don't quite hold the same weight as regular memories. It's almost as if I am recalling something from a dream. Langley and Harris have been telling this story for weeks, each time with more detail. As they speak, I can feel myself being pulled into the memory, watching from a distance as my body jumps off the balcony. I can feel the phantom wire tightening around my neck. Even now, I can faintly feel the scar where the wire cut into me. I wish I could erase all these memories from my head. These memories are simply additional ghosts to add to the already existing ones.

She spoke with an unapologetic tone about my past actions and the scars left behind. I couldn't help but stare at the faded marks on my arms, remnants of a past I can't quite remember. She listed off each tool I had used to inflict these wounds: sharp knives that once seemed like toys, jagged glass bottles that shattered and cut deep, and even a seemingly innocent potato peeler that left its mark. The scars told a story of pain and desperation, of moments where I couldn't have seen any other way out. My hand subconsciously traced along the raised lines, feeling ashamed and exposed under her belittling gaze. I wanted to lash out, to scream at her to stop, to leave me alone with my scars and my secrets. Despite the shame that welled up inside, I couldn't stop the flare of loathing and bitterness that her words triggered. Who was she to judge me, to lay bare this darkest moment they say is mine with such callous ease? She spoke as if she knew me, as if she understood the depths of hopelessness that would have driven me to mar my own flesh. But how could she possibly comprehend the weight of the demons that haunted me, the relentless whispers that urged me to punish myself for sins both real and imagined? I recognised some of these scars from the Philippines, but others were only familiar to me from the horrors I faced in Ethiopia. And despite everything, a part of me longed for her to continue—to unearth every last painful memory until there was nothing left to hide. Maybe then, with all my wounds exposed, I could finally begin to understand.

"But now," she said softly but firmly, "you have a chance to heal. To find a way to live with the scars of the past and build a future." My gaze dropped to my chest, where a faded scar resembling a bitemark peeked out from under my chest hair.

"I remember," I whispered. " Can I ever honestly recover from this?" My voice choked, already knowing the answer to be impossible.

"Only you can answer that, Tommy," Langley responded. "But I believe that with time, support, and treatment, you can find a way."

My mind was in turmoil. I constantly questioned everything. Was there any hope for redemption? I had to do right by Zahra, seek vengeance for her death, and find a way out of the darkness. A graphic memory came to mind—the image of a bloodstained knife clutched with trembling fingers. As I drew the serrated edge across my quivering flesh, with morbid fascination, I observed the way it incised my skin. At first, mere droplets of blood appeared, but soon it transformed into a dark, viscous flow—a macabre fog of crimson cloaking my skin. Chills crawled up my spine as I recalled the razor's sting and its momentary respite from the gruesome thoughts that infested me. Every scar on my body acted as a map of my past, taking me back to the moments of pain and trauma. I could still feel the sharp sting of the blade piercing my skin.

Langley's words cut through the haze of my thoughts, pulling me back to reality. "You have to talk about it, Tommy," she urged.

"I can't... I'll never forgive myself for what happened."

She paused and then continued calmly, "It's normal to feel guilty after losing someone." But I couldn't let her words sink in. My fists clenched as anger boiled inside me.

"I could have stopped it all," I seethed, my voice shaking with emotion. "I should have been there to protect them—to die with them." As I spoke, my anger grew stronger, and I ranted on, spewing out my self-hatred and shame. Langley's hand rested on my shoulder, offering a comforting touch as she spoke.

Her gaze held genuine empathy as she spoke, "Tommy, you can't change the past; however, you have the power to shape your future and choose a path of healing and forgiveness." She shifted in her seat, clearly feeling uncomfortable discussing such painful topics; her fingers nervously tapped against each other. But as she spoke, her words cut through the haze of my thoughts, pulling me back to reality.

"I can't... I'll never forgive myself for what happened."

She paused and then continued calmly, "It's normal to feel guilty after losing someone." But I couldn't let her words sink in. My fists clenched as anger boiled inside me.

"I could have stopped it all," I seethed, my voice shaking with emotion. "I should have been there to protect them—to die with them." As I spoke, my anger grew stronger, and I ranted on, spewing out my self-hatred and shame.

My heart sank as I recalled Zahra's story—or more accurately, Ethiopia's story. The memory of the beautiful girl's heartbreaking sobs, just before she passed in my arms, rang loud in my head. She was Samuel's daughter, a fact that I try to block out of my mind. I want to shut down all thoughts and memories. Despite everything else, she is worthy of memory. Yet doubts are beginning to seep in, amplified by the presence of white-coated people around me. Gut-wrenching images of streets ravaged by war and faces filled with desperation have replaced the peaceful landscapes and bustling markets. In my mind, I can faintly hear the sounds of gunfire and cries for help. It was a chronicle of unthinkable cruelties, where people of all ages were treated as mere objects subjected to cruel and inhuman treatment. The same horrific phrases repeated over and over: 'abducted', 'armed factions', 'unspoken pain', and 'infinite scars'. These weren't just random acts of violence; there was a sinister pattern emerging. The kidnappings, the torture, and the feeding of bodies to the hyenas were all part of a calculated strategy to break the spirit of the people. By targeting the most vulnerable, the warring factions sought to destroy the very fabric of society itself. They didn't care who they took, whether it was women or children, from homes or schools. Their tactics resorted to conscription, human trafficking, and financial extortion. For those who dared to resist, torture and death were swift and merciless.

"Where are they?!" I shouted in frustration, my voice trembling on the edge of a breakdown.

"Take me there," I demanded, my words punctuated by grief and urgency. She remained calm, despite my outburst.

"I can't imagine your pain. "Tommy, I know this is hard for you. But we need to stay in control. You need to accept the truth of what happened to you and Zahra."

"Don't you dare say her name!" I seethe, barely able to control my anger. I feel the urge to lash out, but I force myself to stay in place.

I could see two large men approaching my door, prepared to enter if necessary. She raises her hand to them, and they visibly relax, stepping back.

I scream, "Fuck off!" and fix my gaze on them. Langley quickly shifts her position, blocking my direct view of them.

"I swear, I'll do whatever it takes to get answers. But please try to stay calm. We have to face what happened and the pain it's caused—for you and others.

"Tell me where my wife is!" I screamed, a primal roar escaping from my throat like a wounded animal's cry. "I'm sick of asking that same fucking question. Where the hell on earth am I?" I screamed as I rose to my feet, lifting my head towards the ceiling and letting out another scream of pure anger.

Langley's face twisted in shock, her grip on the clipboard loosening as her glasses slipped down to the tip of her nose. She let out a small gasp and fumbled awkwardly with her pen before quickly scurrying out of my room. Her two bulky goons had already entered my room, and now they trailed closely behind her, their shadows looming over her petite frame.

I spat, "Just get out! Leave me the fuck alone!" I was shaking with rage. The sound that came out was choked and shrill; nothing short of a snot and saliva rage. But they had already left; I could hear their footsteps fading away. Then the click of the door locking behind. Alone now, I couldn't escape my thoughts. Darkness consumed me as the guilt and blood stained my hands. "It won't wash away," I sobbed uncontrollably into my pillow. "I'm sorry, so sorry." The weight of it all was crushing and suffocating, and I felt like I could no longer bear this never-ending nightmare. All I wanted was an end—to life itself.

Chapter 89

*"We are what we are because we have been what
we have been."*

Sigmund Freud.

I had no clue about the current day or month. The saying, 'You'll look back and laugh at all this,' popped into my head. I would tell myself or anyone struggling, "Just keep moving forward." My muscles were weak, and every movement seemed to drain me of all my energy. I felt like I would never be able to move again. While I wouldn't usually be so dramatic, this was how I felt. I knew I had to make it to the small toilet; I didn't want to soil the bed for a second time.

"Coma for a year." Marie had said. The story they were spinning left me devastated and unable to accept it. Did I really try to end my own life? Flashes of memories haunt me, the remnants of two different pasts. Each session with Harris or Langley reveals more horrors than I thought possible. The look in their eyes never faltered; they were either good at what they did, or they were telling the truth. Either way, it didn't change the fact that Zahra was dead, and it was my fault. Parts of their stories mirrored my own—the death of my father, Zahra's departure for Ethiopia, my mom's illness. We all agreed on these details, just as I recall them... up until that point, at least. However, the manner and timing of Zahra's murder remain unclear. They keep telling me that a group of armed men murdered her and her entire family in their hometown in Northern Ethiopia. According to them, a family friend visited our home in Cardiff to deliver the news of her death. A part of me feels as though their version of events is a detached memory, but not my own. It belongs to someone else's past. It's akin to those dreams that you can't remember upon waking—the ones you just know were horrific because your heart is racing, and your body is drenched in sweat. It sounds eerily familiar, but the truth remains that I was by her side when she and her family were brutally slaughtered in an open field in the Highlands. 'My wife, Zahra, went to

Ethiopia,' the doctors both had told me, voices speaking in sync. There was an attack by gunmen. She and most of her family...'

Their words haunt my mind, creating conflicting information that confuses everything I believe to be true. What they are telling me couldn't have happened. It didn't happen! Did it? My head throbs with the intensity of my thoughts. I can still see death's cruel claws taking Zahra's life. It is the harsh reality that I cannot escape from. I grind my teeth and squeeze my eyelids shut, fighting the urge to open them, afraid of what I might see. Time had forgotten me, a cold reality. My life was continuing on. My eyes welled up with tears, and one escaped, tracing down my cheek like a line of blood. Along with it came an ear-piercing quiet, which only heightened my feeling of being trapped in a limbo of uncertainty.

I'm out of my body, suspended, weightless, disconnected from everything but the sight of myself below by my front door. It's surreal, like I'm watching someone else entirely. I can see my face—pale, drawn tight, as if all the colour and life have drained away. After checking the peephole, I unlock and open the door. Standing in front of me is a woman, though I can't quite place her. She wails, shattering the silence of the hallway below. As I focus, she is shrouded in a black and red patterned scarf, clutching a bulging bag. Her shoulders shook with sobs. Our eyes met, and I could see the pain we both shared—she as the bearer of tragic news and me as the receiver. She's speaking, but her words come out muffled, like I'm hearing them through water. I can't make out the specifics, but I can tell it's bad. Her lips quiver, tears streaming down her cheeks as she tries to compose herself. I watch as my whole-body trembles, my head shaking in denial. My throat tightens, and I can see fear and pain reflected in my eyes. I'm sobbing, too. My body shudders with each breath, each sob, but I can't feel it. From this vantage point, it's all so strange, so distant. Then I hear it clearly—my wife. Zahra, she's gone. That's what this woman is telling me. That's why I'm collapsing right before her eyes. My chest heaves as I try to take it in, and I watch myself crumble, folding over as if the weight of those words crushes my very soul. The woman reaches out to comfort me, but I've already slipped into unconsciousness. My body sways, then collapses, hitting the floor hard. And still, I hover above, a silent witness to my own collapse. I can see her standing over me, tears streaming down her face, but then everything goes black.

Panic sets in as I struggle to make sense of the jumbled memories swirling in my head. Time appears to be uncontrollably spinning, blending together moments from both the past and present. My anxiety intensifies. I feel lost, desperately trying to hold onto a semblance of reality. All of a sudden, I remember. It's Tigi. Everything became clear; I was waiting for news about Zahra. And then the phone call came, but I hung up on her. Tigi must have come to my apartment because she knew I wouldn't listen to her over the phone. She came to tell me what had happened to Zahra. I recall coming to consciousness in my hallway, but I have no recollection of speaking with Tigi. When I checked through the peephole, there was nobody outside, and I didn't open the door. Despite this, the images I had just seen were incredibly vivid. What was going on? Why did it seem so vivid and genuine? Was I mistaken all along?

CHAPTER 90

I am transported back in time, standing in my childhood home, surrounded by the familiar scent of my mother's perfume as her strong arms hold me in a tight embrace. My young self, perhaps ten years old, received the devastating news of my grandfather's passing. The tears well up in my eyes once more, as a bright bolt of lightning strikes outside.

In an instant, I'm fifteen again, standing by the train tracks with a group of shocked classmates, watching helplessly as our friend's lifeless body is carried away. The sound of his mother's uncontrollable sobbing is tearing at my heartstrings.

And then, just like that, I am now by my dad's deathbed, holding his cold hand as I plead for mercy to a higher power.

Another flash of light, and Zahra appears before me, her intense gaze locking with mine just as it did at the airport all those years ago. Every word that spills from her lips is like a cold hand crawling up my spine, leaving me in an icy chill.

"Where were you?" she asked. Her voice sounded different somehow.

Her eyes narrowed and her nostrils flared as she accused me, her voice like a scalpel slicing through my heart. I couldn't relate to anything—no sound, no emotion, not even the sweet scent of her perfume, adding to the confusion in my head. Where was I? Who was I? I searched her face for answers, but it remained motionless, betraying nothing. I shook my head, trying to clear my thoughts and make sense of the conflicting emotions within me. When I looked once more, terror gripped me. My mouth opened to release a blood-curdling shriek that could rival the tormented cries of the underworld itself. Zahra stood there again, but this time only a mangled and bloodied mess remained of her once beautiful face. A mere shell of the woman I once knew. Her jaw dangles limply by a few tendons, exposing shattered teeth coated in blackened blood. A grotesque spectacle of contorted flesh and bone undulates before my eyes. Her image glitched, like a twisted presence from another world. My skin prickles, every hair standing on end as the anxiety builds, wrapping tight around my chest. I want to scream, but my voice won't come. It's real. It feels real. Too real. I'm drowning in it, the sensation pressing down on me, suffocating. There's no way out. Nothing works. I'm trapped.

I'm out of body once more, watching myself moving from bar to bar, I can almost hear the suffering—the faint, whispers of a painful past. These are arenas for dark impulses. An opportunity to let my pain flow freely. The clinking of glasses becomes a call to arms, beckoning me to unleash my anxieties. Scars litter my flesh, most self-inflicted, desperate attempts at escape from reality. And Zahra...her memory, encouraging me towards violence. Outbursts are sudden, without warning, triggered by something as small as a glare or a simple nudge. It ignites an intense fire inside that cannot be contained. Blood will be split, whether by my hand or another's. Fists find their targets, leaving behind bleeding and raw knuckles. Each landing with pinpoint precision, the sickening thud of flesh connecting with flesh, brings me a shiver of satisfaction. Did I really do this? Blood was spilling like a river of red. I watch as it sprays from split lips and noses. I hear the glass shatter on impact as it connects with multiple skulls Despite being disconnected from my physical form, it's hard not to revel in the spectacle before me. And when the red mist finally cleared, all that remained were scattered bodies, broken like rag dolls in a child's tantrum.

Suddenly, I am no longer in the blood-stained bar. Instead, I am standing before a shattered mirror, my own reflection is a distorted and twisted version of my former self. My hands were stained with blood, both real and imagined. The whispers grew to a roar as they called me a monster. I could no longer separate myself from the creatures that haunted my nightmares, for they now lived within me. War was no longer an external force; it had become a part of who I was. And in that moment, I saw no difference between myself and the creatures of my nightmares. We were both stained with blood, but theirs belonged to the realm of myth and legend while mine was all too real.

Once again, my vision shifts, and I find myself still outside of my body. Tears well up in my eyes, obscuring my view. I watch myself step out onto the balcony. 'No!' I try to shout, but no sound escapes me. No one is here to hear me anyway; it's just me watching helplessly as I am about to do something that I never thought would happen. I grind my teeth and squeeze my eyelids shut, fighting the urge to open them, afraid of what I might see. This place was a desolate limbo; no enemies lurked here, I am alone, just a spectator to what is about to unfold. I watch from a close distance, my hand hovering just out of reach. I try to grab hold of myself and put a stop to this insanity. But I am paralyzed, unable to move or intervene. My other self is wearing a ragged vest stained with blood and ripped in several spots. My attention is drawn to several open wounds on my body. The most severe one is a deep gash on my chest, blood is seeping out and soaking into my pants. The scar is familiar; I trace my fingers over its familiar shape now, as I watch myself walking towards the balcony's railings. According to Langley, in a state of overwhelming grief. I had used a potato peeler, painfully scraping away the tattoo on my chest. It was an act of brutal self-mutilation. My heart weighed heavily as I watched. In my trembling hand, I held a thin wire coiled like a rope. I drape one end over my head and notice that I'm shaking, crying, and muttering unintelligible words to myself. I couldn't even make out what I was saying, it sounded like a prayer of some sort. I observe my other self scale the railing and stand on the other side of the balcony, now shuddering uncontrollably while securing the wire to the railing. With a hard tug, I test its strength. When I finished this task, I spotted myself letting out a deep sigh of relief. I lean back, using my arms to brace against the railing behind me. For some reason I seem to be looking out in the distance, frantically, searching for…something. Suddenly, there's furious banging on the door from inside the apartment, along with voices shouting my name. I try to join in, but my voice fails me. I'm completely helpless and unable to do anything at all. And just before my expected release to a certain death, Zahra appeared before me like a ghostly apparition. She stood beside the other me, haunting yet beautiful against the events unfolding before us. Tears glistened in her eyes as she briefly locked her gaze with my eyes. Before she turned to confront my alternate, who clung TO the edge of the balcony. I could see the urgency in her eyes, silently begging me to stop. It was as if her very soul was pleading with me, beyond words and comprehension. Time stretches endlessly as I wait to see what happens, each minute feeling like an eternity. I steel myself, preparing for the worst, knowing that any moment could be my last. I can't help but wonder, if this alternate version of myself makes the leap, will it be the end for both of us? I nervously gulp, going over every moment that brought me to this point. I can't stop replaying them in my mind, like a bad dream I can t wake up from. It s as if I m fading into the background of my own life. What was going on? I am staring at another version of myself from a parallel world. I am stunned, questioning what thoughts and emotions are going through this alternate version of myself. Their expression mirrors my confusion and fear. Then, Zahra's voice cut through, her urgent pleas for me to step back and reconsider my actions finally breaking through. She seemed so far away, yet her words were crystal clear. I longed to pull her into a tight embrace one last time, but my limbs were frozen. All I could do was watch helplessly as she tried to save me, well, a version of me.

Suddenly, my paralysis was broken as I saw the other version of myself take a step forward and plummet into a dark space, until the wire tore into my skin, biting at it as I was abruptly stopped midair. I dangled from the balcony, held up only by the pressure on my neck. My chest constricted as I witnessed the scene before me, mirroring the agony of the man dangling lifelessly from my balcony. I struggled to catch my breath, grappling with the reality of the situation. Was this real? Had I truly just witnessed my own suicide? No, it couldn't be. This had to be another one of my waking nightmares. I squeezed my eyes shut, willing the macabre vision to dissipate, but when I opened them again, the sight of my own body dangling lifelessly from the balcony sent a shudder through my core. It swung gently a surrealistic pendulum marking the passage of time. The face, my face, stared back at me with glassy, accusing eyes. In that instant, a wave of revulsion and self-hatred crashed over me.

I stumbled back from the railing, my breath coming in ragged gasps as conflicting emotions warred within. Disgust. Shock. But also…relief? It sickened me. How could any part of me feel even a shred of relief at seeing my own broken body swaying gently in the night?

This time, I found myself at a gathering. The table was set with a feast, but the food was rotten and covered in mould. The people at the table were arguing, their voices rising to a fever pitch, but I couldn t understand what they were saying. Their faces I recognised, were twisted in anger, and suddenly as if on cue, they turned to look at me with empty black eyes.

The scene changed once more, finding myself in a sullen circle with old friends, our eyes fixated on the lifeless forms in front of us. My heart constricted as I saw my own lifeless body among them. A large, shallow grave shaped in a perfect oval accommodated the neatly arranged corpses in rows. Zahra and Mita flanked me on either side, their faces contorted with grief. Solomon and Samuel stood across from us, their expressions mirroring ours. In between was Samuel's daughter, her tears falling onto the lifeless forms below. It was a devastating vision, one that would haunt me for years to come. We stood there, resembling the accused at a murder scene. I felt an odd sensation that I can't quite explain. It was a strange mix of fear and guilt, but I knew deep down that I had nothing to be afraid or guilty about.

A force yanked me back to reality, sharp and relentless. My eyes snapped open, and terror surged through me, raw and cold. My mouth gapes open in a silent scream. Everything is foreign. What happened? Images blurred, flashed, and then slipped away like a half-remembered dream. I am lost and scared, my breaths shallow. I was alone in this strange, suffocating room. The walls loomed close, thick with grime and streaked with years of neglect, as if they'd soaked up the memories of a thousand people who'd felt just as trapped as I did now. I sighed wiping the sweat and tears from my face. "Get a grip," I whispered to myself, forcing each word out. "One…two…" I counted under my breath, grasping for anything solid, anything that could pull me back from the edge. But even as I counted, another fear gnawed at me, a deeper ache I couldn't ignore. I was starting to forget her. Her voice, once so clear, was fading. I could almost hear her again, speaking softly, her lips brushing against my ear, her touch lingering at the back of my neck, her kiss—gentle, slow, searing. But even those memories felt like they were slipping, unravelling thread by thread, leaving only the ache where she used to be.

CHAPTER 91

Phantom forms shifted and contorted, their images glitching in and out of focus. Strobe-like pulses of light shot out from each shape. The bolts were intense, like flashes of lightning, but these shot upwards and in all directions. The bursts are blinding, burning into my retinas. The glare—Fuck, the light—stabs at my skull, searing through my brain like a blade. I squint, blinking rapidly, but the world shifts like 1 m underwater. There s also a beeping sound. A constant, rhythmic chirp inside my head, in sync with the pounding of my heart. It s too loud, but it s distant, too. Like it's coming from inside a tunnel. I groaned, trying to push this nightmare away. But it stayed, squeezing until I struggled to take breaths. Sounds filter in, distant and warped. The wind whispered, as if Zahra's spirit was trying to speak with me, guiding me towards something, maybe the truth. And for a brief moment, I closed my eyes and let myself drift, where I could see her again, touch her soft skin, hold her close, breathe in her scent, and taste her lips one last time. Zahra, where are you? I pleaded in desperation. I hear her voice loud and clear. 'They are everywhere.' 'What are?' I pleaded. 'Monsters' she roars with such brilliance. A warning from beyond the grave. Like flipping through channels on a TV, snippets of memories swirl around- faces, places, emotions—but they re fragmented and erratic, pieces of a puzzle 1 m no longer able to fit together. Then, a show I did not want to see again. Graphic images of hyenas devouring my family's lifeless bodies. Their hollow leer and maniacal cackling drowned out everything else. "This is what happened," Zahra said with conviction. "Trust what you saw, what you felt, trace the scars on your body, please remember, remember, remember..."

"I see them!?" I shouted: "The hyenas... they're everywhere." I hissed. Then someone else spoke in a voice that mimicked my own, 'You are lost, and so are your memories. You will never find your way back."

The rhythmic beeping of a machine nearby took over. And voices—muffled and indistinct—seem to dance around me, growing sharper and more defined as seconds pass. Words like "wake" and "dreaming" float through the cloud, but they slip through my grasp, unable to hold meaning just yet.

A voice broke through. "Tommy? Are you okay?"

A face appeared before me, her expression tense and agitated. I felt trapped and surrounded; their voices were a mix of support while others barked orders.

"It was just a nightmare," a woman said in a soothing tone, trying to calm me down.

My throat felt raw and unused as I spat out the words, "Zahra...my wife. You took her from me! You killed her! Murderers!" The rage boiled inside me as memories flooded back. I remember. I do. They are fucking impostors. They are the beasts in my visions. I wanted to kill them all. Nothing in this place was real or good. And absolutely nothing living was worth living for. Life was unmeaning, and everyone needed to fuck off and die.

Her soothing voice was a stark contrast to her iron grip on my hand. "Mr Thompson," she began, her eyes searching mine for any hint of recognition or understanding. "Your priority is healing right now." The room hummed with constant beeps and whirs of machines, a reminder of where I was. I screamed in protest, and struggled against her hold, but she clamped down tighter on my shoulders, pinning me in place. I felt the rough leathery straps binding my wrists and ankles, constricting painfully.

A strange man suddenly appeared next to me, instantly checking the straps on my wrists before speaking. "Listen to me, Tommy. I'm here to help," he said urgently. "You have to trust me."

"Trust you?" I bellowed; I could feel my eyeballs striving to leave their sockets.

"You killed everyone I loved!" I struggled against the restraints, tears streaming down my face. I lashed out at him. "Let me go! I'll kill you all if it's the last thing I do!"

"Relax, getting worked up will only make things harder for you," he sneered, his repulsive face contorting into a smirk. His eyes appeared to have an eerie red glow, but I guess it was just my imagination.

"Fuck off!" I yelled, lunging toward him. I attempted this several times, but the straps bound my body tightly, nonetheless, I continued fighting against them with all my strength. Only my head was free to move. I attempted to bite into his flesh, refusing to give up. And in a final act of defiance, I spat in his face, desperate to make any kind of contact. After fighting with all I had left, I finally gave in to exhaustion and allowed myself to relax. As I did, I felt a slight sting in my arm, most likely from a sedative that was meant to calm me down. Any sort of life now was a distant dream, an impossible feat.

"Take some time to rest, Mr Thompson. We will leave you in peace for now so you can reflect on your actions." A woman dressed in all white spoke, her face lacking any distinguishable features. It quickly became apparent that I was no longer in my room, or more accurately, my cell. Instead, I found myself back in the hospital-like room where I first regained consciousness.

Her words triggered a strong emotion within me. "Peace?" I snorted cynically. "There's no way I'll ever find peace, not today, not ever!" The nurse's starched uniform clung closely to her figure as she walked across the antiseptic room, she turned, her eyes locked onto mine.

"We're here to help you, Mr Thompson," she said, her voice laced with authority. "But we need your cooperation to make progress." She flashed a condescending smile before continuing, "Dr Langley will be here soon. You don't have any issues with her, do you?"

I clenched my jaw and forced a deep breath, trying to ignore the condescending tone of the nurse's words. I had heard it all before.

"Tommy," the nurse called out, her tone firm and commanding. "You may not see it now, but life has given you another chance. Not many get that opportunity. Don't waste it."

I took a deep breath, struggling to maintain my composure as she walked away. Inside, I was seething with anger and resentment. Chance? What did she know about chance? Her words only fuelled the fire inside me, teetering dangerously between control and complete breakdown. I grapple against the suffocating darkness, gasping for air as it threatens to take me once again. I refuse to give in. I fight against its grip. My fingers stretch and claw at the restraints, desperate for a hold onto something solid. But it is useless, as if gravity had doubled its strength and is pulling me deeper into my bed. It starts slowly, the way sleep always does. My eyelids are leaden, and I can barely hold on to the waking world.

It's peaceful at first, a quiet descent into nothingness. I welcome it, even. I try to embrace the quiet, but I know what awaits me will be far from peaceful. I didn't expect a peaceful journey into unconsciousness, and as I feared, it spiralled into a state of fear once more as I grasped where I was - forsaken in the harsh grasslands of my past horror, every step I take warps the landscape into a warping array of colours, like a kaleidoscope. A memory, maybe. Or is it something I made up? It doesn't matter. I can feel the warmth of a sun that isn't here, the breeze on my skin, like I'm standing in a field or on a beach. It's not real, but it feels real enough. I let it pull me deeper, further away from this room, this bed. It's like slipping underwater, the real world muffled, distant. But suddenly, as if I wasn't meant to experience any emotions, my world goes dark. The footsteps start then, slow and deliberate, echoing louder with each step, but I can't see where they're coming from. Panic surges, a deluge of pure fear. My mind screams at me to wake up, to shake myself free, but it's like I'm wrapped in chains, my mind slipping further into the nightmare's grip. Every second stretches out, misery, with no escape. I should wake up. I know that now. I have to wake up. My heart pounds as I take it in.

Just as the darkness began to close in, I heard a voice, distant at first. Harris cleared his throat; his voice broke through the fog of my drugged state, and I struggled to focus on his words. There was something about the way he moved too—controlled, deliberate, as if every step, every gesture, had been rehearsed. Even when he smiled, it never quite reached those calculating eyes. He was wearing one of those ID badges clipped to his coat pocket, but I couldn't make out the name from where I sat. Just the letters "Dr" and a blurry photo that was probably as polished as the rest of him. And then there was this faint smell of antiseptic that lingered around him. Not overwhelming, but enough to remind you that everything in this place was scrubbed clean, including the people. He adjusted his glasses as he addressed me. His white lab coat swished around his legs as he approached my bed. He spoke in a no-nonsense voice, trying to maintain professionalism. My gut tightened with anxiety, and I knew I had to keep my composure if I ever wanted to escape this hellhole. With a clipboard in hand. He smiled, a little too wide, like he'd practised it in the mirror before coming in.

"How are you feeling today?" he asked, voice calm, clinical.

I inhaled sharply, locking eyes with him. "Are you fucking kidding me?" I asked, disbelieving. "How long did you sedate me for this time?" I spoke quietly, trying to keep my tone in check. The last thing I wanted was to be unconscious again. I needed answers, and I needed them now. A multitude of new questions swirled around in my mind. Where are the monstrous hyena humanoids now? Did you create them? Why are you lying about Ethiopia? And the familiar ones that always went unanswered: Where am I? Who are you people? Where is Zahra, or at least her body? Then, as if he was reading my mind, he answered me.

"Your questions will be answered soon enough, but the loss of Zahra is still a painful truth. At least, for you it is. Sadly, there is no physical resting place for her." He said matter-of-factly, I watched in horror as his lips curved into a thin smile that didn't quite reach his eyes. "Anyway, it would have been inconvenient to collect each of her body parts. So, there was no need for a burial. You know this, Tommy. After all, you were there." At the mere mention of my wife's name, my stomach clenched and turned, making me physically sick. His smile grew wider, and now I could see the satisfaction had reached his eyes. It was terrifying, he found pleasure in delivering this news.

Guilt and unspeakable horror flooded through me as I remember her terrified face, viciously torn away from mine. My voice trembled as I whispered Zahra's name, my memories still fresh and tainted with evil. A storm of emotions raged within the darkest parts of my heart as I asked the question. "Why?" The word dripped with the blood of a thousand nightmares.

Harris exchanged a knowing glance with his brutish colleagues before responding, "Why not?" He cackled darkly, as they turned and walked away, their laughter taunting my spirit. I lay alone on the bed, tightly bound by leather restraints, trembling as I struggled to keep my emotions in check. Not because I felt shame in crying, but because I refused to give them the satisfaction of witnessing my sanity crumble to dust. Despite this resolve, I could not stop the tears welling up, hot and bitter like molten iron flowing down my cheeks. Every word he had spoken was a dagger stabbing into my soul. I wanted to scream, to rage against the travesty of it all, but my voice was trapped in my throat, choked by grief. How could these cruel creatures of darkness be so cold, so cruel? To take a life, to shatter a family, and then laugh about it as if it was some sick joke. The image of Zahra's lifeless body, torn and desecrated, flashed through my mind like a vulture circling a carcass. I fought desperately to maintain composure as self-pity gnawed at the edges of my sanity. I squeezed my eyes shut, attempting to block out the horrific visions that tormented me. But they persisted, searing themselves into every corner of my mind like the mark of the damned. Zahra's once vibrant face - now an unnerving mask of terror and agony - haunted me relentlessly; her ravaged body strewn across the cold earth like a discarded plaything. I could still feel her blood on my hands, the sickening warmth of her life force seeping through my fingers. The weight of her lifeless body in my arms. The knowledge that I had been there, powerless to save her, was a weeping wound, a deep scar that would never truly heal. I strained against the restraints, my muscles burning with futile effort, but they held fast. A scream of rage and anguish tore from my throat, raw and primal, echoing off the cold, sterile walls of my prison. In this wretched place of darkness and pain, I had failed her. Failed to protect her from the monsters who had taken her life so cruelly. The weight of that failure crushed me, suffocating me as surely as the stone walls of my confinement. I gasped for air, choking on my own sobs. The world around me was nothing more than an unending nightmare, a twisted mockery of all I had once held dear. A black fear hung in the air like a funeral shroud as I stared at the ceiling of my accursed cell. Its cold sterility seemed at once alien and familiar - a reminder that this was no place for joy or hope. With every breath, I longed to be free of this cursed existence, to break free from these binds made by the sins of my past. And still, the question remained: "Why?" It echoed through every thought like an unearthly wail, a mocking whisper that would haunt me until the end of my days. I grind my teeth and stare at the ceiling, trying to ignore the pain radiating through my body. The white coats bustle around me, their words blending together in a static-filled chorus. All I can think about is Zahra's lifeless body, her family torn apart, and my own shattered world. But amidst the chaos, one thought rises above the rest: I will seek justice for Zahra, no matter what it takes. This war is not over; it has only changed its combat zone. I am Tommy Thompson, armed solely with the devastating experiences of my past, both real and imagined. These memories will serve as both my shield and my weapon against this evil. I understand now that the people wearing white coats here are not doctors, but something else entirely. They are monsters, no better than the creatures that brutally tore my Zahra apart. I observe as they silently communicate with uneasy looks, unsure if they are assisting a man who is teetering on the edge of madness. With burning hatred in my heart, I stare into their eyes one by one as they come into my line of sight. I am fully aware of the brutal journey that lies ahead, a descent into darkness filled with depravity and a desperate search for redemption. My anger drives me as I seek revenge against those who have harmed me in this place. My mind races with memories of our time together - the laughter, the love, the plans for the future that will now never come to be realised. But at this moment, those memories become my fuel, my resolve to claw my way out of this hell and make things right. I snarled, my voice trembling and my teeth bared, as the very air surrounding me seemed to grow heavy with darkness.

"Fuck you all." I knew I was in no position to make threats, especially not one as bold as promising to slaughter them all. And I knew they would probably kill me soon. Since they knew, if given the chance I'll hunt down every single one of them—human, beast, deity, or monstrosity. I'll get my retribution, even if it means facing death itself. With nothing left to lose, I welcomed the thought of death's icy embrace. There was no more fear, a distant memory now. I welcomed the prospect of death.

In a sudden and aggressive move, two immense figures emerge out of the shadows, their large hands gripping my arms with an iron grip. Despite my desperate struggles, I am no match for their brute strength as the others remove the restraints on my wrists and ankles. Their massive hands held my arms with an unbreakable grip. I thrashed against their savage force, but before I could even catch my breath, a sharp needle pierced my neck, draining my body of all energy in a matter of seconds. I was powerless, completely at their mercy, as they hauled me away like a lifeless ragdoll, my limbs now dead weights, useless and limp in their grip. My sight is blurred, and my mind reels as the cluster of shadowy figures encircles me, their expressions twisted in cruel masks. Langley's voice cut through the mist, but her words felt vacant and distant. The world tilted and blurred. Flashes of light seared my eyes. Rough hands groped and prodded. Metal clanged; hinges screeched. A voice, sharp, familiar, but I can't place it. I blink again, and things start to sharpen around the edges. There's a face hovering above me—eyes wide, red-rimmed. I know that face. I just... I can't... It looms over me, drawing near. I recognise the personal scent of Harris: that strong antiseptic smell that always loitered around him. My focus was drawn to something hanging from his neck. It couldn't be what I thought it was, could it? I attempt to scream, but I am completely paralyzed - even my tongue won't move. My breathing becomes shallower and slower as I fight to stay awake.

"You could have been one of us. But now..." He trails off, letting the unspoken threat hang in the air. Harris's words pierced through my foggy thoughts. Fuck. My mind and body were at war, unable to process what was happening. I desperately searched for my cross, the one that Zahra had given me as a protective charm. She told me it would help protect me. There it is hanging around Harris' neck, mocking me. A sharp pain throbbed in my head, clouding my ability to think clearly. Any movement caused a whirlwind of dizziness, leaving me trapped in panic and struggling to catch my breath. What could I possibly do now? Everything's blurry—just a haze of light and shadow, like I'm underwater. For a second, I can't make sense of it. My mind is sluggish, like I'm moving through mud. My head is pounding, and there's this awful, dry taste in my mouth, like I've been chewing on cotton. I try to swallow, but my throat feels like sandpaper. Every breath feels like a countdown to something terrible. Something ancient and malevolent lurks just out of sight. It's too dark to see, but I can hear it breathing—rasping, hungry, waiting. The darkness isn't just around me—it's inside me, festering. The shadows spin and writhe, taking on a life of their own. I can feel their icy touch on my skin. Harris' laughter echoes through the darkness, a cruel, mocking sound that makes my blood run cold.

"You're too late, Tommy. She's gone. And soon, you will be too." I want to run, to escape. But there's nowhere to go, even if I could move. Zahra. My beautiful, brave Zahra. I failed her. I was supposed to protect her, to keep her safe. But instead… I struggle to make sense of Harris's words, his face swimming in and out of focus. I'm completely at their mercy, trapped inside my own skin, a helpless prisoner. I wanted to scream. But when I opened my mouth, no sound came out. Just a pitiful, choke… A figure leaned in closer and closer. It was definitely Langley; I could smell her signature scent mixed with something strange - a musky, wet dog smell. Her voice was laced with venom as she whispered in my ear, repeating her previous threat: "Tommy, I told you she would be mine. Remember? Her blood still coats my tongue, even now." In a sudden moment of clarity, it all clicked. It was her, fucking Langley! A ferocious beast, a ruthless predator. She had taken murdered my wife. For what? What purpose did it serve? "Fuck, how did I not know these things existed? All this time, they've been walking among us. I need to stop panicking. I need to focus. I heard a maniacal laugh—no, it was a cackle; it was faint but snapped with static. It couldn't be. Could it really be? Fear took over, completely at her mercy. Blood pounds in my head. Madness ravaged my mind, causing me to scream without sound. In spite of my limited vision, I can make out a silhouette standing before me—a twisted, hunched-over creature with a mouth full of barbed teeth and luminous blood-red eyes. Panic claws at my chest as I struggle to distinguish reality from a hazy dream. I open my mouth to scream again, but again no sound comes out, only a feeling of choking. The gurney careened down the hallway, my neck snapping back as my eyes fixated on the flickering fluorescent lights above. With each jarring turn, a wave of nausea and fear washed over me until we came to an abrupt stop. I was thrown back to reality, and dread washed over me as my eyes adjusted to the dim, musty room. All hope evaporated, leaving only the oppressive terror of what was to come. A disgusting and all too familiar stench of decay filled my nostrils, transporting me back to that fateful day in Ethiopia, where my entire world was altered forever. The walls seemed to press in, trapping me in this unspeakable horror. Harris towered over me. I think it is him. It mimics Harris. It's immense, his body expanding with an otherworldly glimmer. Their eyes are bulging out of his skull. A swarm of figures surrounded me, their faces twisted into grotesque masks as they studied my convulsing body with sick fascination. Each seizure wracked my body with excruciating pain, and the lights above flickered maniacally, casting an unsettling greenish hue on everything. Their growls and grunts fill my ears—a baying of evil that will tear apart the very fabric of reality itself. My seizures intensified, the figures around me mutating through the haze of torment, I caught glimpses of their true forms— ancient, malevolent entities that had no place in this world. Their whispers wormed into my mind, promising a perpetuity of suffering if I dared to resist. Then, Harris's face slunk closer, his features now a twisted mockery of the man I once knew. His mouth stretched into an impossibly wide grin, revealing rows of razor-sharp teeth. "You cannot escape us," he hissed, his voice a guttural rasp. "Your soul belongs to us now." The greenish light pulsed faster; each flare caused a sharp pain to shoot through my entire body. The fiendish creatures closed in, and the pain intensified, my body was completely beyond my control thrashing and writhing on the cold, inflexible floor. Harris—or the thing that had once been Harris—reached towards me with elongated, spindly fingers. Its touch burned like ice, sending jolts of pure, unfiltered terror coursing through my veins. I wanted to recoil, to flee, but I was powerless. I wanted to look away, to shut out the horror, but my eyes remained transfixed on the abomination before me.

Their eyes blazed with a fire, pupils dilated and flickering with madness, and their bodies convulsed like marionettes controlled by unseen evil forces, limbs twisting and bending in unnatural angles, and flexing as if attempting to break free from their forms. It was hell—a living nightmare—that I couldn't escape from. The humiliation hurt, intensifying under the blinding lights. They had ensnared me in this satanic place. The thirst for revenge pulsed through every part of me, drowning out any rational thought. And just when I thought it couldn't get any worse, the room fell into silence, and I heard a voice I knew all too well. It growled like a fierce animal, the same one that had haunted me day and night, that had cursed me every waking hour and summoned terrifying visions every time I dared close my eyes.

"Take it easy, Tommy. We're not done with you yet."

The screams inside my head grew louder, shattering the empty promises I had made to myself, and to those I loved. My relentless pursuit to save Zahra had failed. More people had been killed and had suffered because of me. An infernal call to action that ravaged my spirit and left nothing but a husk of who I once was. In the grip of death, I lay here, my mind frantically racing away from the searing pain. It's all my fault. I should have been by her side; I should have foreseen this tragedy. In this cold darkness, the bloodcurdling howls of wandering souls I know will forever repeat in my mind. The gurney began to move once more. The wheels squeaked as it glided down the sterile hallway. The fluorescent lights buzzed above, as my mind drifted back to Zahra. Once again, I found myself at the airport, holding her hand tightly as we walked under the same flickering lights that now illuminated this prison. Her hand was warm in mine, and her smile lit up her face. It was our final moment of happiness before everything fell apart. I could feel tears pricking at the corners of my eyes as each memory flashed through my mind with painful clarity. Then, the picture shifted into a dreamlike haze. Once again, Zahra and I were wrapped in each other's arms, laughing and kissing like we used to. In that blissful moment, everything felt right again; everything was as it should be. I held onto that memory with all my might. But then, reality shattered my visions. I squinted as I opened my eyes, greeted by the sight of an empty ceiling. My body was still strapped to a cold and inflexible gurney. I could feel a presence around me, poking, prodding, whispering, growling, but I barely acknowledged them.

Zahra's bright smile and gentle touch were the only things occupying my thoughts. I held onto those precious memories for as long as possible, but they started to slip away from me like sand through my fingers. I squeezed my eyes shut and fought to keep them just a little longer, trying everything in my power to hold on to them for a few more precious moments. And, then through the drug-induced mist, I saw the silhouette of a feminine figure standing over me. Her delicate fingers brushed against my cheek with affection, igniting sparks of joy that warred with my grief. The woman leaned in close, it was Zahra, her warm breath caressing my ear as she whispered,

"Relax, Tommy. Let me take away your pain." Her voice was like a lullaby, soothing and irresistible.

THE END

www.ingramcontent.com/pod-product-compliance
Lightning Source LLC
Chambersburg PA
CBHW072055190726
48294CB00005B/1526